SAPPHIRE

To Sandy
Thanks for your support
and friendship.

B. D. EDKINS

Sapphire

SPINNAKER BOOKS

Additional titles by B. D. Edkins

Hollow Wings

Waltzing with the Dark Angel

ISBN – 13 978-0615950150

ISNB –10 0615950159

First Edition: January 2014

For my Grandchildren:

Alex, Travis, Isabel and Elizabeth
The next generation…

Special thanks to Verna Carter for her endless support. A shining light in an otherwise dark tunnel of editing!

"Civilization is but a thin veneer stretched over one of life's most deadly creatures."

Anonymous - Zhou Dynasty - 222 BC

"Violence, naked force, has settled more disputes in history than any other factor, and the contrary opinion is a wishful thing at its worst. Breeds that forget this basic truth have always paid for it with their lives and freedoms."

Robert Heilnlein, author (1907 - 1988)

"Anything created for the greater good has the exponential propensity for a greater evil."

The Prelude to an Apocalypse by Albert Chastine (Date unknown)

PROLOGUE

The world had become, problematical. Trust was in a downward spiral. Trust in governments, trust in religious sects, trust in corporations, were to name but a few of the more visible perpetrators. Monetary systems were failing or had already failed; deception the easy path, nondisclosure the new mantra.

Some saw it coming, but then history had shown us that, some is never enough to make a difference.

The exact time line is but a blur so I have written down the events as they were passed on to me. If I am off in the timeline or sequence of events, I apologize, but please remember that the results remained the same.

North Korea launched a fully armed, long range nuclear missile at a small South Pacific atoll in what it had called the ultimate proof to the world that they had joined the ranks of the world's nuclear powers. Soon after launch they lost complete control of the missile. The missile detonated inside southern China with a devastating death toll. The North Koreans quickly blamed jamming interference on the United States, not only causing the missile to go off course, but also their inability to destroy the missile or its payload before it reached China.

- While the world was still reeling over this event, a nuclear explosion at the Iranian, Rark plant is quickly blamed on Israel as 'An outright attack on the people of Iran.' Iran promises retaliation.

- A new strain of the Middle East Respiratory Syndrome (MERS virus) becomes pandemic in the Middle East and Central Europe. Deaths attributed to the virus quickly rise into the hundreds of thousands.

- In a separate event another virus reaches pandemic proportions as computer systems crash worldwide. No one knows its origin or a way to stop it.

- Nations across the globe close their borders defending their sovereignty with deadly purpose.

- In the pursuing war the first thing to be targeted are satellite communications. Within thirty days there is not a single operational satellite left in orbit. Within a year, what's left of the world becomes segregated into isolated nation-states.

Table of Contents

The 9 Districts of New America

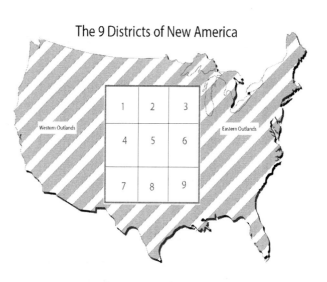

CHAPTER 1

THE LAB

CORE CITY, NEW AMERICA 2087

The shooter was in the prone position, his right eye focused on the figure in the crosshairs. His spotter squatted next to him gazing through his scope.

"Range," the shooter asked.

"450 on the tag."

"Target one, 450," the shooter confirmed.

The spotter panned the area around the two targets. From his position he could make out the silhouette of several members of the strike team hugging the other side of the brick wall not five yards from the targets. He scanned the visible windows of the house. All seemed quiet.

He tapped the shooter on the shoulder. The shooter raised a single finger in response.

"Team leader," the spotter whispered into the com link, "position is good."

"Roger," came the response, "you are

green to…"

The projectile left the muzzle of the rifle with a muffled "puff". The target's knees buckled as he fell. A split second later the second target lay next to the first. Neither showing any sign of life.

The spotter surveyed the area around the two targets while the shooter scanned the windows of the house, his eye still focused through the scope of his weapon.

"Team leader, both of the dogs are down."

"All teams move out," was the response.

The front and rear doors of the home caved inward with a stifled blast as highly condensed air was released from the charges. Simultaneously, two windows on opposite sides of the house crystallized into tiny shards of fiber and glass as assault troops made their way through the openings. Their work was quick and methodical. Anything moving was met with an immediate controlled burst of weapons fire. The assault weapons made no more noise than the sniper's rifle had.

The teams converged on a small room toward the center of the home. They had seen this room in many raids before. The walls and ceiling were sprayed with a blue-gray pasty material. Scattered in the paste were metallic speckles that glisten like diamonds when any of the flashlights mounted on the men's weapons illuminated them. A thick wall to wall mat made of similar material covered the floor. Where the mat met the walls, the seams were filled in with the blue-gray speck filled putty. It was difficult, if not impossible, to see where the walls and floor met.   There was no furniture in the room except for two makeshift tables approximately eight to ten inches from the walls. Each table was cluttered with an array of Personal Data devices and tablets connected by a hodgepodge of wires feeding into a central computer. The computer was plugged into a home-made 'filter box' which was plugged into the wall outlet. The wall receptacle and plug were also smeared with the putty. Constructed as it was, the room was effectively 'dark' to all types of surveillance equipment.

Several of the team's weapons were trained on the two figures, a man and a woman, laying face down on the mat. Both figures had their arms stretched out from their sides, the palms of their hands facing upward, their fingers spread apart. It was easy to see that neither had a weapon.

Suddenly a roaring sound similar to a rocket engine came from within the computer. The outer box glowed fiery red as smoke poured out of the air vents.

"Foam!" One of the men shouted.

Instantly another man began spraying the computer.

The foam and the rocket noise stopped at the same time. When the smoke cleared the computer was nothing but a lump of fused metal melting its way through the plastic surface of the table. The solider with the foam sprayed the table a second time until the melted lump hit the floor beneath the table.

"I was afraid that the *fuser* was going to be a dud," the male said, looking over at the female.

The female chuckled lightly until one of the men kicked her in the ribs.

"Silence!" he continued, "You are both under arrest for violations of the restrictive hardware act."

"I don't guess it would be smart for me to ask to see your search warrant?"the man asked, already bracing himself for the answer.

A swift kick to his ribcage was quickly followed by a black nylon hood shoved over his head. The woman's head was also covered prior to the two of them being handcuffed, jerked to their feet and pushed through the door. They were quickly guided to a small van, thrown into the back where their handcuffs were attached to a thick gauge wire lead protruding from the floor. The hoods were removed just prior to the rear door of the van closing with a whoosh.

The two of them were able to rise to a sitting position before they felt the van begin to move.

"What's your guess?" the woman asked faking a smile, "Life in prison?"

The man seemed to think about the question for a few seconds, "I wouldn't think so, maybe a few years in a rehabilitation center."

"Rehabilitation center? You mean a re-indoctrination center."

He shrugged his shoulders and immediately

winced at the sharp pain in his rib cage. "It's our first offense," he offered as his reasoning. "We'll be released after a few years as model citizens. No matter what, this is still America."

She smiled again with no more conviction than the first time.

Neither heard the small vents in the side of the van open, nor did either of them hear or smell the gas as it entered. Within seconds, both lay on the floor, dead.

CHAPTER 2

THE COUNCIL

The Central Exchange building towered over the rest of the structures surrounding it. Built twenty-four years ago it was the oldest building in Core City. The old axiom of business follows the money was certainly true in the case of The Central Exchange. The structure was twenty-two stories high and was located in the center of the city. It was home to: the Central bank, Solar Collection Systems or SCS for short, the energy consortium, Core Systems Medical Network and Sapphire, the communication group. The rest of the building was occupied by countless offices of law firms, marketing companies, research groups and consulting firms. The crowning jewel of the Exchange building was the offices of the Core Council located appropriately on the entire twenty second floor. It was here that the Directors of each of the four powerhouses, banking, energy, medical/research, and communications conducted their affairs. The Directors did not officially have offices on the twenty second floor, but each Director kept an active staff as well as private quarters for their use. There was a fifth associate member of the council, Commander of Core Security. Core Security did not have a large office staff as did the other Directors. Instead, it housed the security detachment on the twenty first floor that monitored and maintained security for the Council and the rest of the building. The Commander of the Core Security had his own office in the security complex in the western sector of the city.

There were no government offices in the Exchange as this was prohibited in the new constitution. All government offices were located on the East side of town in Government Plaza. The Plaza housed all three branches of the government as well as the district governors from each of the nine outlying areas.

Marci (Mars) Tansy, Director of the Sapphire Group, walked down the hallway of the twenty second floor her heels tapping out their usual cadence announcing her arrival. It had been said that just the sound of her heels drumming along the floor was enough to send support staff and even some managers scurrying to the safety they could find in the restrooms. Even if it weren't true, the thought made Mars' lips curl upward into a curt smile.

The morning sunlight pierced the e-glass of the windows occupying the upper four feet of the outer wall. The filtered rays cast long shadows across Mars' figure projecting a ghostly silhouette along the stone walls. It seemed to her that even her own shadow was attempting to keep its distance.

Mars straightened her three piece twill suit as she approached the private board room reserved for the Directors use. At thirty-seven she was the youngest member of the Core Council by eight years. Stephen Pyrs, Director of the Central Bank was forty-five and junior in age by fourteen years to the next two members Iris Kinsley, Director of Solar Collection Systems and Dr. Ned Grady, Director of Core Systems Medical Network. The fifth member of the group was Martin Adelric, thirty-nine years old and Commander of the Core Security. Martin Adelric was also the only Associate Director on the council and this is why Mars never considered him a true member of the council. In her mind, as well as the other three permanent members of the council, Core Security was useful, but not a profitable venture. Stephen Pyrs often considered them as bank guards; Dr. Grady had never seen a need for them. To Iris Kinsley they were the night watchmen at her solar collectors. *And for her*, Mars thought, *Sapphire's private army*.

The double doors to the board room parted at her approach. She was taken aback to see Martin Adelric already in the room. He was standing over the buffet table surveying the lunch that had been prepared for them. Commander Adelric looked over his shoulder at Mars and offered her a cursory smile.

He had anticipated the look on Mars' face. As a rule, she was always the first member to arrive for the meetings. "I was starving," he offered as an answer for his informal breach of Mars' protocol of always being the first in the room, "I didn't have any breakfast."

Mars approached the table. "A nice layout," she answered not caring to comment on his statement.

"Are we late?" Director Kinsley asked, as she entered the room.

Stephen Pyrs was just a few steps behind her. "No, we are all early as usual," he said approaching the buffet. He locked eyes with Mars, "But not as early as some."

"I guess I'm in last place," Dr. Grady stated as he entered the room.

Director Kinsley logged into her terminal at the huge oak board table. She looked at the members of the council going through the buffet line. Commander Adelric had a full plate and was heading to his seat. "Commander, did you beat Mars here?"

"Not by much," he stated taking his seat.

Dr. Grady placed his hand on Adelric's shoulder as he passed by. "You skip breakfast again Martin?"

The group chuckled as they too began to

take their seats. That is, except Mars. She had never liked the informality that some of the members seemed to foster within the council. Once Dr. Grady had taken his seat the light began to dim. The familiar sound of the board room doors securing themselves was quickly followed by the security field being activated.

An iridescent security field seemed to appear out of thin air on the ceiling above the board table and at a parallel point on the floor beneath the table. The thin shimmering lines moved concentrically away from their center points on the ceiling and the floor. Each circle continued to spread up and down the walls and along the floor and ceiling until each had stopped at a spot directly below or above where it had started.

From the center of the table a holographic resemblance of the Sapphire gem appeared. It turned slowly around in a circle. Several of the gems facets sparkled as if they had caught an unseen beam of light as it traveled around.

"Good morning Directors," the feminine voice of Sapphire stated.

Each of the directors returned the greeting.

"Doctor Grady," Sapphire said evenly, "you have not logged onto your terminal."

Grady laid his fork on his plate as he

placed his left hand on the reading device and punched in his personal code on the keypad with his right. "Sorry," he mumbled with a partial mouthful of food.

"Thank you, Doctor," Sapphire stated with just a hint of gratitude, "the room is now secure."

"Shall I begin?" Sapphire queried.

It was Iris Kinsley's month to act as chairperson of the council. "Please begin Sapphire," Kinsley said.

"Thank you Director," Sapphire replied, "I have the most recent numbers from my monitoring of the blogging network. Core Council approval rating is up two tenths of a percent at 83.4%."

There were whispers of approval amongst the Directors.

"The government approval rating is holding steady at 67%, but there is a personal abnormality within the government worth noting."

"What is it?" Kinsley asked.

"President Ziven's personal approval rating has increased 11% in the last week. It now stands at 87.7%"

"What?" Pyrs asked, looking directly at the hologram in the center of the table. The image of the Sapphire gem now had a chart displayed in its center. Even without looking closely, Pyrs could see the noticeable upward tick of the President's trend line.

"Explain," interjected Mars in a calm tone.

Sapphire began displaying standard press photos of the President and his wife. "His polls began to climb last week when his wife gave birth to their first child, up 1.765% to be exact. This week's increase began when the presidential family released these photographs and videos of the President cuddling his new son. The population across all districts reacted very favorably to the connection of the President and his family. In three days this video received over 800,000 hits on Core-tube."

"This is unacceptable!" Doctor Grady blurted.

Mars' eyes narrowed at the outburst. "What did you expect? We have made sure that supporting, no," she said hesitating momentarily, "*Promoting*," she corrected, "strong family values were to be at the top of both government and religious agendas."

"That's correct," Pyrs interjected. "We even increased monetary incentives to families displaying strong family unity."

Iris Kinsley tapped the table to ask for silence. "Pyrs and Mars are correct. We do want to promote strong family values, but we cannot have the government showing stronger approval numbers than this council."

"Especially not the President," added Mars, "he may start to believe that he runs this country."

The sound of contemptuous laughter filled the room.

Kinsley raised her hand to silence the group. "Agreed," she said forcing a smile.

"Any suggestions?" Commander Adelric asked, speaking for the first time since the session started.

Kinsley and Mars locked eyes momentarily. She then looked around the table to the other three members.

"A scandal?" Grady offered.

"What type did you have in mind?" Kinsley asked.

Pyrs' eyes took on a hunted look. "A good sex scandal will always take the wind out of one's sails."

Dr. Grady winced at the thought. "Wait a minute. You're saying we should use a sex scandal to deflate the high numbers the President has just received for being a great family man?"

Commander Adelric peered critically through the hologram at Grady. "Sex scandals have the desired effect."

Mars nodded her approval. "And sex scandals can be easily fixed without further damage to the target."

Director Kinsley gave Mars a mute nod of approval indicating that she continue.

Mars took the cue, "If we had it released through a filtered source that President Ziven had an affair with another woman during the last few weeks of his wife's pregnancy…"

"Sapphire, calculate the hypothesis," Kinsley commanded.

"A sex scandal, properly initiated, could result in a fourteen to twenty-three percent drop in the President's approval ratings over the next six weeks."

"Sapphire," Mars added, "worst case scenarios."

The dark blue gem continued to rotate for several seconds before answering. "Such a scandal would not bring the demise of the President or cause him any long term marital problems. The conclusion is that he will recover from the scandal"

"You think his wife is going to be happy about an affair?" Grady sneered.

"There is a high probability that his wife would not believe the scandal and stand firmly by the President. There is also a high probability that her personal approval numbers will increase because of her support."

"Projected endgame number for his wife?" Pyrs asked.

"Endgame will see her approval ratings

move up to 72.67% which will be higher than the projected Endgame numbers for the President. I estimate President Ziven's will level off at 69.95%."

"What is the chance that the council is blamed by the government or the public for releasing the scandal?" Adelric asked.

"Less than 3.5%," Sapphire quickly computed. "It is illogical that the Council would initiate the scandal as they have often publicly supported families and have always put a high degree of pressure on the government to be a patriot for family unity."

"Agreed," interjected Mars, "when the desired affect has been accomplished, the council can publicly express their support for the President. Shortly afterward we can have one of the small press outlets spread a story debunking the alleged scandal."

"That could work out in our favor," Kinsley thought out loud. "His numbers would recover somewhat, but not to present levels. After all, there will still be doubt in the minds of some citizens."

"And," Pyrs piped in, "supporting him in a time of personal need could raise the councils own numbers."

"The projected short term change in the council's numbers would be 1.1 to 1.6 percent favorable," Sapphire offered.

"Then it's agreed?" Kinsley asked the

group.

Each member of the council pressed the green circle on their tablets.

"The council is in perfect accordance," Sapphire stated for the record.

"Good," Kinsley stated flatly. "Mars, you will make the necessary arrangements?"

Mars smiled and nodded in agreement.

"Let's move on then," Kinsley said, leaving thoughts of the President behind.

"Sapphire, update criminal data, please," Mars queried.

"Overall criminal activity remains within the acceptable range. Acceptable is based on the definitions established by this council. Shall I review the definitions?"

"Not necessary," Kinsley replied.

"Very well," Sapphire stated. "The following is a breakdown of the major categories." Again Sapphire displayed the numbers for all to see.

"Violent crimes, no computable data."

"What does that mean again?" Dr. Grady asked.

Mars sighed, before answering, "The number is so small that it lies within the margin of error."

Dr. Grady's right eyebrow rose slightly.

"It would be something like," Pyrs offered, "a 1% result with a plus or minus 1% margin of error."

"That means that it could be zero or 2% then," Grady argued.

"The number is so small that it's not worth wasting time on," Mars stated flatly. "Continue Sapphire."

"Illegal drug use is down 6 percent to 8.55% since the Medical bio scan has been reprogrammed in all personal com-devices."

There was a spontaneous outbreak of applause directed toward Dr. Grady.

"Well done, Ned." Iris offered, holding her hands a little higher in the air while continuing to clap.

"Yes, well done," echoed Pyrs and Commander Adelric.

Mars managed a weak smile.

"It was easy once we were able to home in on certain markers within the individual's bio-scan," Dr Grady said, taking advantage of the moment. "As you know, the new PDs perform a bio-scan and fluid test twice a day. When the scan detects the sign of drugs in the body, the person's medical file is immediately checked to see if the drug was prescribed for that person."

"But what if…" Pyrs started to ask.

Dr. Grady continued already anticipating Pyrs' question, "Their immediate family's records are also checked. If the person has not been prescribed the medication or it was intended for another member of the family,

Core Security is notified."

Commander Adelric nodded in agreement. "We are also notified if it is a drug of unknown origin or an illegal substance. At that point," Commander Adelric sneered, "stronger measures are taken to destroy the source of the substance."

"And I thought you," Kinsley gestured toward Dr. Grady, "just gave out flu shots."

Light laughter filtered through the room. "What is the progress of the conversion to the new devices?"Mars asked.

"We figure the conversion will be completed within the next ten months," Grady assured her.

"Excellent," she smiled, "Sapphire, please continue," Mars commanded.

"Acts against society have increased by 4.45%" Sapphire said continuing.

The jovial atmosphere created by the earlier news faded quickly. Commander Adelric sat up in his chair and leaned a little forward. The body language of each director changed as if a dark cloud had moved in overhead.

Mars cleared her throat, her voice was stiff, "Breakdown into sub-categories, Sapphire. Cover only those sub-categories that have affected the statistic.

"Category one," Sapphire began, its voice changing tone and pitch to reflect the seriousness of the situation, "Mindful disregard of social blogging, up 11.6%."

"Have you verified that figure?" Pyrs asked.

"Statistic verified and confirmed," Sapphire stated. "There has been a noticeable increase in individual citizen's blatant refusal to post to the Core blog once a week as required by the Competent Information Act."

Pyrs quickly began typing on his keypad. "There seems to be a corresponding increase in the number of citizens that have lost level one credit incentives for failure to post. Also, there is a slight increase in the numbers who have reached level two violations and have lost tax deductions. "

"Continue," Kinsley stated.

"Wrongful use of graffiti, particularly the use of anti-government slogans, up 7.88%." Sapphire waited for comment. When there was none she continued. "The production, sale, and use of alternate identifications up 5.25%."

"We shut down another ID lab last night," Adelric interjected as he keyed the video.

There was silence as the members of the board watched the entire event as recorded by the security team. The video ended as the doors on the security van closed.

"Their computer was destroyed before

we could secure it." He then continued, "Our crime scene teams are going over all of the confiscated materials as we speak."

"You have nothing to show for last night's raid except for four dead bodies and two dead dogs?" Mars asked curtly.

Commander Adelric cleared his throat, "Not exactly. We know that none of the four were actual citizens of New America."

"Outsiders?", Kinsley asked, the shock clearly readable on her face.

"It looks that way."

"Asian, or perhaps European?" Dr. Grady asked.

Adelric shook his head, "We don't think so. We're checking their identities right now, but we expect them to lead to dead ends. Of interest though, the two that we secured in the van spoke American English."

"Did you think about keeping them alive long enough to discover where they were from?" Mars taunted.

"Mars please," Kinsley interceded, "you know the standard order when it comes to Outsiders."

"That's right," Dr. Grady said supportively. "If they were Outsiders they could be carrying the virus."

"We haven't seen a case of the virus in over nine years," Mars said flatly. "Besides, from what the Commander is saying, it sounds like they are from the old protective zone."

"We haven't seen a virus case in nine years because we kill all Outsiders on contact," Adelric smiled.

Mars did not respond, but instead regarded Adelric with a fixed, level stare. "Sapphire, replay the video."

The board watched a second time and then a third. "Notice the wall and floor covering," Commander Adelric said, acting as the commentator."

"Sound proofing?" Pyrs asked.

"Surveillance proofing is more like it," Adelric responded. "That room was totally dark to any type of surveillance equipment."

"That sounds pretty sophisticated for a couple of Outsiders," Mars commented. "How did you locate them?"

Adelric frowned, "I've said this before. No one should underestimate the capabilities of the Outsiders." He let his words sink in before continuing with a sigh. "We got lucky. We picked it up on Sky-watch, our satellite surveillance network." Commander Adelric tapped on his pad. "Watch this vid. This is a composite video of our surveillance over the last three weeks."

The room darkened as Sapphire began the video. As in any satellite photograph, the video started at the farthest distance from the house. At this magnification the home was no more than a small pulsating yellow dot. Quickly Sapphire zoomed in until the house filled 80% of the screen.

"Enhance," he ordered.

The home soon became nothing more than a ghostly skeleton.

"The hot points in pink or red," he said, "are heat signatures. The stationary ones are the stove and oven in the kitchen and the clothes dryer in the laundry room. The five pink, blurry hot points are the people moving around and the two dogs outside."

"The satellite can determine the difference between people and appliances?" Kinsley asked.

"No," Adelric answered. "The appliances are stationary and give off a constant amount of heat when used and are noted by the darker red coloring. People and animals moving about are harder to pick up thus the lighter shades of red or pink."

"Amazing!" Dr. Grady said.

"Actually, if a person were to run through a surveillance field at a fast clip, you may not pick them up at all," he answered, intently watching the video. "Now watch this. Sapphire, advance to…,"he continued looking down at his personal pad, "117.4"

The scene jumped to a new portion of the video. There were now four people in the house. The two dogs were now at the rear door.

"There are only four people now," Mars observed.

"Correct," Adelric agreed. "Now watch this next part."

One of the figures moved toward the rear door of the house. The red-pinkish blur became lighter as the figure moved. Once at the back door the figure stopped and again turned a darker hue of red. It was obvious that the person was allowing the two dogs into the house. Together, the dogs went into the kitchen and scurried around for a few seconds and then decided to move on. Their quick movement was picked up as a trail of pinkish dots.

"Watch this," Adelric noted.

The two animals moved toward the center of the house and seemed to vanish.

"Where did they go?" Pyrs asked.

It was Mars who answered the question, "They're in the darkroom."

"Yes," Adelric almost whispered as if the people on the video might have been able to hear him, "and…now!" his voice becoming louder as he pointed toward the video. They all watched as the fifth person emerged from the darkroom with the two dogs following closely behind.

"Amazing," Dr. Grady said a second

time.

"We put the house under constant surveillance for three weeks and...Sapphire, bring up the composite picture please." The video was quickly replaced by a still picture of the house. "This is a composite of the three weeks of observation, overlaid to make up this fused image."

It was easy for everyone in the board room to understand the image. While the ghostly blue shadow of the heavier beams of the structure were easy to see, most of the rooms were now highlighted with a reddish/pink shade. Only a small, square section of the house was totally void of any color.

"Ladies and gentlemen," Commander Adelric sighed, "the ID lab."

The conference room lights became brighter as the picture faded within the Sapphire gem.

"Commander?" Mars asked.

"Yes."

"You only killed four people and the two dogs," Mars said thinking out loud.

Kinsley drew the conclusion, "Then one of them got away."

"Yes," he answered solemnly.

CHAPTER 3

REBECCA

Rebecca stood dangerously close to the edge of the cliff and scanned the ravine floor some three hundred feet below her. Currents of hot air rushed up from the depths of the ravine, danced carelessly through her copper colored hair, and continued upward to be used by an eagle gliding seventy-five feet above her head. For the moment everything was as it should be. Well, almost.

Rebecca instinctively touched the small casing housing the tiny camera mounted atop her safety helmet. Through the camera, Sapphire could see everything she could see.

Scanning the area to the east, she could make out on the horizon, one of the massive solar collectors hungrily eating up the energy beam being aimed at it from the solar collector hovering above the Earth.

"Do you wish to know more about the Solar

Collection System," Sapphire asked in its usually neutral voice. "Or, if you like, more information is available on the solar condensers and directional beams."

Rebecca looked to the far west and could barely see the next SCS. At this distance, the directional beam looked more like a golden strand of hair. Where the hair touched the collector, there was a diamond sparkle. "Yes, please," she stated, not caring about either.

"The Solar Collection System or SCS for short, was first activated...," Sapphire began.

Rebecca removed her climbing helmet and placed it on the ledge pointing toward the western SCS. Her deep auburn hair danced around her face as it was caught by the updraft.

"Rebecca, you have removed your helmet," Sapphire stated, "It is very unsafe to remove your head gear while climbing."

"Sapphire," Rebecca said fluffing her hair, "I am not climbing right now. I am taking a break for a few minutes."

"It is still prudent to remember the safety outline for climbing."

"Sapphire, I can quote the outline verbatim to you if you like."

"As you know, that is not necessary, Rebecca."

"Haven't I asked you to call me, Becca?"

"Yes you have, Becca," Sapphire almost huffed. "The fact still remains that at this height it is unsafe to remove your helmet."

"If I fall from this height my helmet is not going to do me any good. Why don't you continue with the information about the SCS while I sit over here, away from the edge, and drink some of my water?"

There was a slight pause as if Sapphire was considering the request. Rebecca knew that Sapphire was nothing more than a super computer and that the pause was intended to make the machine seem more human. "Alright then," Sapphire said, "as I was explaining to you The SCS system…"

Rebecca lowered herself to the ground and used a large boulder as a backstop. She didn't have to look around to find the rock she was looking for. It was sitting not a foot from her right hand. She looked back at her helmet to make sure that the camera used by Sapphire was still pointing away from her. It was not likely that the camera or helmet could turn itself around to look at her, but ever since the raid four months ago, she took no undue risk. Four of her friends were dead and she still did not understand why.

How had they been discovered, she wondered? Even more disconcerting was the fact that she hadn't died with them. It was by pure chance that she wasn't in the house when the security teams had entered.

"Becca, are you paying attention?" Sapphire asked.

Rebecca's eyes shot over to her helmet. It was still pointed in the direction of the westerly SCS. "Oh, sorry, Sapphire, I just closed my eyes for a second. I must have dozed off."

"Are you tired from your climb?" Sapphire asked.

"No not really," Rebecca chuckled, "It's just that the air is so clean up here and the warm breeze feels so good. I just drifted off."

"I understand," answered Sapphire. "Do you want me to stop?"

"Oh no, continue, please," she answered. "I find it very interesting. As a matter of fact, please save the video and information for my weekly blog."

"I was hoping you would say that," Sapphire stated, "The citizens in your blog group always love the video of your explorations."

"I was just thinking the same thing," Rebecca lied. "Please continue."

"Alright," Sapphire agreed. "As I was saying, the solar energy collected from the twenty-seven towers supply New America with one hundred percent of its energy needs."

Rebecca palmed the rock and looked underneath. There was nothing but dirt. She laid the rock back down a few inches to the right and then began to slowly sweep the soil away with her hand. The paper wasn't buried very deep; just enough of a layer of dirt to hide it from any prying eyes.

Prying eyes, she thought, *I'm sitting atop a monolith 300 feet above the ground with the only access being a difficult climb for even an experienced climber like myself.* But four of her closest friends were now dead. Discovered in a safe house that they all thought was secure from any prying eyes. She glanced over at her helmet. Sapphire was still lecturing about the intrinsic values of the SCS.

Rebecca carefully unfolded the piece of paper and read the message. Her heart sank as she read the very first line: 'Remain in place. Assembling new team.' She had hoped that with the total demise of the team and equipment she would be recalled. *Let a fresh team take over,* she thought, *somebody who hadn't lost all her friends.* No sooner had she completed the notion when she began to feel guilty. She had been able to maintain her deep cover without the slightest hint of discovery. Her staying in place would make it easier for the new team not only to enter New America, but also to get a jump start on a new lab. *It makes perfect sense,* she thought, *and maybe I'll be sent out once the new team is established.* After all, the teams spend months working together before they are assigned to an operation. She would be nothing more than a fifth wheel and a total stranger. If it were my team coming in I would want *me* gone as soon as possible. Besides, there is no guarantee that I am not being watched right now. The security forces could be tracking my every move; just waiting for me to show them the way to a new team coming in.

She gazed up at her helmet. Sapphire was no longer lecturing. "Sapphire?", she asked weakly.

"Yes Becca."

"Why did you stop?"

"I thought you had fallen asleep again and I didn't want to disturb you."

Rebecca relaxed. "I was ah…," she said, as she looked down at the paper in her hand, "more in a meditative state than sleeping. Thank you for not disturbing me though."

"You are welcome, Becca. A good recreational outing should include both physical and mental stimulation so that the body can recharge."

"I agree," she said as she reread the last line of the message. *Mat-337.* She would decode that later when she didn't have so much of Sapphire's attention. "Are you ready to make the descent, Sapphire?" she asked as she poured the rest of her water over the piece of paper. The reaction of the water and the chemicals infused into the paper started an immediate reaction.

"Of course, Becca."

"All right then," she grunted as she stood up. She glanced down at the paper one more time to make sure that it was destroyed. "Let's see if we can beat our previous descent record."

"Without involving a freefall, I assume," Sapphire quipped.

Rebecca chuckled. "Yes, please, I don't believe a fall is allowed in the safety manual."

CHAPTER 4

JAX

THE OLD "PROTECTIVE ZONE" 2087

"Jax, what is your current location?" the implant whispered in his ear. In all the years he had the implant he was never sure if he could really hear a voice or if it was just his brain making him think he could hear it. It didn't matter, either way he had received the transmission and it would require an answer.

" Fountain flats", he sub-vocalized, "approximately six miles from the campus." Jax had kept a steady pace as he jogged along the rugged terrain of Fountain flats. The flats were one of his favorite places to run. The diverse landscape gave him the opportunity to take a position on the high ground and survey the area for miles around as he jogged or darted into one of the low lying crevasses if he felt the need to conceal himself. Of course there was no hiding from the implant.

"Return to campus, direct." he heard the implant think. "Go to Doctor Roger's office. Ask for a Colonel McKee."

Jax smiled, returning to campus direct only meant that he was to take the most direct track back to campus. He was free to choose that path for himself. He would continue his jog in the most direct path allowed by the train. It would be a little more of a challenge than the way he had intended to return, but he was happy for the challenge, no matter how small. "Returning, direct," he said to himself. "ETA 35 minutes. Contact Colonel McKee on arrival." There was no answer from the implant, there never was unless it was necessary.

Jax continued his pace as he adjusted his track to bring him on a course back to the Campus. The sun was almost directly overhead. Jax could feel the heat of the sun penetrate the thin veneer of his copper skin and magically charge the lean muscles that moved just below the surface. It was exhilarating. Effortless he threaded his way through the rock, brush, and rough ground that attempted to impede his progress.

The desert was alive and nothing escaped his senses. The rattlesnake sunning himself on a nearby rock; a new colony of termites building their home, the small lizards darting amongst the available cover. Everything was noted and cataloged. For a brief second he was saddened at the thought of having to cut his run short. Very few things gave him such a feeling of freedom. He thought about his past assignments as he made short work of the six miles separating him from the campus.

He jogged up the stairs of the admin building and entered. He would have liked to have taken a shower and changed his cloths before the meeting, but direct meant direct.

From the outside, the buildings composing the campus resembled the bombed out skeletons of the war. Shattered windows and broken doorways accented by brick rubble marked the main entrance to the underground facility. The hallways were empty this late in the day. Most had been gone for almost three hours. Except for the hum coming from the two auto-cleaners and the squeaking noise coming from his cross trainers as they attempted to grip the newly polished floor, there were no other sounds to be heard.

As Jax got within the range of the proximity scanner he could hear it announce his arrival. "Ajax Martin has arrived and is awaiting permission to enter your office Doctor." The system announced in a very pleasant young lady's voice.

Jax paused and waited only a fraction of a second before the door disappeared and he was invited to enter.

"Come in, Jax," the familiar voice of Doctor Rogers beckoned. "Another forty-five seconds and I would have lost my bet to the Colonel here." Jax could hear the Doctor say as he entered the office. Jax smiled. Being around the Doctor always made him smile. He had come to not only respect the man for his vast knowledge, but also to admire him for his uncanny way of making everyone feel like he was a part of his closest family.

Jax walked through the entrance, passed the small desk where Doctor Rogers admin assistant sat during normal business hours and into the main area of his office. Instantly the smile left Jax's face as he noticed the woman standing to the right and slightly behind Doctor Rogers.

Things began to happen very rapidly. In a matter of seconds, Jax had scanned the room assessing the situation. There was no one else in the room except for the two people standing fifteen feet directly in front of him. The only exit accessible to him was the way he had come in, but leaving that way would require him to turn his back to the woman long enough for the proximity reader to identify him and allow him to exit the room. Although that would only take a second to do, he knew that would be too much of an advantage to the woman if she made a move against him. Jax noticed that the woman was dressed in a standard military uniform. Tight fitting as it was, there was no room to conceal a weapon. At best, Jax surmised that she was carrying a throwing blade or knife. The best option for Jax was to defend an area just a few steps to the right of his current position. He made the adjustment without thinking twice. This put a solid wall to his back while placing the Doctor between him and the woman. Any attempt to get at him would involve her having to get around

Doctor Rogers and that would be all the advantage Jax would need.

Jax paid no attention to Doctor Rogers now. His only concern was the woman. Jax was sure that she had noticed his deliberate movement to the right, but made no attempt to adjust her position. This puzzled him, the fact that she had given up any chance of a surprise attack.

"Jax, are you all right?" the Doctor asked.

Jax did not answer or take his eyes off the Colonel. If there was going to be a break in the standoff that had developed between the two of them; it was going to be at the expense of the Colonel.

"Jax, did you hear me?" the Doctor asked again, "Are you all right?"

"I don't think he was expecting me, Doctor?" Colonel McKee said without making any type of move. "Could Jax and I have the use of your office for a while, Doctor?"

Jax readied for her attack. He knew that once the Doctor moved it would allow her a better avenue toward him. At least it would have to be a frontal assault and Jax knew he was in the best position he could be to defend himself under the current situation.

Doctor Rogers stared at Jax for several seconds not sure what had come over the boy.

"Doctor?" McKee asked without taking her eyes off of Jax.

"I'm sorry, Colonel. I guess you're right. I'll

just head down the hall to the lounge. I'll be there if either of you need me."

Neither Jax nor McKee actually saw the Doctor leave the office, but knew he had gone when the door closed. Both stood perfectly still waiting of the other to make the first move.

It was Colonel McKee that made the first move. Slowly she raised her hands from her sides upward toward her chest. Jax could tell that her movement was deliberately slow so that it would not provoke him in any manner. "My name is Colonel Emily McKee," she said. Jax remained transfixed on the woman and her movements.

It only took him a second to study and record her facial features. He guessed her age to be late twenties or certainly no older than thirty-one or two. Her jet-black hair was cut in a boyish bob. It was feathered in the back, her bangs trimmed neatly across her forehead framing her high cheekbones. Her eyes were cobalt in color, cat-like in shape, they sparkled with a blend of curiosity and intelligence. He knew that she could instantly appear fierce or feminine as the need required.

Colonel McKee kept her eyes on Jax as she slowly turned her palms inward toward her chest and touched her breasts lightly. In the next second she then turned her opened hands outward and forward for Jax to examine.

"Jax, I mean you no harm," she said, still holding her outstretched hands for Jax to examine. "I've come here to talk to you about our need for your services."

Jax watched her motions very intently. For some reason, the strange gesture she had made had a relaxing effect on him. Her voice was even and non-threatening. He did not break his defensive stance, but somehow knew that the situation had de-escalated somewhat. He also knew that the next move was up to him.

"Sorry, Colonel," Jax said, dropping his hands to his side as he straightened up some. "I'm not sure what that was all about. But, I..."

"It's OK, Jax," McKee said forcing a smile. "I have that effect on a lot of people. It's probably why I'm still single."

"I guess the heat in the desert was a bit too much today," Jax offered in the way of an apology.

"How hot was it out there?" McKee asked.

"114," Jax replied.

McKee motioned for Jax to take a seat in one of the overstuffed chairs in front of the Doctors' desk. "114 degrees and you jogged six miles in less than thirty minutes?" McKee asked as she took the chair closest to her. "That's impressive."

'Not as impressive as your breasts crammed into that tight uniform', Jax thought to himself. "It wasn't that bad," he said aloud, "I've been doing it for years now. I guess I'm just used to it.

Colonel McKee picked up a view pad from on top of the Doctors desk and touched the transparent sheet. "So your real name is Ajax? That's quite an ancient name."

"Yes, but everyone calls me Jax."

"Why Ajax, possibly family reasons?" McKee prompted.

"None that I know of, Colonel. I guess my parents just like the name."

"I see you have a set of twin sisters. Older, right?"

Jax shifted in the chair. It always seemed that the conversations would end up centering on his sisters. "Yes, by two years," he answered.

"Do you share any of their talents?"

"Not really. I will sometimes get a premonition of what someone is thinking or a feeling about what's going to happen, but nothing like the two of them."

"Like you had when you first saw me?"

Jax's face reddened. "Something like that," he answered.

"Do your sisters connect very often?" McKee asked, changing the subject.

"Often enough to have my parents put on the program." Jax answered.

"Program? Oh, you mean the psychic research studies, but you're not a twin, are you Jax?"

Jax looked down at the floor to avoid eye contact with McKee. "No, I'm not."

"You sound disappointed. It's not your fault that you're not a twin," McKee said smiling. "I don't think you had any say in the matter."

Jax mimicked her smile, "No, I guess I didn't, but I can't help feeling that I was somewhat of a disappointment to my parents."

"It's very rare that a family would have two sets of twins, one in 468,000," McKee stated. "The odds of having two sets of twins with psychic abilities in one family are even worse."

"Yes, I know." he said, "one in three million, but it doesn't stop the psychic research group from trying."

"Did your parent ever voice their disappointment in your not being a twin?"

"Not at all," Jax said shaking his head. "Colonel, are you a psychologist or something?"

McKee laughed out loud, "No, not even close. Currently I'm assigned to the 87th Raider Group. Ever hear of them?"

"Sorry, no," he answered as his face turned red again.

McKee smiled. "Don't worry about it, Jax. I would have been surprised if you had. We're one of the groups that most people never hear about and that's the way we like to keep it. We fall under one of the Special Forces battalions. We kind of get lost in the cracks."

Jax sat up in his chair at the mention of the Special Forces. He had already submitted the necessary e-form application to the military for Special Forces service after his graduation. Doctor Rogers and most of his instructors had added their recommendation to his application. "Are you here to interview me for the Special Forces?" he asked.

"No. I'm here to see if you have what it takes

for a..." McKee paused for several seconds as if considering her answer, "special assignment."

"But Middle-Earth needs soldiers, right? I mean recruiters come to the campus all the time."

McKee was not surprised at Jax's reference to the Protective Zone as Middle-Earth. Many of the younger people had become enthralled with J R R Tolkien's Lord of the Rings. After all, the protective zone lay directly between New America and the wastelands of the West coast. The protective zone, as it was called prior to the establishment of the sovereign country known as New America, encompassed all of the livable land between the East and West coasts. That changed forty years ago when an ad hoc group took power and created the Sovereign country of New America. Anyone who had not sworn allegiance to the new country was quickly labeled as an *Outsider*. The connotation was also used by the new government to mean those infected with the MERS virus. The Outsiders were hunted down and killed or forced to retreat to the area outside of the boundaries established by the New America government. Being in between the new country, where they were not welcomed and the nuclear hot zone of the coastline, they lived in the middle, or as it was quickly becoming known, as Middle-earth.

"New America becomes stronger every day," McKee said flatly.

"And that," Jax interjected looking at her breasts again, "is why you're here; to see if I am good enough for the Special Forces.

"No." she said laughing at his persistence. "Jax, I have another, more general question for you. It's dealing with the male gender of our species."

"All right", he answered unsure what this would have to do with Special Forces.

"Can you explain to me why the male gender of our species is under the general misconception that woman's eyes are located at the tips of her breasts?"

Jax's eyes quickly shot up to meet hers. He could feel the heat on his face as he blushed. Numerous scenarios of what a proper apology would sound like raced through his mind. But, in the end, he went with the safest; "Sorry"

She grinned broadly. "I told you, I need someone for a special assignment." She said looking back at the tablet. "You're at the top of your class in most of your studies."

"Yes."

"Excellent marks in mathematics and computer science. It says here that you have a keen understanding of Political Sciences," she stated as she continued to read. "Top marks in Political theory of the 21st century, top marks in Comparative politics of the third millennium and, of course, top marks in the study of the decay of public administrations during the same time period."

Jax answered with a despairing glance, "I thought it was important to understand how the world was pushed to the brink of total destruction."

"And do you understand?" she asked, raising her eye-brow.

Jax adjusted his position. "I don't have all the answers."

"No, I suppose not," she stated, once again looking down at the tablet in front of her. "And I see here that you excel in physical training as well. Track star for four years, martial arts, marksmanship." Colonel McKee looked up from her tablet and locked eyes with Jax. "You are a very interesting blend of athlete and nerd; don't you think?"

Jax's face hardened as he stared back at McKee.

If she noticed his anger she didn't bother to show it. "But do you know what I don't understand?"

"I think," Jax answered finding his courage, "there's not much that you don't understand."

"That might be true, but all the same, I don't understand how an individual who is so interested in the study of people hasn't participated in a single team sport."

"What?"

McKee pointed toward the pad. "It says here that you are an expert in Martial arts, but you didn't join the school team. You're the second best shot in your class, but turned down a spot on the rifle team." McKee looked up from the tablet, "You're not an introvert. You make friends easily and your instructors all say that you volunteer to help tutor others; whether it's book learning or physical training. So what gives?"

Jax eyed Commander McKee skeptically and pointed to her tablet. "You don't get to be in the top of your class by wasting all your free time," he answered. "Those grades and the physical training don't come naturally to me. I have to spend a lot of time studying and working out. The time has to come from somewhere. Something had to give."

McKee studied him for several seconds. "Alright," she sighed, "I'll accept that for now."

"So I passed the interview?" he asked.

"McKee put the pad back on top of the desk. "I didn't come here to interview you, Jax."

"But you said…"

"I said, 'I was here to see if you were a good fit for a special assignment.' I said nothing about interviewing you for entry into the Special Forces."

"Then why all the questions?"

"Just wanted to see what you were like," McKee smiled.

Jax's right eyebrow rose slightly. "I don't understand then."

Colonel McKee stood. "We'll teach you what we want you to understand." She looked down at her watch. "An hour from now there will be a military transport waiting outside your dormitory. I wouldn't be late. Track drivers aren't known for waiting around."

Jax jumped out of his chair. "Then, I'm in? I got the assignment?"

McKee turned to face him before reaching the

door. "You were in the second we met."

"But, what…?"

McKee walked out of the door. "Use your intuition, Jax, and figure it out for yourself."

CHAPTER 5

JAX'S TRAINING

Jax entered the conference room and headed toward a chair that was closer to the center of the table than either of the ends. He had chosen to sit at the end of the table the last time he had been in the room and, the time before, on the opposite side closer to the other end. If there had been one thing his five months of training had pounded into his head it was the value of inconsistency. Variation became the order of the day; unpredictability the only uniformity of his actions. During mealtime he never sat at the same table, never ordered the same meal twice. He had become quite ambidextrous with his knife and fork.

His speech training had provided him with the ability to speak several regional dialects used within New America. He had learned to change the tone of his speech, to use the everyday vernacular subtleties of the different classes. He had even been taught to change the features of his own phonology, grammar and vocabulary to a point that, when he chose to, the voice patterns recognition system would deny him access to his own quarters. The flip side of this coin had also allowed him to study the voice patterns of others and obtain right of entry into their quarters. This was a talent that he never abused.

He slid into the chair thankful for the support it offered. The training days were long and exhausting. When he wasn't training or studying, he slept. Another talent, if you wanted to call it that, was his ability to sleep anywhere at any time. He had learned the value of resting whenever the moment allowed. He had undergone days of training where the only rest he may have gotten was the occasional fifteen or twenty minutes of sleep while perched atop a wooden crate or lying in a muddy stream. The *where* he slept or *when* he slept no longer mattered as long as he was able to close his eyes at some point and rest.

He was considering closing his eyes for a few minutes when two officers he had never seen before entered the room. Since he wasn't military, he wasn't required to snap to attention, but when Colonel McKee followed the two men into the room he felt himself rising from his comfortable chair.

"Hello, Jax," she said. "Haven't seen you in a-while," she offered in the way of a greeting.

In a-while was an understatement, he thought. He actually had not seen McKee since their meeting in Doctor Roger's office. "It was five months ago," he answered taking his seat again.

"Five months, seventeen days and a half a dozen hours," she said as she took a seat at the head of the table. "I've been busy," she stated, "as, I hear, you have been."

He gave her a slight shrug of his shoulders and a thin smile as an acknowledgement.

"So, are you ready to go to work?"

His training covering the subject of dealing with strangers popped into his head. He eyed the other two officers suspiciously, deciding not to answer the question until they had been properly introduced. "Good," McKee said, her eyes sparkling, "I see the time and effort we've spent on training you has been a total waste."

Again, Jax waited for the introductions. Besides, he thought, sitting silently in his chair might be the most rest he would get all day.

Colonel McKee assumed a posture of superiority, "Jax, these men are here to brief you on your mission. Their names are of no consequence to you as you will more than likely never seem them again."

He waited patiently for the introductions.

"Major Dunnen and Major Streep," she said pointing to each of the officers. "I'll personally vouch for them if it makes you happy," McKee snapped.

"Then, let's get started," he replied.

She smiled broadly, her eyes glinting with

pleasure. Jax knew that the millisecond of pleasure spread across her face was the closest thing he was going to get to a graduation ceremony.

"Gentlemen," she queued.

The taller of the two men punched keys on the control station in front of him. The outline of New America filled the view screen. New America itself was shaded in a light brown color. The borders of the country were marked in a thick red line. "Breeching the frontier and gaining access to New America has become relatively easy."

Jax pointed toward the red border. "I've been told that the area between their territory and the outer zone is protected by an electric fence."

"A solar fence," the shorter officer interjected. "They use their solar power to produce ultra thin horizontal solar beams exactly six inches apart. The fence is twenty-five feet tall and is very effective at stopping any unwanted encroachments into their territory. The fence now travels the entire length of their western border."

"The beams," McKee offered, "can slice through a two inch metal plate without even showing a noticeable drop in energy."

"You call that relatively easy to breach?" Jax asked.

"The fence is impregnable, "the taller officer confirmed, "but we have found a way under it; a way that will deliver you within a few miles of your rendezvous point." Once again the officer touched the keypad. Instantly, the map zoomed outward to a point where the entire west coast of North America was visible. A few more key strokes and a solid yellow horizontal line appeared. The line started deep within New America and continued through the red border marking the fence all the way to a point just off the old LA coastline. "This," he said zooming in on the coast line, "is Santa Catalina Island. Depending on the weather, this land mass will fall somewhere between a two and four on the contamination meter. The island is used by the Core Council of New America to conduct trade with the Asian Commonwealth. Santa Catalina has its own solar collector system; the only one known to exist outside the country's borders."

"I didn't know that there was any contact with Asia."

McKee's lip curled in disgust, "No one outside the Core Council and the Government know about the trade station or the fact that a large population of Asians survived the devastation of the war and MERS Virus. Of course, the government will not allow any visitors into New America. All goods received from Asia are thoroughly scanned and tested before they are allowed to leave Santa Catalina Island."

"So what does this have to do with me getting in?"

McKee's expression changed quickly. "You're going to hitch a ride," She beamed.

"That's right," the tall officer said. "The yellow line marks an underground hyper tube system used by the council to transfer goods to and from the island. Very few people within New America know of its existence."

"Hyper tube?" Jax asked.

It was the shorter officer's turn. "Yes, *New A,* "as he called it, "operates a hyper-tube system. The transportation cars are twenty-five feet long and nine feet in diameter. They function within the near vacuum environment of the tube. The tube system uses an electromagnetic propulsion mechanism that moves the cars at a rate in excess of 800 miles per hour."

"So what," Jax asked, "I'm supposed to go to this island and hitch a ride?"

The short officer shook his head, "you'll catch the cars at a point thirty miles from our present location. The cars come to a complete stop when they change tubes."

"There are actually three separate tubes," the tall officer stated, as he changed the display.

Jax watched as the image on the viewer changed again. This time it zoomed in on the tube system. At this magnification the single yellow line split into three separate lines. "For whatever reason," the tall officer continued, "there are three separate tubes. When the cars reach the end of one tube it stops and is automatically transferred to the next section of the tube system to continue its journey."

The smaller officer spoke next. "As Major Dunnen said, each of the lines travels about one third of the distance. There is a short over-lap where one section of the tube system meets up with the next section. Think of them as three drinking straws lined up on the table in front of you, each covering one-third of the distance from point "A", Catalina, to point "B", New America. Each straw over-laps the next section by about fifty feet, just big enough to allow for the transfer station.

Jax watched as the screen changed again displaying a computer generated model of the transfer operation. As he watched, the twenty-five foot car came to a complete stop in the first tube. Once halted, a doorway in the tube opened and the car began to move laterally on a rail system that delivered it to the next tube thirty yards away. The second tube opened, accepted the car, and then closed. As soon as the door of the tube was sealed the car again shot forward. He knew the process would be repeated once more before the car arrived at its final destination inside New America.

"The transfer takes eleven minutes to complete and luckily for us, the transfer stations are un-manned," McKee said. "During that time period we open the car, place you inside, and you continue on until you reach New America where you will be met by some of our operatives and transferred to a safe house."

The lights came up as the image on the view screen vanished. For several seconds no one spoke. Jax quickly figured out that they were waiting for him to ask questions.

"Well," he finally said thinking out loud, "as you said at the beginning of the presentation, it is an effective way of breaching the border." He looked toward McKee. "So what small detail haven't you told me?"

McKee smiled evilly, "Using the vacuum slash electromagnetic propulsion system the car reaches its maximum velocity very quickly."

Jax's left eyebrow shot up in a questioning slant, "how quickly?"

McKee answered his question with a blank stare. Jax turned his attention to the two officers. "How quickly?" he repeated.

The smaller officer shrugged his shoulder, "you'll take eight to ten g's before leveling out."

"Ten g's!" he shouted as he came out of his seat, "are you all crazy?"

"Our people do it all the time," McKee answered in a somewhat dismissive tone. "Besides, I'll throw in a few motion sickness bags for free."

"Ten g's?!"

The taller officer put his hand out to quiet Jax. "You will be strapped into a body harness that will hold you in a linear position relative to the g-force," he offered. "All of our testing shows that the g-force experienced by the subject in a position where the g-forces are perpendicular to the spine increases the survival rate considerably."

"Right," Jax hissed, "and I come out on the other end with my asshole relocated to the center of my forehead!"

"Our people do it all the time," McKee repeated.

"Your people?" Jax asked incredulously, "am I considered one of your people or am I just an expendable extra?"

"Of course you're one of us."

"How many of *your people* have not survived this little joy ride?" he asked.

"Two," the tall officer answered without hesitation.

"And how many people have you shot through this, this cannon?" he asked, gesturing toward the now blank view screen.

"Twenty," McKee answered.

"Ten percent?" Jax was able to spit out after a millisecond of hesitation. "You lose ten percent?" Jax stood up and began pacing around the small room. "I didn't sign up for this crap," he said, not directing his words to anyone in particular.

"No," McKee said flatly, "you signed up for far worse."

Jax turned to face her, his hands planted firmly on his hips. "Worse than getting shot out of a cannon at ten g's?"

McKee folded her arms over her chest. "Jax, you've gone through all of the indoctrination classes. What happens to those agents that are discovered once inside New America?"

He eased himself back into his chair. "They are never heard from again," he repeated from memory. He started to draw small circles with his finger on the table in front of him. The three officers waited for him to work through his thoughts. "It's a control issue, I guess."

"Control issue?" the smaller officer asked.

"Yes, control," Jax answered. "Once in New America I am in control of my actions. If I die it is because I screwed up, not because I'm strapped helplessly into some type of cocoon and shot down a tube at eleven g's. Twice!" he added as an afterthought. Jax glanced toward McKee for a second and then looked down at the table and again began drawing invisible circles on the table. This time he was drawing them with his other hand.

Colonel McKee looked toward the two officers, "Gentlemen, give us the room please."

The two officers got up from the table in unison and proceeded out the door. McKee waited until she heard the metal click of the door locking behind them before she spoke. "This was my one hesitation in recruiting you, Jax."

Jax was taken a-back at the warm sincerity of her voice. Up until this point she had always come across as the hardcore, testy Special Forcers officer. He knew that he was now hearing the true voice of Emily McKee, not Commander McKee.

"What hesitation?" he asked, "knowing that I wouldn't like the idea of getting shot down the line in that tube?"

"No. Jax," she said softly, "you'll either come around to the idea or you won't."

"And if I don't?" he said sharply.

"If you don't," she shrugged, "I know you well enough now to honestly say that there wouldn't be a single person or reason that could make you do it."

Jax studied her face. "You got that right," he heard himself say.

McKee leaned back in her chair. "Jax, this is going to be a team effort and you quite frankly suck at team sports."

"I never participated in team sports for a reason," he said, defending himself.

McKee smiled wickedly, "alright then, you lack any experience in team sports and therefore, you suck at playing well with others."

Jax chuckled out loud, "fine, as long as we got that straightened out."

McKee found herself laughing also. "You want to pull the plug on this assignment?" she asked, as the smile left her face.

"But..."

"Don't worry," she continued, "I'll find you a spot on one of the Special Forces teams. You'd make a damn good sniper."

Jax closed his eyes and rotated his head from side to side trying to relieve some of the stiffness in his neck. "You know Emily," he said softly, "I've been here almost six months now. I've been instructed on everything from assimilation to survival tact's, but do you know that I've had less than six hours of weapons training?"

Jax raised a single finger into the air. "Actually,"

he said, correcting his last statement, "I've had six hours of familiarization training on the weapons used by the Core Security force."

"Jax, we're not sending you into New America to shoot anyone."

"What then?" he asked, opening his eyes.

McKee leaned forward in her chair. "We're sending you in to start a revolution."

CHAPTER 6

MARS

Mars sat behind an orderly desk twirling a gold colored stylus between her fingers. She studied the figures before her with cold speculation. *It's got to be here*, she thought, *the facts never lie*. She had been in her office ever since the morning council meeting ended. Since then she had been going over every scrap of data that Sapphire could provide on any type of rebellious activities. While Sapphire was a wealth of information and could report it in any format she could ask for, the computer just didn't have the reflective skill set needed to look between the cracks. The computer was indispensable when it came to compiling data. Sapphire could tell her instantly how many times a word or phrase was used. She could evaluate facts and figures; compare methodologies. *But the machine never had a gut feeling or a hunch*, she concluded. The machine was cold and calculating, *something*, she thought, *she had often been accused of.*

In all of the data compiled over the last six

months, there had only been two instances where there was a connection between the public offenders. Once, between a brother and a sister who had made antisocial comments during their weekly posting and the other, when a group of four college students had refused to post to their Core pages. *Hardly a massive uprising,* she quipped to herself. But the video of the raid kept playing through her head. If they were making false IDs; there had to be people who were using them.

She picked up the report on the use of alternate identification. In the four years since the enactment of the "True Identity Act" there had been 247 instances of people being arrested while in possession of an alternate identification. She had Sapphire break down the list into three groups.

The first group was the classification known as "shrouds". In these cases there was an attempt to change an ID by using their original or true identification on their PDs. The hope was to "shroud" their true identity or, in most cases, erase blemishes in their history. There were one hundred and sixty-four convictions in this category.

The second group attempted to create a completely new ID. Group two was considered substandard or the workmanship amateurish. Thirty-seven of the convictions fell into the second category.

The third category comprised cases where the illegally manufactured PD and accompanying ID could be considered professional. The remaining forty-six arrests fell into this category. All of the Class three felons were killed by Core Security when resisting arrest. Four of the forty-six had just been added to the list after last night's raid.

"Sapphire," Mars commanded, "compare all category three offenders for similarities."

Sapphire responded instantaneously. "Excluding the four individuals from last night, the forty-two remaining offenders seemed to have received their identifications from the criminal organization once known as "Jasper". In the last seven years, sixteen members of Jasper had been arrested or killed while attempting various level one felonies. Jasper was finally eliminated by Core Security in the third quarter of last year. There is no evidence connecting the criminals from last night to Jasper."

"Have there been any recent activities that could be associated with Jasper?" Mars asked.

"No."

"What is the confidence level that Jasper has been eliminated?"

"Confidence level is 99.8%," Sapphire reported.

"Are there any crime statistics that show similar mode of operations to Jasper? Copycats perhaps?"

"No."

"What is the probability that last night's felons were the start of a new criminal organization or members of an existing crime syndicate?"

"I cannot calculate the probability, Consular. Although they were manufacturing illegal equipment, the criminal intentions of the four cannot be determined beyond the single crime of producing illegal technical equipment. Their intentions or affiliations remain unknown."

Mars' lips curled with disgust, "Damn Adelric!"

"Consular," Sapphire said softly, "Commander Adelric has just entered your outer office and is heading this way."

Mars tapped the screen to allow Adelric admittance to her office. The doors swung inward closely followed by the authoritative figure of Commander Adelric.

"Martin," Mars smiled as she pointed to a chair located in front of her desk.

"Marci," Adelric said mirroring her smile, opting for a seat at the small meeting area located in the corner of her office.

Mars gave him a long, appraising glance as she leaned back in her chair. "Shouldn't you be out killing off some more leads?"

Adelric crossed his legs and placed his elbow on the table. "I have more than enough men out there taking care of that," he said, brushing off her sarcasm.

"You know it would be nice if you left a few of them alive long enough to interrogate."

"I agree with you completely," he answered smoothly, "but the law is the law and the Purification Act expressly states..."

"Don't quote doctrine to me, Martin," Mars snapped. "I know you feel the same way I do on this issue." She let her response sink in before she slowly stood up and moved from around the desk with just a touch of feline grace. She was delighted to see that Martin was following her hips, not her face. She eased into the chair next to his and slowly crossed her legs. She waited until his eyes met hers. "The virus is under control."

"I'm not Dr. Grady, but if I were, I would remind you that the virus strain is undetectable and lies dormant in a small amount of humans. These carriers could start a whole new plague."

Mars rolled her eyes, "Sapphire, what percent of the population of New America has been inoculated against the MERS virus?"

"100%, Councilor."

"And how many cases of the virus have been reported in the last ten years?"

"There have been no reports of anyone contracting the virus within the time line specified."

Mars gave Adelric a sultry smile, "See, all better."

Adelric stared coldly at Mars. "It's the law."

A spasm of irritation crossed her face. "Dam it, Martin, don't play cat and mouse with me!"

Adelric simply shrugged his shoulders causing Mars to rise from her chair. "I hate it," she hissed, "when you come in here wearing your little tutu of justice and dance around my office."

Adelric gave her a hard look. "Tutu? I never wear a tutu and I very seldom dance," he answered motioning her to retake her seat. She hesitated for a second before acquiescing. "I will not be put on the wrong side of the law," he reaffirmed. "I may be an Associate member of the Core Council but I still report up through the Justice Department and I will not have those bureaucrats over at the Government Plaza subpoenaing me before one of their committee barbecues."

"What do you suggest then?"

Adelric bit his lip. "Change the law."

"That could take forever," she answered, "even with heavy pressure from the council."

"So?" Adelric stated, "time has always been on the council's side."

Mars shifted her position, "not this time Martin. You got very lucky last night."

"As I reported to the council this morning."

She nodded at his comment. "If you had to sum up in a few words; what type of operation did you shut down last night?"

Adelric's eyes narrowed as he composed his answer, "crime syndicate or maybe, paramilitary."

Mars nodded again, "neither of which sounds very good. Which would be your first guess."

"Crime syndicate," he quickly replied. "There were no weapons or military gear found in the house. "I think it was either ID's for money or alternate IDs to cover crimes."

"Could this be Jasper coming back to life?"

"Doubtful," he chuckled, "we blasted those bastards into the ground last year. Twenty-seven confirmed kills, no survivors."

"How can you be so sure there were no survivors?" she asked.

"The group had scheduled a meeting in a desert area deep in District 7. We waited until everyone had shown up for the meeting and were in the building before moving in. Infrared scanners picked up only twenty-seven targets within a four mile radius." Adelric pointed toward the ceiling, "Sapphire was monitoring the operation that night."

"That's correct Commander," Sapphire answered, "there were no other suspect in the area."

"Twenty-seven targets," Adelric stated confidently, "twenty-seven corpses in the body count."

Mars leaned toward Adelric and placed her hand atop his, "Martin, please don't take this wrong, but weren't you damn lucky to catch all of them in one place at one time?"

Adelric slid his hand out from under hers. "Normally, I would be inclined to agree with you, but our undercover agents had been working on this gang for over a year. As a matter of fact, we lost three good agents to those assholes." Adelric leaned back in his chair and crossed his arms over his chest. "In the end we were able to bribe an informant for the information."

"I guess this informant was reliable."

Adelric nodded, "We had used her several times over the course of four months. She was very reliable."

"How did she get such reliable information?

Was she on the inside?"

Adelric laughed uncontrollably, his face beaming. "You might say the head guy was on the inside of her."

"Wha…what?" Mars stammered.

"She was a prostitute, Marci. The boss man's favorite screw."

"I see," she said contemptuously, "I guess that would be hard to refute, I mean the word of a hooker…"

"A hooker that netted us the Jasper crime syndicate," he said interrupting Mars.

Mars looked down at the tablet in front of her. She stared at the figures for several seconds. *The facts never lie*, she reminded herself. "Then we have a new crime organization to deal with," she concluded flatly.

"Sapphire," Adelric said, "have we seen any increase in the amount of serious crimes?"

"The numbers I reported this morning are unchanged."

Again, Adelric shrugged his shoulders at the conclusion, while Mars on the other hand shook her head defiantly. "You don't run a professional clandestine ID shop just to give out free samples to the public. Something is coming and we are unprepared for it."

Her statement brought a deep frown to Adelric's face. A serious and instantaneous increase in the crime statistics would land squarely on his shoulders, especially after being forewarned by

Mars. *Such an incident could cost me my position,* he concluded. "What do you want me to do?"

Mars locked eyes with Adelric, "we need more information."

It was Adelric's turn to stand and pace. "Damn it, Marci, we are right back to where we were twenty minutes ago."

"Actually, Commander, it was fourteen minutes and twenty-three seconds ago." Sapphire said correcting him.

"Shut up, Sapphire!" Mars and Adelric said simultaneously.

The room became deathly quiet for several seconds. Adelric continued to pace around the room attempting to gather his thoughts. Mars waited patiently. *He'll come to the right conclusion,* she thought confidently.

Adelric returned to the table and took his seat. "We can't wait for the law to be changed," he thought out loud, "but if we could get the President to issue a temporary executive order?"

"A *sealed* executive order," Mars added.

"We would need the unanimous approval of the council before summoning the President," he said.

Mars' eyes sparkled, "That shouldn't be much of a problem. In six days I become the chairperson for the council. I can call an emergency meeting to discuss it."

"Getting everyone to meet isn't the problem," Adelric reminded her. "Getting unanimous approval will be another matter."

Mars shook her head, "I don't think we will have any problem out of Kinsley or Pyres," she said, "but Dr Grady could be tricky."

Adelric's nose wrinkled, "He sees the MERS virus everywhere."

"Leave Grady to me," Mars stated. "In the meantime you will need to set up an interrogation facility somewhere outside Core City.

CHAPTER 7

JAX CORE CITY

Jax circled the block faking interest in some of the items in the store windows. 'Little Town' was just eleven years old but rang with quaintness and old world charm, or at least that's what is was modeled after. Four blocks long and three blocks wide it was one of the most popular areas of Core City. He recognized the shop fronts from old videos he had watched while still in college. The narrow shop entrances had an antique warmth and allure about them. The brick facades displayed prominent architectural features of Early American buildings. *Late 1800's*, he thought, *Boston, maybe*, but he wasn't really sure. Boston and been destroyed before he had been born.

The streets were narrow and made of cobblestones. The walkways in front of the stores were red brick, laid in a neat herringbone pattern. Every thirty feet there was a replica of a cast iron gas lamp-post. Of course none of the lamp-posts used gas. The use of natural gas and coal had been outlawed after the SCS was established. Instead, the lamps were illuminated with a very elaborate electrical system resembling the old gas flame. Seven or eight feet up from the base of each of the lamp-posts, two ornate poles jutted out in opposite directions, at the end of each pole hung a large basket of perennials. It was springtime and each of the blocks in Little Town was decorated with a different color theme. The street he had just left had been adorned in reds and pink flowers; the street he was standing on now was decorated with vibrant yellow and gold colored displays. The vendors of each street had carried the color theme of the flowers over to their individual storefronts by decorating with yellow and gold ribbons and had even gone as far as to trim the store windows with similar colored drapes and sashes. The small bistro where he was to meet Rebecca had covered their street side tables with yellow checkered tablecloths.

It wasn't until he glanced up that the festivity was dampened. At the fascia of the buildings, he noticed the hidden surveillance cameras. They were well concealed within the stone and masonry decoration, but there none-the-less. He was sure that there were even more devices throughout the block, but hadn't made the effort to locate them. Also, when he looked down the center of the street he could pick out the Central Exchange building looming in the distance. *Not exactly your Norman Rockwell, Saturday Evening Post*, he mused, remembering his pre- Apocalyptic history.

Jax glanced over at the bistro searching again for Rebecca. He looked at his personal device, *11:20 AM*; there were still ten minutes to go before their scheduled meeting. Technically she wasn't late and certainly not the, 'fashionably late', he was told to expect about her arrival. He moved across the street and walked up to the hostess.

"Hello," she smiled greeting him, "a table for one?"

Jax returned her smile, "Two, please. I'm meeting someone." He thought he noticed a hint of disappointment in her face at his answer.

"Of course," she stated, recovering quickly. She led him to one of the tables on the patio and motioned for him to sit. "Jason will be your server. He'll be out in just a second."

"Thanks,"

Jax sat with the brick wall to his back. The seat gave him an unassailable position and a good 180° field of vision. He looked down at his PD, *11:28 AM*. Their meeting had been arranged through SPARKs; Sapphire, Personal, Adult, Reliable, Konnections. Stupid, he thought, but it was the best way for them to meet. They had both gone through an elaborate ruse of joining the online personal meeting service. Both chatted with and dated several other people before they 'connected' on SPARKs themselves. At first he had hated the whole idea, wanting to get down to business, but it had given him some extra time to acclimate to the New American culture and it was a totally safe way for them to meet. He knew the online dating scheme had to have been McKee's idea. She probably laughed herself sick thinking about little Jax going out on a first date.

He decided he would just add it to McKee's list of 'Payback is a bitch'. Of course the hyper-tube was still at the top of the list. He had made it through the first acceleration with not much more than a mild case of nausea. The second part of the trip seemed to be much faster and more intense than the first. He had lost consciousness and awoke when two men lifted him out of the body sling. Jax smiled at the memory. As they lifted him out of the car he had instinctively reached up and felt his forehead.

"You hurt your head?" the one agent asked.

"No," Jax had laughed, "just checking for my asshole."

"Hell of a ride aint it?" the man bellowed as he helped Jax steady himself.

"Jax?"

The mention of his name brought him back to the present. Startled, he looked up. There, standing but a few feet away, was Rebecca. His first impression was that she was much prettier than the pictures on SPARK. Her auburn hair was cut in a neat pageboy and delicately framed her face. Her eyes were emerald green, bright and intelligent. Her skin, velvety, with just a slight wisp of ginger speckles across her checks and nose.

Jax felt himself rising from his chair. "Yes, hi," he answered as he offered her his hand, "you must be Rebecca."

The freckles across her nose wrinkled as she smiled. "Yes, it's good to finally meet you," she said, as she pumped his hand.

Jax was caught off guard by the firmness of the handshake. His micro-assessment of her had registered her lean shape, but her facial features had fooled him into believing her hands would be as soft. He remembered that the brief on her had described her as athletic. Her handshake had certainly proved that.

Rebecca quickly took a seat to Jax's left. Jax retook his chair.

"Well," he started and was motioned to silence by Rebecca as the waiter approached.

"Hi," he said greeting them, "my name is Jason and I'll be your server today. May I start the two of you off with something to drink?"

Jax motioned to Rebecca.

"A glass of water, no ice, would be a great start," she replied.

"I'll have the same," Jax piped in, "but give me the lady's ice as well as mine."

"You've got it," he said as he walked away.

"It's so nice to finally meet you," Rebecca chimed.

"Same here," he answered, hating the touchy feely crap they were being forced to go through.

The waiter returned with the two glasses of water and placed them on the table.

"Give us a few minutes before we order,"

Rebecca stated, before the waiter had a chance to ask.

"Certainly," he said as he walked away.

Jax watched in amazement as Rebecca picked up her water glass and began soaking the yellow flower arrangement on the table.

"Electronics and water are never a good mix," she explained lowering her voice.

Jax was stunned at her rationalization for drowning the table bouquet. "You think the flowers are bugged?"

Rebecca offered him a sweet smile. "Jax, trust me when I tell you it's better to be paranoid here."

"I guess a little paranoia will go a long way around here," he answered not knowing what else to say.

"A lot of paranoia," she answered, "will keep you alive."

They had shared a pleasant lunch while all the time making light, first date kind of chat. Jax had learned in his studies that it was customary in New America for the male to pay the check, but had just learned that it was perfectly alright to split the check if the woman requested it. Rebecca had and the two of them had half the tab scanned to each of their PDs. Fifteen minutes later found them sitting on a street bench, enjoying ice cream cones that Rebecca had allowed him to pay for.

Jax took another lick of ice cream. "This stuff is really good,' he said. He had never seen so many flavors before and didn't have a clue which to order so he followed Rebecca's lead and got the Neapolitan. He was not disappointed.

"Didn't you have ice cream back…home?" she asked.

He knew that *back home* was referring to the outer protective zone. "Yes, but not like this," he answered, taking another lick. "When's the last time you were home?"

Rebecca lowered her cone, "It's been a long time now," she answered thoughtfully, "five years, I guess."

"Do you miss home?" Jax could tell that she did not like this part of their conversation.

"No, not really," she smiled, "Core City is so wonderful I don't miss the District at all."

He remembered that her profile had stated that she had come from District Nine and taken a job with the middle school system teaching home economics and physical education. Home economics was highly praised by both the Core Council and Government for its connection to good family values. It had been easy for her to get a job with such an extremely desirable skill.

"What about you?" she quizzed, "do you miss your District yet?"

His profile had stated that he was from one of the large farming co-ops located in District One. Coming to Core City was part of his four week vacation ruse. "Would you be surprised if I told you I was already home sick?" he lied.

Rebecca giggled as she took another lick of her

cone. "Just a farm boy at heart hugh?"

"Right now the wheat is as green as can be," he answered. "Almost as green as your eyes," he added.

Rebecca smiled like a young school girl. "Flatterer."

"You're dripping there, son," a gruff voice stated.

Jax and Rebecca looked up into the face of a Core Security agent. Jax had seen several security agents throughout the morning but was still taken aback by the Core agent's appearance. He wore no body armor or helmet of any kind. There were no padded gloves to protect their hands and the most interesting thing was the fact that he had no visible weapon. He did have, like all agents Jax had seen so far, a slightly larger PD than most people carried. His uniform was made from an ivory colored synthetic material that had a slight sheen about it. Over the right pocket was a QR code with his name, Johnny, printed at the upper edge. Over the other pocket was an embroidered patch simply stating, "I can help, just ask."

The PD in Jax's pocket vibrated silently, almost like a faint heartbeat. It was a modification that had been made to the PD by their tech people. The alarm was to warn the owner when they were being scanned. He was sure that Rebecca was feeling the same vibration through the back pocket of her jeans.

"I'm..." Jax stammered.

"Your ice cream," the officer said as he grinned

and pointed at Jax's cone, "it's running down the side there."

Jax looked at his cone and began to laugh. Rebecca repeated the same school girl giggle as before.

"I hadn't noticed," Jax said looking toward Rebecca, "I must have been distracted."

"First date?" the officer asked, as he offered Jax a paper wipe.

Rebecca leaned toward Jax until their shoulders touched. "Yes, does it show?"

"I see it all the time here in Little Town. Would you two like me to take a picture of you?"

"That would be great." Jax said and put his arm around Rebecca's shoulder.

The Core agent held up his PD and framed the two of them in the middle. "OK, smile," he commanded.

They both put on their best 'first date' smile and held the pose. Rebecca reached around and pulled her own PD out of her back pocket and held it out toward the officer. Jax mimicked her motions.

Almost instantly the picture flashed on the screens of their PDs. "Wow, thanks," Jax said.

"Not a problem," the officer said, placing his PD back into the holder at his side, "always glad to help out."

The two watched as the officer began to walk off. Jax's PD vibrated steadily for a full second telling him they were no longer being scanned.

"Shit," Jax hissed.

Rebecca continued licking her ice cream not taking her eyes off the security officer. "Not a problem," she said in a confident tone, "it happens all the time."

"Rebecca, that officer scanned us and took our picture," Jax said incredulously.

Rebecca got to her feet wiping her mouth off on a napkin, "Like I said, Jax, it happens all the time. What makes you think it would be any different for you?"

Jax looked at the officer moving off in the distance. "You mean that was his normal routine?"

"Yep," she answered plainly.

Jax watched him until he was out of sight. He was having trouble understanding what had just happened to them. In his mind they had just been searched without probable cause. He threw his melting cone into the trash container. "Why don't they carry weapons?" he asked as an afterthought.

Rebecca tossed her cone in the container. "They don't need them," she answered.

"Well what would have happened if the scan would have reported that we were criminals or something?"

She touched his arm lightly and started down the street. "Probably nothing more than just happened," she answered.

"Then he would have let us go?"

"No, not at all, he would have tagged us and then later..."

"Later..." Jax prompted her.

"Later," she continued, thinking of her lost comrades, "in a much more *private* setting, we would have met the ones with the guns."

"Unbelievable," was the only thing Jax could think to say.

Rebecca turned to face him. She smiled kindly and offered him her hand. "Well Jax, I had a lovely time today. Thank you for having lunch with me."

Jax studied her eyes and determined she had fallen back into character. "You are welcome," he said taking her hand.

He watched as Rebecca walked away. After a few steps she turned back toward him. "Jax, I'm going hiking tomorrow, would you like to join me?"

He walked up to her and stopped. "Sure, that sounds like fun. Where should we meet?"

Rebecca held up her PD and began typing. After a few seconds she held the PD out in Jax's direction. Jax took out his devise and held it out.

"I marked the entrance to the forest and the beginning of the trailheads," She answered as she activated her device. "I'll meet you there at, say 9:30?"

Jax looked down at his PD. The information was all there. The map even showed him the best route to take from his hotel and offered several suggestions on public conveyance, including a list of times he should leave the hotel to arrive at the scheduled 9:30 meet time. He knew that the various departure times depended, of course, on the method of travel he had chosen. "This looks good, Rebecca," he said, his eyes still fixed on the screen before him. "Can I ask you a question?"

She placed the PD back into the rear pocket of her jeans. "Sure, you can ask me anything."

Jax surveyed the area around them. There were people everywhere, many of them young couples just like them. The sounds of laughter could be heard in several directions. "Help me out here," he said making a sweeping gesture with his hand."I don't see the danger. I don't see the repression I was told about."

Rebecca's expression saddened. "Jax, do you know what's a hundred times more dangerous than a rattlesnake?"

He shook his head knowing he wasn't expected to offer an answer. "I give, what?"

"A rattle snake without the rattle."

Jax immediately had mixed feelings as they entered the forest. There was no doubt in his mind that it was beautiful. He marveled at the magnificent trees, the various plants and bushes that made up the lush green underbrush; *all*, he thought, *competing for the few scattered rays of sunlight that managed to pierce the canopy above.* There were more shades of green than he had ever imagined existed. On the other hand, he found it very constrictive almost suffocating at times. There were places along the trail where he could barely see a few dozen feet into the thick foliage. He caught himself longing for the heat and openness of the desert.

"A credit for your thoughts," Rebecca asked.

"It's very beautiful," he said, looking around.

"But a little claustrophobic?" she offered.

He examined the area again, "Yes, that's a good word to use."

Rebecca pointed toward the upper canopy. "Can you see the sky?"

He looked up again, "Very little of it," he admitted.

Rebecca continued to move forward along the trail. "Then they can't see us."

They hiked along the main trail for a few minutes until they turned onto one of the smaller, less traveled routes that jetted off in another direction. It seemed to Jax that the foliage was closing in tighter and tighter with every step. Rebecca finally stopped and took out her water bottle. She took a deep sallow and handed the bottle to Jax. As Jax drank, Rebecca took out her PD and studied the screen. When she was finished she held it out to Jax to see. "No signal," she said triumphantly. "Now they can't see us from the sky and there's no signal for them to eaves-drop on."

Jax pulled out his own PD and checked the signal strength. *Nothing,* he thought. He took a deep breath and sighed as he let it out. "You know, this is the first time in a week that I don't feel like someone is standing over my shoulder."

Rebecca laughed out loud, "I know the feeling,"

she said as she found a spot on a fallen tree to sit down. "I do a lot of hiking."

Jax sat next to her, "I can see why."

"Really," she asked, one eyebrow rising in a questioning slant. "Yesterday you didn't see any danger."

"I still don't," he answered a little defensively, "not really. I mean, so they scanned us illegally, it's not like they locked us away in some deep, dark hole and beat a confession out of us." Jax stood and with an elaborate gesture pointed around them, "And look, here we are off the grid and I don't see anyone rushing in to get us back under their microscope."

Rebecca remained sitting on the log, her hands folded in her lap, and her legs swinging freely. "I brought you out here to fill you in on some of the finer details of life in New America, so we better start before they do get here."

Jax made a quick scan of the area, "You're kidding, right? They're not coming out here."

She shook her head as she spoke. "They'll be here soon enough. It will be two of them, a bike patrol coming out to make sure we're alright and don't require medical assistance."

"You're..."

Rebecca held out her hand to silence him and continued, "They will scan us again. This time it will include a bio-scan to supposedly make sure we're OK. There will be more pictures taken; the usual, 'Let me take a picture of you two lovebirds.'

or something just as stupid."

Jax returned to the log and eased himself down next to Rebecca. "Bio-scans?" he heard himself ask.

"That's a good place to start," she sighed. "Jax, we now know that everyone is subject to a bio-scan by their PD's at least once a day. Those with the newer PD's have a little more to worry about."

"How so?"

"The casing on the new PD's can collect the oils and secretions from your hands and perform more in-depth testing."

"What are they looking for?"

Rebecca shrugged her shoulders, "Any number of things I guess. The testing we were doing in our lab suggested that they could be performing any number of tests all the way down to the DNA level."

Jax rubbed his palms on his trousers. *Damn*, he thought, *now I'm feeling itchy.* "Well the first thing that comes to mind is that they can do a lot of good with those tests." He was amazed how much he doubted his own words as they were coming out of his mouth, "But on the other hand…" he looked over at Rebecca, "the rattlesnake with no rattle." A cold chill passed through his entire body, "Hey, wait a minute, do I have one of the new model PD's?"

"You're not worried about it," she said sarcastically, "are you?" Rebecca winked and offered a wicked smile.

Jax started to get up from the log but was

stopped by her hand on his arm. "Not to worry, none of us are using that model. At the current rate they are replacing the older models we figure that it will take them another eight or so months to upgrade everyone."

He relaxed as much as he could while digesting this new information. "Tell me more about Sapphire."

Rebecca nodded. "It's their super computer, or computers that monitor and run everything in New America."

"And the Solar Collection System?"

"Everything. There isn't a gadget or device that isn't tied into Sapphire."

"So, you would rate it as their most important weapon?"

She thought about her answer. "It's hard to say. It would be between Sapphire and the Solar Collection System. We're almost positive that Sapphire draws its power needs from the SCS to function, but then the SCS relies on Sapphire for its complex operating system. It's kind of like asking, 'what's more important, the brain or the heart?"

"Well, a bullet to the brain or the heart would do the trick then."

"Yes, we've discussed those options over and over," she said. "A computer virus uploaded to Sapphire could kill the brain, so to speak, or the destruction of the solar collectors would put out their lights."

"But?"

Sapphire is a closed system. No one is allowed to upload anything into the network. All their coding, which is like nothing we have ever seen in prewar software, is locked behind a massive firewall."

"We uploaded pictures and emails all week," he offered.

"No, Sapphire uploaded and distributed all of that. You are not allowed to upload any kind of file format into the system. If Sapphire doesn't give it you, you can't have it."

"Do we know where their network mainframe is?" he asked.

"No one has the faintest idea. We haven't been able to discover its location. Asking those types of questions can get you eliminated before you know it."

"OK, what about the solar collectors?"

"There are twenty-seven of them within the system, all heavily guarded."

"There's twenty-eight," Jax interjected.

"Twenty-eight?"

"Yes, there's one located on Santa Catalina Island just off the old California coast," he answered, watching Rebecca's eyes light up at the new information. "But, that's a subject for another day," he said, motioning for her to continue.

"OK, for our current discussions, we'll stick with the twenty-seven that supply all the power to the districts. It would take an army greater that anything we have to destroy just a few of them."

"And," Jax added, "that would be self-defeating in the end."

"Absolutely," she agreed. "If we stay with our analogy of the human body, and consider each of the districts as one of the body's other functions, they would all perish with the death of the brain or heart."

"Sorry, Mrs. Jones," Jax smirked, "the operation to remove your husband's brain was completely successful, but for some reason he still died."

Rebecca laughed lightly, "A bit melodramatic, but you got the point." She stood and stretched before she turned back to face Jax. "Jax, you and your team have to dig deeper than my team was able to do. I don't know…"

"Whoa, girl," he said cutting her off in mid-sentence. "I don't have a team. It's just me."

The blood drained from her face as she stared open-mouthed. "No…what…you didn't come in with a full team?"

"Sorry, it's just me."

"I don't understand. I thought you were bringing in a new team to replace mine."

"Sorry," he said meaning it more than he expected, "whatever you and your team were doing is finished. I'm not a replacement."

"But my orders were to bring you up to speed," she protested.

"And you are," he answered. "By the way, what was your team doing?"

"Rebecca looked at him with suspicion, "Didn't

McKee tell you?"

Jax had to smile, "I didn't need to know, or more to the point, McKee said it was none of my business."

"That sounds like her," Rebecca nodded.

"She did mention that you were part of a *pop-chain protocol*, but she never told me what that meant either."

Rebecca grinned from ear to ear, "You don't know what a pop-chain is?"

"I think I just said that."

"Back in the sixties or seventies, that's nineteen-sixties, there was a child's toy made out of plastic beads. They came in all sizes and colors, but the one thing they all shared was that each bead had a male and female receptacle. A chain of the beads could be made by connecting one plastic bead to another until you had a string of them."

"Why call them pop-beads?"

"Because, silly, when you pulled them apart they made a popping sound." Rebecca placed her thumb on the side of her mouth and flicked it outward. The resulting friction caused a popping sound. "Kind of like that."

Jax stared at Rebecca grinning. "And how does that have anything to do with military protocol?"

"Pop-chains were made up of individual pieces and could easily be broken and reassembled. So, in other words, if one of us is compromised, or the chain is *popped*, no-one else up or down the chain is affected. The chain can be reassembled."

"I'm still having a problem understanding the military," he admitted. "So, if my next question doesn't activate the 'kill Jax protocol', what was your team doing?"

Rebecca pulled out her PD. "We were manufacturing these," she said, holding up the device. "We made the one you're carrying now."

They heard the rubber of the bike tires grinding through the gravel on the trail long before they could see the two security officers. Rebecca pulled Jax close to her and, wrapping her arms around his neck, kissed him. Jax pulled back slightly and moved his lips closer to her ear. "Please tell me," he whispered, "that they are not going to shove their PD's up my ass for the bio-scan."

As the two riders came around the bend, Rebecca pulled back slightly and looked Jax in the eyes. "Idiot," she whispered as she kissed him a second time.

CHAPTER 8

PRESIDENT ZIVEN

President Joshua Ziven was a tall, lean man in his mid thirties. At six feet four inches his closest acquaintance would describe him as lanky or leggy. It was for this reason that he fit so poorly in the hyper-tube shuttle that ran between Government Plaza and the Core Towers. The shuttle had been designed for four occupants, but Ziven thought that whoever had been the test subjects couldn't have been taller than five feet four. No matter how many times he had ridden in the car, he could never figure out a way to cram all of him in comfortably. The ride was mercifully short, but miserably painful. He had even gone so far as to ask Core Council to have the two forward seats removed since he was the only one ever to travel in the damn thing and he had always traveled alone.

Once again, Ziven found himself crammed into one of the four seats whooshing his way back to Government Plaza. He braced himself for the abrupt stop that was coming and grimaced when the attempt failed. The door slid open revealing the highly polished shoes of his Chief of Staff waiting for him on the tiny platform. Ziven unfolded himself from the car, refusing to take the Chief of Staff's outstretched hand.

"How was the meeting?" asked Robert Lars, Ziven's Chief of Staff and closest friend. Lars turned and pushed the only button on the lift. The elevator only went one place and that was directly to the president's private office.

"Blessedly short," he answered, stretching upward, his hands almost touching the ceiling above. The doors slid open and the two men entered the small car.

"Welcome back, Mr. President," Sapphire said in a smooth silky voice.

"Whatever," Ziven shot back, the only sign of the true level of his anger.

"What floor, Mr. President?" Lars asked the President, snickering.

"Mr. Lars, the elevator only has one stop," Sapphire reminded him.

"Really," he grinned, "I was hoping to go to the pool area."

"There is no pool in this building," Sapphire answered.

The door opened allowing the two men to exit. It closed again but not before Sapphire wished them a pleasant day.

"Bob, why do you tease that thing?" Ziven

asked, sliding into his chair.

Lars took his regular seat without asking for the President's permission. There were no formalities between the two when behind closed doors. "I don't know Josh," Lars answered. "I guess I get some type of sadistic pleasure out it." Lars moved forward in his chair, "Speaking of sadistic, how did the meeting go?"

In a conspiratorial gesture, Ziven's eyes shot around the office, "Sweep?" he asked.

Lars nodded, "ten minutes ago. The room is clean."

Early in the formation of the new nation a fierce debate had taken place between the Core Council and the then sitting President over the privacy of the presidential offices. Both sides had dug in their heels and a dangerous rift became apparent. With the eminent collapse of the fledgling country hanging in the balance, the Core Council gave in. Sapphire was not allowed into the presidential offices except for the PD devices carried by The President and the staff members. It was agreed that the PDs could be muted when entering the rooms. No sitting president had ever trusted the agreement.

Ziven opened the top drawer of his desk and lifted the heavy lid of the inner container. He thoughtlessly threw his PD in. He noticed that Bob's was already there. He let the lid drop, closed the drawer and relaxed.

"That bitch, Marci Tansy is chairperson again," he hissed.

"Ah, Mars, the goddess of war, what edict did she pass down this time?"

Ziven locked his hands behind his neck and stretched, "They want me to sign a sealed executive order allowing them, through Adelric's group, to detain and question *any person of suspicion.*"

"You're kidding. For how long?" Lars asked, skeptically.

"Indefinitely."

"And Dr. Grady went along with them? You know he sees the damn virus behind every bush."

Ziven leaned forward resting his elbows on his desk. "Bob, I swear the man's eyeballs were sweating. Tansy must have gotten to him."

"Hell, Mars owns him," Lars stated flatly.

"Probably, but I can tell you; they're all scared."

Lars rubbed his chin thoughtfully, "I can't imagine why. We haven't done anything to piss them off any more than usual."

Ziven shook his head, "This is not about us. Something else has them spooked."

"Well, if it isn't us, it must be something near and dear to their hearts, if they have hearts. What do they care about other than power and money?"

"Losing power or money," Ziven added thoughtfully.

Lars began rubbing his chin again. "It can't be the SCS, they own it completely and it would take a small nuke to destroy one of the facilities.

"A nuke that no one has," the President added.

"What about Sapphire?"" Lars asked.

"Nope, they own that too," he said, "that's the base of all their power and definitely the source of their income. Everything is tied to those two enterprises."

Lars leaned forward in his chair resting his elbows on his knees. "If it's not about gaining or losing their power base, what's left?"

Ziven closed his eyes thinking momentarily about waking up this morning. The vision of his wife lying there with him, her naked body pressed up against his made him forget the tension between his shoulders briefly. He grew angry again when the thought about how the Council had tried to drive a wedge between him and his family with their vicious lies about his supposed adultery. *They have tried to corrupt my marriage,* he thought, *and I won't forget it.*

Ziven shot straight up in his chair. *Corruption,* he thought. "Someone's stealing from them," he said out loud.

Lars looked up at him, "Stealing what?"

Ziven tapped his desk with this finger emphasizing each word as he spoke. "Either money, power, or both," he said going over the possibilities in his head. "What was that report the Department of Justice gave me a few weeks ago concerning Adelric?"

"The Attorney General mentioned that Adelric had been accessing some of the old DOJ files dealing with the criminal gang known as Jasper," Lars said as he rose from his chair, picked up the phone and pressed one of the speed dial buttons. It was a split second before there was an answer on the other end. "Hi, Maggie, is Mrs. Kelly there?" Lars listened for a second and then smiled and nodded. "Perfect, have her come in to see the President as soon as possible." Lars hung up the phone and returned to his seat. "She's on this floor just finishing up a meeting."

"It has to be someone dipping their fingers into the cookie jar," Ziven said evenly.

There was a light rap at the door. "Damn, that was quick," Lars said, as he got up to answer the door.

Attorney General, Adrian Kelly, entered the room and without speaking. She walked over to the President's desk and as before, Ziven opened the drawer with the two PDs in it and waited for the Attorney General to deposit hers. Once the drawer was secure she spoke. "Good morning Mr. President." She turned to the Chief of Staff. "Bob, how are you doing today?"

Both men returned the greeting and took their seats. Kelly sat in the only other chair in the office, the one matching that of the Chief of Staff. "I guess that since this isn't our regular scheduled meeting time, something must be up."

"Sissy," the President addressed her as he had ever since they had attended law school together, "I know you think that I don't listen to your reports as attentively as I should sometimes."

"Sometimes?"

Ziven ignored the dig. "Could you refresh us on

the report you gave on Aldrich a few weeks ago?"

"It was three weeks ago, Mr. President," she reminded him, "our techs discovered that he was conducting a search of some old files dealing with the now defunct gang that called themselves..."

"Jasper," Ziven interjected. "I did remember that much," he grinned. "What was he after?"

I wasn't sure at first, but I had a few of our people dig into it further."

Ziven was happy to hear that she had inferred that Aldrich was not one of her staff or, by association with her, one of 'his people'.

"Have you come up with anything?" Lars asked.

"The only thing we've discovered so far is that he was zeroing in on a woman named Patricia (Pepper) Mallory."

"Pepper?" Lars asked snidely, "no doubt the Valedictorian of her graduating class."

"A hooker," Kelly said, "at least according to the security reports input by Aldrich's men."

Again Ziven did not miss the inference that, in fact, Aldrich or his security force could not be trusted. "Any thoughts as to why she would be such a high profile subject?"

Kelly shook her head. "Nothing yet, but everything points to the fact that Aldrich was more interested in her than anyone else in the gang."

Ziven pulled out the bottom drawer of his desk and rested his size thirteen shoe on the rim. "They were all killed, weren't they?"

Kelly nodded."Yes, Aldrich's black knights wiped them all out in a single night."

"Must have been one hell of a shootout."

"Do we need to find her before Aldrich does?" Lars asked.

Ziven pulled lightly on his ear. "Aldrich already has three weeks head start on us," he sighed. "With the help of Ms Blue," as he often referred to Sapphire, "he should already have her in the bag."

Lars nodded in agreement, "Sapphire could definitely pinpoint the suspect within a few hours, but up until an hour ago, the Council didn't have the approval to detain and interrogate."

"What?" Kelly asked, looking from one man to the other. "When did this go down? And why wasn't I told about it?"

Lars pointed toward the President. "The President was coerced into signing a sealed executive order giving Core Security the right to detain and question people of suspicion. You were informed within one hour of the signing."

"So it just happened?"

Ziven reached forward and began rubbing his knee. "I still have the dents in my kneecaps from riding in that Core kiddy car."

"Well," Kelly sighed, "if security has her we'll never see her again. You know that, right?"

Ziven remained silent for several seconds before speaking again. "I need you to do two things for me, Sissy. First, find out if they have the woman and second if so, where are they keeping her."

"It won't be any place we already know about," Lars offered.

"It will probably be in a remote section of one of the outer districts."

"You don't think he would go outside the protected perimeter, do you?" Lars asked.

"I doubt it," Kelley stated, "the Outsiders would cut him up into little pieces and knit him into an Afghan."

"I agree," Ziven nodded, "he'll stay inside the protective zone where he can make maximum use of his resources."

"What if, for some strange reason, they haven't found her yet?" Kelly asked.

Ziven composed his answer. "Sissy, what do you have Steven doing right now?"

"He's working on a project for me, but I could make him available."

"Great, keep me informed on this one," Ziven stated as he leaned forward and opened the draw containing the PDs.

Kelly took her queue to leave and retrieved her PD from the drawer. Without saying another word, she nodded her goodbyes and left the room. Ziven sealed the drawer again.

"Bringing out the big guns on this one aren't you?" Lars asked, after the door had closed behind Kelly.

Ziven stared at his best friend. "Bob, I can smell real trouble on this one. I've never seen Mars like she was today."

"And with Mars at the helm of the Core Council for the next four weeks," Lars added, "she can throw her weight around like she obviously did with Grady."

"Exactly," Ziven said as he went to open the drawer again.

"Wait a second Josh," Lars said, putting his hand out to stop the President.

Ziven relaxed. "What's up?"

"I've probably known you longer than anyone alive," he grinned. "You didn't give them and Executive Order for nothing, did you?"

"What makes you say that?" Ziven asked stone-faced.

Lars gave him the 'come on, it's me you're talking to' look.

Ziven placed his hand back on the handle of the desk drawer. "The bastards agreed to get to the bottom of my adultery scandal and debunk the source by the end of the week or I pull the order."

"Excellent," Lars said as Ziven pulled the drawer open.

CHAPTER 9

THE MEETING

Jax studied the map that was projected on the wall. It wasn't a whole lot different from the one McKee had shown him back in Middle-earth with the exception that this map had an overlay of the nine districts superimposed over the land mass. The districts were a simple configuration of identical squares laid out across the middle section of the old United States. They were three across and three rows down. The numbering started in the upper left hand square, went to the right then returned to the left to start the numbering for the next three and so on. So it was a simple layout with the first row being Districts , 1,2,3 the second row 4,5,6 and of course the bottom row being 7,8,9. He had studied early American history in several of his Political Science classes and had learned about the Metes and Bounds system of measurement. The system had been used in the United Kingdom for many centuries and was brought over to the American colonies. The system worked especially well when used to define larger pieces of property where precise definitions were not required. Core City was located in the center of District 5 and was therefore located in the center of the grid.

"Rebecca," he asked not taking his eyes off the map, "can you overlay the SCS locations?'

He heard the keys clicking as Rebecca's fingers pounded out the request on the old key board. "There," she said, as the small red dots materialized.

Jax studied the map more intently. "There are three SCS locations per district," he mused out loud.

"That's true," Peter confirmed, "but if you look closely, they are not symmetrically spread out over the regions."

Peter had been one of the agents that had freed Jax from his cocoon in the hyper-tube and they had struck up an instant bond. There were four other agents in the room besides Peter and Rebecca. Jax felt equally comfortable with each.

"Why do you think it's that way?" he asked the room.

Rebecca's fingers could be heard clicking on the keys again. "If you look at their locations in relation to the larger cities," she said, as the computer circled each major metropolitan area in a blue circle, "it shows that the SCS locations tend to be closer to the density of the population."

"The more people, the more power needed,"

one of the other agents offered.

"Exactly," Jax replied, "and the more security forces required to protect them."

"The solar plants are pretty much equally spaced out in District One." Peter mentioned.

"Not really," Rebecca countered, "District One is mostly agricultural, but two of the plants are closer to the outer perimeter of the square."

"That's right," Peter answered, pointing to the map. "One's up in the northern area and the other to the west."

Jax frowned as he took in the information. "Helping to power the border fences?"

"Possibly," Rebecca answered, "or strategically placed for expansion when the time comes."

"Has anyone heard anything about a new plant being built?" Jax asked.

There was a low murmur of no's throughout the room.

"I asked Sapphire once," Rebecca offered, "she told me that the system only added a new facility when it was required."

"When was the last facility added?" Jax asked.

His question was answered with silence. "Anyone?" Jax prompted.

"I can't remember hearing about a new facility being built in my life-time," Peter offered.

"Nor can I," added Rebecca. "Can anyone remember one being built?"

Again the room was filled with the sound of no's.

"Does it matter?" Peter asked.

Jax sat up in his chair. "I don't know yet, but it is an interesting question. Do we have any information on the capacity of one of these facilities?"

"It's a taboo subject," Rebecca reminded him. "Any questions about the inner workings of the solar system are not welcome."

"You asked," Jax reminded her.

Rebecca shook her head, "No, not really, I asked a simple question and got an ambiguous answer. I've never asked about the hardcore day to day operating system or power output."

"Rebecca's right," Peter added, "they don't exactly offer a daily tour through any of the plants." He looked in Jax's direction. "Is it important?"

"I don't know yet," Jax sighed, "but the more we know about their power base, the easier it will be to devise a plan to bring them down."

"Those things could have endless power," Peter stated.

"I don't think so," Rebecca answered thoughtfully, "I mean the max output is limited to the number of hours that they can collect energy from the orbiting satellites. Once we're on the dark side the beams stop. I've seen them shut down."

"Plus," Jax added, "we have no idea what their energy conversion rate is, but I doubt it's 100%."

"Well," Peter offered, "we know it's enough to power all the cities and the fence."

We're off track, Jax thought. "My original

question wasn't so much as to the energy they put out, but more directly to the point, of Core Security forces committed to each facility."

Peter shook his head in disgust. "Impregnable to anything we could muster."

"Still not my point," Jax said. "What I'm concerned with is the Core Security forces being able to deliver troops to a fight."

"Fight?" Rebecca asked. "I thought you ruled out open combat."

Jax stood and began to pace the room. "Not combat, Rebecca. "Open resistance or better yet, open rebellion. We have to start a rebellion that will gain strength as it grows."

"Ah," Peter smiled, "a rebellion that would be quickly shut down if security forces were able to respond quickly."

"That's right. We start the protest in the outer Districts where the security forces are thinnest. By the time a sizeable force can be moved into the area we'll be gone."

Rebecca folded her arms across her chest. "You're still assuming that you can get enough of the general populace to join your little crusade."

"Why wouldn't they?" Jax gestured emphatically.

"Because," Rebecca shot back, "they are very happy with their lives." "Mostly," she added as an afterthought.

"Rebecca's right," Peter said, "there is no unemployment, there's not any basic food shortage or lack of available medical care. What have they got to protest?"

Jax lowered himself into his chair with a sigh, "So you're telling me that they are all just fat and happy little pigs lying out in the stock yard waiting for their turn to be slaughtered."

"Come on, Jax, we're not saying that," Rebecca said, "but you have to admit that they will have to have something to light a fire under them or this rebellion is going to die on the vine."

"What about Sapphire?" Jax asked. "Is anyone in this room happy with having the system looking over their shoulder everyday or is anyone happy about reporting their private information to that thing?"

"Of course not," someone answered, "but there are many who don't care."

"What about the bio-scans and the information they're collecting?"

"But they sell it as a good thing, Jax," Peter said. "For the overall wellbeing of the community.

"And Hitler sold the Jews on the relocation program."

"Jax is right," Rebecca said, thinking of her fallen team, "and we're forgetting about the people that go missing."

Jax found himself rising from his chair again. "There are basic freedoms, freedoms that our constitution granted us that have been taken away under the guise of 'for the overall good of the people' and they will never get them back from this government."

"A constitution," Peter added "that we of Middle-earth have sworn to protect and defend."

Rebecca felt the pride swell in her. "That's right; this country was taken from us and a new set of rules shoved down the throat of those who were left behind. They have a right to decide for themselves."

A look around the room told Jax that the message had hit home. *Now,* he thought, *we can move forward with the next step.* "Peter," Jax was startled at how loud his voice sounded in the silence, "do we have agents in each district?"

"Several, it's the only reliable way for obtaining good information."

"Excellent," Jax said, pointing back up to the map projected on the wall. "Have the agents begin probing weaknesses in their areas."

"Weaknesses?" Rebecca asked.

"Yes, any sign of malcontent among the population no matter how small, must be reviewed." Jax turned to face Rebecca, "Do we have any PD's that are operational, but not connected to the system yet?"

"Sure," she offered, "we even have a dozen or so that have no uplink capability at all."

"Are they fully functional?" he asked.

"As fully functional as they can be without the connectivity to the network."

"Camera and video able?"

"Yes, but you know we could never upload anything to the system, at least not for very long until it was shut down. And the link would be instantly traced back to the individual PD."

Jax smiled deviously, "No, but we have the capability to print photos, correct?"

"Sure," Peter answered.

"Then we print them and post them."

"You can't post to Sapphire," Rebecca protested.

Jax shook his head, "Not posted to Sapphire, post the printed pictures on walls, lamp posts, anything that you can glue a flyer to. Kind of like the old…" Jax strained to remember the right word from his history class.

"The old…what?" Peter asked.

"Old…" Jax said snapping his fingers as if it would help him remember. "Old…bulk mail system," he finally blurted out.

Everyone in the room stared at him as if he had just lost his mind. "Bulk mail," he said emphasizing each of the words. When he saw that no one had a clue what he was talking about he continued. "Look, prior to the war, the US Postal system would allow people to send printed advertisements through the mail system for a fraction of the cost of a first class letter. It was a very inexpensive method of advertising that would reach thousands of people in a single mailing. The mailings usually had a very low response rate, but it was a numbers game. If you mailed out say 200,000 pieces and got only a one percent response. You still got your message to 2,000 people."

He studied his audience for any sign of understanding. There were a few nods so he continued. "So we take pictures of anything that is adverse to the government position and then print them and post them all over the region."

"It could work," Rebecca offered, "we would have to be very cautious though. Remember the cameras?"

"A little creativity would help avoid them," Peter smiled.

Jax started to feel like he was making some progress. "Alright then, let's get the word out to our people in the field. Peter, can you see about setting up some printing operations in each of the districts we decide to target?"

"I can, Jax," he answered, "but we're not going to target all the districts?"

"Not at first," Jax answered.

"Walk before you run," Rebecca offered.

Jax gave her a warm look, "Something like that." He looked around the room one more time. "Are there any more questions?"

One of the agents toward the back of the room raised her hand.

"Yes?" Jax prompted.

"What's a 'first class letter'?"

CHAPTER 10

MARS' PLAN

Mars hated visiting the twenty first floor where the security forces were garrisoned. In fact, in the past, she had made up her mind that she didn't need to spend any time there and refused to meet with Adelric whenever he extended an invitation. The elevator door opened to reveal the large crest of the Core Security Forces emblem. Mars clenched her fist at the sight of it and turned in the only direction that was allowed to anyone who entered the territory of Adelric's forces.   The hall had been designed to give limited access and movement to any visitors. Mars looked over her shoulder back at the door. There was purposely no call button for the elevator on the wall. If someone wanted out, they would have to have the permission of the officer on duty.

She smiled wickedly as she stamped down the long hallway. *One word from her*, she thought, *and Sapphire would shut down their entire operation.* It's also comforting to know that she, through a command to Sapphire, could recall the elevator at will.

She stopped at the doorway at the far end of the hall and waited for security to finish their check. Her nostrils flared. *He's making me wait on purpose,* she thought, the security check was finished within seconds of her pushing the elevator button for the twenty first floor. *If I hadn't passed the check then, the doors would have opened revealing a three foot by three foot security room instead of the long hallway.* She smiled at the camera she knew was hidden in the door. *For whatever reason,* she fumed; *he's really trying to piss me off today.*

The door opened silently. The towering figure of Commander Adelric was waiting just inside. "Councilor Tansy," he said, greeting her with a slight bow, "I'm glad you could find time to come down."

At least he remembered to address me as councilor this time. Only once before had he slipped and used her given name in public. A mistake he would not soon forget. "Commander Adelric," she responded nodding her head politely, "I'm always happy to spend time with the men and women who serve."

"Of course," he responded pointing to the door opening to their right, "this way please."

Mars followed him through a twisted pathway of halls. One of Adelric's security measures was a wall system that could be changed on command. Walls could be moved easily, in effect, changing the layout of the floor plan. It would be difficult if not impossible to find your way through the maze if you didn't know the system. *But,* she reminded herself, *she held the trump card in Sapphire.*

"Are we going to run around your little maze like a couple of mice or do you have a point in dragging me down here?"

"Right through this door," he said, ignoring her comment.

Mars entered the small room closely followed by Adelric. A spasm crossed her face as she drew a sharp breath. The small hairs on the back of her neck stirred as she felt queasiness in the pit of her stomach. "What?"

"Something wrong?" Adelric asked.

Mars looked around the very small room. There were two padded arm chairs positioned around a small wooden table. Other than the sparse furnishings there was nothing else in the room. "Didn't you feel it?" she heard herself ask weakly.

Adelric motioned her toward one of the chairs. "Sit down here," he said, "the feeling will pass quickly."

Her saliva glands seemed to be working overtime, filling her mouth with metallic tasting spittle. She reached out her hand to steady herself on the arm of the chair. "What's happening to me?" she managed to say as she slumped down in the chair.

Adelric calmly took a seat in the chair facing hers. "It's the result of the field," he said making a vague gesture around the room. "My research people tell me it has to do with how it affects your middle ear. The field has some type of temporary affect on your balance, causing disorientation which, in turn, gives you the queasy stomach you're probably experiencing."

"What field?" she asked, starting to feel a little better. "What are you talking about?"

"This room," he stated proudly, "is shielded from any form of eavesdropping or scans."

"A darkroom?"

"Very similar to the darkroom we discovered the Outsiders using to shield their operation; in a matter of speaking."

Now her natural curiosity was kicking in as her stomach slowly returned to normal. "How did you do it?"

Adelric pushed a small button hidden in the arm of his chair. Almost immediately the door opened and an officer carrying a tray holding two glasses entered. He placed the tray on the table and left without speaking. "I haven't the slightest idea," Adelric said, picking up one of the glasses and offering it to her. "Here, drink some cold water; it seems to help."

Amazingly, she felt better as the cold liquid ran down the back of her throat. "Thank you," she said in earnest. "Electronic shielding is prohibited technology." She reminded him.

"It was," he admitted, "until the President signed that executive order."

Mars' eyebrow rose slightly, "I don't remember

reading any such thing in the order."

"Well," he said, giving her a conspiratorial wink, "you'd have to read between the lines to see it."

Mars placed her empty glass back on the tray and eyed the second glass hungrily. "I consider myself a very good reader and I don't remember reading that part." She considered just taking the full glass without asking Adelric, but had second thoughts.

He pointed to the full glass as if reading her mind, "That one is for you also. I had three glasses the first time I experienced the field, but," he continued as he touched his stomach lightly, "I don't recommend it."

Mars drank the second one slowly. "We were talking about the executive order."

"That's right, we were," Adelric agreed. "The order did say something to the effect that we were to use 'whatever means necessary to find and interrogate person or persons of interest'.

"And," Mars prompted him.

"You, yourself, said that we should hide the interrogation centers so that we draw no attention."

Mars' eyes narrowed, "I know for a fact that this," she said waving her hand around the room, "was not what I meant." A cold chill suddenly shot through her body, "Wait a minute, you're not telling me that you plan to interrogate subjects right here in the Core Exchange building?"

"Of course not," Adelric snorted, "that would

be insane. This was just a test facility used to perfect the field. We are currently installing the equipment in buildings in Districts One and Nine. Of course," he said nonchalantly, "we'll add additional centers as the need arises."

Mars was finally feeling a little better after the initial effects of the field, but now had a familiar old butterfly, in the form of Adelric, floating around her stomach. "So you feel that more centers will be needed?"

Adelric frowned as he reached into his breasts pocket and produced a folded piece of paper. "I have a report on our missing hooker, Pepper Mallory."

Mars understood the significance of a paper document. Whatever information Adelric had on the paper would never be found within the Sapphire computer system. The information would cease to exist the second the paper was burned. *I need to double my efforts in making our society truly paperless, she reminded herself.* She moved forward in her chair, "You found her?"

"I'm afraid that I have some bad news," he said solemnly.

"She's dead?"

He shook his head from side to side, "Well, in a manner of speaking."

"Martin, stop screwing around!" Mars hissed.

"Pepper Mallory was never born, never existed; all traces of the fictitious person are gone."

Mars slumped back in her chair feeling as if Adelric had just knocked the wind out of her. "Wait a minute," she said, "your group would have done a complete background investigation on her before trusting some whore to give you information. What happened there?"

"You're right," he nodded, "a complete investigation was done, but I know now that it was an elaborate shroud."

Mars jumped up from her chair forgetting the size of the small room. With nowhere to go she awkwardly placed her hands on her hips. "You're trying to tell me that this was some crappy shroud job?"

"I think I used the word *elaborate*," he said.

"So, you need a real person to create a shroud. Where's that person then?"

"She died six days prior to the new person taking over her identity."

"Damn it, Martin, as usual you are speaking in circles. Just a minute ago you said there was no one named Pepper Malory. Now you're telling me that she did exist and she or someone shrouded her ID."

"There was a young woman named Patricia Malory raised right here in Core City, but she was never called 'Pepper' by anyone. Not even as a child. Whoever did this surgically wove the persona, *Pepper*, into the young dead Patricia's life." Adelric frowned again, "I have never seen such seamless precision in my entire career."

Mars crossed her arms over her chest. "Then how did you discover this *elaborate* ruse?"

"As you often accuse us of; we got lucky. First,

we had Sapphire conduct an extensive background check on everyone with the name Pepper. When that turned up nothing, we searched for any name that could have been associated with the nickname Pepper."

"And..." Mars prompted him.

"Nothing came up there except for a single anomaly when the name Patricia was searched. It seems that the real victim, Patricia Mallory, had passed away from blunt trauma to the head when she fell from a second floor balcony. It was classified as an accident and there were several witnesses."

"You think she was murdered?"

"No, not at all, I believe it was truly an accident. A death certificate was properly recorded, but then a few days later an exception report was entered stating that her death was recorded in error. Patricia (Pepper) Mallory was alive and doing well in her new profession as a hooker."

"Unbelievable," Mars whispered.

Adelric shrugged his shoulders. "Except for that tiny bit of information, the shroud was perfect."

Mars shook her head as she thought out loud, "They never would have expected that anyone would go looking for her again. I mean, she wouldn't be called to testify against Jasper, you eliminated all of them; case closed."

Adelric leaned forward in his chair and rested his elbows on his knees. "But you're not asking the right follow-up question, Marci."

Her breath caught in her throat, "Why go

through all this trouble to wipe out Jasper?"

"That's the big question. Whoever went through all of this," he said, holding up the sheet of paper, "wanted Jasper out of the way and didn't want to be implicated in their demise."

"So they got your men to do the dirty work. A rival gang?" she asked.

Adelric shrugged his shoulders. "A rival gang that hasn't committed a single crime since Jasper's downfall?"

Marci bit her bottom lip as she considered the possibilities, "What about Ziven? He certainly has people who could have created the shroud?"

"What's his motivation?"

"To undermine the Core Council of course," she spat.

Adelric wrinkled his nose dismissing the notion. "Not enough substance to implicate the government, but there could be a tie between Jasper and our subjects from the dark room."

"What tie?"

"One of Jaspers operations was the manufacturing of fake PD's; mostly to cover up criminal activities."

"You think that the criminals from the other night were working with Jasper; supplying the gang with the fake PDs?"

"Why set up your best customer to be wiped out? No," he said shaking his head, "more than likely they were at cross purposes."

"Cross purposes?"

Adelric took a deep breath and let it out slowly. "What if both groups were producing fake ID's?"

"In direct competition?" Mars interjected.

"No, hear me out. It's possible the two groups were truly at cross purposes. For now, let's say that the darkroom group was working on a plan that could have been jeopardized by the Jasper sales of ID's. In their minds the reckless sale of ID's could have brought the wrath of Core Security down on their heads. After all, we were investigating every lead we could get to shut down the ID factories."

"They could have accidentally been caught in the same net as Jasper's factories." Mars said.

"Or if we kept turning up the heat it would have forced them to shut down."

"And it may well have temporarily forced them to shut down," she said, now thinking along the same lines as Adelric. "They shut down the operations and hoped to wait it out, but…"

"But," Adelric said finishing for her, "it was taking too long for us to shut Jasper down."

"So they gave you the help you needed in the form of Pepper Malory, aka the informant."

"It fits," he answered.

Mars sat back in the overstuffed chair and let the information sink in. *It makes sense on the surface*, she thought, *but to what end?*

"Sapphire," she said nonchalantly, "compute best possible scenario for the following information. One…"

"Marci," Adelric interrupted, "Sapphire can't

hear you."

"What? What are you saying?" she demanded.

Adelric pointed in the air, "The field. Nothing penetrates it."

Stress lines quickly formed across her brow. "You're telling me that Sapphire cannot be used inside your field?"

"It's a switch, not a dial," he offered. "It's either on or off. There's nothing in the middle."

"I won't allow it!" she almost screamed, her nostrils flaring, "Martin, you dismantle this contraption of yours, today."

Adelric placed the piece of paper on the table. His motion was slow and smooth. He had no sooner removed his hand from the object when it burst into a bright ball of white light. The momentary brilliance created by the incineration caused Mars to jump reflexively. "Damn it, Martin, you could have warned me."

"Sorry," he answered unconvincingly, "but without the darkroom your interrogation project won't last as long as that piece of paper did."

"What are you saying?"

"What I'm *telling* you," he answered very slowly, "is that I will not put my men or myself at risk."

"It's your job you take risks every day," she insisted.

"Calculated ones, yes. Stupid ones…No. This little project of yours will go no further without some assurances that Core Security will not be left hanging out to dry."

Mars could feel the sweat begin to trickle down from her armpits. *He's backing me into a corner,* she thought. She was angry that Adelric had played her so well. He had intentionally brought her down to the darkroom where Sapphire could not record their conversation. *Sapphire, is that why she was experiencing such a high level of anxiety? He has effectively blocked my access to Sapphire!* "What type of assurances?" she heard herself ask.

"Written ones, to start," he said, "and full use of the darkrooms."

"You're crazy," she spat.

"He smiled menacingly. "You're on your own," he assured her flatly and stood to leave.

"I could have the council order you to proceed."

"First of all," he said looking down his nose at her sitting there, "I don't work for the Council. I am an associate member. I still work for the government."

"And second?" she asked snidely.

"I could always have the Department of Justice Director or the President himself sit in on the meetings."

"You don't think we could convince the President that you needed to work with us on this?" she asked tersely.

"It would cost you dearly," he said chuckling. "And besides, even if you could get them to go along with you, I'm not sure how effective my men would be in your little endeavor once they find out that you would sell them out if the tide turned against you."

Mars strummed her fingers on the arm of the chair, before looking back at Adelric. "Sit down," she said, motioning toward the empty chair.

Adelric remained standing glaring down the end of his nose.

"Please," she added softly.

CHAPTER 11

THE PLAN BEGINS

Bob Carson skipped up on the curb feeling much younger than the fifty six years old he was. He entered the front door of his neighborhood Core Pharmacy and was instantly greeted by the holographic image of the store manager.

"Good morning Bob," the holo said as it smiled. "Your prescriptions will be ready in about fifteen minutes. I'll have them sent up front for you while you shop around."

"Thanks," Bob answered, as he headed for the men's toiletry aisle.

"Oh, and Bob," the holo of the store manager said in a lower voice as it leaned closer to him, "adult protective underwear is on sale this week." The image winked, "Thought you'd like to know."

There was a faint giggle from a younger woman coming up behind him. Bob turned scarlet, but didn't bother to turn around. He proceeded deeper into the store now feeling twice his age. He rubbed his aching elbow hoping the young woman would head in a different direction.

"Good morning, Stacy…" the holo greeted her as Bob moved on.

Bob finally got up enough courage to look behind him and was relieved to see that the woman had indeed taken a different path. He began walking down the toiletry aisle trying to get his mind off the giggling young woman. He looked at several different types of under arm deodorant knowing full well that he would buy the brand he had used for the last eleven years. He continued down the aisle and was again greeted by the image of the store manager.

"Hey Bob, your wife wanted me to remind you that you were to pick up a bottle of aspirin. The Core Generic brand is on sale today; 20% off with any fifteen credit purchase."

He smiled at the hologram, "Thanks, schmuck," he said, feeling a little better with himself.

"No problem," the image said cheerfully, "and don't forget the adult underwear."

Bob begrudgingly made his way over to the incontinency aisle. *Maybe if I pick up a package the damn holo will quit announcing it to the whole store,* he thought. He leaned down to the bottom shelf and picked up the Core store brand of protective pads. He had tried the brand name ones and had come to the conclusion that since he was, in fact, truly pissing away his money on the pads; he'd go with the cheaper ones. As he lifted the package he could feel the small sheet of paper attached to the other side on the bundle. He turned the package over to see what had stuck to the back side. To his amazement it was a note. *If I know about your little problem, who else does?* It was signed *Sapphire.*

✳ ✳ ✳ ✳

Mary Mc Canney walked down the aisle at her local food store looking at the shopping list Sapphire had made for her on her PD. She was pleased to see that 80% of her needed items were now in her cart. A quick glance at her PD told her that the items in the basket totaled up to thirty-nine credits. She was very pleased also to notice that the same screen showed she was four credits under her budget thus far.

The holographic figure of a beautiful young woman now stood in her path. "Hi Mary," the young holo woman said pleasantly. "Mary we have a great new fragrance in our home line that I think you'll really like." The holo figure held up an aerosol can and sprayed the area in front of her. Mary instantly caught a hint of the new fragrance from an atomized mister hidden on the edge of the shelf.

"Very nice," Mary said aloud, "but not today, thank you."

The holo frowned slightly, "Mary I know that purchasing this wonderful product will put you two credits over on your current budgeted amount, but you can make that up when you get to the dairy aisle. Besides, we'll give you a two credit refund on your next purchase!"

Mary stuck the can in her basket with the full intention of ditching it once she got to the dairy department. She hurriedly dodged two more holo ads and safely made it to the dairy aisle without spending another credit. She stopped in front of the milk section and started looking for bargains. *Maybe*, she thought, *I can make up the two credit difference if I can find a bargain. Then I wouldn't have to put the fragrance product back.* Suddenly, her eyes zeroed in on the last container of white cocoa fudge flavored milk. "Oh no," she said aloud looking around to see if anyone had over-heard her. *She knew it was her lucky day. Cocoa fudge was on the short list and hard to find. The fragrance can and the pack of imitation peanut flavored crackers would go back on the self, she decided.* She quickly picked up the container and placed it in her basket. As she did so a small note dislodged itself from the container and drifted down into her basket. She picked it up and read it.

Cocoa fudge milk is not for fat people like you. Signed, *your friend Sapphire.*

Mason, located toward the center of District One was the home of the District seat. It was a sprawling city which surrounded a two square block park appropriately named Central Square. The buildings bordering the square were restricted by city code to a height of four stories. The park had flourished with different types of trees and shrubbery since its dedication in 2060. In the center of the park stood a large gazebo where many events were held and today was no different.

Today was Founders Day and people had been gathering all day; staking out their territory with blankets and quilts of various colors. The wind had been blowing briskly on and off throughout the day and many had pinned down the corners of their blankets with coolers and other heavy objects. Street vendors weaved their way through the crowds plying their goods to anyone who would give them a chance. Core Security was also making their way through the crowds stopping now and again to chat with the people and take a few pictures for them. Often when they approached a blanket they were met with reserved pleasantries and quiet tones. Today there was more than double the number of security agents than in past years. This year Mason had two distinguished Council Members attending the celebration. Councilwomen Iris Kinsley, Director of SCS and Councilman Stephen Pyrs, Directory of the Central Bank were scheduled to speak to the crowd.

Several bands had taken their turn inside the gazebo and had entertained the crowd for most of the day. Many had enjoyed the music while eating both lunch and later in the day, dinner. Now, at almost 7:00 PM, the District Governor, Mike Tanner was taking the stage to give the annual Founders

Day speech. He checked his PD for the correct time. He didn't want to anger the crowd by taking more time than was allotted, but on the other hand, he had to maintain the strict timetable. The fireworks show was scheduled to start at exactly 8:15 PM and all of the speakers had to be finished by then or lose the crowd to the roar of the explosions and the brilliant colors of the starburst.

"Ladies and Gentlemen," Tanner addressed the crowd. "May I have your attention, please?"

The crowd started to simmer down as he tapped the microphone. "OK," he started, "that's better." A few seconds more and it became as quiet as he knew the crowd was going to get. "Have you all had a great day?" he shouted into the microphone. The crowd responded warmly to his question, but he felt a little disappointed at the shallowness of their enthusiasm. "Have you had a great day?" he shouted even louder than the last time. Again the crowd responded with little higher level of applause.

"That's great," he said, as the wind now picked up again, causing some interference with his voice over the PA system, "I'm glad so many of you…"

The deep Boom, Boom, Boom of the explosions from the nearby roof tops drowned out his words. *Son of a Bitch*, he thought, *those idiots triggered the fireworks too soon*! Boom, Boom, Boom came the second report from the huge tubes.

"Look!" someone in the crowd shouted and pointed into the air. Tanner had to lean out of the gazebo to look up at the sky. The air was literally filled with thousands of pamphlets fluttering in the breeze. It took several seconds before the first of the pieces of paper reached the outstretched hands of the people in the park.

A sea of chatter swept through the crowd as more and more people had their own personal copy of the pamphlet. It was several seconds before one of Tanner's aids scurried up to him and handed him a copy or actually copies of different pamphlets. His heart sank as the taste of bile rose up from somewhere deep in his throat. Each of the four pamphlets had different pictures; each with their own caption. The first was a photograph of a Core Security officer pinning a young civilian to the ground. The second officer in the picture had a riot stick out and was in mid-swing when the photo was taken. The caption read: *The security forces you're not meant to see.* The second photo was very similar to the first but this time one officer had the person's hands pinned behind their back as the second officer was back-handing the individual across the mouth. The caption read: *Is this what they call lending a hand?* The third photo was a picture that he knew well. It was a shot of the Sapphire crystal the national symbol of the Sapphire network. The caption was: *I'm watching you!* The line below the caption asked: *Why let this thing have your freedom?* The fourth, and to Tanner, the most disturbing was a close-up of the crystal. Inside around the edges were shadowy faces suspended within the crystal.

The center face was much larger but the center was blank. The caption inside the blank face read: *Your face here.* The caption under the blank face read: *I'm Sapphire's prisoner.*

Tanner lowered the pieces of paper, crushing them in his right hand. *I don't have any training for this kind of thing!* It took all of his strength to turn around to where he knew the two Core Councilmen were seated. Each had their own copies and were staring at him.

Iris Kinsley's lips were in a tight thin line across her pale, almost ghostly face. Stephen Pyrs on the other hand, regarded Tanner with cold murderous eyes, his clutched hand shaking with an anger that Tanner just knew would boil over at any moment. *I'm a dead man,* he thought. He knew their expressions would be burned into his memory for as long as he lived. *However short that might be.*

Jax, Rebecca and two of his officers from District One were seated around the small table. As a mandatory procedure, the room had been swept minutes before they had entered. Their PDs were left back at their homes to show that they were all where they were expected to be. Their secondary PD's had been locked in the vault located in the floor of the house. They didn't think Sapphire could tap into these units, but there was no room for error. Their standard operating procedure was to treat all PD's as if they were accessible by Sapphire.

"They finally put Tanner in a security truck around three in the morning," Peter said with an amusing smirk on his face.

Roger, Pete's second in command shook his head in agreement, "I swear the poor man was green and looked as if he had been throwing up for hours."

"Who is in charge of the district now?" Jax asked the two.

"As far as the people are concerned," Roger answered, "it's still Tanner."

"That's their SOP," Pete added. "There won't be a formal change in command for at least a month. Until that time the orders will look like they are still coming from him, but the real person in charge is a woman by the name of Sandra Belfore."

"She was Tanner's second in command, correct?" Rebecca asked.

"That's right," Pete confirmed. "She's probably at least twice as nasty as Tanner."

"That's unfortunate," Jax said, "but it couldn't be helped. What's the latest pulse?"

Pete leaned back in his chair. "There's a lot of talk on the streets about the incident. The Core Security force has imposed a *voluntary* 7:00 PM curfew until the culprits can be brought to justice."

"Is the talk in our favor?" Rebecca asked.

Roger shook his head from side to side, "Too early to tell. Most of the chatter is still about the event itself and not so much the actual message."

"It was pretty spectacular if I do say so myself,"

Peter laughed.

The laughter was contagious and Jax even caught himself grinning. "I wish I could have been there," he said. "It will have the Core Security people scratching their heads for days if not weeks trying to figure out how you guys pulled it off."

"How's the other project going?" Rebecca asked.

"Better than expected," Roger said, "customers have been complaining to store managers as well as their local security people about the notes. More than a few stores now have security personnel walking the aisles."

"That's true," Peter added, "but more than just a few of the customers are walking away with a question or two about the truth of the messages."

Jax smiled at the report. "It's good that security is patrolling the stores. It will make the district look more like the police state it is. We can only hope they don't correct their mistake too soon."

"Anything from District Nine?" Peter asked.

"Not yet," Jax answered, "they don't kick off their program for another three days. We want to draw as many Core Security personnel here from up north."

"Then they can travel down to District Nine later in the week."

There was a rapid knocking on the door. Peter walked to the door and looked through the viewer at the person on the other side. "It's Russ," he said to Jax.

Jax motioned for Peter to open the door. Russ entered the room and walked directly over to Jax. He bent down and whispered a short message into his ear.

"Are you sure?" Jax asked out loud.

Russ nodded. "It's been confirmed," he answered.

Jax looked around the table at the three. "Does anyone know who ordered the ambush on a couple of Core Security vehicles earlier tonight?"

CHAPTER 11

EMERGENCY MEETING

Mars could not remember a time when the Core Council had ever called an emergency meeting, let alone one at seven-thirty in the morning. She sat at the head of the conference table staring down into her still full coffee cup. Dr. Grady and Commander Adelric were eating pastries that had been prepared for the meeting. They were talking to each other in low voices between bites of food and slurps of coffee. Their conversation was not secretive by any means and Mars took no offense. *Actually,* she thought, *it was very considerate of the two men not to disturb her.*

Commander Adelric placed his left hand to his ear at the same time, silencing Grady with his right.

"Excellent," he said, "keep me posted." Adelric turned his attention to Mars and made eye contact with her. "Pyrs' and Kinsley's vehicle has just entered the garage level of the building. They will be straight up."

Mars nodded her understanding without speaking. Adelric turned his attention back toward Grady.

It was only a few minutes before Councilmen Pyrs and Kinsley dragged themselves through the door. They had literally driven all night from District One to make it back to Core City for the meeting. Pyrs was in desperate need of a shave and Kinsley, fresh makeup.

"Thanks to both of you for making such a hard trip in order to be here this morning," Mars stated. "Sapphire, the room please."

Within seconds the room was once more secure from any outside surveillance or snooping. Both Pyrs and Kinsley took their seats after getting a cup of coffee and something to eat. Both placed their plates before them freeing up their hands to sign in.

"The room is secure," Sapphire announced.

Mars looked at the group assembled around the table. "Where should we start?" she asked rhetorically, but Adelric spoke up anyway.

"I would like to start by talking about the deaths of eight of my troopers early this morning."

"We heard on the way in Martin," Kinsley said, reaching out to touch his hand, "I am so sorry for their loss."

"We all are," Pyrs added.

"I have not heard of the murder of one of our security forces since the cleansing back in 2059," Mars stated, retaking the lead of the meeting. "It is not only very sad, but an outrage to the peace and tranquility we have enjoyed since the early days."

"They will pay," Adelric said, tapping the table's surface with his finger. "I will find them and they will pay in blood!"

"I think your feelings are unanimous among the council," Mars stated, "but we need to work through this methodically. Sapphire, has there been any increase in violence or civil disobedience in any of the other districts?"

"There have been no new acts since 4:30AM this morning when the two security vehicles were destroyed. All other districts have reported normal activities."

"That's a start," Mars said. "Iris, what have you to report on the SCS?"

"All facilities are running smoothly," she answered. "Security at each facility has been increased to include roaming patrols around the outer parameters."

"Stephen, what can you tell us about the banking system?"

"Everything is still normal. We are currently, with the help of Sapphire, running audits throughout the system."

"Very good," Mars said, "Dr. Grady, anything in your area?"

"Nothing to report here," Grady answered through a mouth full of Danish. "I've checked on any request for emergency medical assistance; nothing that would raise an eyebrow. No shootings, stabbings or deaths reported."

"Other than the death of my eight men," Adelric growled.

"Other than that," Dr. Grady said sheepishly.

"Adelric," Mars asked, "tell us what you've been able to find out about both incidences."

"The attack on the two vehicles happened at approximately 4:20AM about seven miles outside of Mason. The men were part of the additional security detail assigned to the Founders Day celebration. All that we know at this time is that the vehicles were returning the men to their home station when they were ambushed. Roadside charges were detonated and we think it was coordinated with small arms fire from the ditch or maybe the field adjacent to the road. The whole incident didn't last more than a few minutes. We have our crime-tech people on the scene and the bodies have been turned over to the forensic investigators assigned to the case by Dr. Grady this morning."

"They are the best we have," Grady reassured the group. "We'll get to the bottom of this."

"As soon as they have something to report," Adelric continued, "I will issue a follow up."

"And the flyers?" Mars prompted.

"First of all," Adelric sighed, "we don't know if the two events are related."

"Of course they're related," Grady almost shouted, "two serious acts of violence in a single night in the same town. How could they not be connected?"

"We don't know that for a fact," Mars answered. "Although it's likely that they are connected, we should allow Martin and his men to investigate the events. Then and only then will we draw our conclusions."

"Well said," Pyrs added. "Let Commander Adelric perform a proper investigation."

There were mumbles of agreement from everyone in the room.

"Thank you," Adelric stated before continuing. "The investigation of the pamphlets is proceeding. "Sapphire, play the security tapes from cameras 1-117A127 and A131."

On a split screen the events unfolded from two different angles. Both cameras showed a single large truck parked at the rear of a nondescript building. "Pause the tapes," Adelric commanded. Sapphire paused the playback. "This is the truck that transported all of the fireworks to the Founder's Day event. From this single truck all of the launchers were distributed to the top of the buildings surrounding the Central Square."

"Were there guards?" Kinsley asked, "I don't see any guards."

"There were no guards." Adelric confirmed, "We have never had the need to post guards."

"That will change now," Mars interjected.

Adelric shot Mars a scorching look. "Sorry, Martin," Mars said apologetically. "Please continue."

Adelric's voice became strained, "Sapphire, play tape."

The screen progressed for several seconds. Then very quickly, three hooded men carrying large canvas bags over their shoulders approached the truck. Two of the men wasted no time in entering the back of the vehicle. The tapes clearly showed the third man handing his canvas bag to one of the men that had entered the truck and then he remained on guard outside.

"Hold tape," Adelric ordered. "We believe that the two men inside the truck replaced several of the large firework tubes with ones they had brought with them."

"Why do you think that?" Kinsley asked.

"Continue playback," he ordered. "Advance tapes to point… four dash four." The tape skipped ahead to a point where the guard outside the truck took the three canvas bags from the men still inside the vehicle and placed them on the ground. Within seconds he was joined at the rear of the vehicle by the other two men as they exited the truck. The council watched as the three men each picked up a canvas bag and slung it over their shoulders. "Hold tape," he commanded again. "If you will observe," Adelric offered, "the three bags are still full and it is obvious that all three of the men are struggling with the weight of their bags."

"So they replaced a number of the tubes with their own tubes," Mars concluded, "Tubes that were stuffed with the pamphlets."

"Correct," Adelric said. "The tubes in the truck were segregated into four groups; one for each of the four buildings surrounding the square. They merely substituted their tubes for some of the real fireworks tubes and let the workers install them on the roof mixed in with the others."

"And then," Mars surmised, "they set them off remotely when the speeches started."

"Or," Adelric added, "the tubes had some type of timer in them."

"I was there," Pyrs stated, "they all went off together. I don't think timers would have been so precise."

"I agree," Kinsley added, "the explosions on all four buildings went off at the exact same time."

Adelric nodded his head in agreement, "We haven't recovered any of the devises yet, but statements from all of the security forces in and around the square seem to agree with you."

"Have you been able to identify any of the men from the security tapes?" Mars asked.

"No, not a single one. The hoods all come down over their faces. Also, when we tried to zoom in on their faces it was apparent that under the hoods they were wearing some type of cloth face mask making identification impossible."

Mars looked around the room at each of the other four members. *Sheep,* she thought, *no one here besides Adelric could stand up to these thugs. Sure they all can give orders, but none have shown me the conviction needed to deal with this type of violence. And Adelric is too head strong. He would attempt to bully his way through any situation.* She cleared her throat to gain their attention. "Does anyone here not think we are involved with a military or at least paramilitary unit?"

The question caused a great commotion among the membership. Snippets of information were offered in no particular order or drawing any hard conclusions.

"It could be college kids," Grady offered, "some type of prank."

"A college prank that ended with the death of eight security officers?" Mars asked.

"Marci is right," Adelric stated, "the attack was made with all of the precision of a military strike team. It was clean and precise."

"Councilman Mars," Sapphire interrupted.

"Yes, Sapphire."

"I have President Ziven on a secure line wishing to address the council. Should I patch the call through?"

Mars looked around the room for the other attendee's approval. "Patch him through."

The image for President Ziven materialized within the Sapphire crystal. "Members of the Council," the President started, his voice was warm and sincere, "I speak for the entire government when I say I am truly sorry for the senseless murder of eight Core Security personnel last night. If there is anything that the council needs, please let us know."

"Speaking for the entire Council," Mars answered, "we thank you for your acknowledgment of our loss, and when I say *our loss*, I mean every person in this great nation."

The image of President Ziven bowed slightly acknowledging her statement. "Of course, if there is anything we can do to help," he offered.

"Commander Adelric is heading up the investigation with the help of Dr. Grady's forensic team," she answered. "We could use all of the men we could get to weed out the perpetrators."

President Ziven raised his hands in a gesture of helplessness, "As you know, the Secret Service is limited to just a handful of agents needed to protect Government Plaza, but that being said, Commander Adelric has the full support of the Department of Justice."

"Thank you, Mr. President," Adelric answered, "I believe that we have all the man power we need to bring these rogues to justice."

"I have the utmost confidence that you do," the President said. "Chair Mars, do you think that there is any chance that the government may be a future target of these people?"

Now we've come to his real purpose, she thought. "We were just discussing that very thing, Mr. President," she said with a straight face. "At this time we think that any future acts of violence will be directed at the outer districts where they may feel we are the weakest. We don't think that there is much danger of them striking here in Core City."

Ziven shook his head in agreement, "Just the same, I have ordered the Secret Service to increase the security here at The Plaza."

"A wise precaution, Mr. President, Adelric stated. "Rest assured that the Core Security patrols around Government Plaza will be strengthened, discreetly of course, as an added measure of protection."

"Thank you, Commander," Ziven smiled, "I will share the good news with my staff."

"Not a problem," Adelric assured him.

"Again," the President added, his mood turning solemn once more, "Our hearts go out to the fallen." The image of the President faded from their view.

No one seemed to want to break the momentary silence that had fallen over the room. "I'll ask one more time for the record," Mars finally said. "Is there anyone here that has the slightest inkling that the President might have anything to do with last night's attack?"

"Doubtful," Adelric answered. "Like he said, they only have a force of 300 Secret Service Agents and none of them are combat trained."

"Could he be involved in hiring mercenaries?" Pyrs asked.

"Again, doubtful," Adelric said. "Where would they train them without our finding out?"

"What about some of your own officers?" Mars asked.

Adelric's eye-brow rose at the question. "What

are you saying, Marci?"

"Don't get defensive, Commander," Mars said. "I was just thinking out loud. Don't some of your security officers from time to time get recruited into the Secret Service?"

Adelric gave it some thought. "Yes, when an opening becomes available it makes sense that they would recruit a replacement from our ranks. I mean, they are the best people and have all the right training."

"Training that could have been used in last night's attack?" Kinsley asked.

There were several frowns around the room. "Yes," Adelric finally answered, "I guess that could be true."

"I'll ask again then," Mars started.

"Excuse the interruption." Sapphire chimed in.

"What is it this time?" Mars asked caustically. "There are supposed to be no interruptions during a Council meeting, let alone an emergency meeting.

"I'm sorry Ms. Mars, but procedures dictate that I advise the Council of any class four transmissions without delay," Sapphire stated. "I have a class four text for Commander Adelric, should I transmit the message?"

"Transmit," Adelric ordered, as he watched the personal screen in front of him. After carefully reading the text, he looked up from the screen. "This is the initial ballistics report from this morning's ambush," he said. "It seems that the projectiles recovered from the scene have been identified as being a 5.56 millimeter round.

"Who uses that type of round?" Pyrs asked.

"It's the standard ammunition for our MR-7-S assault rifles; used by our Special Weapons teams," he answered.

The noise level in the room rose sharply as the individual chatter between the council members grew.

"Are you saying," Dr. Grady asked, "our men were shot with our own weapons?"

A scowl covered Adelric's face. "What I'm saying Doctor is that the rounds were 5.56 millimeter, nothing more."

Mars studied Adelric's face as she composed her next question. "Commander, what type of round is standard issue for the Secret Service?"

Adelric shook his head. "Mars, you're barking up the wrong tree. The standard side arm carried by the Secret Service is the latest version of the Glock 23 which fires a .40 caliber round. They also have at their disposal a version of the SCAR H Mk 19 automatic rifle which uses a 7.62 mm round."

Mars didn't care for the lecture she was receiving, but had to admit that it didn't seem that the President or his private army was involved in the murders. She hated to admit it, but she did have faith in Adelric when it came to his side of the business. More than once his 'black nights' special weapons group had come in handy. "I can't believe it was our own people," she said.

"And you would be right." Adelric said,

pointing to his private screen. "There is one more factor that you all should know. According to this report there were three shell casings found at the scene that were not 5.56 mm." Adelric punched in a command and a picture of one of the casings appeared. "This," he said pointing to the slowly spinning casing suspended within the Sapphire crystal, "is the shell casing of a 9mm Parabellum round; the standard round used by the rebel outsider gangs."

"Outsiders again," Dr. Grady gasped.

"I'm afraid so, Doctor," Adelric confirmed.

"Commander," Kinsley asked, "what is a *Parabellum* round?"

"It is a round that was invented in the very early 1900's and was still widely used in the early 2000's. There are many weapons," he said, pointing to the projection again, "that use this round and like I said, the standard issue for the Outsiders.

"Was Parabellum the inventor?" Kinsley asked.

The question made Adelric chuckle, "No, the name *Parabellum* is derived from the Latin phrase *Si vis pacem, para bellum.*

The blood drained from Mars' face as she heard herself speak, "The translation is literally, "If you seek peace, prepare for war."

"Precisely," Adelric said.

Mars looked around the room trying to read the thoughts of each council member. Never in their history had any of the previous councils had to face the uncertainties that now faced them. The first council had to deal with the *Cleansing War,* as it was later called. The war that had forced all of those infected with or who were possible carriers of the MERS Virus out of the country. The war had ended successfully. They had been driven out of the land that they now called New America.

"Fellow council members," Mars said with a tone of hard line conviction, "as current President and Chairperson of this council, it is my duty to declare a state of emergency as outlined in the Core Council charter under section 14." She looked around the room once more to check the pulse of the group. Dr. Grady, Kinsley and Pyrs looked at her in stunned silence. Only Adelric was totally unreadable. "As it is outlined in the charter, I will now ask for each member to voice their approval or disapproval of the declared state of emergency." Mars looked toward the image of the Sapphire crystal suspended above the conference table. "Sapphire please call the roll and record the voting."

"Doctor Ned Grady, how do you vote?" Sapphire asked.

"I approve," he answered.

Mars noted that Grady seemed relieved with his vote. *He's probably very thankful,* she thought, *that this didn't happen when he was chair.*

Mrs. Iris Kinsley, how do you vote?

"I approve," she answered, fidgeting in her chair.

Ms. Marci Tansy, how do you vote?"

"I approve," she answered.

Mr. Stephen Pyrs, how do you vote?"

"I approve," he answered.

"All members of the council have approved the measure," Sapphire stated. "The measure…"

"Sapphire," Mars interrupted, her eyes locked with Adelric's, "even though Commander Adelric is not a full member of the council, I would like to record his vote."

"Commander Adelric, how do you vote?" Sapphire asked.

Adelric refused to break the stare with Mars. "As stated by Chairperson Tansy, I am only an Associate Member of this council and therefore have no voting rights. That being said, I will support the wishes of the Council."

"Thank you, Commander," Sapphire said. "The measure before the council has passed with four votes to approve and one abstention from the Associate member. A state of emergency now exists.

CHAPTER 12

JAX'S TROUBLE

Jax sat at the small table tucked in the corner of his room. Over the last six weeks he and Rebecca had continued their mock relationship and had applied for a Cohabitation without Marriage license. The licenses were issued on a case by case basis allowing for a couple to live together without being married. The license was usually issued for an eighteen month period allowing a couple to 'get to know each other' before committing to marriage. The license required the same legal commitments between the couple, but could easily be dissolved if the relationship didn't work out. A *Prearrangement of Separation* document was required to be attached to the license application. Jax wasn't worried about the commitment or the time line as he knew his job would be over before then. The license did however allow them to move more freely and drop many of the external parts of their façade. What Jax hadn't known was that Rebecca was in a true relationship with one of the agents stationed in District Five. So, much of his time in the evenings was spent alone.

He looked down at the piece of paper in his hand and read it for the eighth time. *Stay on mission. Timeline remains firm.*

Colonel McKee certainly didn't waste words, he thought. He had advised her of the incident outside of Mason through their normal commutation channel which had taken two weeks. It was another two weeks before he received her reply. He read the second line of the message, *Not members of the family. Seek out and destroy if necessary.* He laid the paper back on the plate sitting on the desk. Slowly he poured water over the paper until it was completely dissolved into a pasty gel. With a fork he stirred the gel around the plate.

He hadn't waited the four weeks before he began seeking out those who were 'not members of the family'. The only thing they had to show for their efforts was a ninety percent probability that it was not a rogue splinter group from their own team. Rebecca and Peter had handled the search and came up empty handed. It was the ten percent that worried him and what he feared more was the possibility that there may be enemy plants among his own team. Again, they had gone over each and every one of the team members' profiles. As Peter had reported, there were no cracks in the mortar. They were still an effectual team and they were to stay on mission.

He had made sure they had done just that. Dissention among the general populace was growing. Not at the pace he would like to have seen, but as in any grassroots movement, they had yet to pick up the momentum needed to reach their final goal. He was sure it would come as long as he and the other leaders pushed it forward.

He heard Rebecca's approach before she reached the door.

"Jax," she said softly, "you got a moment?"

He turned slightly in the chair to see her standing at the door. She was dressed in a long undershirt that was probably three sizes too big for her, but he was sure it made a comfortable nightgown. He couldn't help but notice that she was of course, without a bra and the outline for her breasts and nipples could easily be made out through the thin material. "Sure," he said, trying to push the image out of his head, "have a seat."

As she sat next to him she looked down at the plate of goo. "Got tired of reading it?"

He glanced at the plate, "Yeh, no matter how many times I read it, the damn words never changed."

She managed a weak smile. "I know exactly what you mean. I got more than my share of those types of messages."

Jax remembered the details of the demise of Rebecca's team. He had not heard it from her of course, but Peter was more than willing to tell the story. The thing that ate at him, and, not doubt, Rebecca and the others, was the fact that they just disappeared. No arrest, no trial, just gone. He remembered Peter telling him about the clean up service showing up at the house the next day. Core Security had spread the story of how the occupants had been stricken down with the MERS virus and that the house was to be quarantined until any trace of the virus was eradicated. The only thing to be eradicated that night was Rebecca's team.

He looked back toward Rebecca. She was leaning slightly forward, her baggy shirt not revealing any of her body. He was glad. "Well, at least the messages only come about once a month."

"Yes," Rebecca chuckled, "if we were using a Sapphire type system, McKee would be looking over your shoulder every step of the way."

"Please," Jax said in mock horror, "I have enough to worry about as it is."

"You're doing great," she answered.

"Is that why you came in to see me?"

She nodded her head, "Yes, I've noticed you don't cut yourself much slack around here. Things are going very well even if you don't think so."

"I think they are going...OK," he answered. "I would be a lot happier if there were more signs of open revolt."

"Open revolt, Jax, is like a volcano. There's usually a whole lot of shaking and rumbling going on before the top ever blows. And our gauges on the street tell us that there is, in fact, a whole lot of rumbling going on."

Jax thought about the morning reports from the districts. What Rebecca said was true. There were more open signs of disfavor with the current government. People were heard talking openly about some of the repression by the Core Security; something that had never happened before.

"That's true, Rebecca, but we are three years away from an election."

"What does that have to do with it?" she asked.

"Well, for one thing, grumbling malcontents seem to be louder during an election year. Elections are synonymous with change and change can come in many forms."

Well, you haven't been here during an election. Here elections are synonymous with stagnation." She tucked her feet up under her shirt and wrapped her arms around her knees.

Jax couldn't help but notice her smooth skin and muscular thighs when she moved. *Damn*, the thought, *I'm going to have to make my room off limits to scantily dressed women.*

"We even had reports of ballot stuffing in several districts," she continued, not noticing his discomfort.

"Ballot stuffing?" he said, pushing the thoughts of her legs as far back in his mind as possible. "Balloting is done through Sapphire," he reminded her.

"Yes, but that doesn't stop election fraud."

Jax shook his head, "How can you be so sure."

Rebecca shifted in her seat. "We initiated several exit polls during the last election."

"Exit polls?"

"Yes, you know, asking people how they voted, checking on election results."

"And these exit polls confirmed the fraud?"

Rebecca leaned forward on her chair. "Jax, in the last election one of the candidates running against the government's incumbent was from the small town of Veles, in district three. Two hundred and sixty-four people voted in Veles that day including the candidate, his wife and two of their sons."

"So?"

"So, when the results were posted two hundred and sixty-four people had voted for the incumbent. The opposition party received zero votes."

Jax pulled lightly on his ear following Rebecca's reasoning. "You would think that the man would have gotten at least one vote, if not four."

Rebecca stared at Jax, "Two hundred and sixty-four to zero. I later had one of our informants ask the candidate about the results."

"And?"

"The candidate told the informant that he and his family must have pushed the wrong button on their PDs. The informant said he was laughing when he said it, but the hurt was obvious in his eyes." Rebecca shifted in her chair again, causing her shirt to rise, exposing more of her thigh. Jax stood up and walked across the room to avoid being in a position to see her legs any further.

"Why would anyone have done that?" he asked, as his thoughts traveled to a place they shouldn't.

"To send the man a message of course," she

sighed.

"A message, what kind of message is that?"

"Jax, the incumbent took 68% of the votes. He didn't need those four votes to win. As a matter of fact, they could have stolen four other votes from somewhere else if they needed them."

"But they didn't," he thought out loud, "they took his vote to tell him he never had a chance."

"Yes," she said, standing and walking over to him, "and because of it he will never run against them again."

Suddenly loud voices could be heard coming from down-stairs. Instantly both Jax and Rebecca were holding pistols aiming them toward the commotion making its way up the stair case. Several weapons were hidden in each room of the house and everyone within the house knew where each gun was in case of an emergency. Jax made a mental note to add a few automatic rifles to his room. The sound of footsteps continued up the stairs.

Peter entered the room almost slipping as he back-pedaled at the sight of the two guns pointing at his head. "Jax!" was the only word he was able to get out of his mouth. Instantly Jax and Rebecca pulled their weapons away from Peter's head. Peter was no longer in sight.

"Peter?" Jax asked, pointing his gun at the door again.

"It's me," he said not showing his face.

Jax kept his gun trained on the door. "I know it you, dumb ass. Are you alone?"

"Yes, Chris and Phil are waiting down-stairs. Can I come in now?"

Rebecca moved to a better firing position.

"Come on in," Jax ordered.

Peter entered the room with both of his hands up in the air. His face was ashen. "Sorry, I wasn't thinking."

Jax lowered his pistol, taking note that Rebecca's weapon was still pointing at Peter's head.

"Come in, Pete," he said. As soon as Peter cleared the entrance Rebecca shot out of the door in a crouching position. A second later she re-entered, the gun at her side. "All clear," she stated releasing a long breath. Jax looked at Peter with disgust, "Wasn't thinking! You damn near were never going to think again. What the hell is going on?"

"Bad news," Peter said, lowering his arms.

Jax stuck his pistol inside the waistband of his pants. He looked over at Rebecca and her long undershirt. "OK," he sighed, "if it's bad news I need some tea." He looked toward Rebecca. "Get dressed and we'll meet you in the kitchen."

Chris, Phil and Peter were sitting round the large table as Rebecca entered the room. Jax was standing at the stove waiting for the water to boil. "Anyone else want tea?" he asked, not taking his eyes off the pot.

Rebecca eased herself into her usual chair. "I do."

"I'll take some coffee, if you have it," Chris said.

Rebecca got up from her chair and went to the

pantry.

"If it's too much trouble…" Chris said, having second thoughts.

"Don't be silly," she answered, putting the coffee grounds into the pot.

"So what's the bad news?" Jax asked, while filling both Rebecca and his cups with hot water. Rebecca leaned over him and picked up her cup. He noticed that she had changed into a pair of jeans and a regular t-shirt, but her bare breasts pressing against his back told him that she hadn't bothered to put on a bra. They both returned to the table, Rebecca removing the pistol from her waistband and laying it on the table. Jax did the same.

"The coffee will take a few minutes," Jax said as he dipped his tea bag into the hot water. He looked up at Peter. "Bad news?"

Peter looked down at the table not wishing to meet Jax's eyes. "Core Security," he said gritting his teeth, "has opened a clandestine interrogation facility in district nine."

"Well, Jax said as he blew on the hot tea, "it's not very clandestine if you know about it."

"But…" Peter stammered.

Jax held up his hand, "It's alright, Pete. I was just jerking your chain for scaring the shit out of me. Tell me what you know."

"Two different sources in District Nine have told us that they have seen unusual security activity around an abandoned warehouse in the lower district."

"So?" Rebecca asked, as she got up and walked over to the stove.

"We sent a few men in to check out their story," Peter started.

"Don't tell me they were captured," Jax said, almost choking on his tea.

"No, no, nothing like that, but they did observe several unmarked cars enter the facility under the cover of darkness."

"Did you scan the facility?" Rebecca asked, returning to the table with three coffee mugs in one hand and the coffee pot in the other.

"They didn't have the scanning equipment with them," Chris answered as he took the mug from Rebecca.

"We sent four men back two nights later," Peter continued. "Our team counted six people entering the facility."

"And when they had the scan set up," Chris continued, "they were only able to locate two of them."

"Could they have gotten out another way; undetected?" Jax asked.

"We don't think so," Phil said, entering the conversation for the first time.

"Why's that?"

"I was one of the four, Jax," Phil answered. "We had four very good observation points picked out around the structure. If someone had left from another exit I think our night vision equipment would have detected them."

Rebecca sat with her legs crossed under her. She sipped at her tea. "Is there an elevator in the building? Maybe there are several floors below ground level."

"Good question," Jax interjected. "Our portable scanning equipment wouldn't have been able to detect any underground activity."

Phil poured himself a second cup of coffee. "Too hard to tell without the risk of giving away our position. But the other possibility is that they're using some type of shielding to hide their activities."

"Shielding?" Rebecca asked.

"Either way," Jax said, heading back to the stove for more hot water, "whatever they're doing it's not your run of the mill information booth."

"So what do you want to do?" she asked.

Jax returned to the table with the kettle of hot water. "Expose them of course," he said, refilling both of their cups.

"And how do we go about doing that?" Peter asked.

Jax closed his eyes for a second mentally walking through the facts he had just received. He looked around the table at his team. "If they're using the building as an interrogation center it means that people are going missing. So we start looking for people in nearby towns that have lost someone."

"That won't be easy," Peter said. "I mean, if they can't locate them with the help of their PDs…"

"Easier than you think," Rebecca stated confidently. "When they can't be located through Sapphire and their PDs, loved ones will be expanding their search options. They will be asking others questions about their whereabouts."

"One place to stake out is the local security stations," Jax added.

"You don't think they'll take the people they bagged there, do you?" Chris asked.

"No, not at all," Jax answered. "But once their loved ones have exhausted the normal channels they will be going to the stations to report the missing person." He rubbed the temples of his head as he developed a plan. "Peter, have our people start listening closely to the chatter on the street. Tell them what they should be looking for. Do the same thing around the security stations. Discretion is going to be key. I don't want anyone performing exit polls outside the stations." The comment brought laughter from everyone seated at the table. "Also," Jax said, looking toward Rebecca, "let the other District Commanders know what we found in Nine. If there's one secret base, there's bound to be more."

"This could be a break-through for us," Rebecca said winking at Jax. "It could really turn up the heat."

Jax smiled at her as he stood up from the table. "Now," he said, picking up his pistol and empty tea cup from the table, "if there's no more emergencies I'm going to bed."

CHAPTER 13

MARS VS. ZIVEN

"Have you completely lost your mind?" President Ziven spat the words out with as much contempt as he could muster. Once again he found himself at Core Towers facing Chairperson Mars, her eyes almost bulging from their sockets as he spoke.

"Watch your mouth," she cautioned him. "I don't have to put up with insults from you."

Ziven stood in front of her desk towering over her. "Insults?" he asked acidly, "The only insult was to my intelligence when I allowed you and that idiot Adelric to open these damn things." He tossed the tablet onto her desk.

Mars tried not to look down at the tablet now in front of her, but failed. She picked it up and stared at the photos on the page. She had already seen it but couldn't help but study it again. The center of the pamphlet had a large picture of their supposedly secret interrogation center located in District Nine. It was easy to see the two well armed Core Security guards standing out in front of the double doors. *Ziven is right,* she thought, *Adelric was an idiot to allow his men to be seen.* She looked at each of the four other pictures around the center photo. Each was a picture of a person, according to the pamphlet, missing and presumed to have been illegally brought to the facility for detention and interrogation.

"Did you know that an additional three members of the security force have gone missing?" she stated icily. "We found one of them a few hours ago in the woods outside of Core City. His throat was cut."

Ziven pushed his jacket back behind him and placed his hands on his hips. Mars had seen that very pose a hundred times before. It had almost become the President's signature stance during his election; an election that the Core Council had allowed him to win figuring he would be the easiest candidate for them to control.

"Right now, Ms. Tansy, I wish they *all* would disappear," he said flatly.

She slowly stood, her mouth twisting in an ugly grimace. "Be careful Ziven," she said sourly. "This council will not tolerate any ill will that you may harbor toward them."

President Ziven stood his ground. "Or what,

Marci?" he sneered. "You're going to make up some more lies about my family and me? Or maybe, you could have that buffoon Adelric have me go missing?"

Mars knew that the conversation had gotten totally out of hand. Inwardly she knew that, no matter how much she hated Ziven and his little band of jackals, they would have to stay in place until the crisis passed. Then, when the new election came, they could artfully emasculate the towering giant. She had to force herself to relax. "Mr. President," she said trying to placate him, "I'm sorry for my aggressive behavior, but" she said, pointing to the paper lying on her desk, "these criminals are a true threat to us all. A threat to our way of life and now they have us at each other's throats. We need your help to solve this issue."

Ziven relaxed slightly but didn't remove his hands from his hips. "The Government's numbers are falling...*My* numbers are falling," he added, pointing his finger at Mars. "You need to get your arms around this situation quickly and get that idiot Adelric under some type of control."

Mars forced her best smile. "It won't happen again, I promise you."

Ziven let his arms fall to his sides, his shoulders relaxing. "All right," he said, "I'll do what I can from Government Plaza."

She nodded her appreciation. "Between the two groups we should be able to clean up this mess."

Ziven's eyebrow raised slightly, "And Adelric?"

Mars looked down at her PD. "The Council is meeting in five minutes. I'll take care of him." She moved from around her desk and motioned Ziven toward the hall. Together, in silence, they walked to the room containing the elevator that would take him down to the tube. Mars offered him her hand. "Mr. President," she said smiling.

He took her hand and shook it as the elevator doors opened. "Ms. Tansy."

She stood in front of the doors her hands folded in a demure fashion in front of her. As he entered and turned to face her she spoke a final time. "Mr. President, we now know that these criminals are Outsiders sent into the country to cause disruption."

"I already knew that much," he smiled. "Oh, and next time, I think we should meet in my office."

She bowed her head slightly. "That would be nice," she said sweetly, "I haven't been in the Oval Office since the last time we installed a new President." The door closed without further conversation.

Mars walked into the council chambers at a full clip. Even at her current distance from the table she could see the image of the pamphlet suspended within the crystal. "Secure the doors," she ordered. Sapphire complied instantly. Mars took her seat at the head of the table and signed in.

"The room is now secure." Sapphire stated.

Mars looked around the room at each of the council members. They all looked tired even Commander Adelric. *They look*, she thought, *almost defeated.* The events of the last few weeks had taken their toll on a group of people who were not combat hardened. They were civilians, business people who had been able to get their way through power, money, and manipulation. None of them, she mused, had ever thrown a punch or for that matter, been punched. Oh, they had been metaphorically punched in the gut by a sour deal or some miscalculation, but none of them had ever tasted blood and the Outsiders were out for blood.

"I just had that righteous ass Ziven in my office," she said.

Mars paused, waiting for any type of response from the group. There was none. "He threatened me…us with our jobs if we don't do something to reign in these terrorist."

"He doesn't have that authority," Pyrs stated flatly.

"We all know that Stephen," she hissed, "but he can make our lives miserable and I for one don't treasure the thought of waking up each morning wondering what the hell he's done while I was asleep."

"Did you make any headway with him?" Kinsley asked.

"He's agreed to help shore up support at The Plaza; if that makes any of you feel better."

"Hardly," Pyrs sneered. "How far can we trust

him?"

Mars thought about the question. The thought of having him assassinated came to mind. "Not very far," she shot back. "He's more interested in protecting his own ass. So as long as we are all in the same boat we can expect some level of cooperation from him and his band of chimpanzees." She turned her attention to Adelric. She had given a lot of thought to what she would say to him while she walked down the hall. He too was a valuable player at present and she blamed herself for giving him too much leeway on the interrogation facilities. "Commander, what is the situation in District Nine?"

Adelric cleared his throat. "Luckily we received the pamphlet information at the same time as everyone else. As it is a good three hour ride out to the warehouse, we were able to evacuate the building and cover our tracks before the first group arrived."

"You were able to move out of the building that fast?" Dr. Grady asked.

Adelric nodded his head, "Fortunately there isn't a lot of equipment involved in an interrogation. The equipment we do have is very mobile in nature and quickly moved."

"And the people you were interrogating?" Mars asked.

"There were only two and they were moved with the equipment."

Mars assessed the situation for a minute. "Well

it seems like the damage control was effective."

"That's correct," Adelric answered, "by the time the civilians got out to the building there was nothing to see or link us to the accusation on the pamphlet."

"This might have worked out to our benefit," Pyrs smiled. "These terrorists cry 'wolf' and the people go out to the warehouse and there's no wolf to be found. I think it put a big ding in their credibility."

"Sapphire," Mars commanded, "what are the current numbers on the Core Council and the Government."

The Council's numbers have dropped to a fourteen month low of 67.6%" Sapphire stated displaying the data for all to see. "The Government approval ratings are at 61.1%."

"Sapphire," Kinsley asked, "why is the Council's number so low?"

"My calculations show that the council's recent public support of President Ziven during his adultery scandal has generally had a negative effect. The populace does not see a big enough difference between the Government and the Core Council. At present the elasticity of the numbers is negligible. "

"So we're kind of tied at the hip," Kinsley said.

"How were we to know back then that all this crap was going to happen?" Pyrs offered defensively.

"We couldn't have," Mars said in support of the group. "But Iris is correct; right now we have to be very careful when it comes to the Government."

"More than usual?" Grady asked.

"I'm afraid so," Mars answered. "Ziven will only go along with us because his people are telling him the same thing Sapphire just told us. If either group goes down they are going to take the other group with them."

"We're fighting a phantom," Pyrs stated. "It's hard to land a solid punch when you have a ghost as an opponent."

Grady shifted in his seat. "More like a poltergeist."

Mars shot straight up in her chair. "That's it," she exclaimed. "The problem is that these terrorists have no face. There's no substance to them."

"I think that's what I just said," Pyrs stated.

Mars stood and began to walk around the conference table. "To the general populace the Outsiders' are just a subconscious voice nagging in the back of their head. They have no tangible being. The public doesn't see them as we do."

"Hell," Grady added, "they don't see them at all."

"That's exactly right," Mars said, as she continued to walk around the table. "There is an old adage in business that goes something like this; if you want to stay employed you can let the boss know your name or your face, but never both."

There was light laughter at the remark. Mars took her seat. "The problem is no one knows their names or their faces."

"So?" Adelric asked.

"So," Mars smiled wickedly, "we give them a name and a face."

"What are you implying?" Adelric asked sarcastically, "hello, my name is Joe and I'm a terrorist."

Again the room filled with suppressed laughter. Mars slapped her open palm on the table making everyone in the room jump. "Yes!" she said, "a little simplistic, but that's the main idea. We give them a name and a reputation as a group of ruthless terrorist that will stop at nothing to bring down the lawful government."

"Give them someone to point a finger at for all their problems," Pyrs added, "Genius!"

"Do you have a name in mind?" Grady asked.

Mars shook her head, "No, not at the moment, but we should be able to come up with something sinister."

"And their acts of terror?" Kinsley asked.

Mars frowned, "I don't know yet, but *the council* should be able to come up with a few plausible ideas."

"Let me say something right now," Adelric said, taking the floor. "Mars, this idea of yours is good and the council needs to back it 100%."

Mars swallowed hard, she had never heard such conviction come from Adelric before. The closest thing was the day he learned about the ambush of his men. She made a mental note not to underestimate the man in the future.

"Of course we'll back Mars," Grady said, "don't we always stand together?"

Commander Adelric's face hardened, "Dr. Grady, we are dealing with people who would kill you for the sugar in the bottom of your coffee cup. This is a war, no different from the Cleansing War of thirty years ago. People died in that war fighting to maintain our way of life and I'm afraid that people will continue to die in this one. One of the hardest tasks required by a leader is their ordering soldiers into a situation where there's a good chance they will die. We all," he said with an emphatic gesture toward the council, "will be called on to ask people to put their lives on the line."

Mars studied the room. The council had never had to make the decisions that would now be asked of them. She wondered which members would crack under the strain of what was going to be required. She would have to be ready to push those aside that could not or would not do what was required of them. "Thank you, Commander, she stated as she looked at each member of the Council. "Understanding what is being asked of you; is there anyone here who wishes to resign from the council before we accelerate this war to the next level? There will be no shame in resigning, but there will be no going back if you stay."

"Kind of a, take it or leave it proposition then," Pyrs said.

"That's it exactly, Steven. People are going to die and we may be the ones ordering their death."

Dr. Grady cleared his throat. "A surgeon may sometimes be called upon to sacrifice a limb of a patient to save their life. During the Cleansing many a person was sacrificed to ensure that the virus did not spread to the whole population." He looked toward Iris Kinsley for support."Those of us that were involved with the purge remember the pain and suffering."

Kinsley nodded her head; her eyes began to water, "I promised myself back then that what we were doing was right. In the end, our plan prevailed. I now pledge myself once again to endure whatever pain is ahead of us."

"What about Ziven?" Pyrs asked.

"We keep him and the others in the dark of course," she said without a moment's hesitation. "If we handle this correctly the operation will look like the terrorists are behind it. Why would that idiot Ziven think any different if we don't tell him?"

"And," Adelric added, "if this plan blows up, I promise you it will blow up in Ziven's face, not ours."

CHAPTER 14

THE MARKET CELEBRATION

Jax and Rebecca walked hand in hand through the crowd of people. Anyone observing them would remember the cuteness of the young couple. The Old Town Market Celebration was one of the best attended public events of the year. Hundreds of people filled the narrow streets reveling in the festive atmosphere enjoying the spirited music filling the air and tasting every type of food and candy available. Children and adults alike wore multicolored decorations painted on their faces by a more than willing street artist. Many wore gaudy hats adorned with colorfully dyed feathers and small plastic knickknacks sparkling in the noon day sun. It was three days of celebration for the coming spring and it seemed that everyone in Core City wished to be a part of the festivities surrounding the event.

Jax was surprised that the Core Security was taking such a low profile during the event. But as Rebecca reminded him earlier, after the recent bad press they received, the government may well be thinking it wiser to be less conspicuous. It didn't mean there weren't plain clothed officers in the crowd. *Hell*, he thought, *some of the very couples holding hands around him may actually be security forces in disguise.*

Rebecca pulled him toward one of the street vendors selling popcorn. "I think, "she said smiling, "this may be my one true addiction."

Jax purchased the largest bag the vendor offered and held it out toward Rebecca. "Well don't let it be said that I wouldn't support a popcorn junkie."

Rebecca smiled warmly and dug into the bag. "What time do you have?" she asked Jax as she continued to munch on popcorn.

Jax knew what she was really asking. The pamphlets would be released in approximately twenty two minutes. Jax gazed upward scanning the roof top of one of the nearby buildings. He could just see the top of a Core Security person's head as he patrolled the roof. After the incident in Mason earlier in the year, no roof top was ever left unguarded or at least under strict surveillance. Since they no longer had access to the roof tops or the fireworks that would be fired from them, Jax's team had devised another clever means of delivering the message to the crowd.

On every street there were at least eight huge

rectangular boxes suspended fifteen feet above the revelers heads and anchored to the walls with heavy cables. The boxes were dispersed in a pattern that allowed the music coming from the speakers to be enjoyed by everyone. No matter where a person stood or sat within a four block radius, they could listen to the music coming from the main stage area. It was inside these boxes that, when the time came, the pamphlets would burst out and float down to the waiting crowd. Peter had nicknamed them the 'party poppers'.

"About twenty minutes," Jax said, "do you have to go to the ladies room?"

"Nope, I'm good...

In the nanosecond that followed, Jax caught the flash of white light and the howl of the explosion. As played out in Jax's mind, they were almost simultaneous. The deafening roar of the explosion suddenly seemed to be muffled as the shockwave hit Rebecca and him, knocking both of them off their feet. Stunned as he was, he had a clear perception of Rebecca floating through the air, her popcorn filling the air around her face. His body could not react fast enough to grab Rebecca or soften the blow as he hit the blacktop. He shook his head as the metallic taste of blood quickly filled his nose and mouth.

He blinked several times trying to clear his vision. The sounds of people screaming seemed distant and disconnected. The cries of a young child grew louder as he shook his head trying again to clear his vision and hearing. Suddenly the sounds rushed in from all sides. There were the screams and shouts of people lying around him; some had managed to get to their knees but could move no farther. Sirens squealed in almost every direction as first responders were already moving among the wounded, shouting orders to people Jax could not see.

Rebecca! Was his first clear thought as he began searching around where he was now sitting. It only took a second to spot her lifeless figure several feet away. She lay face down on the asphalt; her right hand tucked under her torso, her left still gripped the almost empty bag of popcorn. Jax tried to stand but was hindered by his equilibrium that had not fully returned to normal. He managed to crawl and pull himself next to her. His hand trembled as he reached toward her neck. As gently as his shaking hand would allow, he reached around her neck and felt for a pulse.

Rebecca gasped for air the second Jax's fingers touched her neck. She managed to roll over on-to her back and began coughing desperately trying to fill her lungs. She lunged for him as soon as she recognized his face. He caught her head and held it close to his chest. "Easy," he rasped, "you may have internal injuries."

She locked eyes with him, "What about you?"

He gave his own condition a momentary thought, "I… I don't know." He looked around at the chaos. It was the first time he noticed the smoldering store front across the street. "We have to get out of here.

Rebecca nodded against his chest. "Can you stand?" she asked.

Two large hands suddenly gripped both of his shoulders from behind. "Are you alright?" a booming voice asked. Jax winced in the vice like grip that the person had on him. He quickly learned that it wasn't the hands of one person but two.

Chris moved around in front of him and studied Jax's face for several seconds. He then waved his hand in front of Jax's eyes, "can you focus on my hand?"

"Let me have her," Phil said on the other side of him. Jax relaxed his hold on Rebecca as Phil picked her up gently. Chris helped Jax to his feet and steadied him until he was sure that Jax was not going to fall again. "We've got to get out of here," Chris whispered in Jax's ear.

"Which way?" Jax asked, still somewhat disorientated.

Chris held him around the waist as Jax painfully placed his arm over Chris' shoulder. "Follow Phil," Chris ordered and led Jax away from the turmoil around them.

As the four reached one of the alley-ways leading out of Old Town and away from the crowd, they heard the muffled bangs of the party poppers as they went off. The level of screaming intensified once again.

"Shit!" Jax moaned, without looking back.

✳ ✳ ✳ ✳

Jax felt the presence of someone entering the room. He forced his eyes open. A crusty film impeded his vision. He tried to reach up to wipe it away but found that his arm was somehow strapped to his side. He blinked several more times. He tried to raise his other arm, but it too was immobilized.

"Sheila?" he rasped recognizing her as the young woman who had asked him about the first class letter.

"Hi boss," the young woman said leaning over the bed.

"Hey," he answered, "where are we?"

She smiled at him as she waved a small penlight in front of his face. The beam of light moved from one eye to the other and back again. "You're in the best place you could be," she said with a broad smile, "home in your own bed."

"Rebecca?"

"She's in her bed," she confirmed. "The two of you took a real beating."

"No joke," he answered, "I think my parachute didn't open."

She straightened up and turned off the light. "Parachute?"

Jax grinned from ear to ear, "Never mind."

She motioned toward his ribcage, "How's your side?"

Again he instinctively tried to raise his hand to

touch the area where she was pointing but failed. "Why are my hands tied down?"

"We didn't want you hurting yourself any more than you already are so we secured your arms." She leaned over again and began unfastening the restraints. "I think we can remove these now, but be careful with your left hand you still have an IV in it," she said untying his hands. Jax watched as she lowered the bed sheet and unbuttoned his shirt.

"Holy shit!' he said, his eyes widening at the large bruise covering the right side of his ribcage. He focused on the white bandage which was about a three inch square. There was evidence of blood seepage on the dressing.

"I had to remove a large shard of glass," she said noticing his gaze. "You were damn lucky it struck perpendicular to your ribs. If it had gone in at an angle parallel to your ribcage it probably would have slipped in-between the two ribs and stopped somewhere in your heart."

"You removed it?" he asked. "You're a medic?"

"Nope," she said, as she gently peeled back a corner of the dressing.

"No?" he asked incredulously.

"I'm a doctor," she answered, "and I have to say, that up until now, there hasn't been much for me to do around here."

"I didn't know we had a doctor."

"We have three," she said examining the wound. "We couldn't let any of our team members end up in a Core Clinic or hospital now could we?"

"I guess not," he answered trying to relax. "Is Peter or Phil here?"

She continued dressing the wound, "They're both downstairs."

"Could you…"

"I told them," interrupting Jax's thought, "I would come down and get them once I was finished my doctoring."

Jax took a deep breath and winced at the sharp pain in his side.

"I wouldn't do that for awhile." she said, seeming pleased with her work. "I'll check in on you later this evening. In the mean-time I'll go get Peter and Phil."

"Thanks, Sheila or should I say, Doctor."

"Either will do," she smiled and started toward the door. "Oh, by the way," she said turning back to face him, "I'd talk real fast if I were you."

"Why…why is that?" he stammered.

"I pushed a sedative through your IV so that you would sleep tonight." She winked, "I'll send them right up."

Jax didn't have the strength to protest nor did she give him time to. Sheila was true to her word. Jax looked up to see the two men standing in the doorway. "Come on in," he said softly.

The two men entered the room and approached the bed with all the reverence of one entering a church.

"Hi, how're you feeling?" Peter asked.

"Like I've just been blown up," Jax grinned.

"Hey listen," he quickly interjected, "Doc Sheila just gave me a cooler so I don't know how long I'll stay awake."

"Yeah, she told us on the staircase," Phil said.

"So, before we get into things, I just wanted to thank Chris and you for getting Rebecca and me out of there."

"No problem," Phil blushed.

Jax nodded slightly, "OK tell me the details."

Peter rubbed the three day growth on his chin, "sixteen dead another four in critical condition and not expected to live and twenty six wounded."

"Not counting you and Rebecca," Phil added.

"Damn," Jax sighed, "what the hell happened? Did one of the party poppers malfunction?"

"Not hardly," Peter said. "The poppers didn't have enough explosives in them to do any real damage. Someone planted one hell of a bomb in a flowerbed in front of that restaurant. It went off about twelve minutes before the poppers."

"From what we've been able to find out," Phil added, "it was plastics."

"Shit!" Jax slurred, "has anyone taken credit for the bombing?"

Peter looked at Phil and then back to Jax. Phil dug a pamphlet out of his rear pocket and handed it to Jax. "I guess you could say we did."

Jax reached for the piece of paper with an unsteady hand. Phil caught his hand and guided the paper into this open palm. Jax drew the paper back and read aloud.

"We are tired of the people of New America not

taking us seriously. More will die if the government does not meet our demands."

A bile taste rose from his gut and burned the back of his throat as he looked at the signature.

"The Raven", he mouthed weakly.

"That's all that's been on the Netcast News since the incident," Peter offered.

"That, and the government vowing to bring us to justice," Phil added.

It took more strength than he had to crush the pamphlet in his hand so he let it fall from his fingers. "We didn't do this," he hissed.

"Well, we're being set up to take the fall for it," Peter answered.

Jax nodded weakly feeling the effects of the sedative, he felt light headed; his eyes fluttered.

"Jax?"

His eyes shot open, trying to focus on the blurred faces of Peter and Phil. "Sorry," he offered dimly, "must have dozed off."

Peter reached down and touched his hand. "Listen, Jax, you rest and we'll talk tomorrow."

"Wait a sec" he slurred, his words running together, "I need you to find me…"

"Find what, Jax?" Phil asked.

Jax opened his eyes as wide as he could and blinked several times. He was still having trouble comprehending Phil's question.

"What do you want us to find?" Phil asked again.

Slowly Jax's eyes fluttered and began to close. "Find me…four or five…angels"

✳   ✳   ✳   ✳

The bright morning light was diffused by the ivory colored drapes covering the window. Jax still found the room very bright as he finished wolfing down the breakfast that Chris had brought. Jax took the opportunity to thank Chris in person as he had Phil three days ago. *Or, at least,* he thought, *he vaguely remembered thanking him.*

Sheila had come and gone before breakfast. She was pleased with his condition and had reported that Rebecca was also doing well. He was savoring the last piece of buttered toast as Peter entered the room.

Peter pointed to the toast, "Well, if you have to get blown up to get real butter around here, I'll stick with the fake stuff."

"I'm with you on that," Jax laughed. A sharp pain on the right side of his ribcage suppressed any further laughter. "Damn, I've never had a cracked rib before," he said, "it even hurts to smile."

Peter pulled up a chair next to the bed. "I know what you mean," he said rubbing the left side of his chest. Two cracked ribs when my harness worked loose in the hyper tube."

"We have to find a better means of transportation for the future," Jax thought out loud. "Where are the others?"

Peter nodded in agreement, "I'm hoping that we can just walk out of here when this thing is over."

Jax's eyebrow rose slightly, "It's a long walk back."

Peter stood up and removed the tray in front of Jax. "I'll chance it, besides; they probably owe me so much vacation time I could take a few months off anyway."

"Peter, we don't get vacation pay."

"Oh yeah," he said, placing the tray on the dresser, "I forgot."

"Why don't you get the others and we'll get started."

The words were no sooner out of his mouth when the others started filing in. Jax was surprised to see Rebecca come through the door with the aid of her boyfriend, Mat. He was very happy to see her and to his surprise, had no feelings of jealousy toward Mat at all. It quickly dawned on him that the only feeling he truly had for Rebecca were those shared by close friends.

"Good to see you up and moving," he said to her.

She shuffled over to an overstuffed chair and, with Mat's help, eased herself down.

"Well, kind of moving around," Jax said as an afterthought.

She smiled at him. "I was told by Sheila that this will be my one and only trip for the day."

The others entered the room and formed a semicircle around the bed. Jax looked over at Peter.

"Any updates since I passed out the other night?"

Peter nodded gravely. "One more confirmed dead this morning. That brings the death count up to seventeen."

Stress lines formed across Jax's brow, "Anything on the Netcast News?"

Peter shook his head, "Not much, they're starting to move into the life stories of those killed.

"They've put out a reward for any information leading to the arrest of *The Raven*," Phil added.

"Raven," Jax hissed, "a large, carnivorous, bird of prey that will devour almost anything it can get its beak into."

"Yes," Rebecca added, "a bit of a scavenger I'm afraid."

Jax shook his head slowly, "I have to give it to the government, I didn't see this one coming."

"So you think the government's behind the bombing?" Chris asked.

"Of course they are," Peter said. "They weren't happy with just killing a few of their own security people so they moved on to bigger game."

"Peter's right," Jax said. "In their minds, they just sacrificed a few pawns to try and get us in checkmate."

"Those were real people who died."

Jax looked over to see Sheila standing in the doorway. "To you and I, maybe," he said, "but to a government that's not run by the people or for the people, it is an entirely different situation."

"Then you expect more to die?" she said, crossing her arms over her chest.

"Sheila," he said looking at her but making sure everyone else in the room knew he was talking to all of them, "they will not stop until they grind us into the ground. They cannot afford to leave a single one of us alive."

"What do you want us to do, Jax?" Peter asked.

Jax had spent most of his morning, even while eating, recalling everything he could remember about the dictatorships of the late 20th Century and those that flourished in the early days of the 21st Century. He made mental comparisons between the ruthless styles of leaders like Stalin to the more subtle regimes of a leader like Putin. He thought of the leadership styles of Gaddafi, Mubarak, Castro and Garcia. He tried to remember those that were successful and those who had given up their positions in death. In the end he found himself longing for the stack of textbooks he was forced to leave back in Middle-earth.

"Where do our operations stand as of today?" he asked the group.

"We've shut down everything we could, Jax," Peter volunteered, "we… I felt it best to lay low for awhile."

"Excellent!" Jax stated, "you were absolutely correct in going dark." He looked directly at Peter. "Good call, Peter," he said in a congratulatory tone. "So none of our people are in danger of being discovered?"

Each of the district leaders shook their head in response to the question. Jax turned back to Peter,

"How far are we on the mall operation?"

"Everything is ready to go, but we were unsure how you would like to proceed."

"You said that the Government has been on the Core-net?"

"Yes, the President himself," Peter said.

"What about the Core Council? Any remarks from them?"

"Yes, the Chairperson, Marci Tansy, was on this morning offering the Council's condolences to the families of the victims. She also stated that the Council was making available some emergency funds for the families."

"Did either make any references to the other group?" Jax asked.

"That Tansy woman said she thought that the Government would quickly resolve the issue," Phil interjected.

"Nothing from the President about the Council?"

Peter shook his head, "I don't think so. Why do you ask?"

Jax slowly lifted his hand to his face. He rubbed his nose and then lowered his hand back to his lap. "I was just seeing how the two groups were reacting. Seeing if they were in lock step on the way the Government was handling the situation."

"You don't think they're at odds over this, do you?" Rebecca asked.

"It would be better for us," Jax answered.

"Divide and conquer?" Chris asked.

"Yes, something like that, but at the present," he said, "we have to deal with our severely tarnished reputation."

"Ravens," Rebecca stated, "killer of small children and pets."

There were murmurs among the group. Jax could sense their uneasiness about the label that had been thrust upon them. He knew that the bad press would affect the group inwardly as much as it affected the people of New America. The Government had thrust a double edged sword into the gut of their organization. Jax knew it was his job to repair the damage. He now understood why McKee had chosen him instead of a hardened combat leader. She had foreseen this type of attack and knew someone like him would be better suited to repair the damage and probably come out on top. They were in a battle of wits and no assault rifle could inflict the type of damage necessary for them to survive. Jax knew that he could come up with the counter attack that was now needed. In fact, the answer had come to him the other night shortly before fading into the drug induced slumber.

"Peter," he said, turning to the man, "Did you find my angels for me?"

Peter's jaw dropped open as he gawked at Jax in disbelief. "I...I..."

"You were serious about that?" Phil almost shouted.

"We...we thought you were hallucinating that night," Peter finally was able to say. "Phil and I didn't take you seriously."

"You asked them to find you some angels the other night?" Rebecca asked. "Did you think you were going to die in your sleep?"

The comment was just what was needed to break the tension in the room. Everyone laughed at the statement, including Jax.

"Hey", Jax chuckled as he pointed to Peter and Phil, "I was really doped up when I talked to these guys. I'm surprised I made any sense at all."

"You didn't," Peter said, as the room burst into laughter again. "Phil and I just let it ride."

"Yeah," Phil joined in, "we didn't go shopping for angels this morning."

Jax raised his hand and waved it slowly, "It's OK, he said. "I had the right idea but, the thought didn't come out correctly."

"I'll say," Peter replied, showing his relief. "Want to tell us what you were trying to say."

"What I wanted was for the two of you to find us four or five *angelic* looking men and women among our teams. I want the kind of faces that an artist would use as models to paint the inside of a chapel."

Peter turned and looked a Phil.

"Don't look at me," Phil protested, "not unless you need a model for the devil."

The room erupted in laughter again. Snide comments were tossed around the room at just about everyone's expense. *Excellent*, Jax thought, *the laughter is bringing the group back around. That,* he mused, *and the fact that they all understand that I have some crazy idea as to how we're going to turn this disaster around.*

CHAPTER 15

THE PRESIDENT'S DISPLEASURE

The demeanor of the group sitting around the small conference table was deathly solemn. President Ziven and the other two men in the room had removed their coats immediately after returning from the morning Netcast. Ziven had further loosened his tie and unbuttoned the top button of his shirt. Chief of Staff, Bob Lars and Pitney Ryan, Secretary of Intelligence, had loosened their ties but, at a second's notice, could go back in front of the cameras. The two women, Attorney General Kelly and Secretary of State, Bretta Glace still wore their traditional three piece suites as if they were getting ready for a Net-conference rather than returning from one. All five of them had deposited their PDs in the safe box before entering the secure room.

"I don't want to do that again," Ziven said solemnly, as he took his seat.

"None of us do, Mr. President," Kelly assured him.

Ziven looked at the four of them after they had all settled in. "OK, you're the best and the brightest we have so it's time for you guys to start earning your pay checks. What have we discovered?"

Pitney Ryan opened a paper folder in front of him. Pitney had the looks of one who would rather read a book than attend his own birthday party. His mousy facial features were further accented by the wire rimed reading glasses that he often wore. The others would describe him as being fit, but not athletic. If there was a true tell into the man's demeanor, it was his shark-like eyes. Pitney Ryan was no one's fool. Ziven had once described him as someone who could smile warmly as he devoured you whole.

"The explosives used in the bomb were definitely pre-apocalyptic manufacture," he said, not looking up from the file. "We had a large supply of it when we entered the shelters back then."

Ziven knew Ryan wasn't speaking of himself personally when he stated that 'we' had entered the shelters. Ryan was only thirty-two years old and wasn't even born when the government shelters were opened, but both his grandfather and father had secured a place in the shelters when the end came. "Is it all accounted for?" Ziven asked, already knowing the answer.

Ryan shook his head. "Not nearly as well as we would like. During the Cleansing war our logistical supply line was breached several times before we pushed the Outsiders into a full retreat. Some of the stuff could easily have fallen into their hands."

"Does the Core Security have access to this type of explosive?" Bob Lars asked.

Attorney General Kelly answered the question, "Yes, when the war was over and we decided that our military and civil police forces were to be combined into a single organization, it was the Core Security that was put in charge of merging the groups and collecting all of the weapons."

"You have to remember, "stated Secretary of State Glace, "it was a new nation rising out of the apocalyptic mess left by our ancestors. The new government, even though they had twenty years to plan for the rebirth, were strapped for manpower and other resources."

"Hell," Lars said, "it took the government another eight years to secure all the weapons left in the hands of the civilian population. And it was another five years before we began manufacturing the MR-6 and MR-7 assault rifles to replace the pre-apocalyptic stock pile."

Ziven rubbed his face with both hands. "So the explosives could have come from anywhere."

Ryan locked eyes with Ziven. "I wouldn't say anywhere, Mr. President. This stuff could only have come from two sources, either the rebels or our Core Security forces."

"So," Ziven sighed, "we've narrowed our two main suspects down to... two."

"There's another factor to consider," Ryan said. "The shelf life of this stuff is only about two to three years unless kept under strict storage conditions."

"What type of storage conditions?" Lars asked.

"Well, the stuff we kept in the shelters was stored in a vacuum environment where all conditions were kept static."

"And once out of this static environment?" Kelly asked.

"Then," Ryan said, "the clock is ticking, so anything the Outsiders could have today would be very unstable if usable at all. I would be willing to bet that they are manufacturing their own explosives by now, just like we are."

"Pitney," the President said, still rubbing his forehead, "I've got a raging headache, could you get to the point."

"Mr. President, our ballistics test shows this stuff to be pre-apocalyptic, so that means it has been kept in very good condition; something I don't think the Outsiders could accomplish."

"But," Ziven said, thinking out loud, "whoever set off the bomb wanted us to think it was someone who had these types of explosives available."

"Again," Lars added, "either the Outsiders or Core Security."

Ziven moved forward in his chair, "OK, let's cut to the quick here. Give me a percent probability on which group pulled the trigger."

Ryan shrugged his shoulders, "Seventy-thirty," he said. "If I had to guess I would say Core Security, but I wouldn't want to go on Netnews with it."

Ziven flopped back in his chair, "Crap."

"But there are three more pieces of evidence," Ryan offered; "the explosive residue taken from the speaker boxes and the pamphlet paper."

"You said three," Kelly reminded him.

"Well yes, let me rephrase that. The explosive residue and the two different types of paper used in the two pamphlets."

Ziven sat up again, "they were different?"

"Yes," Ryan said, "the explosives used in the speaker boxes didn't match any profile we have on record and it was definitely not the same substance used in the detonation that killed all these people." Ryan looked around the room momentarily, sizing up his audience. "The two parchment samples we discovered at the scene were both manufactured in New America, but different paper stock."

"And I'm willing to bet," Glace added, "the print and ink didn't match either."

A wicked smile grew on Ryan's face. "You're right about the print, totally different font style. We're still doing an analysis on the ink type used."

"So," Kelly mused, "we have two nearly simultaneous events happen, but all of the evidence points to the fact that they are not related."

"Boy, that's a long shot." Lars said. "Both groups are intelligent enough to throw enough twists and turns in this thing to have us chasing our tails."

"Or, it could be extraordinarily bad timing for

someone," Ziven stated. Looking toward Kelly, he asked, "nothing new on our hooker?"

"No, sir," she answered, "it's a dead end. We are certain that Patricia Mallory's identification was stolen at her death and the pseudo ID of Pepper Mallory was created." She continued as she raised her hands in a hopeless gesture, "but as to what end, we haven't a clue."

"And Commander Adelric hasn't made any more inquiries?" Lars asked.

"Nothing," Kelly confirmed, "it seems to have fallen off his radar."

"I can imagine," Ziven said thoughtfully. "Well ladies and gentlemen; is there anyone here that doesn't think this is going to happen again?"

They shook their head in unison.

"It is also insanity," Ziven said as he stood up, "to think that it will come to a peaceful conclusion."

Ryan looked up at the President. "You know, Mr. President, back during the horrific times just before the apocalypse, when my Grandfather entered the shelter he brought with him a plaque. He gave it to my father and in turn, he gave it to me. The quote is still as valid as ever."

"What did it say?" Kelly asked.

"It was a quote from Nietzsche," Ryan said, his brow wrinkling as he conjured up the passage. *"Insanity in individuals is something rare – but in groups, parties, nations, and epochs it is the rule."*

Ziven shook his head sadly. "It's too bad, Pitney, that we couldn't have fettered group insanity and left it in the bunker before we came out."

Mars marched down the hallway having mixed feelings about the news reporters she had just left in the main auditorium of the Central Exchange building. They always seemed to get under her skin, no matter what the subject. Today turned out to be especially difficult when that brash reporter, Albright, had the nerve to question her on the monetary relief the Core Council was offering the victims.

The conversation still rang in her ears. He had used words such as patronizing and condescending when referencing the paying of money as a means of reducing the families suffering. She made a mental note for the fourth time to have Pyrs look into the reporter's finances. *If he's receiving any type of subsidy or public funding*, she thought, *I'll have Pyrs cut him off at the knees. Or maybe, she mused, Adelric will discover that he is a sympathizer with the terrorists and have him hauled off to one of the interrogation centers.* The thought brought a broad smile to her face. She would speak to Adelric at the first opportunity.

Mars entered her office at a full clip but suddenly slowed as Adelric and one of his officers stood upon her arrival. "Commander," she said as she walked around her desk and took her seat, "I was just thinking about you."

Adelric placed his hand on his chest and began rubbing it as if in pain. "Is that why I have this feeling of being roasted over an open pit?"

Mars managed to laugh lightly as she leaned back in her chair. "Humor," she said, "you must have gotten your monthly allowance early."

Adelric bowed slightly not wishing to joust further. "Excellent Netcast," he said instead. "Sapphire has just told me that the Council's number went up quite nicely."

"They would have been much higher if it hadn't been for that snot nosed little reporter," she shot back.

"I don't think anyone even noticed," he said, with a dismissive gesture.

"I noticed," Mars spat. She looked at the other officer and then back to Adelric. She didn't like having strangers in her office. "Why are you here Commander?"

Adelric made a gesture toward the officer sitting next to him. "This is Captain Ellis. He is in charge of one of our *special* facilities in the outer districts. His facility has been very effective in obtaining the information we are seeking."

The news, of course, was of great importance to her, but she only showed a faint interest, "Please continue, Commander, I have an extremely busy schedule today."

Adelric nodded to the young officer to take over. "Ms. Tansy, we have had a recent breakthrough with some of the people we've been questioning."

"And," she prompted.

The young man cleared his throat before continuing. "We now have several sketches of some of the suspected terrorists."

"And," she prompted again, showing her impatience.

"We think that we will have at least one or two of them in custody by the end of the week."

For the first time, she allowed a little of her pleasure to show. "Excellent, Captain," she beamed, "have you uploaded the sketches into Sapphire?"

"I've had Captain Ellis delay in doing so," Adelric interjected.

Mars sat forward in her chair. "Delayed? Why delay when we can have these criminals incarcerated now?"

"If we upload their sketches they will be broadcast all over the net. Since we don't know their current location they could easily go to ground if we tip our hand too soon."

Mars eased back in her chair again. "Good thinking, Commander. You know we want them badly, but on the other hand, patience seems the best way to handle this right now."

"Correct," he answered, "also, once we spot them we can begin to track them. They should be able to lead us to the bigger group."

Mars let her imagination run wild. Catching a few of these terrorists could lead to the down-fall of their entire organization. She pictured their leaders bound and kneeling behind her as she went on Netnews to tell the entire country that they, not

Ziven and his little government had brought the terrorists down. If she had her way, Ziven would find out about it during the broadcast. It would certainly cut him down a few notches until the next election.

"Please keep the Council advised on this matter Commander," she said, as she stood up and directed the two men to the door. "I would like to see this matter ended before the Fourth of July."

"I think there's a good chance of that happening," he said as he left.

Oh, Commander," she said, motioning Adelric back to the door of her office."

"Yes?" he said, returning alone.

Mars leaned toward him and in a whisper said, "Commander, I have been informed by a reliable source that the young reporter, Mr. Albright, may be a sympathizer with the rebels. It certainly warrants further investigation."

Adelric studied Mars' face for several seconds then looked over his shoulder at the young Captain.

"I'll have Captain Ellis look into it."

CHAPTER 16

SOMETHING TO THINK ABOUT

Jax sat at the kitchen table watching the heating element beneath the kettle glow as he waited for the water to boil. The red-orange glow of the element was true and steady attesting to the ample power supplied to the unit. Much of the power available in Middle-earth had been produced by generators powered by propane. There were still great stock piles of propane, gasoline and oil available at the fall of the United States. The end had come so quickly that the huge supply of fuel far outstripped the number of people using it. He had heard that Middle-earth had millions of barrels of propane alone. He missed the flickering bluish flame of the fire back home.

"Enough water on for two?" Rebecca asked as she entered the kitchen.

Jax turned to see Rebecca dressed in a very comfortable looking warm up suite. He looked down at his shirt, open to the waist, revealing the white gauze bandages wrapped around his rib cage. He began buttoning the shirt up as she took a seat next to him.

"Don't get all dressed up on my account," she smiled.

"I asked Sheila if she had a more formal bandage, but she said we were all out."

"What are you doing up so late?" she asked

"Couldn't sleep," he answered quickly, "so I came down here to get some tea and think awhile."

"I'll leave if you like."

"No, no. It's good that you came down." Jax slowly started to rise from his chair.

"Stay put," she insisted and was up and to the stove before he could move any farther. Rebecca quickly filled two mugs with hot water and returned to the table.

"Thank you," he said as he took the mug. "I was thinking about Sapphire."

"Sapphire, what about it?'

Jax gazed into the bottom of his mug as he dipped the tea bag. "It controls everything around here. Without it, New America would be helpless."

"Is that what you want?" she asked frowning. "Bring the entire country to its knees?"

"Not like you're saying it, but it could make our job a lot easier." Jax placed his hands around the mug and let the warmth of the ceramic soak into his fingers. "Some of the things we're doing would be so much easier if you could upload some of our programs onto the system."

"It's funny to hear you say that," she said, from behind the rim of her mug.

"How so?"

"Well, you're sitting here complaining that Sapphire has got the people in a pair of electronic shackles that they can't break free from. Then, on the other hand, you are wishing that Sapphire was ours to shackle the people the way we want."

Jax thought about her analogy. He really didn't want anyone restricted. "That's not true," he said softly, "I just wish the playing field was a little more evenly balanced."

"No you don't!" she said bluntly, "Ajax Martin, I've known you long enough now to understand that you would never be happy with a level playing field."

That was the first time he had heard his full name in almost a year. It surprised him even more that Rebecca had known his family name. Full names were not often used in the field. Someone had once told him it was a soldier's way of depersonalizing one another. If someone died, it was just another Bill or Terry gone from the group. Last names related to families and no one liked to think about families. Personally, Jax thought that line of thinking was a load of crap.

He looked at Rebecca sheepishly. "I do like a good fight," he admitted.

"We all do, that's part of why we're here," she said as she got up and brought more hot water. "Have you ever heard any of us talk about defeat?"

He thought about the question. "No, actually I've never heard that word used by anyone in this command."

Rebecca refilled both mugs and sat down. "So what do you want to do about Sapphire?"

Jax shrugged his shoulders. "You've been here longer than most. What do you think we can do?"

Rebecca's eyes had become glassy. He knew she had drifted off to a place where Jax had never seen her go. "About eighteen months ago," she started slowly, "a couple of our programmers were here helping us set up a PD shop. Somehow they were able to get a look at the Sapphire proprietary system sign on. It was nothing like they had ever seen before or even dreamed of. They tried to hack into the system numerous times, but failed."

"Did they just give up?"

Rebecca shook her head, "they both went missing along with three others."

"Did we try again?" Jax asked.

"I understand that they sent their work back to Middle-earth and that it's being studied."

"No program is impossible to hack into," Jax insisted.

Rebecca looked at him squarely, "One of the programmers told me that it was like reaching the sign on screen and there was nothing there but a bowl of soup. Then the next time you went to sign in it asked you to answer a question. *How high is up?* or *How do you know when you've gone too far?* or *What is the opposite number of red?*"

"All good questions, Jax said, "let's blow it up then."

Rebecca rolled her eyes in frustration, "Have you seen a building around here with a sign on it saying: Halt, do not enter. Top Secret building containing the Sapphire mainframe and components?"

"It has to be around here somewhere."

"We've been looking for years," she stated.

"What about the Core Exchange building?"

Rebecca shook her head. "Dead end, we had an agent infiltrate the complex as an electrician. After six months he reported back that there was no sign of a computer complex at all."

"It could be hidden out in one of the outlying districts, like the interrogation facility."

"Rebecca nodded in agreement. "We've thought of that, but have come up with nothing."

Jax let his frustration show. "Well then, let's move on to some very real targets, the solar collectors. I would like to get a close look at one of them."

"Definitely more tangible," she agreed, but still heavily guarded."

"I'm sure we could convince them to send some of their troops into a nearby town that, say was involved, in a full scale riot."

Again Rebecca agreed. "Very possible, if you

can start the riot. I don't need to tell you that our reputation needs to be polished up before we could get anyone to follow us into a full blown protest."

Jax thought about her words as he went over their current operation in his mind. It was one of the craziest ideas he had ever come up with, but in the current situation it could work. "What do you think of the angels?"

Rebecca's face beamed for the first time, "Jax, it is without a doubt one of the most bizarre ideas I've ever heard of, but I got to tell you, I think it's pure genius. Whatever made you think of something like that?"

A devious look came over his face. "I think it was, partially the drugs and then a good amount of theatrics and a little bit of the old con man tricks. Of course, it doesn't hurt that these people have been put to sleep by Sapphire."

"Put to sleep?" "Yes, absolutely, these poor people are fed propaganda on a twenty-four hour basis. Through the Core Council and their use of Sapphire, they are told what to eat, what to wear, what to do, where to do it." Jax pushed his mug away from him in a helpless gesture, "They even report what they do on a weekly basis to the damn machine." He pointed his finger toward Rebecca, "I'll bet you there's more to Sapphire than we currently know."

"Like what?"

Jax threw his hands into the air and instantly regretted it. The pain in his ribs shot through his entire body forcing him to retract his actions immediately. "Damn", he hissed, holding his side as if that would control the pain.

Rebecca frowned empathetically but kept her mouth shut. Jax slowly brought his breathing down to a normal level as he mentally tried to relax the muscles in his entire body. "Damn, that hurts," he said recalling her question, "I'm not sure, but there has to be something." He continued to adjust his breathing and finally removed his hand from is ribs. "All the history I have read on the United States shows that the American people tended to be very complacent and self-centered."

"Really," Rebecca said, her eyebrow rising, "everything I've read shows just the opposite. They were great explorers, and pioneers. They had a reputation of never backing down from a fight. If anything, they were compassionate, not complacent."

Jax shook his head, "You didn't look at the underlying cause and effect. Let's look at the history of American warfare. In every major war the Americans were pushed to the brink before they struck back: The Civil war, Spanish American war, World War one and two; it wasn't until they had exhausted every means to stay out of the war no matter how slim the chance was before they took the final plunge. There was always an external catalyst that pushed them to the boiling point."

"I would call that an admirable trait, wouldn't you?"

"Yes, but it can also be a major flaw."

Rebecca pulled her feet up under her and wiggled around until she was comfortable. "How so?"

"Complacency," Jax answered, "you said it yourself. These people have most things they want. There are few basic food or medicine shortages. Unemployment is none existent, major crime is under control."

"Again," Rebecca said making a vague gesture in the air, "Then what are we doing here?"

"What happens to you if you don't post to Sapphire at least once a week?

"There are several levels of monetary punishment that a person would go through."

"So at that point, their warm and fuzzy little world is shaken up," he smiled. "What happens when you continue to refuse?"

Rebecca thought about the question, "I don't know, I guess it could lead to some type of stricter punishment."

"So, the government's not just going to cave in and say that they don't have to participate, right?"

Rebecca picked up her cold mug of tea, frowned and set it back on the table. "No, they never 'cave' as you put it."

Jax gingerly stood up and retrieved the pot of hot water. "Do those damn PDs track your every move?"

"Yes."

Are the Core Security allowed to use their PDs

to search you with no probable cause?'

"Of course."

"What would happen if I said, screw it, I'm not taking my PD with me this morning?"

Rebecca recited the law verbatim as she placed a new tea bag in the hot water Jax had supplied. "A person who does not have their PD in their possession at all times is subject to penalties under the law."

"What would have happened to us if we had decided to *shack up* without applying for a cohabitation license?"

"Subject to penalties under the law," she paraphrased.

"Seems to me that everything you do is," Jax held out the two fingers on each hand and made a theatrical gesture emphasizing the quotation marks, *subject to the penalties of some law.*"

"I happen to agree with you, but look at the many benefits."

"The bird in a gilded cage," he smiled.

"What?"

"No matter how nice the prison is, it's still a prison."

"People living in a society are often required to give up some freedoms in order for the society to function cohesively," she quoted from something she remembered reading."

"That's true, but where do you draw the line?" he asked, "What would happen to you if you wanted to explore the wastelands?"

"It's not allowed."

"What if you wanted to change professions?"

"Not allowed."

"Wanted to marry another woman?"

"Not allowed."

"What if you and Mat wanted to have five children together?"

"It's not allowed," she frowned.

Jax leaned forward, "So what freedoms have I not given up? Or better stated maybe, what is allowed? My right to turn oxygen into carbon dioxide? My right to eat and drink as long as I don't crap on the floor? "

"Jax, we've had this conversation before and it got us nowhere. We're doing what we can to open their eyes, but it's not working."

"That's why I'm desperately trying to discover ways to move that complacency meter without reverting to killing people." He sighed in frustration…"we need to show them that their comfort zone is a fabrication of lies built around a list of the government demands. They're being fed propaganda and told it's candy."

Rebecca's eyes lost their luster, wounded by the frustration expressed in Jax's words. She knew that Jax had been and would have to continue being their guiding light. If that light were to go out she worried about who would replace him and what the next strategy would be to bring down the barriers surrounding New America. She felt that the people of Middle-earth were ready to stand up and fight if necessary. "Do you think the angels will help bring that about?" she offered changing the subject somewhat."

Jax shook his head, "I'm confident that the angels will help repair our reputation, but it's too early to predict what value they will have after that."

Rebecca picked up the two empty mugs and washed them in the sink. Jax still sat motionless obviously lost in thought. After clearing the rest of the items off the table she turned off what lights Jax had turned on and returned to the table. She placed her hand on his shoulder. "OK, we have a big day tomorrow," she said, helping him to his feet. "Let's go to bed."

Jax lead the way up the stairs. "OK," he smiled. "But I'm warning you, I don't think I'm ready to perform great feats of sexual aerobics yet," he said, carefully making his way up the stairs.

"That's OK," Rebecca said from behind him, "it's not going to happen anyway."

"You're not going to believe me but I was really hoping you were going to say that," he chuckled lightly, but not lightly enough. "Ouch," he said holding his side as he reached the landing.

"Jax..." Rebecca started.

Jax turned to face her.

"I still don't think you should go tomorrow," she said.

He offered her a reassuring smile. "It will be fine. No explosions this time."

She smiled and nodded her head knowing she would not be able to change his mind. "OK, see you in the morning," she answered heading down the hall to her room.

"Goodnight," he called to her as he crept into his own room.

Next to the Core Exchange building, The Central Mall complex was the largest structure in all of New America. Covering eighty-two acres, the complex had almost two million sq ft of retail space. The complex consisted of four equidistant spurs jutting out from the center arena. Each spur was a three story building housing over 125 stores and restaurants. The center attraction of the mall was its hub or center arena where three major hotels were located. The hub could handle any number of events simultaneously. A theme park wove its way through all three stories of all of the spurs as well as a jungle river ride enjoyed by people of all ages. The center arena was center stage for numerous cultural events produced throughout the year. Once every six years the center arena was host to the national elections with instantaneous results being displayed on the mall's four million credit, multi-media projection systems, visible to everyone who was in the mall.

Transportation to the mall was provided from every District by way of an underground tram stations. The trams were an early version of the hyper tube system and could deliver passengers to the mall at a speed of 150 miles per hour. In various places in the mall, Sapphire was advertising the future upgrades to the trams. The project was to start soon and be completed over the next three years. At the end of the renovation period the speed would be increased to 215 miles an hour and each tram would be able to carry over 250 passengers at a time.

Next to the Core Exchange building and the SCS facilities, the tram had the highest level of security in the country. No passengers were allowed into the lower tram buildings without undergoing intensive scanning. The surveillance system and emergency lock down procedures were said to be the equal of those in operation at all of the SCS facilities.

The above ground entrances were too numerous and did not have the high-tech security system that was located on the tram level. Core security did house a full detachment of troops right in the mall and they, along with the Sapphire surveillance system, provided security.

Rebecca stood in front of one of the dress shop windows. The merchandise display system had scanned her for her exact measurements and was now displaying one of the dresses on a holographic reproduction of her. As Rebecca twisted and turned, the holographic reproduction twisted and turned with her. She flipped her long hair over her shoulder the system mimicked her movement. When she turned away from the window a new likeness of her was now in front of her. She was now looking at herself from the rear. Rebecca placed her hands on her hips a shifted her legs several times. The holo in front of her did the same. "Does my butt look too big in this?" she asked Jax.

"Your butt wouldn't look too big in anything," he answered, leaning on his cane. His cane displayed a 3D sticker that confirmed that it had been checked out by security. The sticker would detach itself upon his exiting the mall.

Rebecca grinned from ear to ear at the comment. Her holo turned to Jax and winked its approval at the remark.

"You come stand here," she said to Jax.

"Please, Rebecca, no."

"Come on, Jax," she insisted and pulled him to where she was standing.

When Jax looked at the display; instead of seeing himself in the dress he was given a look at the sales price and several lay-a-way options.

"How much is it?" she asked, trying to see what he was seeing.

"Isn't it telling you the price?" Jax asked.

"No," she frowned, "I have to go into the store to see the sales price. The holo knows you men are too lazy or afraid to go inside and therefore it gives you the information out here.

"Let's move on," Jax suggested. "Center mall is that way and it's going to take me awhile to get there."

"Thank you," Rebecca said to the holo as she

moved away.

They passed a BBQ restaurant that displayed several of the daily specials right before their eyes. From some hidden location a flavor mister shot a quick puff of mist that smelled like the restaurant's signature sauce. Both Jax and Rebecca's mouth began to water. As they moved closer to the center court they passed a woman's lingerie store.

"Stand right here," Jax said to Rebecca.

"You wish," she answered and continued toward the hub carefully staying outside of the holo's scanning range.

Jax smiled and whispered to himself, "Yes I do."

"I heard that," Rebecca said, not bothering to look back.

Soon they were standing on the top floor looking down at the center hub of the complex. There were no special events happening at the mall this weekend so the main floor was divided up into several sections. One of the sections was still an ice skating arena. Under the ice the phrase 'Last weekend' was flashing in a multiple array of colors. A second section was a group of vendors selling pre-apocalyptic antiques and memorabilia from the tops of their folding tables. A large holo sign over the area spoke of the authenticity of the goods and guaranteed that everything had been found in the waste lands. Jax knew the goods couldn't have come from the western wastelands as the solar fence would stop anyone from traveling in that direction.

As for the eastern wastelands, he couldn't say. If what he had heard was true, the eastern seaboard of the United States had taken the brunt of the nuclear attacks. What was once called the thirteen original colonies was now the original radiation slag land. He surmised that most of the goods had been worked up from old pieces found within New America. New American companies had taken advantage of the materials remaining in the old cities. They had torn down every scrap of material and used it in the reclamation process. This very mall could have been constructed from what once was the City of Chicago for all he knew.

Lights began to dim throughout the mall. The four million credits, multimedia system was preparing for some type of show. A good eighty percent of the shoppers stopped and looked around them. The mall was known for its excellent presentations, especially during the holidays, but that's not to say that their off season mini-shows weren't something to behold.

Clouds began to form and role through the different levels. The flicker of lightning and the rumble of thunder came from within the formations. Quickly several of the larger clouds began to rise in the configuration of thunderheads. The intensity of the lightning and thunder grew. Many of the onlookers jumped when the lightning flashed and the thunder crackled. The crowd showed their appreciation by clapping or cheering with each progressively intense event. Soon five distinctive thunderheads were forming through the mall. Each thunderhead was as tall as two of the malls levels. The sound of the wind picked up and the clouds began to move rapidly across the open area, that is, all but the five huge thunderheads which remained stationary. As the wind began to howl the thunderheads transformed into whirling tornadoes. Suddenly the wind died down and the once dark swirling masses that were the tornadoes grew brighter until they were almost too bright to gaze upon. Jax and Rebecca both had to shield their eyes from the light. Almost as quickly as it started it ended. The bright light dissipated leaving five figures each standing on what looked to be a thin layer of cloud.

Jax knew all five of the figures but he was truly stunned at the splendor they portrayed. Each was dressed in what looked to be silver blue-gray robes, the material shimmering with their slightest movement. All five looked around the crowd, offering radiant smiles. The glow around them portrayed goodness and kindness and their faces had a celestial purity about them. Jax couldn't believe that these were the same people he interviewed two weeks ago.

"Jax," Rebecca whispered so close to his ear he could feel the moisture of her breath, "they are unbelievable."

Jax just nodded as he himself was transfixed by them.

There were two women and three men. It was

the youngest and most angelic of the two women who spoke first.

"People of New America," she began. "We are the Guardians."

The mall was so quiet Jax could hear the hum of some distant machinery. He was finally able to break eye contact and look around for a split second. Even though he knew what they were going to say, he didn't want to miss a word. It was obvious that no one else wanted to either. Even the security personnel were mesmerized by their presence.

"We have watched over you in silence" she continued, "since the falling of the apocalypse."

"But now", boomed the voice of one of the male figures, "Your government has committed such great atrocities upon its own people that we can no longer be silent."

The second women moved forward. "They have killed their own and try to censure us for their sins."

"They have murdered your friends, your families and your children," stated the fourth person his voice filled with grief, "and in doing so have cowered behind a factious creature they created known as The Raven."

"By doing so," stated the final figure, "they have picked their own demon and damned themselves into becoming the carnivorous creature that they have conjured.

The first figure stepped forward. Tears now ran down her cheeks. "We stand ready to help you fight the greed and immorality that they represent."

Together they bowed and spoke the final words. "We are the Guardians."

The wind quickly picked up again pushing the clouds. As quickly as it had started, it ended. The five figures melted into the swirling clouds and vanished.

For several seconds there was only silence. Jax could hear several people sobbing before the roar of thousands blended together. There was cheering while others voiced concerns. He was truly stunned by their performance and turned to get Rebecca's response. His voice caught in his throat as he noticed the tears pooling on the rims of her eyes. She blinked pushing the water over the edge and cascading down her cheeks. Before he could speak she reached out and drew him close, burying her head in his chest. He gave her a brotherly hug and patted her softly on the back. Finally she raised her head and deflected her eyes from his. "I feel like a total ass," she sniffled.

"Well, not total," he managed to choke out.

From out of thin air she produced a tissue and blew her nose. "Sometime you can be such a jackass."

"Ah," he sighed, "the rigors of command."

She looked around the mall trying to regain her composure. "Are you hungry?" she asked. "I'll buy you a BBQ dinner."

They started to walk back toward the restaurant. "Hey," Jax said, "maybe this time we can stop in front of the lingerie store."

"No," she said and continued walking.

"Just for a second?" he pleaded.

"No," she reaffirmed. "You're lucky to be getting BBQ."

CHAPTER 17

MARS' RAGE

The glass shattered against the far conference room wall. All of the council members sat frozen in their chairs diverting their eyes from Mars. A few loose tendrils of her hair, usually perfectly styled, hung down before her eyes. Her voice rose to a murderous falsetto. "Those bastards have pushed us as far as I am going to let them." Her eyes flared as she looked toward Adelric, "Step up your efforts to bring some of them in. Push your informants for better information if need be. I want those bastards behind bars tonight!"

Adelric knew better than to voice a reply. Instead, he simply nodded at the command. The others squirmed in their seat not wishing to invoke her wrath any further.

Mars paced as she thought. The room became deathly quiet.

"Excuse the interruption." Sapphire stated.

"What is it?"

"I have President Ziven on hold. Shall I put him through?"

Mars ground out the words between her clamped jaws, "I told you that there were to be no interruptions until further notice."

"Yes, Ms. Mars," Sapphire answered in her usual calm voice.

"Sapphire, Mars asked, "have you finished profiling all of the shoppers at the mall this morning during the event?"

"Ms. Mars," Sapphire answered, there were 21,267 people at the mall during this morning's event. I am currently comparing their facial ID points to the 1,872 persons that were at the Old Town bombing as requested...

"Fine," she interrupted, "Let me know as soon as you have the results."

"And the President?" Sapphire asked again.

"It's the third time he's phoned." Pyrs reminded her.

Mars closed her eyes, her face growing pale. "Hold *all* calls as you were ordered to do," she hissed at the computer.

"You're just going to piss him off," Kinsley stated, "more than he probably already is."

Mars offered a dismissive gesture as her answer. There was a low level chime alerting

Adelric that a message had come to his console. All eyes turned to him.

"I have the short report from our tec-group," he said as he scanned the screen in front of him. He looked up from the machine. "As you know, the message was broadcast over the mega view system a total of three times. Each message was a slight variation of the first message that broadcasted the first time at 11:32 AM. Forty minutes later a slightly different variation of the first message was played. The third happened exactly forty minutes after the second."

"Does your report say why the view system operators couldn't shut it down?" Mars asked acidly.

"The system operators," Adelric continued, pointing down to the screen, "said they were temporarily locked out of the system."

"Then why didn't they just pull the plug? Cut the power?" she said, her voice raising a full octave after each question. "Turn off the damn lights!?"

"As you know," he said calmly, "a complex the size of Central Mall has a redundant failsafe system so that the power cannot be just shut off on a whim."

"A whim?" she shouted. "You call the crap they spewed out a whim? Why didn't your men evacuate the mall?"

"These systems," Adelric continued ignoring Mars' rant, "have a complex shut down protocol to prevent total panic among the shoppers and store personnel. Every time they attempted to shut the power down, the system told them that there was no reason to do so."

"Don't they have an override code?" Pyrs asked.

"It didn't respond," Adelric sighed.

Mars plopped down in her chair and flicked her dangling hair out of her eyes. "Go on," she ordered, regaining some of her composure.

"At the end of the third projection, the system performed a reboot, wiping out whatever programming had been entered."

"Let me guess," Mars said sarcastically, "when they regained control of the system there was no trace of the rogue program."

"Not entirely," he answered punching a few keys on his keypad. The Sapphire crystal image now contained a dark silhouette of a raven's head and the words: *Compliments of the Guardians*.

There was a low murmur among the council members as they voiced their concerns.

"Ms. Mars," Sapphire asked.

"You have the comparisons?" Mars asked.

"I am still compiling the data," it answered, "but I am informing you that President Ziven is currently starting a press conference."

"On screen!" Mars barked.

The multimedia screens around the room flashed to life. Each screen showed the same image of the Presidential Seal. Within seconds, the seal vanished and was replaced with the image of

President Ziven sitting behind his desk in the Oval Office.

"My fellow Americans," he started, "by now you have seen or have been told of the events at the Central Mall today."

"Sapphire," Mars yelled, "Shut him down!"

"No!" yelled Pyrs, locking eyes with Mars, "It's too late for that," he explained.

"Your orders, Ms. Chairman?" Sapphire asked.

Mars slumped back in her chair, "Let him continue."

"We are currently looking into the allegations made by the persons calling themselves *The Guardians*. To date, we have not concluded our investigations of the Old Town massacre. But, I am willing to say that we may have been rash in our earlier press releases in reference to The Raven and the distribution of the two different pamphlets that were found at the crime scene. So far we believe we have been able to ascertain that the Guardians and the Ravens may indeed be two separate organizations."

"Oh shit," Mars hissed.

"It is unclear at the present time," the President continued, "if the two groups are working together or at cross purposes, but both groups are being considered armed and dangerous. I will ask you to remain calm and allow Attorney General Kelly and her personnel to investigate this further. If anyone has any information that may help our investigation, please do not hesitate to call the

Attorney General's hotline now listed at the bottom of your screens." President Ziven gave his audience a warm, reassuring smile, "Together, we can get to the bottom of this tragedy while remaining a strong, peace-loving nation. Good night and bless you all."

The screen went dark.

"Would you like to view the broadcast a second time?" Sapphire asked.

"That won't be necessary", Kinsley stated. "Comments on the President's remarks?"

"The Guardians and the Raven are the same people," Pyres offered, "We know that much."

"Of course they are the same people," Mars said. "But how to prove it."

"Simple," Adelric offered, "I'm sure once we arrest the members of Raven, we will not hear from the Guardians again."

Mars eyed Adelric suspiciously, "you do remember that we are the ones who created The Raven."

"So what," Pyrs said understanding Adelric's meaning. "We may have named them but, now there's a name and soon enough we will be able to put faces with the name."

"I can promise you", Mars said holding up a still photograph of the five Guardians, "that these people are not the ones we are after. They're probably paid actors who just did what they were told to do."

"Ms Mars," Sapphire interrupted, "I have finished compiling the data as requested.

"Don't make me wait," Mars said.

"There are eleven matches between the people who were at the Old Town festival and also present at the Central mall during the time stipulated." Sapphire explained. "Given the parameters you stipulated, five of the people identified have been eliminated. Three of these people were over the age of fifty-five and two of them were below the age of fifteen. Here are the images of the six people that remain." Sapphire said as she displayed two rows of pictures. The top row was the individual pictures of the five people recorded in Old Town. The bottom row was the images of the same people shown at the Central Mall.

"Excellent," Adelric said, "if we are right about the criminals being present to witness their crimes, then these people are prime suspects."

"Why would they do that?" Kinsley asked innocently.

"It's a known physiological trait," Dr. Grady stated, "that in the past, known criminals have had a tendency to either witness their crimes or return to the scene after the crime is committed. These criminals were often captured when photographs or videos of several like crime scenes, say arson, were compared and revealed the same person lurking in the crowd."

Look at the second one from the right," Adelric said, pointing up to the photos. The top picture shows him at Old Town looking quite healthy. The photo below shows him leaning on a cane;

obviously he has had a recent injury."

"Say, being caught in the Old Town blast?" Mars smiled wickedly.

"Yes, exactly," Adelric said. "Look at his face. It's obvious he is still in some pain."

"So?" Pyrs asked.

"So," Mars said, connecting the dots Adelric had lain out, "if you were recently injured in a blast, would you be out at the mall so soon afterward unless you had a compelling reason to do so?"

"To watch the show he helped put together," Pyrs said catching on.

"Sapphire," Mars said coldly, "I want names and addresses of the woman in image number four and the man in image number five as soon as possible."

"The woman?" Dr Grady asked.

"She's obviously with the man in both pictures," Adelric stated.

Mars stood and began to gather her belongings. "Sapphire, I also want the following to be initiated immediately. First, I want the media system at the Central Mall to be placed under your control. Nothing is to be broadcast without the Council's express permission." She turned to Adelric, "Replace all of the mall personnel working in the media section or at least assign agents to them at all times. Second, have all broadcasts coming from Government Plaza placed on a ten minute delay. I want to be able to shut that loud mouth down next time." Mars started toward the door, "Commander, inform me the second you have those two people in custody."

* * * *

The Black Nights quietly moved into position around the house. In the control van a block away, the mission commander viewed the blue prints of the large two story home. The home contained four bedrooms and three baths and a very large kitchen-family room, there was also a basement in the home that caused him some concern. Because of the rush imposed on him by Commander Adelric, he did not have time to order the repositioning of a satellite to check for heat signatures. He had no idea how many people were currently in the home nor could he tell if any modifications had been made to the structure. His stomach contracted at the thought of the negative possibilities.

"Team One to Team leader.." his earpiece hissed.

"Go ahead Team One."

"We have eyes on all four sides now," the team relayed. "Our P-scanners are showing three possible targets inside the home."

"Roger, I read three, repeat, three possible targets," the Commander confirmed. "Location of targets?" he asked.

"We have two targets located in the family room area with the third person on the second floor either in a bedroom or possible bath."

"I copy," he answered, double clicking the

microphone. "Team Leader to Team six."

"Team six, go ahead."

"Team six what is you status?"

"Team Leader be advised," the leader of Team Six said in a very calm voice, "we have secured the perimeter around the block. There is no movement at the present time."

"Roger Team Six, when I give the word seal off all street and points of exit."

"Roger that," came the reply.

The Team Commander looked over his shoulder toward the agent seated at the console. The electronics covered about half of the right side of the van. "Jerry," he asked, "give me an update of satellite coverage."

The tech shook his head as he answered, "Sorry, sir, we won't have a sky-spy for another ninety minutes."

The Commander looked at his situation board. In the upper right hand corner the display showed the three digital numeric clocks. The first showed actual time, the second showed the time remaining before sunrise and the third showed the mission lapse time. "It will be daybreak before that damn bird gets into position," he said to no one in particular. None of the other three occupants in the van offered a suggestion. The Commander knew that the early morning commuters would be rising soon. Traffic on the streets would pick up dramatically.

"Team Six to Team Leader," the ear piece

hissed.

"Go Team Six. This is Leader."

"Sir, we have signs of activity starting in several of the homes around the target."

"Roger that," the Team Leader confirmed, "All teams stand by."

Jax and Peter sat at the kitchen table not speaking. They had stopped drinking tea or, in Peter's case, coffee over two hours ago. That was when Rebecca said good night and went upstairs.

Jax and Peter had gone over the schedule of the next week's events a dozen times since Rebecca had gone up and they had now exhausted every detail of the plans.

"We'll leave mid-morning," Jax said. "After the morning rush hour has died down." He and Rebecca were returning to one of the safe houses in District One. Peter, with the help of Chris and Phil, would stay behind and carry on with the operations in Core City.

"I'll get to work on having Matt join you there," Peter confirmed.

Jax nodded his understanding. He had told Peter to make sure that Matt was moved to the same location as he and Rebecca. Things were going to start getting dicey and he felt Rebecca and Matt deserved the time together. He tried to convince himself that Matt was a good soldier and could be used in the upcoming missions in the North, but deep down inside he knew he was doing it for Rebecca. He had never seen her happier than when she was with Matt. And for his own edification he reminded himself that Matt was indeed a hell of a good soldier.

"We'll send you a few reinforcements once we get up there," Jax said for the eighth or ninth time.

Peter nodded looking very sleepy.

Jax had made another discovery over the last few days. He had tried for months to push the thoughts out of his head, but they became stronger every time his mind began to wander. He had feelings for another officer that he couldn't shake. After things quieted down some, he promised himself that he would explore his urges further when the opportunity made itself available.

"Pete," Jax began, I will be…

"All Teams go!" the Team Commander shouted into his mike.

In coordination with every team, the front and rear doors of the house blew inward with a muffled pop. Simultaneously, windows on opposite sides of the home shattered inward. Four different teams breached the house like synchronized swimmers performing their routine flawlessly. They quickly shuffled through the home, clearing each room as they moved. Team Three encountered an unknown person running down the stairs toward them. Two quick shots to the chest dropped the suspect, her momentum carrying her to the bottom of the landing. A third shot to the back of the head ensured that she would not get up. Team three continued up the stairs stepping around or over the young woman's body.

Team One and Two met on opposite ends of the kitchen. Six laser sights were trained on the two figures sitting there.

"Let me see you hands!" screamed the leader of Team One.

"Show us your hands, show us your hands," was repeated by the second team leader.

The two suspects were pushed to the floor as black cloth bags were secured over their heads; a foot placed on the back of their covered heads reinforced the notion that they were not to move.

Several members of the strike team shouted simultaneously throughout the house, "Clear!...Clear!...Clear!"

The team leader of Team One keyed his mike, "Three, sit-rep?"

"Three here, second floor cleared. One body at the base of the stairs."

"Understand," Leader One confirmed, "Team four, sit-rep."

"Team four," the leader answered, "basement cleared, but you'll want to see this down here."

"Secure your position team four," he answered. "I'll be there shortly." He double keyed his mike. "Team One to Team Commander, house secured, two prisoners in the bag: one enemy KIA."

The Team Commander relaxed and smiled is he pushed the mission stop clock. "Transportation rolling," he confirmed. "I want those people secured in the van and out of here in two minutes."

"Roger," answered the Team One leader.

Jax and Peter quietly walked up behind Rebecca who was looking through a thin slit in the blinds of her bedroom. Peter and he peered out through the slit. From their vantage point they could see the unmarked security van pull into the yard of the house across the street.

"Very efficient," Rebecca said. "Three minutes and forty-seven seconds."

"Yes very," Jax added, "a precision operation."

"What do you think is going to happen when they discover they just arrested one of the Attorney General's staffers and his family?" Peter asked.

"The crap will come down in buckets," Jax answered, walking away from the window. He looked back at Rebecca and Peter, "I'm going to get some sleep and you guys should too."

Both left their position at the window. Rebecca walked the two men to the door.

"Remember," Peter added as he headed toward the guest bedroom, "you guys are scheduled to be on the road by 10:00 AM.

Jax waved his hand over his head as he entered his room. "I hope Chris and Phil got all of that on video."

CHAPTER 18

ATTORNEY GENERAL KELLY

President Ziven leaned forward in his chair, his elbows resting on the desk while he rubbed his hands in a circular motion. His thin lanky structure coupled with his current posture gave him the appearance of a rather large Praying Mantis. He watched the events unfold on the multi-screen. He witnessed teams of men in black body armor creep into position. It was obvious that the four cameras were stationary and set up to record night time activity using night vision equipment. At times the details were so crisp that Ziven could count the creases in the men's uniforms. There was no sound, but none was needed to understand what was happening. Core Security's *Black Knights* were preparing to raid a home.

This was not just any home. It was the residence of Albert Lotte, Associate Attorney General of New

America. Albert, age forty three, lived in the house with his wife, Carmen, age forty one and their daughter, Dena, age seventeen. It had been their residence since Dena's twelfth birthday.

Ziven sat back and watched all four views at once. He inched forward as the order to enter must have been given. He had to admit that he was impressed with the precision with which the team breached the perimeter of the home. There couldn't have been a three second difference between each team gaining access from their assigned entrée point. The cameras didn't follow the men into the house, but stood vigilant watch from their fixed positions.

"Oh God!" someone in the room sighed as several bright flashes lit up one of the windows. Not five seconds later a third flash could be seen. In his mind Ziven knew that young Dena had just died a horrible death. The sounds of sobbing could be heard from around the room. In the darkness of the office several people blew their noses and sniffled trying to hold back the sorrow they were feeling. Shortly after the flashes an unmarked van pulled up in front of the house. Within seconds two hooded people were roughly ushered into the back of the unit and whisked away.

The cameras continued documenting the events unfolding for several more minutes. They recorded the two government vehicles pulling up at the curb and Attorney General Kelly and her husband, Roger, exited one of the vehicles. Four Secret Service men exited the other. They were met on the front lawn by two of the Core Security Black Nights and barred from entering the house at gunpoint. Attorney General Kelly then produced her credentials and handed them to a third security officer who had stepped out of the house and was obviously in charge of the team.

Everyone in the room continued to watch in silence as the team leader keyed his communication devise and called for instructions. The large flat black surveillance van pulled up and the commander stepped out of the side door. Ziven could tell that there was a heated conversation happening between Attorney General Kelly and the Commander. She tried to step around the man at one point and was stopped when one of the security men pointed his machine gun at her nose. Instantly the four Secret Service men reached for their weapons, but were halted by a wave of Kelly's hand.

"Now watch the back door," someone said.

Ziven's eyes switched to the view covering the rear door. He watched as two armor clad security personnel exited the rear door carrying their weapons and a black canvas bag. The first man easily cleared the rear fence and accepted the bag from the other. Once the second man joined him on the other side of the fence, they moved out of view of the camera. Ziven's eyes returned to the front lawn. He could tell that the group commander had just received a message on his headset; he then waved to his men ordering them to step aside and allowed Kelly and her people to enter the house. No one was prepared for the sight of Kelly quickly exiting the house, leaning over the porch railing, and throwing up.

"OK," Ziven sighed, "turn it off."

The light came up to full brightness as the screens disappeared into the ceiling.

"Where's Sissy now?" he asked Lars.

"She's with Albert and Carmen," he said. "The last time Kelly checked in they were at the hospital."

Ziven tilted his head slightly. Lars knew he wanted more information. "Carmen is taking this very hard," Lars answered. "They had to sedate her."

"How's Albert doing?" the President asked.

Lars frowned and shook his head. "He's hanging on by a thread," he answered. "Kelly said that he almost lost it when they sedated Carmen."

"And what about Kelly?"

The frown on Lars' face changed into worry. "Mr. President, I'm more afraid of what she might do."

"How so?"

"I think she would gladly walk into the Central Exchange building and take out the entire council if you ordered it," Lars said flatly. "She might do it anyway; orders or not."

"Do we have people watching her?"

"Yes, Sir."

"Who notified Kelly that the raid was happening?" Ziven asked.

"An anonymous call-in from a neighbor," Ryan answered.

Ziven looked around his office. "Alright," he said in a kind but stern voice, "I would like Mr. Lars and Mr. Ryan to stay behind. Thank you." He waited until the others had left his office and closed the door. Ziven turned to Ryan. The man had his nose buried in a stack of printouts. "Pitney, what was in that bag?"

"Hard to say, Mr. President," he answered, "but my guess would be the Lottes' PD's. We haven't been able to locate them at the house."

"What about the four cameras we recovered?"

"Standard Security issue," he sighed. "They were being operated by a remote receiver. Whoever was operating them could have been sitting on a neighbor's back porch or under a tree somewhere. If we could have been there we might have been able to get a fix on his location, but now?"

"OK, Pitney, give me your best guess," the President asked.

"It was definitely the underground," he said, without hesitation. "These guys are no band of street thugs. They are highly trained operatives."

"I agree with you," Ziven said, "but, give me your reasons for saying so."

"Sir, they have run rings around the Core Security forces. The incident this morning was just additional proof of that."

"What do you mean?" Lars asked.

"Adelric's men thought they were raiding a rebel safe house."

"You confirmed that?" Ziven asked.

Ryan nodded his head ever so slightly. "I'm willing to bet that the actual safe house is within five houses of the Lotte's home."

Ziven moved forward in his chair to speak but Ryan answered his question in his next breath. "We're doing a house by house now," he assured the President.

"How did Adelric's men get it so wrong?" Lars asked.

"The rebels probably painted the Lotte's home using it as a decoy."

"Painted?"

"They hid several of their illegally manufactured PD's inside the home knowing Sapphire would pinpoint their location using them," he explained, "They probably got a real laugh out of the fact that they were able to use one of our people's homes; a bit of irony on top of the humiliation." Ryan gestured toward the blank screen. "My guess is that the pirated PD's were in the black bag that went out the back door. "

"You mean to tell me that they planned what happened to the Lotte's?

Ryan shook his head, "I believe so but," he emphasized sternly, "I don't believe they thought that anyone would get hurt."

"Why in the hell do you believe that?" Ziven

asked hotly.

"Well, we know that they have the original video from the raid. I'm sure we only received a copy of it."

"I'm not following you," Ziven said, still steaming.

"Neither do I," admitted Lars.

"A copy of the raid video was sent to Kelly's office this morning around 11:20 AM."

"Go on."

Do we know if anyone else received a copy?" Ryan asked. "Or has the video been released to the general public in any manner?"

Ziven looked at Lars. "Nothing yet, Sir," he replied.

"So what of it?" Ziven asked.

"Sir, I believe that they fully intended to show everyone what our government does under the cover of darkness. They planned to have the Guardians release the vid to reinforce their position against us."

"So what happened?" Lars asked.

Ryan looked down, "Dena happened. They never believed that the security forces would ever kill their own people, certainly not an Associate Attorney General's daughter."

"Ryan, are you trying to tell me that these rebels have a conscience?" Ziven asked incredulously.

"Mr. President, these rebels know they didn't kill all of those people in Old Town and they used the Guardians to try and dispel their guilt. And I believe they did not intend for Dena to die. They just wanted to ridicule us one more time."

Lars stood up and began pacing around the office. "So, when they reviewed the video they figured out that someone was killed in the house during the raid. Of course they didn't know that it was a young girl at the time, but they had good reason to believe that one or more of the Lotte's had been killed in cold blood."

"That's correct," Ryan confirmed.

"So instead," Ziven said picking up on the theory, "they send it to us as evidence against the Core Security."

"That's my best guess, Mr. President," he continued. "That vid has two very damning pieces of evidence on it. One, it is totally clear that the entire operation was run by the Core Security and two,..."

"Adelric's men were concealing something in that black bag from us." Lars said finishing the sentence.

"I want to know for certain what was in the bag," Ziven commanded.

"We don't even know if Core Security still has it. They could already have destroyed whatever it was," Ryan said.

"Sir," Lars said, "you could call Commander Adelric in and demand to know what was in it. Show him the video if he denies it exists."

Ziven shook his head. He knew Mars would never release any information to him willingly and he had just decided that he would not pay for it or anything else in the future. "They'll just lie about it." he said.

"I agree," Ryan said. "At best, they will tell you that it was some type of *secret* equipment they were using or something just as insulting."

"Morning, Mr. President," Attorney General Kelly said as she entered the office. She nodded to both Lars and Ryan.

The three men stood as she entered. Lars and Ryan waited for the President to speak.

Ziven came from behind his desk and wrapped his arms around Sissy, "Claire and I are so sorry for Albert and Carmen's loss."

Kelly held her composure, "Thank you, Sir. I expressed your condolences to them several times this morning." She looked at the other two men. "I conveyed all of our condolences to them."

"Have a seat, Sissy," Ziven offered. "We've been going over the facts all morning."

Kelly took a seat next to Lars on the couch. Ziven pulled up a chair where he could look at everyone in the room. "Have you seen the video?"

She nodded her head, "Yes, at the hospital earlier this morning."

Ziven chose his next words carefully, "You...didn't...let Albert watch it?"

"No, Sir," she assured him, "he doesn't know of its existence and I'm not sure he should."

All three of the men nodded their understanding. "Have you come to any conclusions?" Ziven asked.

Her eyes narrowed as she clinched her jaw, "Yes, Sir," she said coldly, I think that Commander Adelric should be staked out over an ant hill and have his balls set on fire."

"Funny you should say that, Sissy," Ziven said showing no emotion, "that was at the top of our list also."

"It was only slightly more preferred," Lars added, "to our second choice of public impalement."

Kelly's smile was heartless, "That would be fine too as long as you added setting his balls on fire."

The three men tried hard not to laugh but failed. They quickly regained their composure.

"So what's your take on the video and last night's events," Ziven asked, bringing the group back to the more serious matter at hand.

"Well," she started, "it was definitely taken by the people who call themselves The Guardians." She shifted in her seat, "I believe they had every intention to broadcasting it to the entire nation at some point."

"Had?" Ziven asked.

"Yes, Sir, had," she replied. "I don't think they'll show it now."

"Interesting you would say that," Ryan said, "what makes you think they won't show it?"

"Not their style," she answered.

"Don't you blame them for Dena's death?" Ziven probed.

Kelly took a deep breath and let it out slowly. "I'm still processing the events of last night. I left the hospital because I knew sitting there with Albert was really screwing with my head. I had to get some distance between us so I could evaluate this situation as the Attorney General and not the friends of Albert and Carmen."

Ziven shifted position in his chair. "Sissy, I've known you for a long time. You had plenty of time in the car ride over here to sort this mess out; so spit it out."

"Alright," she agreed. "If I look at it from a cause and effect point of view, the rebels are at fault for doing what they did. If they hadn't, Dena would still be alive. If Adelric's men would have used brains instead of bullets, again it wouldn't have happened and Dena would still be alive."

"Go on," Ziven prodded.

She looked around the room at all three men. "Sir, I feel like we're in a school yard caught between two bullies throwing rocks at each other."

Ryan nodded his agreement, "They're fighting and we're taking all the hits."

"But the irony of it is," Lars added. "The rebels think we're the other bully. They don't even know what the council's involvement is in this mess."

Ziven pulled lightly on his ear as he processed the information. After several moments he spoke. "Alright Lady and Gentleman," he said firmly, "time for a lightning round. Kelly, you're first."

"Steven is in place and I think we move forward

with our operation," she quickly answered.

"Lars," Ziven prompted.

"I agree," he stated flatly. "We can't stay out in the open like this. It's time to go on the offensive."

"Pitney?"

Ryan pushed his spectacles further up on his nose. "Our plan is a good one," he stated. "The longer we wait, the harder it will become to stay in the game."

Ziven looked at each member of his Cabinet. Once again, he was very pleased with his choices. He was looking at the people that would help him pull the country through this mess. "I agree," he said. "It's time we roll up our sleeves and kick some ass." He pointed to Lars, "get our public relations people on board, Bob. They have to be ready to react as soon as we require it. Don't tell them anything more then they need to know to get the word out."

Ryan raised his index finger. "What's up, Ryan?" Ziven asked.

"Sir, you do remember that Sapphire has us on a ten minute broadcasting delay, right?"

"What?" Kelly asked venomously.

Ziven nodded. "Yes, I remember," he said turning to Kelly. "Pitney found out that Sapphire has been programmed to insert a ten minute delay in all our broadcasts to allow the Council to censure our releases."

"Son of a bitch!" Kelly hissed.

"Yes, exactly." Ziven replied giving Kelly a

conspiratorial wink.

CHAPTER 19

TIME TO THINK

Jax sat in the back seat of the car along with Rebecca. It had been a long night waiting for the security forces to storm the house. Personally, he wouldn't have waited until four in the morning to get in position. It may have been that Sapphire had not been able to match up Rebecca and his identities until much later than he anticipated, but he doubted that scenario. Sapphire was one hell of a machine.

Rebecca was sound asleep on his shoulder. They hadn't made it out of the city limits before she closed her eyes and slumped toward him. He had tried to close his eyes several times but the vision of the muzzle flashes lighting up the window in the Lotte's home haunted his thoughts. They had no official confirmation as to who had been killed, but just the sight of the two men carrying out the body bag was enough to confirm to him that one of the Lotte's had been killed. *That was not supposed to happen,* he thought to himself again. *The best laid military plans are ended when the first shot is fired;* he remembered, not knowing if he had gotten the quote correct or even who had said it.

Jax felt the small lump in his pants pocket. It was one of the only two copies of the video they had taken last night. The only other was with Attorney General Kelly or the President by now. He had planned to use it in their Guardian campaign but, now it served as a grim reminder that any decision he made had consequences.

"Jax," the driver said, "you awake?"

"Yes," he answered softly as not to wake Rebecca.

"You're going to want to see this," the driver said as he slowed the vehicle down. They were on a two lane road somewhere out in the countryside. Jax could see no buildings or structures in sight.

Rebecca sat up and looked around. "See what?" she asked.

Obviously, he thought, *she wasn't as dead to the world as he had believed.*

"On the right side of the road," the driver pointed just ahead. Chris, sitting in the passenger seat in the front blocked their view for several seconds. Eventually, the armored personnel carrier came into view. Or, more to the point, what was left of the carrier came into view.

The driver's compartment was a mass of charred, twisted metal.

"They took the driver out first," Chris commented.

"Looks like a hand held rocket launcher," Rebecca added. "Possibly a ZM-3."

Jax looked at the damage to the compartment. "I agree," he said, "the round wasn't armor piercing but certainly carried a punch." The side of the carrier was raked with heavy machinegun fire. The rear compartment door lay open. There were signs that someone had waited until the rear hatch was opened then concentrated their fire into the opening. There were noticeable wet blood stains on the rear step and bumper of the vehicle. *This strike was carried out by professionals*, he thought, *and recently.*

As they reached the front of the vehicle Jax yelled, "Slow down!" The driver brought the vehicle to a crawl as they moved past.

"I'll be a son of a bitch," Chris said. "Do you see that?"

Jax looked at the hood of the vehicle, "How could you miss it." There, neatly stenciled in black was the large outline of a Raven's head.

"There's no writing," Rebecca commented.

"There's no need for words," Jax responded.

As if reading Jax mind the driver spoke, "That wasn't here yesterday when I drove down to Core City. It must have happened sometime after I passed here last night."

"You're right, I'm guessing in the last three hours. They haven't had time to haul it away," Jax said looking around. "OK, move on." He didn't think it was a good idea to linger.

"That's the third one I've seen this month," the driver stated. "But the first one I've seen with the Raven painted on it."

Jax had been receiving reports from almost every district of attacks on Core Security facilities or vehicles. *Thankfully,* he thought as the image of the body bag being removed from the Lotte's home entered his head, *up until now there have been no civilian casualties.*

"Chris," Jax said evenly, "this strike was done by a team of professionals. I want you to look into these attacks. If any of our people are behind this, I want to know."

"We've been keeping a tight handle on it, Jax," Chris said without looking toward the back seat.

"We haven't had the slightest hint that any of our guys are involved."

"That's right, Jax," the driver added. "I don't think we have any ZM-3s in our inventory."

Jax glanced at Rebecca for confirmation. She shook her head, "No ZM's and certainly no heavy machine guns that could have done that," she confirmed.

"I remember having a couple of hours training back home, Jax mentioned, "on familiarization with Core Security weapons."

"We all had that" Chris said, "its standard operating procedure."

"Are you thinking that some of our guys are stealing weapons and turning them on security forces?" Rebecca asked.

"It's possible. How many new people are we getting each month now?" he asked the group.

"It's up to thirty or forty a month now," Chris answered.

Jax turned to Rebecca. "How many PD's did your groups make before I came in?"

"Thousands," she answered, wide eyed.

"Can you inventory them for me?"

Rebecca shook her head, "Not possible," she said. "There were several groups manufacturing them. No one group knows where they are all hidden. Remember Pop-chains? It will take me awhile to contact the people who can pull the numbers together."

"All right then," he said to no one in particular. "You guys keep your ears open. If we have a rogue splinter, I want to know about it."

The mobile check point had been slow most of the day. They had moved their position several times and had only stopped seven vehicles. The security leader looked down at his PD. It would be dark in a half an hour and he was getting hungry. He looked over at the man standing behind the barricade. He was in full body armor and armed with an MR 50 automatic assault rifle. "Ten more minutes," he signaled to the man, "and then we'll close up shop.

The man smiled and waved his understanding. The weapon was very heavy and required a large sling to help the carrier manage the weapon without the use of a more fixed mount-like tripod, but the weapon was what they called a show stopper. Two men were assigned to stop the vehicles thirty yards in front of the barricade while the third person armed with the MR 50 stayed behind the barricade ready to fire on anyone who refused to stop and be searched. The MR 50 would quickly stop any vehicle that wasn't heavily armored.

The three men had been taking turns manning the barricade, allowing the others to remove their heavy body armor and take the lighter duty of searching any vehicle that came their way. That way no one person had to stand in the oppressive armor and tote the heavy weapon all day.

A car crested the hill and slowed as it approached the two security officers already waving it to a halt. The woman behind the wheel was dressed in a bright yellow sun dress which cut mid way across her chest causing the upper half of her breasts to swell in a very provocative manner. Her golden hair was styled in a feather cut curling slightly at the bottom toward her chin. Her broad smile was sweetly expressive as the solider approached.

Maybe the day isn't a total loss, the security officer thought as he approached the car.

"Good afternoon," he said as he approached the driver's side of the car. The other officer moved around the passenger side of the vehicle checking the back seat as he made his way toward the trunk. "Security check," he smiled warmly. "Please exits the car and allow me to look at your PD. Also, if you would, please open your trunk for my partner."

The young women reached over and picked up her purse off the seat beside her. "Of course Officer," she said as she opened the door of the car. Exiting the vehicle she swung her legs toward the door until they were facing the officer. She spread her legs slightly, enabling her to reach down along the side of the seat and release the latch to the trunk. Her legs were parted just enough for the office to notice that she was wearing a small pair of yellow panties. *This is my lucky day*, he though, his eyes glued to her skimpy panties.

As she stood he followed the line between her legs, up her abdomen and thru the middle of her breasts. Within a few seconds he was again looking at her eyes. He had been so mesmerized by the lines of the woman's body that he hadn't noticed the small automatic in her hand until it was too late. He froze looking at the end of the barrel. A muffled pop came from the direction of the trunk as the second officer lifted the lid. He crumpled to the ground instantly.

The man at the barricade stretched his neck to see what was going on at the car. A sharp whistle behind him drew his attention for just a second. It was long enough for the man standing behind him to fire his weapon. The trooper crashed to the pavement under the weight of the MR 50. The man walked up to him, bent down and began loosening the shoulder strap of the weapon. He looked up momentarily when the woman with the yellow panties shot the last officer between the eyes.

He tucked his weapon in his belt as he lifted the MR 50 and began walking toward the car. The man that had been hiding in the trunk was already moving toward the security vehicle. He was now armed with a stiff corrugated stencil and a can of black paint. It only took him a few seconds to spray the driver's door of the car with the image of the Raven's head. He walked back toward the blond holding the stencil away from his body. "Don't want to make a mess," he joshed to the blond.

She looked at the dead officer lying at her feet. "No," she answered sliding the gun back in her purse, "don't want to do that."

The three climbed into the car and drove around the barricade.

Mars sat behind her desk with her eyes closed. She had instructed Sapphire to lower the overhead lights and block any incoming call for twenty minutes. That is all the time she allowed herself to relax. In the past week several new attacks had been successfully conducted against the Core Security forces. As of late, a black Ravens head had been stenciled on the vehicle as a reminder of who had committed the atrocities. *It may have been a mistake to give the rebels a name,* she thought.

It had been a dual mistake on her part as now much of the violence directed toward the security forces was attributed to *The Raven* while the Guardians were making a more peaceful appeal to the overall general public. The Guardians' popularity had been growing like a weed. The image of the five people had been popping up all over the districts reminding the populace of the numerous faults of their government. It had reached a new height this morning when almost three hundred students at the university had staged a forty five minute sit-in at the student center. They were wearing silver blue-gray clothing of various sorts in support of the Guardians. Sapphire had reported a marked increase in the use of graffiti around the nation. Most of it was now done using the silver blue-gray color representing the rebel group. There was, of course, the deathly black being used with anything to do with the Raven.

As predicted, the Council's popularity was falling along with the government's. *Maybe*, she thought, *if we were to drop Adelric from the council and have him and the Core Security report back directly to the Attorney General.* She quickly dismissed the thought. If need be the council could offer the population Adelric's head and still maintain effective control over the nation's armed forces. They would then be free to pick a more suitable person for his position. "Sapphire," she said softly.

"Yes, Ms Tansy."

"Prepare a file on Commander Adelric. Please note any actions that could be considered a dereliction of duty or incompetence on his part. The file is to be marked, for my eyes only."

"Yes, Ms. Tansy."

The cover up of the death of Dena Lotte had been very successful. *If*, she mused, *being personnel threatened by the President of New America can be considered successful.* His agreeing to keep the incident under wraps just proved that he was as weak as she had believed. He had given in and she paid nothing for it. Plans to initiate a management change in the Oval Office were already underway. She had held a private Council meeting without Adelric and Dr. Grady. *Pyrs, Kinsley and I control the real power on the Council,* she reminded herself, *eventually our control of the money, energy and media would move the needle in their favor. Without their support in the next election, Ziven would be trampled by the competition. And, as in any election, a new broom sweeps clean. All of his loyal followers would soon find themselves out of jobs.*

"Excuse me, Ms. Tansy," Sapphire said softly, "it has been twenty minutes. Shall I bring the lights up?"

"Bring them up to half power," she ordered. "What was the final result of the student sit-in?"

"After the prescribed forty five minutes, the

students dispersed as scheduled without incident. There was a sizable amount of pro-Guardian graffiti left behind, but as you instructed, it was removed immediately after they disbanded."

"Excellent," Mars stated. "Were you able to ascertain who the movement coordinators were?"

"I have pinpointed several students that have a high probability for being involved with the coordination of events."

"Perfect," she smiled, "audit their online postings and blogging. If there is the slightest infraction of any kind, remove all core funding from those identified. Have their parent's personnel files scrutinized and impose the appropriate sanctions if you discover any discrepancies."

"And if no infractions are uncovered?"

"Contact, Martha Rodgers in the Identification Review Section," she answered without hesitation, "She will supply you with what you need."

"What level of infractions would you like Mrs. Rodgers to apply?"

"Level six," Mars said then changed her mind, "no, make it level three. I don't want to arouse too much suspicion."

"I understand," Sapphire answered, "is there anything else?"

Mars thought about Adelric. "Where is Commander Adelric at the present time?"

"He is currently in District Eight looking into the latest attack on the Core Security forces."

Mars frowned at the information. *Leaving Core City at a time like this, she mused*, "He has personally gone into the field to perform an investigation?"

"Yes, one of the officers killed was the son of his oldest brother."

"I see," she answered flatly. "Have him report to my office once he returns. I want…"

"Ms. Tansy," Sapphire interrupted, "Commander Adelric is receiving a class five distress transmission from the District Four Armory Facility."

Mars shot straight up in her chair. "Show me," she commanded.

The screen in her office flickered once before showing the enormous face of the security agent that had placed the emergency call. His face was a greasy, dark marbled color of soot and smoke residue. The only contrasts to the black deposits were the scarlet red blood trickling down from several abrasions and cuts on his face.

"…repeat, we've had a breach!" he shouted over the sound of automatic weapons fire. "They,

they were in the compound before we knew it."

The man had his PD so close that the screen would blur out of focus and then sharpen again, when the distance between his face and the device allowed it. "They're everywhere!"

"Calm down son," Commander Adelric stated in a cool, calm voice of his own.

"You fucking calm down!" he officer shouted. "We're getting slaughtered here."

"How much of the complex is still under your control?" Adelric asked still not raising his voice.

The man shook his head causing the tiny PD camera to go in and out of focus again. The sound of the automatic gun fire was getting louder. "Nothing, almost nothing at all," he panted, "most are dead, gone."

"Do you still have control of the auto destruct mechanism?" Adelric raised his tone to a much firmer commanding voice. "Can you activate the self destruct?"

Again the man shook his head, "Control room was lost in the first volley. We're just hanging on by a thread."

"Sapphire," Mars asked, "can you activate the self destruct for that complex if commanded?"

"Yes," affirmed Sapphire.

"Cut me into Commander Adelric," she ordered.

The screen in front of her split into a dual view. The right half still showing the injured solider, the left half was the image of Commander Adelric peering at his PD. His face was taught and menacing.

"Hey Bitch," the solider yelled, "get off the link!"

Mars disregarded the man's ranting, "Commander," Mars said trying to maintain a firm voice. We have been monitoring your distress call. Sapphire has informed me that it can activate the auto destruct at your command."

"You can't do that!" the solider shouted at his PD. "We still have men who are alive. We still hold a piece of this fucking place!"

Instantly Mars' screen showed a full screen image of Adelric. She knew that Adelric had put the soldier's call on mute.

"How many weapons are we talking about, Commander?" she asked.

Adelric's facial features contorted into a pained expression, "too many."

"Then, you have no choice," Mars said firmly.

The screen split again. "Get your men out of there," he warned. "I'm activating the auto destruct in," he paused as he checked the chronometer on his PD, "seven minutes."

The injured solider shook his head, "Not enough time... give us more time!"

Mars pushed the override command on her terminal.

"Auto destruct is at your command," Sapphire informed her.

Mars pushed the enter key as she spoke, "End transmission, Sapphire."

The screen went black. "Inform my driver and bodyguards that we're traveling to District Four within the hour," she commanded as she stormed out of the office.

CHAPTER 20

NEW REPORTS

Jax sat at the table he had set up in the basement of his new home. He, like Rebecca, had been given a new PD and identification. He marveled at the complexity of the environment he and the others lived in. Years ago, the plan had been put into motion when groups, like the one Rebecca had been a part of, began manufacturing the PD's that they were now using. Identifications had been created for hundreds of bogus people to be used later when needed.

These PD's took on a life of their own as the factious people were skillfully moved from place to place, attended to school, graduated and found jobs.

The required weekly postings were being taken care of by a network of computers. Team members were assigned to take the appropriate photographs and load them into the system. When a weekly post was required, the text and accompanying photos were uploaded into Sapphire.

When the plan was constructed, the orchestrators had decided that most of the IDs were to be spread out in the more rural areas where diction would be much more difficult. All of the identified had been model citizens with very mundane lifestyles. The purpose had been to stay under the radar and avoid bringing any attention to them. Jax was amazed to find out that they had actually killed off ID's in accordance with the limits of numerical probabilities. Nothing had been left to chance.

The final step of the plan was put into motion when it was discovered that a totally new model of the PDs was being produced. It was easy enough to get their hands on one but, they soon learned that they lacked the ability to counterfeit the new devices. Scientists back in Middle-Earth estimated that it would take twelve to eighteen months to reverse engineer one. Their best estimates were that the entire population would be converted to the new device within a year.

"Hey," Rebecca said as she entered the basement.

Jax looked up from his work and smiled. "Hey yourself," he said gesturing toward a very large overstuffed chair close to the desk.

Rebecca pointed as she made her way across the room. "Damn, that's a big chair."

"I know," he said, "I don't know how they got the damn thing down those stairs."

Rebecca sat down. "Whoa, this is very comfortable."

Jax grinned, "I've fallen asleep in it more than once."

She wiggled further into the depths of the chair. "I could get used to this."

"If it comes up missing," he said pointing at her, "I'll know where to look first."

"I've just returned with the weapons inventory you asked for," she said.

"Judging from your expression, I'm guessing that everything is not in order."

"The weapons check out down to the last bullet," she reported.

"What's the bad news then?"

"How do you know I have bad news?" she huffed.

Jax looked down at the work in front of him. "I've lived with you long enough to know when something's bothering you," he said softly. "You and Mat seem to be getting along swimmingly, so it's not that."

Rebecca crossed her legs and began bouncing the upper leg. "You know, one of these days you're going to be wrong about me and I'm going to bask in the glory."

"I look forward to it," he said with a smile, "but in the meantime, tell me what's on your mind."

I also conducted a PD inventory," she started to say then corrected herself; "I've asked several people in the know to conduct an inventory of PDs under their control."

"Alright, let's have it."

"We currently have 647 PD's in stock," she stated. "When you came through, we had 887."

"OK," Jax said wishing she would get to the point, but another thing that he had learned about Rebecca, other than her various moods, was not to push her when she was giving a report.

"I estimate we have been receiving new recruits at an average of forty five per month."

"Five months times forty five people is…" Jax started calculating.

"Two hundred and twenty-five," she supplied.

"OK, then, 225 plus the current inventory of 647 is…" he said calculating the number.

"Eight hundred and seventy two," she interjected.

Jax eyes narrowed, "I hate when you do that," he said without being able to muster much conviction.

"I know," she smiled, "it's one of the little pleasures that I get out of our relationship."

"So you're fifteen off on the count," he said, ignoring her comment. "So, someone screwed up on their inventory. Have you asked for a recount?"

"I planned to do that after I had some lunch."

"Good," Jax said, looking back at the work in front of him, "case closed."

"Not really," she said and continued. "I decided to go over to the embarkation station and spread my work out on one of the mess hall tables."

"Rebecca, I don't want to sound rude," Jax said, placing his stylus down on the desk. "But does the story have a happy ending?"

She continued ignoring his sarcasm, "One of the cooks joined me for a cup of coffee. We've known each other since basic training."

Jax interlaced his fingers and rested them on the desk. "And?"

"When he saw what I was working on he told me that there had been over 800 new recruits through the station in the last five months."

"Impossible," Jax said tersely, "we would have known about something like that."

"Why?" she asked.

"Because we're in charge of this operation," he responded quickly. "I would have been informed of the increase."

"What if they're not part of our operation?" she asked. "What if they are part of the next phase?"

"I would have been told of that also," he answered, showing his annoyance. "I *should* have been told," he added as an afterthought.

"Pop-chain," Rebecca almost sang. "Besides, the personnel at the embarkation station don't work for us. They are here to process anyone who comes through the station. Not everyone coming in is part of our group."

Jax slumped back in his chair. "I don't believe it," he said, knowing that he was just kidding himself. "What aren't you telling me?" he said, studying her face more closely.

"Jimmy," she answered, "the cook, recognized a couple of the guys coming through the chow line."

"So?"

"He knew them from back home," she said slowly, "They were members of McKee's shock troops. Jax, I believe they are here to prepare for the start of the next phase."

Jax's eyes wandered around the room as he worked through the information that Rebecca had just dropped in his lap. "They would need PD's."

"What for?" she asked, pushing him toward the conclusion she had already made.

"They would need them to get around."

Rebecca shook her head, "Only if they needed to infiltrate a town or city. The others would just hide out in the countryside until needed. These are attack troops," she said. "They don't need a PD pinpointing their exact location to Sapphire 24-7."

"They would still need to recon the cities."

"Well maybe 225 of them do have PDs," she reminded him, holding up the inventory report. "I don't have a breakdown as to where they have gone, but I'm guessing they are in the larger cities throughout the nine districts."

"Shit!" he exclaimed.

"Nothing's changed for us," she reminded him. "We still have a job to do and if you think about it, it only makes sense that they are moving into position as we come closer to reaching our objective."

"Well it certainly would be easier if these guys weren't running around blowing away security troops on a weekly basis," he snarled. "McKee could have warned me." He raised his hand to interrupt Rebecca's next sentence. "I know, Pop-chain." He was suddenly lost in thought again. "OK," he said, "let's get our District leaders together. We can at least inform them that they need to be more cautious going about their business."

Rebecca struggled to get out of the massive chair. "I'll call them in," she said, as she finally got to her feet. "And, Jax, we don't know if these guys are out there killing anyone."

"I will work on getting confirmation from the Colonel as to what her troops standing orders are at the present."

"That sounds good," she said heading for the stairs.

"Wait a minute, "let's meet in District Four. It's sparsely populated and I'm hoping we're less likely to run into any problems."

Rebecca headed up the stairs. "District Four it is."

✱ ✱ ✱ ✱

Mars stood next to her vehicle studying the destruction that was laid out before her. The driver had refused to allow her to get any closer than their current location. He had warned Mars that there were still live rounds buried in the rubble. Several fires could be seen from where she stood. She was just about to reprimand him when several explosions hurled projectiles and debris into the air. Some of the rounds came closer to them then she would have liked.

She held her PD up. "Sapphire, how many guards were assigned to the facility?"

"The District Four Armory is manned by eleven men per twelve hour shift," she informed Mars. "There are a total of thirty-six men assigned to this facility."

Not anymore, she thought as she surveyed the damage. She had been under the misconception that there had only been one building on the site. The main building, which she had figured out, was the actual armory, was little more than a smoldering crater in the center of the compound. Groups of firemen had aimed their power hoses in such a manner that it caused the jet streams of water to shoot up into the air, arc over several hundred feet of debris, and cascaded into the center of the armory area. She noticed that the equipment was unmanned and that the firemen were standing several hundred feet away from the trucks.

There were quite a few smaller buildings which must have housed troops or acted as maintenance facilities. They had fared better than the armory. She speculated that only the armory contained a self-destruct mechanism. The intensity of the blast had turned everything else around it into rubble.

The Chief of the first responders' team approached Mars with a slow steady gate. The man was older and, she thought, more seasoned than the rest. This was probably not his first large emergency. She waited for the man to reach her remembering the recent explosions.

"Ms. Tansy," he said touching the rim of his helmet.

Mars took notice of his name tag. "Mr. Wellford," she said, "what are the first reports coming from the armory?"

He gave Mars a strange look then looked back over his shoulder. "Everyone's dead," he said calmly, "no one could have survived the concussion of that blast. Hell, I was fifteen miles from here when it went off and I heard it clear as day."

"Are you at least looking for survivors?" she asked tersely.

"We've only just breached the outer perimeter,"

he offered. "Entering the Armory itself is still too dangerous. There's still a chance of a major explosion. We'll wait and throw a lot more water on it before we send anyone near the crater."

"Major explosion?" she asked, "it looks like the armory is totally destroyed. What could be left?"

The Chief took off his helmet and brushed his hair back with his hand. Exhaustion showed in all of his movements. "Ms. Tansy, I've been Chief of the First Response Team for eight years now. At least once a year, me and the other men from District Four have come out here and participated with the Core Security on mock events that mimicked this one. Do you know how much ordinance was buried in the ground?"

Mars pointed to the large crater, "there's nothing left of the building. How much could still be in there?"

Chief Wellford tucked his helmet under his arm. "Ms. Tansy," he said pointing to the crater, "that structure goes three stories below ground. The floors were constructed in such a manner as to prevent something like this from happening. The weapons and explosives were segregated into smaller rooms with heavily reinforced walls and doors. The theory was that an explosion or fire in one of the smaller rooms would be prevented from setting off a chain reaction, destroying the entire facility."

Obviously, she thought, *he doesn't know that we triggered the self destruct. He believes that this was some type of freak accident. There is no need for him to know differently.* "Whatever happened, Chief Wellford," she said, "it doesn't look like the failsafe plan worked."

Chief Wellford studied her face for several seconds. "Hmmm," he offered as a response. "There could be an entire room down there that hasn't been touched yet. A room with enough explosives stored in it to kill anyone who goes snooping around too soon. By the way," he said, turning and pointing to the far building closest to where the remains of the barbed wire fence had stood, "see that building way over there?"

Mars had to move slightly to see around him. "Yes."

He turned back to her and locked eyes, "that was security housing for the off duty men."

"So," she said, tiring of the conversation.

"That's as close as we've allowed our teams to get to the armory."

"What about the fire hoses?" she asked.

He nodded, "Oh, we allowed a couple of volunteers to get the water jet equipment in close enough to pour water into the hole, but as soon as the trucks were in position we pulled our teams back."

"Commendable," she answered. "You must give me their names so that can have citations drawn up for them."

"Hmmm," he answered, "anyway, over there in that building, a few of my men went in to look for survivors."

"Did they find anyone?" she asked, with a definite tone of concern. "*They can't be allowed to talk with any survivors*, she worried.

"Oh they found several people," he answered. "Funny thing though," he said, locking eyes with Mars again. This time his bloodshot eyes sent a chill down her spine. "We discovered that they all had been shot. Several times, I might add."

Mars was lost for a reply. Anything she could or would say would be a lie and he would see right through it.

The rapid pop, pop, pop sound coming from deep inside the armory caused everyone to instinctively take a few step back. Mars was grateful for the timely intrusion. Her answer was further delayed as her driver walked up behind her and whispered close to her ear. "Commander Adelric's convoy will be coming over the ridge in sixty second," he informed her.

She turned back to the Chief smiling,

"Commander Adelric," she said pointing to the ridge.

As if on cue, the top of the first armored personnel transport crested the peak of the ridge. Commander Adelric's body was half way out of the top turret; one hand gripping the rim of the opening while the other hand leaned on the twin 50 caliber machine guns. *Crap*, she thought, *I don't need this warrior shit today.*

Mars displayed a huge smile and waved toward the transport as it whined to a stop. Adelric held his hand up high and made a circular motion that Mars did not understand. Instantly, the armored vehicle coming up behind Adelric's lead vehicle began to move to the left and right, each vehicle alternating in their direction. Soon the eight vehicles were dispersed across the area.

Mars watched as Adelric removed his head gear, dropped down into the vehicle and, in a few seconds, emerged from the rear hatch. He walked up to the group as he removed his gloves. Mars smiled as he reached them. "Good morning, Commander," she said offering her hand.

Adelric ignored her as he stepped past and put out his hand toward the Chief. "Morning, Scotty," he said, shaking the man's hand vigorously.

The chief grabbed Adelric's hand with both of his, "Morning, Marty," the Chief beamed. "No trouble on the trip in?" he asked.

Adelric made a sweeping gesture toward the surrounding armored vehicles. Each had a similar machine gun arrangement to his. "Not with this much firepower," he said proudly.

"It's like I told you, Marty, "the Chief said without waiting for the question, "it's a damn mess."

Mars walked up to the two men, her face betrayed her anger, "Commander," she said in a firm tone, "may I have a word in private?" she asked, stepping several paces away.

Adelric followed her. "Yes, Ms. Tansy,"

Mars resisted pointing her finger at the man, but the anger was still evident in her voice. "If you ever ignore me again," she threatened, "I'll..."

"Marci," he interrupted, "if you *ever* kill another one of my men I will make sure the Attorney General brings you up on murder charges!"

She knew his threat was a hollow one, but the words still had the effect that Adelric wanted. "I had to push that button," she hissed defensively, "you were going to wait until it was too late."

Adelric pointed to his chest, "It was my men and my decision. Another five or six minutes might have meant the difference between life and death for some of those men." He pointed to the large crater. "The weapons would have been destroyed in that blast no matter what."

"I did what I thought needed to be done," she said without remorse.

Adelric's eyes burned into her face, "You better hope that you are never in a similar situation and I have my finger on the button," he said with a cold, chilling tone.

She refused to back down. "Is that a threat?" she asked.

Adelric looked over at her vehicle. Her driver was standing next to the rear compartment. "Go back to your tower," he said flatly, "I'll take over here." He walked back to where the Chief was standing before she could respond.

Mars turned curtly and walked to her vehicle. "I'll see you back at the office then," she said, as if they were the dearest friends and got into her vehicle.

The two men watched as she and two cars of security personnel drove away. "Is that what our Council has turned into?" Chief Wellford asked his old friend.

"I'm afraid so, Scotty," he sighed.

Jax decided he wanted to drive and so Rebecca sat next to him playing her role as the faithful wife. They had left before daybreak and had driven straight through. Shortly after ten in the morning they noticed the towering column of black smoke rising from somewhere off to the right. They had past the time speculating what could have caused such a fire and finally decided on a fertilizer plant explosion. Rebecca still had a thought that a grain silo explosion could also cause that kind of damage. Either way they had agreed to stay clear of whatever it was. They didn't need to be around emergency vehicles or risk having their faces caught on the Special Netcast that was surely going to happen.

Actually, it gave them a small measure of comfort knowing that all of the surrounding security vehicles were going to be miles away.

"Cars coming," Rebecca said, pointing ahead.

"Got it," Jax acknowledged checking to make sure his gun was still on the seat next to him.

The three large black colored sedans approached at a speed that Jax knew was in violation of the posted speed limit. All vehicles' speed was monitored by Sapphire and the operator would be issued a citation instantly if they exceeded the posted limit. The mechanism in their car had been bypassed.

Jax maintained his speed as the three vehicles shot by causing a whomp, whomp, whomp sound as the air pressure changed with each passing vehicle.

"They must have a pile of speeding tickets lying on their floor by now," Rebecca jested.

"Something tells me," he said, looking in his rearview mirror watching the vehicles get smaller, "they aren't worried about the speed limit."

"Jax." Rebecca said, as they crested the small rise.

Jax returned his eyes to the road in front of him just in time to see the security roadblock ahead. He handed Rebecca his gun. "Put this away," he said, as he slowed the vehicle.

The road block setup was different from what they had been told to expect. Instead of the normal three security soldiers manning the checkpoint, there were six officers with an additional heavily armored transport vehicle pulled forty feet off the side of the road. A seventh soldier manned the machine gun mounted on the turret.

The officer waved Jax to a stop and approached the driver's side. Jax noticed that the man kept his hand on the grip of his pistol hanging from his belt.

"Good afternoon," he said, as he approached the car. Jax watched out of the corner of his eye as the other officer moved around the passenger side where Rebecca was sitting. They noticed that the second officer was checking the back seat as he made his way toward the trunk. "Security check," he almost sang. "Would the two of you please exit the car and allow me to look at your PDs. Also, if you would, please open your trunk for my partner."

"Sure," Jax said, as he opened the door and exited the vehicle. He was keenly aware that several of the rifles were pointed in his direction with an equal amount pointed at Rebecca.

Rebecca slid across the seat and exited the car on Jax side. He helped her to her feet. Both extended their PD's to the officer. The man quickly tapped the units against his. He started looking at the data he had just received. "William and Becky Lions," the officer stated.

"Yes, sir," Jax answered for the two of them.

"Where are you headed on this fine day?"

"To my sister's," Rebecca answered. "She's getting married this weekend and I'm the matron of honor. Hey, who were in those cars that shot by?" she asked, hoping to change the subject.

"Augh, some high brass from Core Central," he answered, tapping keys on his PD.

The officer who had checked the trunk came around the side of the vehicle and was now standing next to Jax. "Nothing," he said to his partner. He turned to Jax, "Hey do you know that your spare is flat?"

Jax winced knowing what was coming next in their prearranged script. "Billy Lions," Rebecca scolded him, "I thought you said you got that tire fixed last week."

Jax shrugged his shoulders at the two officers as Rebecca continued. "You knew we were headed to my sister's this week. What would have happened if we had gotten another flat?"

Jax pointed to the two officers, "These guys are around; they would help us if we got a flat," he said, turning to the soldiers again. "You guys would have helped, right?"

The officer not checking the PD smiled kindly, "We're not supposed to do that kind of things anymore, sorry."

Rebecca hit Jax with her purse, "See, you can't be counting on these men to be stopping and helping us out. They got their own jobs to do," she said, whopping Jax with the purse a second time. "I ought to make you run behind the car the rest of the way to Sissy's house."

The officers checking their PDs lowered his and clipped it back on his belt. "So, you guys are spending the weekend at your sister's wedding?" he smiled.

"That's right officer," she said. "Now we ain't staying at Sissy's house because they ain't going away on a honeymoon or nothing like that so they'll be staying at home, "Rebecca said winking at the solider. "We'll be staying over at my Uncle Taylor's house."

"Well there isn't anything like a good old country wedding," he said pulling on his ear. "But you two aren't going anywhere," he said as four weapons were leveled on the two of them.

"Hands on the top of the car!" he commanded.

"What's wrong, officer?" Jax said, trying to maintain the pretense. "I'll get the damn tire fixed if it makes you happy."

The officer grabbed Jax's right hand and brought it around behind his back. Jax felt the cuff tightened around his wrist. Within seconds the routine was repeated for his left hand.

Jax looked over to see that Rebecca was already restrained. Black hoods were forced over their heads and tightened around their necks.

"What did we do?" Rebecca whimpered from beneath the hood.

"You are both wanted for questioning in connection with rebel activities within Core City.

You have also been charged in the bombing of Old Town and the death of Dena Lotte."

"We don't go down there," Jax protested as he was jostled toward the van.

"We ain't never been to Core City," Rebecca said.

The two of them were pushed toward the benches lining both sides of the compartment. Jax heard his shackles being attached to something on the floor. He couldn't hear Rebecca but, he assumed she was close by.

"You know where to take them," the officer said, as he closed the hatch. Jax noticed a slight hissing sound as the door sealed shut. Seconds later he was jolted sideways as the van began to move."

"Ain't never been to Core City?" Jax said, mimicking Rebecca's words. "Was that supposed to persuade them to let us go?"

"Well," she answered from a position directly in front of him, "I figured if we sounded as dumb as we looked they would have thought they had made a mistake."

"I see," he stated. "Got another plan?"

"Nope," she shot back, "it's your turn."

Jax resisted the urge to try the strength of his

bonds. He concluded it would cause damage to his wrist. "Can you see anything?" he asked.

"Nothing, pitch black."

Jax leaned back on the bench as much as he could. "Guess we better get comfortable," he said. "No telling how long of a ride this is going to be."

"I wish I was sitting in that big chair back in your office," she chuckled nervously.

"Yeah," he answered, "I wish you were there also."

They had driven for about forty minutes as far as Jax could tell before the van began to slow. He braced himself for a jerky stop. He wasn't disappointed.

"Are we there yet?" Rebecca asked, trying to keep her spirits up.

"Don't know," Jax said, trying to hear anything that might be happening outside the compartment they were in. "This thing must be airtight," he said, "I can't hear a thing."

"We might be at another check point," Rebecca suggested.

"Or, at the front gate of the interrogation

facility," he offered as an alternative.

Neither was ready for the jolting start of the van and both of them hit the floor. Jax grimaced as a sharp pain shot through his chest. "Shit," he cried out struggling to get to a sitting position."

"What's wrong, what happened?" Rebecca asked in the darkness of her hood.

"Old war wound," he answered. "It's gotten a lot better but it's still a bit sensitive when I'm unexpectedly slammed down on a hard surface."

"There's some pain killers in my purse if you can find it." she offered.

"I imagine it's in the cab of the van along with our PDs."

When there was no response from her he concluded she was trying to save her energy. There was no doubt in his mind that they were going to need it. The van continued down the road changing speed several times but it never stopped again. Jax was sure that they had made at least three turns over the last two to three hours or so. He felt the noticeable deceleration of the vehicle and braced himself. The vibration of the electric engine slowed then stopped.

Neither of them spoke waiting for the next chain of events to begin. They didn't have long to wait. The rear door of the van hissed as it was swung open. Jax could feel the coolness of the evening air. Someone entered the back of the van without speaking and unlocked his shackles from the floor. They guided him to the rear of the van and he was surprised when a gentle hand guided his head downward to avoid the rim of the door. Two sets of hands quickly grabbed him on each side and lowered him to the ground. Once he had his own footing they released him. A single hand took hold of his forearm and lead him away from the van. He stumbled along in the dark for several minutes. A voice close to his ear spoke softly. "Step up," the woman said.

Jax exaggerated his moves as he entered the building. They were guided down a hallway and continued down two flights of stairs. They walked a short distance then were brought to a halt. Jax heard the sound of machinery start up. *An elevator,* he thought. He heard the door open and they were guided inside.

A hand guided his fingers to a railing attached to the wall. "Hold on to this," the woman said, "we're going to drop quickly."

Jax thought his stomach was going to come out through his mouth as the elevator dropped in what Jax could only describe as a freefall. After a few seconds it started to feel like his body had finally caught up with the floor of the elevator. This only lasted for a few seconds before the gravity of their fall was quickly slowed causing his knees to buckle slightly.

"That was fun," he said stepping out of the lift.

"I'm glad that's over," Rebecca added.

"We have one more to go," the woman said.

They were led down a short corridor and helped through a small doorway. He heard the sound of elevator machinery once again. Again he was led into the elevator and helped with the placement of his hands on the rail. The second elevator drop was identical to the first one, only this trip seemed to last twice as long.

They exited the elevator and he took several steps before a hand impeded his forward progress. There was the sound of metal against cement as several chairs were drug across the floor. He felt the edge of the chair push against his calves. "Sit down," the woman instructed. Jax complied and adjusted himself on the seat. The restraints round his wrists were once again fastened to a metal chain. He pulled up lightly on the chain until it came to a stop. The other end was definitely attached to the cement floor.

A hand unfastened the hood and removed it from behind. There wasn't much light, but it still took him a few seconds to adjust his eyes. The first thing he saw was Rebecca sitting next to him. They exchanged smiles as a sign of their being OK. He noticed that Rebecca also had been shackled to the floor. In front of them was a small folding table. On it rested two metal tumblers filled with what appeared to be ice water. From the condensation on the tumblers and the small puddle of water around their base, he judged that the glasses had been sitting there for some time.

Jax looked around trying to peer into the darkness. Both he and she were bathed in the soft light of a single directional light coming from the ceiling some thirty or forty feet above them. He could not see more than twenty or so feet into the darkness in any direction.

"Welcome," the voice was scrambled and while easy to understand, Jax could not tell if it were a man or a woman. He could tell that the voice was coming from directly in front of him or at least, that's where the speakers were located. "You are hard people to get a hold of," it continued.

"Sorry," Jax said, "maybe you should have invited us to lunch."

"Now why didn't I think of that?" the voice asked. "Do you know where you are?"

"In a world of shit?" Rebecca answered.

"Quite possibly," the voice agreed. "The water, on the table, is for you."

They both looked at the tumblers but made no attempt to pick them up.

"They are quite alright, I assure you. You must be thirsty after the ride here."

Again, neither Jax nor Rebecca made a move toward the cups.

"If I had wanted to kill you, I have a thousand options at my disposal and I certainly wouldn't have wasted my time by dragging you here." The voice assured them. "And if I wanted to drug you I would just have one of my assistants jab you in the arm with a needle. What I am trying to do is build a little trust between us."

Jax held his cuffs out toward the voice, "Fine, remove these please."

"The key word in that sentence was *build*," the voice informed him.

Jax picked up the water and began to drink. It was amazingly refreshing. "Do you have a ham sandwich to go along with this?" he asked. "We haven't eaten since breakfast."

"We can talk about food later. Right now let us talk about the destruction of the Armory."

"What armory?" Rebecca asked, as she picked up her water.

"The District Four armory that was destroyed this morning."

"Sorry," Jax stated, "don't know anything about that." Suddenly it dawned on him. "That big column of black smoke we saw today. Is that what you're talking about?"

"The same."

Jax turned to Rebecca, "Boy, we were way off on our guess." He turned back to the voice. "We were guessing that it was some type of industrial explosion; a fertilizer plant or perhaps a grain silo."

"So you're saying that you had nothing to do with that?"

"I think we just said that," Rebecca answered. "But if you would prefer a more direct answer then, no, we had nothing to do with that."

"So, can we go now?" Jax asked.

"Do you know," the voice asked, "that Commander Adelric has been conducting an extensive search of the archives; researching methods of interrogation and torture? He has come up with several that are as despicable as they are painful."

"If you want to learn about torture," Rebecca said, motioning toward Jax, "Then try living with this guy for a couple of months."

Rebecca's words reverberated off the concrete walls then died out. Her outburst was met with utter silence; that is, until the voice began to laugh uncontrollably. It was soon joined by at least two others.

Jax looked over toward Rebecca as the laughter continued, "I didn't think it was so funny, he said. Rebecca merely shrugged her shoulders.

The laughter dissipated and then again there was silence. After a few seconds they heard a metal click. A second overhead light in the direction of the voice began to warm up, slowly illuminating the area in front of them. Soon they could make out the figure of a man sitting behind a small table. At the rear of the room, to his left and right were two other men standing. The seated figure removed a device from in front of his face and laid it down on the table. He stood up and moved from behind the table to a spot almost directly under the light.

"Hi, my name is Joshua Ziven."

CHAPTER 21

THE ACCOUNTING

Jax and Rebecca had been removed from the large room and taken to separate rooms where their handcuffs were removed and they were fed. Each was taken to facilities where they were allowed to freshen up before being escorted to a small conference room where President Ziven was waiting.

Jax nodded at Ziven as he entered the room and took a seat. Rebecca entered within seconds of Jax. She smiled at Jax and bowed her head slightly in recognition of Ziven. The two men that were with Ziven in the larger room were now seated on either side of the President. All three, Jax noticed, wore slacks and casual shirts. There was no place to hide a weapon within the shirts he noted.

"I'm sorry there was no ham, but I assume the meal was adequate," Ziven said, starting the conversation.

"Yes," Jax answered, "thank you. Now, if you would just give us our check we'll pay and be on our way."

"This is Robert Lars," he said, pointing to his right, "and Pitney Ryan," pointing to his left. "They work for me."

"Robert Lars, Chief of Staff and Pitney Ryan, Secretary of Intelligence." Jax stated. "Hello."

Both men nodded and smiled. A wide grin also crossed Ziven's face. "You've done your homework," he said. "Shall we get down to business?"

"And what business might that be?" Jax asked.

Ziven looked back and forth between Jax and Rebecca. "I'll give you the dramatic answer to that question first," he said. "I want you to help me steal back my country."

"I didn't know it was missing," Rebecca said.

"Well," said Ziven, thinking out loud, "it's more a case of smoke and mirrors than actually missing."

Shock registered on Jax face as the truth came to him. "You're running a puppet government," he said, his amazement betrayed by his tone of voice. "You guys don't run the government."

"That's not quite true," Ziven stated. "We run the government; we just don't run the country."

"If you don't," Rebecca asked, "then who does?"

"There's an old adage," the President stated, "where you find the money, you'll find the source of power."

"The Core Council," Jax said. "Rebecca and I had been wondering about that. The money and the power are resting with the Core Bank, the SCS, and Sapphire Corp. but we thought that you guys were involved in some type of partnership, if not direct management."

"Your first clue should have been the lack of a Treasury Department within the government."

"You don't control the money so why have a money department," Jax said shaking his head. "I hate to ask this, but could you start at the beginning. I'm a little simple minded."

"I seriously doubt that," Ziven smiled, "but I planned to start there anyway so let's begin. What I'm going to share with you is known to a very select few," he started. "I didn't say that to threaten you whatsoever, it's just one of the many facts that I'm going to lay on the table for you. The plan was conceived sixteen or so years before the Apocalypse. It involved some of the wealthiest and power hungry people in the country. They bound together to form a brain trust that had major strangleholds on industries such as energy, technology, military equipment and medical. They would sequester any new invention that would threaten to weaken their position. They manipulated anything necessary to keep them on top. Of course this was all done very quietly."

"But I understood that technology was growing in leaps and bounds back then; almost out of control," Jax interjected.

"True and that was part of their dilemma," Ziven continued. "For centuries members of the, let's call it, *The Trust*, were able to manipulate industry as well as the government in order to maintain their position. Keep things in balance, so to speak, and continue to increase their wealth and power base."

"So what happened?" Rebecca asked.

"Tapio happened," he said. "He was a Finnish Ph.D., who developed the Tapio algorithms among many other things."

"Bots?" Jax asked.

"That's right," Ziven grinned, "see, I knew you were smart."

"What are bots?" Rebecca asked.

"Well, I can give you the political sciences person's answer," Jax offered.

"Go ahead," Ziven said.

"Well an algorithm is a step by step procedure for calculations either computer science or mathematical. A bot or robot was a group of algorithms strung together to perform a certain task."

"You got the main idea," Ziven said, "although the bots we are talking about contained billions of calculations. The Tapio bots dealt with trying to predict certain outcomes using mathematical formulas. Of course Tapio used mega computers to run the bots."

"Certain outcomes of what?" Rebecca asked.

"In his case, world events."

"Is that even possible?" Jax asked, "what you're saying was his bots could mathematically predict what was going to happen?"

"Kind of, but let's move on and I'll try to answer that. The real genius of Tapio's work was his Theory of 21. It was better known as The 21 Pillars of Predictability. Tapio had created 21 bots containing billions of algorithms. Each bot was designed to monitor and predict a certain global situation." Ziven looked up at the two of them, "are you keeping up?"

"Kind of," Jax answered, "keep going we'll stop you if we have any intelligent question to ask."

"OK, lets skinny this down some and get real simplistic. Let's say that we create a bot that can predict a daily event. The event is predicting the color of the blouse our young female neighbor is going to wear to work. Amazingly this bot is correct 98% of the time. Then all of a sudden, the percentage begins to drop, 90, 80, 70 percent. It finally drops to a percent which Tapio called the *threshold of unpredictability*. Our algorithm is no longer working. Something dealing with our subject has changed. The only choices we have to rewrite the bot to encompass the new parameters, abandon it, or wait for it to stabilize."

"So?" Rebecca asked.

"OK, let's move back to the 21 Pillars. Each of the 21 bots are designed to predict 21 certain global situations. At any time a few can hit the threshold of unpredictability but eventually return to within normal parameters. They are all constantly in a state of flux. The 21 bots are interconnected and are combined to form a single mega algorithm to predict one single event."

"Armageddon," Jax answered and quickly added, "can't be done."

"Well that's not for you or me to say," Ziven continued. "Based on Tapio's theory, when a certain number of the bots hit the threshold of unpredictability within a certain time period, a global disaster was imminent."

"That doesn't make any sense," Rebecca said, "how can you predict the end of the world?"

"Let me take a crack at it," Lars said.

Ziven relinquished the floor to Lars. "Rebecca, let's say there is a gearwheel in a machine that has 21 cogs or teeth on it. This gear is working just fine and the bigger machine (the world) which the gear is an integral part of, performs well. Now one day a tooth breaks off. Because its only one tooth the gear will still perform its job within the machine. But suddenly another one breaks off and then, another one. If enough of the cogs break off the gear, the machine will break down... Armageddon. So what Tapio said was if you could predict when the teeth would break off you would know when the machine would stop."

"So." Jax asked, "what does this have to do with this Trust?"

"He worked for them," Ziven stated, "the Trust *owned* Tapio. They had the money and computers to make Tapio's pillars operate, and the one thing the Trust didn't like was unpredictability."

"So you're saying that the Trust saw the end of the world coming, decided to duck into a bunker and wait it out?" Rebecca asked.

"Not quite," Ziven said. "Let me give you one more analogy. Jax, let's say your speeding down a country road. You drive over a crest and there, right below you, is a fork in the road. You have a choice of three directions in which to go. Which do you choose, remembering you only have a couple of seconds to choose or crash and die."

"I guess I would pick the one that looked the safest or easiest to navigate."

"Fair enough," Ziven smiled. "Now we replay the same scenario, but this time you see the caution sign telling you that there's a fork in the road a mile up ahead. What do you do?"

"Well I would slow down and pick the road that would get me to where I wanted to go."

"Exactly." Ziven grinned. "Tapio's Theory of 21 was the Trust's caution sign."

The possibilities were racing through Jax head. "So they saw what they considered to be Armageddon looming in front of them and they chose their own path?"

Ziven's face turned to stone. "What if they didn't like any of the paths offered to them?"

"They would try and create the path they liked," Rebecca said slowly. "Before the end?"

"Why not," Ziven shrugged, "they had been creating their own path for centuries. What was going to stop them from doing it with the end of mankind staring them in the face?" Ziven leaned back in his chair. "You both remember your pre-Apocalypse history?"

"Yes," they answered in unison. Jax motioned to Rebecca to continue.

"Alright I'll give you the short version," she said. "World monetary systems were collapsing, the major countries had arsenals of nuclear weapons and the smaller countries all wanted them. Religious tension and fighting was at an all time high. Terrorism was becoming out of control. World governments were bogged down in spiteful politics. Legal systems were failing to protect the very people they were intended for." She stopped to catch her breath, "Did I leave anything out?"

"A few things," Ziven chuckled, "but you captured a good part of it." He turned to Jax, "What pushed them over the brink?"

Jax recalled his studies. "There were the two nuclear accidents," he said.

"Accidents?" Ryan asked, speaking for the first time. "You think they were accidents?"

"Alright, let me rephrase that. There were two nuclear incidents. One in China and one in Iran."

"Sounds bad," Ziven prompted, "was that it?"

"No," he continued, "at almost the same time a mutated strain of the Middle East Respiratory Syndrome became pandemic. Thousands of people died."

"Hundreds of thousands," Ryan corrected him.

"Hundreds of thousands of people were dying," Jax restated.

"And the computer virus," Rebecca added.

"That's right," Jax agreed, "computer systems were crashing on a global scale."

"And then what happened?" Ziven asked.

"It gets very fuzzy at this point because of the failure of computer systems and the tremendous death rate, but I guess there was a global meltdown."

"You're right," Ziven said grimly. "Ryan, tell them what we know."

Ryan cleared his throat. "There were retaliatory nuclear strikes. China against Korea; Korea against the United States; The United States against Korea; Iran against Israel; Israel against Iran and Syria. There were unconfirmed nuclear strikes in Russia and Chechnya. The last we heard was that the major powers were destroying every satellite in orbit trying to knock out the other guy's spy and targeting equipment."

"And then darkness fell," Ziven said, holding his hands out as if giving a sermon.

Jax looked toward Rebecca and then to Ziven. "So you're trying to tell us that this Trust had something to do with it?"

"Alright," Ziven sighed, "I'm going to give you some hard facts. Then we'll take a short break. You and Rebecca can discuss what we've shared with you between yourselves and then we'll get back together. Does that sound fair?"

"Rebecca and Jax both nodded their agreement. "Ryan," Ziven prompted.

Ryan leaned forward, "Number one, The Trust owned a bio-tec company that did major military research into chemical and biological weapons. This company developed a biological agent code named ME2. This virus was engineered to be easily spread from person to person. The incubation period was two to three weeks with the carriers displaying no signs of being infected. Once the virus became active death came quickly. They also created the antiserum. If a person was inoculated prior to contact with the virus, there was zero chance of infection. Certain members of the, Trust and their families, certain key U.S. Government employees and their families as well as key members of different Trust corporations were inoculated just weeks before the outbreak." Ryan held up two fingers. "We know that the Trust had purchased certain solar technology and sequestered all information about that technology. This technology is now the basis for the SCS equipment." A third finger went up. "The Trust was also heavily leveraged into computer technology. What they didn't own they purchased. What they didn't purchase, they had no need for. There were rumors that a major technological discovery was made in the software market. Later, after the company was purchased by the Trust, the rumors were debunked. The corporation stated that the technology they had been duped into buying didn't work. No lawsuits were ever filed against the persons who had sold them the technology. This system is known today as Sapphire. They also had interest in several of the world's largest computer protection companies. These companies made their living by protecting people and business from computer hacking and virus. And finally," Ryan said, folding his hands in front of him, "when we come back I will take you on a tour of this facility."

"Facility?" Jax asked.

Ziven stood up; his move was quickly mirrored by Lars and Ryan. "Jax, you are currently sitting in one of the Trust's main apocalyptic bunkers."

✳ ✳ ✳ ✳

Mars twirled her stylus between her fingers as Commander Adelric read down the inventory. She had lost interest in the destroyed armory soon after learning that during her absence, there had been fourteen additional acts of graffiti and vandalism committed just in Core City alone. She had asked that the matter of the armory be tabled and that Commander Adelric provide the individual members of the council with an electronic copy of the weapons inventory, but she had been overruled.

"92 ME 50 heavy machine guns," Adelric continued reading down the list, "2,500 pounds of plastic explosives, 4,000 rounds of tear gas, 2500 anti-armor land mines and 2,500 flares," he concluded.

"There were enough weapons there to supply a small army," Kinsley stated. "How many assault rifles did you say?"

Adelric ran his finger down the list on his pad. "3,200 MR-7 assault rifles," he confirmed. "And yes, the purpose of the armories is to keep us in a ready state of preparedness if there was ever another intrusion from the outsiders."

"And how many rebels were killed?" Mars asked, trying to move on. She was ready to have

Sapphire issue a press release to the public stating that they had killed a certain number of rebels to date. Sapphire was not to mention the armory in the release.

"None," Adelric stated, "at least none that we know of."

Mars shot him a quick look after he made the comment. She immediately knew by the look on his face that she had just been set up.

"None?" She said, knowing she would have to weather whatever storm was brewing. "That's incorrect; I was at the site of the explosion and saw with my own eyes the damage. No one could have survived that blast."

"That is correct," Adelric said evenly, "but we now believe that the rebels had retreated from the site sometime before the self destruct was activated."

"But, Commander," Pyrs asked, "how could you possibly know that. From everything we've been told, anyone who was in the bunker was killed."

"I don't know who told you that," he said looking at Mars, "but they should have waited for the official report."

"Then, the weapons, they weren't destroyed in the blast?" Grady asked.

"No, sir they were not."

"How do you know?" Pyrs asked again.

"Our analysis of the site showed several discrepancies between what we found and what we *should* have found," he said.

Mars tightened her hand around the stylus in her palm. *He's enjoying this too much*, she thought, *what could he have possibly found in that rubble?*

"What type of discrepancies?" Kinsley asked.

Adelric adjusted his position in his chair, "The first thing was the total lack of any evidence that there were rebels inside the complex when it was destroyed."

"I don't understand," Pyrs said, "what type of evidence?"

"We found only Core Security issued uniforms, or pieces of them inside the building."

"You've certainly lost enough men in the last few weeks," Mars interjected, "that the rebels could have been disguised as our own troops."

"We have lost twenty-seven troopers in the last thirty-two days, including my own nephew," Adelric stated.

The statement brought condolences from every member of the council except Mars who only glared at him. *I should have known he would use that fact as leverage at some point.*

"In only two occasions had the uniforms of five men been removed from their bodies," he continued. "Five men did not attack that armory. Our forensic teams have finished their initial pattern reconstruction of the attack. They have concluded that the compound was breached in three different areas. It is also believed that the attacks were well coordinated and began after a smaller group of rebels penetrated the outer security undetected and had actually entered the main armory building. This small team entered the building and disarmed the general alarm system just prior to the main assault starting. Based on our electronic mapping, we estimated the rebel force consisted of at least twenty men." He looked at Mars again his eyes nothing more than narrow slits, "That's fifteen men more than the number of missing uniforms."

"Is that all the evidence you have, Commander?" Kinsley asked.

Adelric directed his glare toward her, "No, there is more. I have just supplied you with the total inventory of the ordinance in that facility. After going through the carnage, the teams also concluded that there are insufficient numbers of destroyed weapons or parts of weapons to account for the large number of weapons stored." Adelric paused several seconds allowing his audience to digest the information. "We now believe that the bulk of the weapons were removed prior to the blast."

"Again," Mars said, "I visited the site. With the amount of damage caused by that blast I don't see how you could tell exactly what was in that bunker when the blast went off."

"As you often like to quote," he answered, "statistically speaking, the debris at the site was totally inadequate to account for the number of weapons stored. But, I will defer this point until we have a more accurate figure for the council," Adelric said as he began punching keys on his key pad. "Now please look at this picture of the solider that placed the emergency call." The dirty face of the man was displayed for all to see. Adelric pointed to the figure, "This man made the call that Ms. Tansy and I both witnessed. We both heard his distress message." Adelric looked around the room at the different members, "Would any of you like me to replay the call in its entirety?"

"I don't think that is necessary," Mars answered, "I can verify that that was indeed the man we spoke with." *Bastard,* she fumed, *he's drawing me in deeper!*

"I've had Sapphire run this man's face through our identification process, twice," he emphasized. "This man is not and never has been a member of the Core Security Forces. In fact, he is not even recognized as a citizen of New America."

"So, why do that?" Grady asked.

"Here is what the forensic teams and I both believe happened," Adelric stated. "The actual raid on the facility happened under the cover of darkness much earlier in the evening. They probably had control of the facility by one or two in the morning. After the complex was secure, they started moving the ordinance out of the facility. Once they had taken what they wanted, the main body of the task force left."
"Main body?" Kinsley asked.

"Yes, we think that most of them left with the weapons sometime before daybreak. They left a few people behind to make the fake distress call. Around eight-thirty, this man," he said pointing to the figure again, "dressed up in one of our uniforms. I believe the uniform was taken at the site evident by the blood and grime visible here in the picture. He made the call while his comrades stood in the background adding the needed sound effects of a battle raging." Adelric enlarged the picture of the man. "Look behind him. Notice that all you can see is smoke, nothing else of the facility. It my opinion, they were nowhere close to the armory when he made the call."

"So that they weren't caught in the blast," Pyrs offered.

"That's correct. They made the call and we destroyed the complex."

"But why go through such an elaborate ruse after you already had the weapons?" Grady asked.

"That was precisely why they did it," Adelric answered. "They needed time to make sure they got away. By destroying the facility, they knew it would take us several hours, if not days, to be able to enter the bunker complex. They left just enough weapons and ammunition in the bunker to give the impression that it was too dangerous for our men to go into the building as long as there were rounds still exploding. They were able to buy themselves at least eight to ten hours head start before we even started looking for them."

"What would have happened if you hadn't destroyed the facility?" Pyrs asked.

Adelric rubbed his chin. "If Ms Tansy hadn't triggered the self destruct, we might have gained five or six hours on them. With our knowing what to look for, moving that much ordinance over an open road would be easy to spot

"Point of clarification," Mars said, raising her stylus. "Just for the record, it was Commander Adelric who remotely activated the self destruct from his personal PD, not me."

Adelric's face flushed with contempt. "Excuse me," he said coldly, "I'm positive that it was Ms. Tansy who activated the destruct mechanism. A simple check of the records will confirm the sequence of events."

Mars' heart leaped as she prepared to close the trap. "Sapphire, please verify the sequence that lead up to the execution order to destroy the District Four Armory."

"At 8.47 Commander and Ms. Tansy were involved with, what they thought was a member of the Armory security forces. At 8.52 Ms. Tansy suggested to Commander Adelric that he wait until more information was available before giving the order to destroy the facility. At 8.54 Commander Adelric informed Ms Tansy that it was his decision and his alone whether to destroy the facility or not. At 8.55 Commander Adelric activated the destruct order from his personal PD. If the council would like I can replay the communication sequence from that morning."

"I don't think that will be necessary," Mars stated as she looked around the room. All the members except Adelric shook their heads negativity. Adelric just stared blankly at Mars.

"Commander," Mars said compassionately, "I can understand your moment of temporary confusion and don't fault you whatsoever." She turned to address each member of the council, "It should be remembered that Commander Adelric was, at the time, out in the field investigating the murder of his brother's only son. That alone would be enough stress for anyone. Add to that the sudden news that thirty-six of his men were dead or dying could easily scramble the timetable of events for any of us."

Adelric sat quietly as the members chatted about the events and finally agreed with Mars' assessment. Dr. Grady leaned over and placed his hand on Adelric's shoulder. "Totally understandable, Martin," he said in a professional tone. "It was the right decision to make."

The Apocalypse bunker turned out to be enormous. They went through several areas of housing, large commissaries and food storage rooms. They were amazed at the labs and workshops scattered throughout the complex. There were even exercise facilities and sun rooms used to simulate the outdoors. The hospital facilities were spotless and even though much of the equipment was missing, it was easy to see that it was at one time top notch.

Ryan had told them that the upper echelon of course had larger living quarters and private dining and exercise facilities. He informed them that it would be too time consuming to show them the entire complex, but there were a few more things he wanted to squeeze into their tour.

He took them to an area that seemed to be smaller in size. The ceiling began to get closer and closer until they were standing in a room that was no more than eight feet wide, ten feet long and the ceiling, Jax guessed, was approximately eight feet tall. The room was empty but there were obvious signs of use along the walls and floor where equipment or desks had been situated. Across the room was a large metal hatch with heavy latches to secure it in place. In the top third of the door was a small view port with what was apparently two inch thick bullet proof glass. He estimated that the hatch itself was at least two feet thick. Jax also noticed that the locking mechanism was probably on the other side of the door.

Ryan pulled on the huge metal handle and with surprisingly little effort, pulled the door toward him. "This way," he said, allowing Rebecca and Jax to go first.

Jax was stunned at the size of the room or, more adequately, cave on the other side of the door. It has been chiseled or jack hammered out into a large almost egg shaped cave. The door had opened up onto a metal platform. On the far side of the platform was some type of metal vehicle that could seat, he estimated, nine people. There were three rows of benches one behind the other with room for at least three people per bench.

Ryan held out his hand to Rebecca first. "Here," he said, handing her a pair of ear plugs commonly used at a rifle firing range, "I don't know if they used these back then, but this ride is going to be very noisy."

Ryan ushered them into the second row of benches while he climbed in behind the steering wheel. He turned the key and the gas motor roared to life. A flip of a single switch activated powerful headlights, illuminating the long tunnel in front of them. Jax could not see the end of the tunnel as the light was soon sucked up by the darkness. Ryan released a hand lever and the car slowly began to move forward. After just a few seconds the car was speeding down a pair of metal tracks into the darkness. Jax estimated that they had traveled at least ten miles when the car began to slow. The small station they were now entering was identical to the one they had just left. Rebecca and Jax exited the vehicle had offered their earplugs to Ryan.

"Hold on to them," he said, "you'll need them for the ride back.

Ryan's words offered Jax a certain level of comfort knowing he was at least not going to die here at the end of this long dark tunnel. Ryan walked over to a small electrical box and began flipping switches. When he finished he walked over to the large hatch. Again, as before, the door was made of concrete and steel measuring some two to three feet thick. This time, Jax lent him a hand in opening the door. Jax was surprised at how smoothly the door moved aside.

Instead of leading into the small room, the hatch gave way to a very long and narrow hallway. The hallway was constructed of large iron cross beams painted in light green color. At just over six feet tall, Jax was forced to bend down to avoid hitting his head on the overhead cross beams.

"This entire portion of the facility is suspended on a huge coiled spring system," Ryan pointed out as they made their way down the corridor.

They followed Ryan to the far end where they again walked through an already open hatch. "Down that way," Ryan said as he pointed off to the left, "is the operational control room." He motioned them down the hallway, "What we came to see is at the end of this hall."

At the end of the hall was another door the stood open. Jax found himself standing on a small metal walkway. The rest of the room was like nothing he had ever seen before. First of all the room was in a shambles. Pieces of some type of metal structure were scattered below them. He looked up to see a tremendous circular chimney rising over one hundred feet above his head. He looked down toward the rubble to see at least another hundred feet below. He didn't know what they had burned in the chimney or how long ago they had last used it, but the smell of smoke still lingered in the air.

"Try not to touch the sides," Ryan cautioned,

the soot is on everything and its hell to get out of your clothes."

"How far is it to the other side?" Jax asked, noticing a small section of gangplank still attached to the cylinder directly across from where he was standing.

Almost sixty feet across," Ryan offered. "Over two hundred feet from the bottom to the very top."

"What did they incinerate in here?" Rebecca asked.

"Incinerate?" Ryan asked.

"Yes," Jax said, "was this their method of destroying garbage and waste? I'm assuming that somewhere at the bottom is a system of furnaces used to super heat garbage and waste which I imagine there was a lot of."

Ryan began to laugh out loud. "A super trash burner," he said holding his side as he continued to laugh, "I can't wait to tell Bob and the President when we get back."

"What's so funny?" Rebecca asked. "Are we missing something?"

Ryan waved his hands in front of himself, "No, no, I'm sorry," he said trying to get his outburst under control. "I didn't think. I should have known that the two of you would never have had the experience of seeing a facility like this in your entire life."

"Well, what is it?" Jax asked, trying to maintain his composure.

Ryan was finally able to straighten up, "This is a launch silo for sending missiles into outer space. There are over two dozen of them scattered around the countryside."

"This is where they launched the ICBM's?" Jax asked, showing his utter excitement.

Ryan shook his head, "The ICBM sites were able to launch Intercontinental Ballistic Missiles armed with nuclear payloads, but sites like this one were built by the Trust to launch the SCS equipment into orbit. I guess you could say that one-half the equipment is here on Earth while the other half is out there. Having a source of almost endless clean energy was one of the Trust's top priorities when establishing New America."

Jax and Rebecca looked around the silo in disbelief. *Ryan had been right about one thing,* Jax thought, *I could have tripped over this place and never known its purpose.*

"If you don't have any more questions," Ryan stated, "we can head back to the conference room."

"I do have one question," Jax said. "Why are you showing us all of these things?"

Ryan smiled and pointed toward the hatchway. "Why don't you save that question for President Ziven?"

The trip back seemed much shorter. So they were once again in the small room that Ryan had called a conference room. He excused himself and left to find the President.

Rebecca walked around the small room casually. "What do you think?" she asked.

Jax was seated at the table drawing concentric circles on the table top. "I'm not sure what to think," he said, continuing to doodle on the metal surface. "I'm giving our chances of getting out of here at around thirty percent."

Rebecca folded her arms over her chest. "That's not very good odds."

"It's a lot better than the zero percent I gave us upon arrival."

"I mean, why waste all this time showing all of this," she said, making a grand gesture, "then shoot us?"

"I don't know," he shrugged, "maybe in his own way he wanted to justify our execution."

"Well, that would certainly put a crimp on our relationship building."

President Ziven entered the room followed by Lars and Ryan. Jax noticed that Ryan was now carrying a medium size paper bag. Ziven took a seat across from Jax. Lars and Ryan took the two chairs at either end of the conference table. Rebecca sat at Jax's side.

"So what did you think of your little tour?" Ziven asked.

"It's funny you should ask that," Jax answered. "I had just told Rebecca that "I'm not sure what to think."

"Fair enough," Ziven answered. If he was upset with Jax answer, he didn't show it. "Do you now believe me when I tell you this was a Trust's apocalyptic bunker?"

Jax shook his head. *I don't see why I shouldn't be totally honest in my answer*, he thought. "Joshua," Jax started then caught himself, "Is it alright if I call you Joshua?"

Ziven nodded, "I've certainly been called worse. Please continue."

"Well, Joshua, I have a high level of confidence that this was in fact an apocalyptic bunker, but I don't see anyone's name on it. Not a single plaque stating 'Keep Out, Property of the Trust'. Why couldn't it be one of your bunkers?"

"Your bunker... meaning the government's?

Actually, there weren't separate bunkers. There was no *theirs and ours*," Ziven admitted. "Government personnel that were afforded places in the bunkers received them because the Trust believed they would serve a purpose."

"What purpose?" Rebecca asked.

"Just what you discovered hours ago. They need a buffer between them and the general populace. They were poorly equipped to handle the distasteful task of herding the general public. The past governments had done that so well. The Trust could filter their demands through the government; to test the people's reaction. If the people didn't like it; the government took the blame."

"If they liked it?" Jax asked.

Ziven held open his hands. "Then the Trust got what they wanted with little or no cost to them."

"So," Jax started slowly, "if I remember correctly, you want to take the government back. Kick the Trust out."

Ziven frowned. "I see where the fault lies," he said. "What I failed to get across to the two of you is that when I say, we. I mean *we* the people of the United States."

Jax studied Ziven's face and body langue. His eyes shifted between the three of them. "And what do you get out of all this?"

"I guess if I did need to get something out of this," Ziven chuckled, "it would be that fact that I would probably go down in history as the modern day George Washington.

Lars jabbed his finger toward Ziven, "I've know this guy most of my life, Jax," he said laughing. "He does have a small ego problem."

There was just enough laughter from everyone in the room to lighten up the mood. "I don't mind him saying that," Ziven winked. "I'll have Ryan put him on the rack again when we get back to Government Plaza."

Lars looked at the antique wrist watch he wore, "Which should be leaving soon, Mr. President."

"So," Jax asked, "where does that leave us?"

"Alright," Ziven sighed, "I have two more things to give you, and then the two of you will be blindfolded, driven several miles from this facility and released. There will be a car there for your use."

"Just like that?" Jax asked.

"Just like that," he assured them. "Then you are free to do as you like, but I will warn you," he said becoming very serious, "if you choose not to help us, the two of us will continue on our own separate paths until, at some point, we will be standing across from each other under a different light."

"Fair enough," Jax said. "Show us what you have."

Ryan opened the bag without waiting for Ziven's order. He removed a plastic bag containing a PD. He placed the item on the table and pushed it toward Jax.

Jax picked up the bag and began to open it.

"I wouldn't open that." Ryan said sternly. "At least not outside a proper lab facility."

Jax laid the bag back on the table.

"It's OK to handle in the bag," Ziven said. "Do you know what that is?"

"It's the latest model of the Sapphire Personal Device," Rebecca said.

"That's correct," Ryan offered. "Then you also know that within the next year everyone will have this model."

"Yes," they said in unison.

"We've already seen one of these," Jax said, sliding the bag back toward Ryan.

"Not like this one," Ziven assured them. He turned to Ryan, "Let me have the map."

Ryan reached into the bag and removed a large folded map and handed it to Ziven. Ziven began unfolding the map and turned it so it was right side up for Jax and Rebecca. "I'm sure you recognize this," he said.

The map was no different than the one they had back at the house. It showed the continental United States with an overlay of the nine districts. "Yes." Jax answered for the two of them.

"I'm going to show you a new way of looking at this map," he offered. "Here are the nine districts, surrounded on each side by what is effectively known as the waste lands. In a few months Core Security, with the help of the SCS, will complete the perimeter fence."

Jax was stunned that Ziven would share that type of information with them. They knew very little about the eastern wastelands or the defenses. Jax's heart sank. *I don't think we're going to get out of here alive after all,* he surmised. "Alright," is all he could think of offering as a reply.

"What a lot of people forget is that a fence has two sides," Ziven grinned. "It functions well at keeping *most* people out," he said, eyeing the two of them. "But, it also keeps people in."

"I don't want to be rude," Jax said sincerely, "but what is your point?"

"You've seen the empty silo. All of the SCS facilities and their satellite are in operation. They can only supply a finite amount of power," he said pointing to the general area of the districts, "and we only have a finite amount of space. What happens when the current population reaches a level that the two can no longer support?"

Jax thought about Santa Catalina Island and the SCS station there, but decided not to mention it. "I guess you would have to turn off the fence and expand."

Ziven nodded, "That's what we would do. Or at least, that's what my predecessor would do, but that's not the Trust's answer to the problem." Ziven pointed to the plastic bag, "That's the Trust solution to the problem."

"New PD's?" Jax asked.

Ryan pushed the devise back toward Jax and Rebecca. "This device has the latest advanced bio-scan software," he said, "It can detect the tiniest of genetic flaws within the human body. Genetic abnormalities that you would like to rid your body of."

"That's impossible," Rebecca said, "no one can change the genetic code at the DNA level...can they?"

"Correct," Lars interjected, "they can't, but what if you could eliminate the genetic flaw at the carrier level?"

"Jax looked at Lars skeptically. "Are you saying that these new devices will kill the user if they detect a flaw?"

"No," Ziven answered, "something less drastic and more… covert. What we discovered is that this device will be used to sterilize the user, preventing them from passing on the flawed gene."

Jax shot Rebecca a quick glance looking for confirmation of what Ziven had just said.

Rebecca's face paled, "I don't believe it."

Ziven pointed to the device. "Take it with you, study it," he offered.

Possibilities raced through Jax's mind. The amount of data was too much to digest in such a short time period. *We need more time to study all of this*, he decided. "Why don't you build more SCS facilities," he asked. "Expand the perimeter as you increase your power output?"

Ziven shook his head, "The Trust no longer has the technology or the manufacturing facilities to build new rocket boosters or satellites. Unfortunately for us, all of the booster and rocket construction facilities were along the coast lines and were destroyed. It would take too long to regain that type of knowledge and skills needed to reconstruct everything."

Jax stared at the device sitting before him. *The*

best thing to do, he figured, *was to take the device and run. If Ziven was on the level they could take this with them and get it in the proper hands for analysis.* "What else do you have for us in your bag of tricks?" he asked.

Ryan removed a small memory wheel from the bag and placed it on the table. "This is for you to use as you see fit," he offered.

"What if we don't take you up on your offer to help?" Rebecca asked.

Ziven rested his elbows on the table and interlaced his fingers together, "As I've already told you, you will go your way and we will go ours."

"And the memory wheel?" Jax asked.

"It contains, among other things, information on how to contact us if you so choose. Ziven then offered them a gracious smile, "As for the rest of the information on the wheel; think of it as a consolation gift if we aren't able to come to terms."

"Anything else before we leave?" Jax asked.

"I have one more thing to ask," Ziven smiled. "Pepper Mallory, do you know her?"

Jax shook his head, "never heard of her. Who is she?"

"A shroud," Rebecca answered.

Jax immediately gave her an inquisitive look.

"Before your time, Jax," she answered turning to face Ziven. "We created her to eliminate a small problem we were having a few years ago."

"A problem with Jasper?" Ryan asked.

Rebecca shook her head, "Yes, Jasper was producing fake PD to be used by their crime organization. Core Security was putting a lot of pressure on Jasper trying to destroy their labs."

"And this pressure," Ryan asked, "was putting pressure on your lab?"

"That's correct. We didn't have the man power to eliminate the threat being posed by their operations so…"

"…you allowed Core Security to do it for you," Ziven said, completing her sentence.

"Yes," she answered, "why do you ask?"

Ziven leaned back in his chair. "It just ties up a few loose ends for us," he smiled.

"May we go now?" Jax asked.

Ziven motioned toward the door. "We're looking forward to working with you," he said as a means of saying goodbye.

Jax and Rebecca nodded their goodbyes and

headed out the door. As soon as they had cleared the hallway and entered the elevator Jax turned to face Rebecca. "Pepper Mallory?"

"Pop chains," she answered, looking around the car.

CHAPTER 22

ADELRIC'S PROBLEMS

Commander Adelric sat at his desk reviewing the transmission for the countless time. No matter how hard he tried to wish the video to change, it never did. The physical evidence showed that he, not Mars, had activated the self destruct. He had given it to his top technical specialist to evaluate. There had to be some small flaws omitted when Mars had Sapphire re-write the history of the event. He was sure that his vindication was somewhere in the recording, but as he suspected, his own technicians did not have the unlimited access needed to reveal the truth.

He turned back to the report in front of him. Two subjects had been detained at a check point only miles from the Armory blast. The two had matched the ID profiles of the two suspects wanted in connection with the Core City events. They had both been detained and shipped off to the District Four Interrogation facility. Somewhere between the roadside checkpoint and the interrogation facility the van carrying the two had been hijacked and the driver and guard had been murdered.

Forensic teams had been dispatched to the site of the hijacking. Their report showed no signs of the vehicle having been forced off the road or that there had been a struggle. Both security personnel had been shot at close range. It was suggested by the forensic people, and he agreed, the van was most likely flagged down by persons disguising themselves as CSF personnel. The two deaths had been added to the growing list of casualties throughout all of the districts.

Finally, there were reports of rebel casualties as some people being stopped had resisted. Adelric frowned as he continued to read. In all of the reported deaths there had only been three weapons recovered. He sadly admitted to himself that there was a very good possibility that his men were becoming trigger happy. In some ways he couldn't blame them. Far too many of their comrades were being ambushed and killed. He had overheard two of the men talking about it. *It is better to be alive to say you're sorry than to be dead and tell St. Peter I screwed up,* he recalled.

His mind wandered back to the armory

destruction. He had received a unanimous vote of confidence from the Council on his handling of the event, but what he really feared was how the 'Three' would vote in their next closed door meeting. In many ways he knew that the five member council was merely a facade to the real power wheeled behind the scene by Mars, Pyrs and Kinsley. Deception and manipulation were the twin blades they used like finely sharpened weapons. As skillful as any gifted surgeon, they would perform an operation with flawless perfection. Most often their victims had not even known they had been struck until it was too late. *I will not be just another fatality*, he swore to himself, *I may not be as devious as them, but I am certainly as deadly.*

Jax shifted his weight from one side to the other pushing himself deeper into the stuffing of the big chair. It had taken them the better part of two day to return to their headquarters. As promised, they had been released on a back road near the invisible border between corner of District Four and District Two. What Ziven had forgotten to mention was the fact the Rebecca and he were going to be subjected to a sleeping gas soon after they had entered the back of the van. They woke up six hours later in the front seat of the car Ziven had promised would be waiting for them. Rebecca found a map in the storage compartment with a small note attached. *Sorry for the sleep, needed some protection against you*

figuring out where you were. There's some food in the rear compartment. It was signed 'Jay'. The map did show their location as well as the known patrol areas of the Core Security. It was decided to keep to the back roads through District Two avoiding all check points marked on the map.

They had abandoned the car on the side of the road about five miles from a predetermined safe house operated by their group. It wasn't really a house, but more of a hidden cache of clothing, food and weapons. They ate, changed clothes and left. After hiking for almost a day, they hid the PD and the memory wheel and continued. People would be sent back to retrieve the two items. People, who would have the equipment and training to scrutinize both items for any hidden transmitters or locating beacons.

That had been six days ago. Jax now had the memory wheel in his right hand and held it out in front of him. The PD and a copy of the information contained on the wheel had been sent back to McKee. He had also included a full report on their time in captivity. He had requested Rebecca to file a separate report to McKee so that she would receive the information from two independent sources therefore reducing the chance that their reports would have been biased by the other.

Rebecca came down the stairs and walked over to a chair near to where Jax was sitting.
"I was hoping to find you behind your desk," she

said, "that way I would have had first shot at the big chair. Peter, Chris and Phil are on their way over now."

So far only he and Rebecca had seen the information on the wheel. They had reviewed it several times before they went into any lengthy conversation about what they had seen and read. Now it was time to share it with the others.

"I seriously thought about sleeping here last night," Jax answered, pointing down to the chair, "but it's too far away from the bathroom."

The three men came down the stairs making enough noise for at least double their number. Greetings were quickly exchanged and seats taken. It had been Chris' first time in Jax new office.

"Have you shrunk, Jax, or is that chair really that big?"

The others laughed and made a few appropriate snide remarks. With some effort, Jax leaned forward and dropped the wheel in a multi media device on the floor at his feet.

"This is the memory wheel that was given to Rebecca and me after meeting with Mr. Jay," he said, pulling a remote out of his shirt pocket. Everyone knew that Mr. Jay was the code name for President Ziven. "The first message is self explanatory he said as he activated the holographic player. Almost instantly a holographic representation of a women appeared. She sat rather uncomfortably on a high back stool. She was small in stature and could not have sat back on the stool and still have her feet touch the bottom rung. So she sat on the front half of the seat, her short delicate arms forward allowing her fragile hands to rest on her knees. When Jax had first viewed the holograph he thought she was the most unremarkable looking woman he had ever seen. Rebecca had summed it up best by stating that she had the perfect presence of a spy. The woman could get lost in a crowd of two, Rebecca had commented.

The woman nervously nodded her head slightly as if someone behind the camera had just given her a queue. "Hello," she said softly, "My name is Carmen Lotte and Dena Lotte is…was my daughter."

Rebecca had seen the recording a half a dozen times but still managed to tear up at the woman's introduction. She looked out of the corner of her eye in Jax's direction. He was pinching the bridge of his nose, rubbing his eyes in the subdued light. She choked back her own tearful breakdown.

"We are being told that this recording will be watched by The Guardians and that," she gulped swallowing her sigh, "that you would…could help me bring to justice the people who took my Dena from me. You have our permission to use this information in any way you see fit. My husband and I ask nothing from you other than this one thing." Tears began to cascade down her pale cheeks, but she refused to wipe them away. Finally a hand entered the picture from the left side offering her a tissue. She took it and nodded her gratitude. She dabbed her eyes and smiled weakly toward the camera, "this is the fourth time in the last twenty minutes that I've tried to make this holo," she apologized, "you would think I wouldn't have any tears left by now."

Rebecca could not hold it back any longer. A huge sigh escaped her as she covered her mouth with a handful of tissues. No one in the room made a sound or took their eyes off Mrs. Lotte.

"My husband and I have shared some information on this wheel that will help you get to know what a wonderful young woman Dena…was. Please take the time to get to know her and you will understand why we ask so shamelessly for your help." With an unsteady hand she wiped her eyes. "I don't want someone else's Dena," she cried, her lips trembling, "to die like my baby did. Please, I know you can help. Thank you."

The holo faded. Jax cleared his throat, "Does anyone want to see it again?" he asked. The room remained silent as Jax dug in his pants pocket. Finally he produced a small piece of paper. "This is a reply from Colonel McKee," he said, "it's the fastest reply I have ever gotten from her. I'll read it to you." He unfolded the paper and began to read. "Thanks for the gifts. I'm sure the kids will love them. The family pictures were great and I think mom was right; you should help take care of her baby. Of course she is my favorite, but then I'm extremely prejudiced as I'm sure you are. Oh, PS, I sent you a present. "

"Wow," Peter exclaimed, "that's the most I've ever heard her say since I got here."

"Same here," Jax said climbing out of the chair. He popped the wheel out of the player and handed it to Phil, "Phil you and your team review all the information on this. I want to know in 48 hours how you and The Guardians plan to approach this."

Phil took the wheel and slipped it into his shirt pocket, "Right, Jax, we'll have a draft for you as soon as possible."

"We think we have an opportunity for distribution," Peter said, "That is, as soon as Phil is ready.

"Excellent." Jax said as he crossed the room stopping at the door leading to the storage area under the stairs.

"So, Jax, what kind of gift did McKee send you?" Chris grinned. "I've never heard of her sending anyone anything but an ass chewing."

"Funny you should ask that, Chris," he said unlocking the door. "I understand from Rebecca that you were originally trained as a spotter. Is that correct?"

Chris looked toward Rebecca, "Yeah, but that was some time ago before I volunteered for this duty."

Rebecca smiled like the Cheshire cat. "All duties as assigned," she said.

Chris turned to see Jax remove the sniper rifle from the closet. "Good, you are going to stay here and help me with Auntie McKee's early birthday present."

Chris walked closer and studied the rifle. "You got a spotter scope?" he asked stepping around Jax to gain entrance to the small room. Chris exited with a flat black case in his hands. He placed the case on Jax desk and opened it. He immediately began checking the equipment as he had been trained to do. "Who's my shooter?" Chris asked.

Jax balanced the rifle with both hands testing its weight. "It's me and you, man."

Chris didn't look up from what he was doing, "Do you have a flanker picked out?"

Rebecca stepped in-between the two of them, "That would be me," she said placing a portable holograph machine on the desk. She quickly inserted the disk in the machine and stepped back as the image began to materialize. The figure was about twelve inches tall and slowly began to spin.

Chris glanced over and did a double take, "Is that who I think it is?" he asked now staring at the figure.

Jax eased the butt of the sniper rifle down on the desk top. "It's none other than the killer of young children, Commander Adelric."

"Damn, Peter said as he walked up to the desk to get a better look at everything. "What's Mr. Jay going to think about you punching Adelric's lights out?"

"I've been told," Jax said lifting the rifle up to his shoulder, "that it's not our problem to worry about."

CHAPTER 23

GOING SHOPPING

Klackman's Super Stores held two major titles within New America. The first is that each store covers over 274,000 square feet of total shopping area making him the owner of the largest retail stores in the country. The second title is that Klackman's has eighty seven stores spread out over the nine districts, three times as many as their next competitor.

Each store stocks everything the consumer could want in a full-service supermarket, including dairy products, garden fresh produce, fresh meat, poultry, pond raised seafood, delicatessen, baked goods, and frozen foods. Klackman's also offer a full Core Urgent Care Center, Pharmacy, and Optical Center. Each super store also offers numerous alcove shops, such as Sapphire Personal Device stores capable of issuing; repairing or replacing a person's PD. Restaurants ranging from fast food to fine dining are also available in most units.

So it is easy to conclude that their stores became extremely busy on a Saturday morning. This was one of the main reasons Mars enjoyed shopping during that period. The fact that she, Pyrs, and Kinsley were all major stock holders in the corporation also influenced their shopping habits. But it was here; on a busy weekend morning that Mars felt that she could get the best pulse of their society. She had never accepted the concept of having your finger on the pulse was the right thing to do. She truly believed that if you wanted to stay abreast of what was happening, you had to be a part of the pulse.

So, Saturday morning grocery shopping was her chance to see what was happening. *It doesn't hurt*, she thought, *to be seen out in public either.* Being recognized as a member of the Core Council and out shopping with everyone else only helped to bolster her personal approval ratings on Sapphire. It would have been easy enough to manipulate her personal approval numbers the same way she had changed the details of the Armory incident, but the personal blogs and photographs posted by other shoppers was priceless.

She continued to push her cart down the aisles

picking out the few things she needed. She could have allowed Sapphire to run an analysis of her past shopping habits, compare that against her home inventory and have the appropriate items delivered to the house. But the council had decided many years ago that having the populace interact with each other in public forums helped promote a feeling of unity. The Council well remembered the tremendous isolation caused during the pre-apocalypse times by people spending too much time in front of a computer. Video games and violent forms of entertainment were still banned from the Sapphire network. Instead, family home games and outdoor activities were promoted and incentivized. Limited online shopping was allowed, but special 'in store' discounts and promotions never available to the online stores, more than helped to tip the balance in the store's favor.

Mars looked down at the cart's display checking on which items she still needed to purchase. She very seldom checked the total amount feature of the display as it meant little to her. She and the other Council members paid the same prices as any other shopper in the store. They felt it important that shoppers saw that they were all treated the same. This was also true when it came to utility bills. Mars would receive an invoice once a month and approve payment on line. The utility rates that she paid never varied as much as a single credit from anyone else. The council also made themselves available to public audits when it came to payments. Of course, certain adjustments were made to their accounts once they were inside the Core Financial system. These adjustments were made deep within the cogs of the system and usually showed up in their accounts as expense reimbursements.

Mars continued to plow through the different holo advertisements not bothering to stop or speak with them. As head of the largest communication and marketing company she knew too well how the system worked. All holo advertisements contained algorithms set up to interpret a person's facial expressions as well as their speech patterns and body langue. Within nano-seconds the bots were able to analyze the customer and adjust to a profile that was most likely to appeal to them. Mars had learned on more than one occasion that she was not excluded from their affects when she had chatted with a holo and ended up walking out of the store with an item she did not intend to purchase. They now either received a curt smile from her or she ran them through with her basket.

The Klackerman's company theme began playing throughout the store. The music was very soft at first but grew louder as the holo of the Klackerman's chairperson began to materialize in place of all the advertisement halos. Old man Klackerman was fond of appearing in the stores and thanking its customers for their patronage. Also, the appearance of old man Klackerman could occasionally bring an unadvertised discount or promotion.

"Hello everyone," the many halos of him throughout the store waved. "It is so nice to see you all back again. "As our way of saying 'thanks' for your patronage, we at Klackerman's have some very special things for you today."

Mars rolled her eyes. *The pudgy little man never gave a thing away in his life*, she sneered, *If he was offering you something, he had taken it away from someone else*. The Council knew of his gray advertisement tactics but looked the other way because of his support to them. *After all*, she thought, *78% of his advertisement budget was spent with the Sapphire marketing group*.

"Today," the pudgy figure gleamed, "I have a special guest for you and without further delay here are The Guardians!"

Mars gripped the handle of her basket so tightly her knuckles turned white. The figure of Klackerman was quickly replaced with the single youthful appearance of the spokeswoman for the group. Mars' hand dove into her purse and retrieved her PD. A simple tap and Sapphire was there. "Shut down all advertisement halos in Klackerman's."

"Sorry, but the advertisement system within Klackman's is a multi-sponsored, overlapping private network that does not use our system."

"Hello, my friends," the blond headed figure smiled throughout the store, "It is always good to see you all."

Mars talked softly, but firmly to her PD. "Shut down the power to the store."

"Do you wish to shut down the power to this unit or every Klackerman's store?" Sapphire asked.

"All too often these days," the angelic figure said, "I must share some troubling information with you."

"Are all of the stores displaying the message?" Mars asked.

"Yes."

"Then shut them all down." she hissed.

"I'm sorry Ms Tansy, but shutting down the different power grids supporting the Klackerman units would mean cutting power to 38% of the country. That type of action could be very dangerous to the power substations and the SCS overall power grid."

"I have someone who would like to speak to you all today," the Guardian said. "A member of your own community."

"I don't give a damn," Mars almost yelled, "I'm ordering you to shut it down."

Sapphire responded instantly, "A shut down of that magnitude would require a vote from the executive council," Sapphire answered flatly. "Would you like me to contact the other members for an emergency vote?

"Yes," Mars answered between clenched teeth, "and by the way, I vote in favor of the shut down." With nothing else she could do, Mars looked up at the holo.

A new figure had materialized alongside the blond speaker, an image of a younger woman. She was dressed in casual pants and wore a pullover sweat shirt displaying the emblem of the Core Central University. Around the emblem were the words, Core University Freshman Class.

Mars did not recognize the young lady. She held up her PD and spoke softly, "Identify the holo," she ordered Sapphire.

The figure of the Guardian stepped back and motioned for the young woman to take center stage.

"Hello everyone," the young girl said waving, "My name is Dena Lotte and up until recently I was a student of Core Central College," the young girl raised her two center fingers on her right hand and pushed them toward the sky. "Go Central!" she yelled.

Throughout the store other students and alumni

shouted their response, "Go Central!"

Mars jumped at the roar of the cheer.

The face of Dena grew sad. "The reason I said that I was recently a student was," she said solemnly, "because six weeks ago, in the middle of the night, Core Security Forces stormed my home." Footage of the security forces massing outside of Dena's home began to play behind her. There were cries of outrage from the shoppers when the armored troops began their assault. The image of Dena motioned toward the video. "These men illegally broke into our home; arrested my mother and father and as I ran down stairs to see what was happening," she continued as the video now showed the muzzle flashes through the Lotte's window, "I was shot three times and was murdered."

The shoppers became deathly silent, their eyes glued to the nearest image of Dena.

"Poor girl," a woman standing next to Mars sighed. Mars abandoned her basket in the middle of the aisle and, ducking her head, made her way to the exit.

The image of Dena's arms came together in front of her as she placed her hands together, "I will miss my mother and father," she wept, "and I will miss all my friends at Core Central." She continued, "I have but one request for everyone that is watching. Please help yourselves and your children, don't let these murderers do to your family what they did to my family. Don't let…"

The lights throughout the store shut down along with every counter or display that depended on the central power. Scattered, throughout the store, emergency lighting flickered to life and then suddenly failed pitching the store into total darkness. From out of the void people slowly began activating their PDs and held them aloft. An eerie blush light filtered through the store. "For Dena!" someone in the crowd yelled. "Dena!"came the reply over and over. Louder and louder the crowd cheered, "Dena, Dena, Dena!"

Mars sped away from the shopping center in no particular direction. Once she was far enough away she would decide where to go. *The office*, she concluded after a moment of clear thought. Traffic slowed and finally came to a complete standstill. She activated Sapphire through her car device. "Traffic status," she commanded.

"All lanes of traffic in your area have come to a full stop," Sapphire informed her. "Traffic controls in this section of the city are non operative."

"I see that," she screamed, "what's the delay?"

"District Five Power grids, three, seven, eleven, twenty-two and thirty-six have been shut down by Executive Council order," she responded. All districts are experiencing the same type of power shut down. Shall I list the affected grids by district?"

"Crap!" Mars shouted slamming her fist down on the steering wheel. "Lift the executive order and return power to all grids," she sputtered.

"It will require a vote of the Council to repeal the current executive order," Sapphire explained. Mars' face contorted as a spasm of irritation, distorting her features, "Do it!" she yelled savagely, "just damn do it!"

"A vote to return power to all grids has been issued to the Executive Council members." Sapphire informed her.

"Councilman Tansy," Sapphire asked, "how do you vote on returning power to all previously affected grids?"

"Yes," she hissed.

"Councilman Tansy, you have priority calls from Councilman Pyrs, Councilman Kinsley, Commander Adelric and President Ziven. In what order would you like the calls answered?"

Commander Adelric stood by the barricade in front of the Tower Exchange building monitoring communications traffic on his head set. Skirmishes between SCF troops and mostly students had broken out on or around the CCU campus and continued through the night. Standard procedure was to secure the Towers building at the first hint of trouble.

Adelric began to pace behind the barricade as reports from other districts began to come in. It seemed, for the moment, most of the trouble was centrally located on CCU campus. District disturbances were being reported as minor but growing.

Jax tracked Adelric's movement through his scope as the man marched along the barricade. Chris lay next to him feeding him information on atmospheric conditions and distance. Jax was very confident that he could make a good shot as Adelric paced back and forth, but his training had told him to wait. Sooner or later, Adelric was going to head back toward the main entrance of the building. In Jax and Chris's current position, that would offer them the optimum target. One that was moving in a straight line away from them. The head shot that Jax was planning would require all of his skill as well as every advantage he could think of. The target moving from left to right was not something he wanted to fire on. He removed his eye from the scope and rested.

"He'll head back inside soon enough," Chris

whispered, "then we'll have him."

Jax nodded his agreement.

Mars stood at the conference room window her arms crossed over her chest. From where she was standing she could see at least nine columns of smoke rising in the distance. Riots had broken out within one hour of Dena's broadcast. Of course it started on the Core Central University campus first. Students marched through the streets of the campus shouting Dena's name as they broke windows, turned over cars and spray painted Dena's name on every building they passed. CSF personnel were dispatched to the campus to restore order, but the presence of the CSF threw the student body into an outrage. Several CSF vans were either sprayed with Dena's name or set on fire. Twenty-three students and CSF troopers were sent to the surrounding area hospitals. A curfew was finally declared at sundown.

It seemed that wherever the CSF troops were, an outbreak would start somewhere else in the city. Throughout the night clashes between troops and rioters erupted across the city. The clashes would last five to ten minutes and then the rioters would disappear into the darkness. By morning, things seemed to be returning to normal.

Mars returned to the conference table where Pyrs and Kinsley were waiting. None of them had slept more than a few hours in the last twenty-four and it was beginning to show.

"Things seem to be settling down out there," Mars said, retaking her seat.

"Of course you mean until the next time," Pyrs stated. "Our current approval ratings are in a freefall. Do you want Sapphire to display the current numbers?"

"That won't be necessary," Mars snipped. There won't be a next time," Mars assured the two of them. Sapphire is currently going through all of the independent media licenses within the country. Any group that has more than two multimedia devices registered to their name is now going to be monitored by Sapphire. No communication broadcast through the advertising network will be allowed without first being reviewed and released by this office.

"What is the feedback from the advertising companies?" Kinsley asked.

"They have no choice," she said arrogantly, "if they want to keep their licenses."

The other two members of the Executive Council nodded their heads in agreement.

"Ms. Tansy," Sapphire interrupted, "President Ziven has just started giving a live broadcast."

"Shut it down!" she shouted. "You were told

not to broadcast anything from Government Plaza without inserting a ten minute censor delay."

"President Ziven is not broadcasting from inside the Government Plaza," Sapphire informed the council, "he is speaking live from the steps of the Administration Building at Core Central University," she said smoothly. "He is addressing a crowd of over five thousand people and is being carried by fourteen different flash media reporters."

Flash reporters had always been a problem in Mars' mind. They were independent reporters with little or no staffs for support. Their equipment was as shoddy as their tactics. They had been nicknamed *Flash* reporters because of their quick, impromptu methods of interviewing and then later reporting their stories on the minor, seldom watched sites. Their methods and stories were little more than a cheap imitation of professional reporting.

Mars had brought the matter of closing them down several times to the council with little success. Her last attempt, over a year ago, to shut them down was defeated when the Attorney General, Adrian Kelly, had stepped in and threatened to file legal action against the Core Council on the grounds of a violation of the reporters First Amendment rights. While the constitution of the United States had been rewritten back in 2054, the battle to remove or alter the First Amendment, met strong opposition. However, the Second Amendment originally stating:

"A WELL REGULATED MILITIA, BEING NECESSARY TO THE SECURITY OF A FREE STATE, THE RIGHT OF THE PEOPLE TO KEEP AND BEAR ARMS, SHALL NOT BE INFRINGED," WAS CHANGED TO READ, "A WELL REGULATED SECURITY FORCE, BEING NECESSARY TO THE SECURITY OF THE NATION, WILL SOLELY MAINTAIN THE RIGHT TO KEEP AND BEAR ARMS."

"Display the broadcast," Pyrs ordered.

The image of the President appeared on the viewer. He was just finishing up his thanks to everyone who had come together in a peaceful manner. "And now," he continued, "I would like to have Attorney General, Adrian Kelly step forward and speak to you about Ms. Dena Lotte."

The roar of the crowd was almost deafening. Several Flash reporters panned the crowds from different angles. People were still crowding into the parks and streets surrounding the Administration building.

"Sapphire, how many people did you say were present?" Kinsley asked.

"At the start of the presentation there were 5,346 citizens identified through their PDs. That number has increased to 6,678 and is rising quickly."

Mars placed her hand over her mouth and continued to watch in silence.

"Thank you fellow students and alumni of Core Central University," she said. Kelly then smiled broadly, raising her right hand above her head, her two fingers fully extended. "Go Central!" she screamed into the microphones in front of her.

"The crowd went wild, screaming at the top of their lungs. "Go Central! Go Central! Go Central!"

Don't tell me, Mars said weakly, "she's a damn graduate of Central University."

"Both Joshua Ziven and Adrian Kelly attended Core Central University School of Law. Both graduated with top honors," Sapphire informed the group.

The crowd had now broken into the University fight song. The noise was so loud several of the Flash reporter's cheap microphones could not handle the volume and began cutting out. The message was clear though; the people liked Kelly.

"That was great!" she said raising her hands over her head and lowering them gently. The volume of the crowd lessened. "I wish this was a joyful reunion with my fellow class mates, but my heart is filled with sadness today," Kelly said. She gestured toward President Ziven and Chief of Staff, Lars. "We all worked with Mr. Lotte and we all knew both Carmen and Dena," she said. "I asked that President Ziven address you today, to tell you about the Lotte family, but he felt it was more appropriate that I, someone who worked with Albert every day, speak with you."

The crowd applauded and whistled their approval.

"My readings of the crowd," Sapphire stated, "show high approval of the President's choice to allow Attorney General, Adrian Kelly to address the issues concerning the Lott family. The government's numbers are expected to rise sharply."

"No shit," Mars hissed, "the damn man's a great politician if nothing else."

"Friends," Kelly continued, "I worked side by side with Albert Lotte and I knew Carmen and Dena almost as well. The Lotte's were law abiding citizens and they were model Americans." She paused and wiped a tear from her eye, "Dena was a beautiful young woman. You know, I have a picture on my desk of Dena when she was ten. In the picture she is sitting behind my desk with an ear to ear grin across her face. She told me she wanted to become the Attorney General some day. In short, she was telling me that she wanted my job," Kelly laughed.

The crowd laughed along with her.

Again, Kelly wiped away the tears forming in her eyes, "and I wanted her to have it. I wanted her to have the chance to grow up and become what she had dreamed about; not have that dream stolen from her by a thoughtless act of violence."

The crowd chanted, "Dena! Dena! Dena!"

Attorney General Kelly raised her hands to quiet the crowd. "A great injustice has happened. An injustice, not just against the Lottes or Dena, but against all of you!" she said, pointing out into the crowd. "Against every law abiding citizen of this great country who believes their homes should not be violated in the middle of the night." The crowd broke into applause and whistling.

"Have we located Albert and Carmen Lotte?" Kinsley asked, her eyes glued to the viewer.

"The whereabouts of Albert and Carmen Lotte are still unknown," Sapphire supplied.

"They were turned over to agents of the Secret Service a few hours after the incident," Mars said. "The Lottes and the agents never made it to Government Plaza."

"They were kidnapped?" Pyrs asked incredulously.

"Evidently so," Mars answered. "The Justice Department said they hadn't sent anyone over to pick them up, and had never heard of the two agents that signed for their release."

"This is damn unbelievable!" Pyrs said, turning

his attention back to the broadcast.

Attorney General Kelly stepped back from the microphones and allowed President Ziven to move forward.

"Excuse me, Ms. Tansy," Sapphire started.

"Stop!" Mars ordered keeping her eyes on the President.

"I have a priority mess…"

"I said stop!" she ordered again. "I want to hear this."

All three of the members of the Executive Council moved forward several inches in their chairs as if they were not going to be able to hear clearly from the previous positions.

President Ziven stood in front of the microphones and looked out onto the crowd. "I stand here today not only as your President, but as a concerned citizen. And, he added in a solemn tone, a friend and co-worker of Albert Lotte. We will get to the bottom of this and we will find the person or persons responsible."

The crowd rallied to his words. Ziven held his hand into the air. "What I ask of each of you today is for your patience. Patience while we get to the bottom of this. Give us the chance to bring these people to justice." He took several steps away from the microphone while waving to the masses. "God bless America!" he yelled as he and the others walked into the front door of the Administration office.

"That investigation," Pyrs said, jabbing his finger at the table in front of him, "is going to lead right back to this council."

"It will lead," Mars insisted, "back to Commander Adelric and the Attorney General's office. I can promise you that much."

"Councilmen," Sapphire interjected, after the allotted time delay prescribed within her protocol, "the priority message, shall I relay it?"

"Relay, the message," Kinsley huffed.

"Eleven minutes and forty-two seconds ago, Commander Adelric was shot by an unknown assailant outside this building. He has been rushed to Core Central Hospital. His current condition is unknown at this time."

CHAPTER 24

ANGEL OR DEMON

Commander Adelric lay in the hospital bed, his head and neck stabilized by a plastic brace system that was constantly monitored and adjusted for maximum efficiency. His vital signs were taken and scrutinized by the latest technology available. The left side of his head and neck showed signs of massive bruising, his left eyes still swollen partially shut. He wasn't sure if his jaw had been broken or for that matter, if he still had a jaw. Then he remembered being informed by the doctors that he had been placed on a sedation drip that would keep his muscles in a calm and restful status. Of course, he had also been told that it would keep him in a condition of drowsiness.

The bed had been adjusted slightly to allow his

head to be higher than the rest of his body. From that position, if he moved his eyes to the right, he could see through the small window in the door, the heads of the two SFC guards stationed outside. *I'm not sure if that is one guard or two*, he thought, *my vision is so blurred that I could be seeing double. But then, if there were two guards wouldn't I be seeing four?* Something deep in his subconscious told him it wasn't important and to let it go. Listening to the feeling, he closed his eyes and felt his body become lighter, his thoughts carefree.

"Hello, Commander," the tiny voice said softly.

Adelric smiled without opening his eyes. The nurse had come in two or three times already to check on him. She was a lavishly endowed woman with a thick sultry voice. He frowned when he thought of her cool, *No*, he thought, *clammy hands.*

"Are you awake, Commander," she asked.

The gentle soft nature of her voice tended to make him drowsier. "Yes," he slurred remembering her question but still not opening his eyes.

"Good," she said, "I thought it was time that you and I should talk. You're very lucky that bullet only grazed the side of your helmet. Another inch to the right and it would have taken your head off."

Adelric resisted the urge to open his eyes. "Yesss" he slurred, "lucky." He remembered her question, "Talk?" he asked.

"Yes, talk. Wouldn't you like to talk face to face with a Guardian?" she asked.

"A Guardian," he grinned, "talk to a Guardian?"

"If you would like," she cooed.

Adelric attempted to open his eyes. He had to blink several times to clear his vision enough to focus on the woman standing over him. *She's beautiful*, was his first thought as he took in her pure, innocent appearance. Then a moment of clarity reminded him of her status. "You're not supposed to be here," he heard himself say. "You're..." he struggled through the fog searching for the right word, "enemy."

"I'm not your enemy, Martin," she assured him, "you know who the real enemy is."

Adelric watched as her angelic face turned into the hard, pitch black image of a Raven's head, its shimmering black marble eyes almost devouring him. His eyes widened at the sight of the animal. "Raven!" he screamed glancing over to the guards that were still stationed outside his room. "Raven!" he shouted again wondering why they were ignoring his alarm.

"They can't hear you, Commander," she assured him. "In your present condition I can barely hear you."

Beads of sweat materialized on his forehead and began trickling down his cheeks. He focused on the two guards trying to will their attention in his direction. "Raven," he whispered hoarsely.

"Commander?" she said.

He slowly turned his gaze back in the direction of the woman. He relaxed when she appeared to be the cherub he had seen before. "Raven," he slowly said hoping she would not transform to the horrible creature again.

"Yes," she nodded, "the Raven is the true enemy."

"Raven," he repeated not blinking.

"But," she frowned, "why does the Raven want to harm us and now you?"

"Raven," he said, swallowing hard. "Marci…" He closed his eyes and drifted off into a dreamless sleep.

Mars stepped off the elevator and walked over to the nurse's station. "Where is Commander Adelric's room?" she asked the young lady behind the desk.

The nurse looked up at Mars and smiled. It was obvious that she did not recognize Mars. She pointed to the right. "He's down that hall, but he's not allowed visitors."

Mars looked down the hall in the direction the nurse had pointed. The large double doors to the wing were closed. Standing in front of each of the doors was an armed CSF solider, their rifles held at a 45 degree angle across their bodies. "He'll see me," Mars said, with a condescending smile pasted across her face.

Mars turned and for the benefit of the nurse, marched down the hall with an arrogant feline grace. She continued her graceful stride until the two guards stepped forward and blocked her path.

"I'm here to see Commander Adelric," she explained.

"Sorry," the guard to her right stated, "no one is allowed in to see the Commander."

Mars managed a thin smile, "It's alright solider," she said pressing forward, "I'm Councilman Tansy."

The two guards stepped together, their huge shoulders touching. Mars' nose was just inches from their chest when she stopped. "Sorry, Ms. Tansy," the guard said firmly, "*no one* is allowed in."

The idea of retreating even one step infuriated her, but their current positions would force her to look up at the guard's face. She had no intention of being dominated by the man. Mars took the one step backwards needed to look the guard in the eyes once again. She held up her PD in front of his face.

"Councilman Marcy Tansy," Sapphire stated through the device while showing Mars photo on the screen, "Chairperson of the Core Council. Security clearance; Level five."

Mars locked eyes with the guard. "Now move," she commanded.

Neither guard budged an inch. "Sorry, my orders still stand," the man said calmly.

The left door behind the guard slowly swung outward and an officer that Mars had never seen before stepped into the hallway. He was a good-looking young man in his late twenties.

Mars gave him her best flirtatious smile. "Finally, "she said softly, "someone with a brain bigger than a bullet. I'm here to see Commander Adelric. I'm Ms. Tan…"

"Yes, Ms. Tansy," he interrupted in a commanding, but not unpleasant voice, "I know who you are, but no one is allowed to see the Commander at this time."

"I am the Chairmen of the …"

"Core Council," he finished for her, "you are not allowed in."

The door behind the officer opened a second time. Attorney General Kelly stepped through the opening and round the group not bothering to stop. "Thank you Lieutenant," Kelly said over her shoulder as she moved toward the nurse's station.

Mars' eyes blazed murderously at the young officer, her finger nails pressing into the palms of her hands. *I'll be damned*, she fumed inwardly, *if I'm going to ask that Bitch for permission to enter.* She held her PD up one more time as she heard the light hearted chatter and laughter coming from the nurse's station. "You understand, Lieutenant," she spat, "that this infraction is being recorded?"

The chime on the elevator rang and the doors slid open. "Thanks again, Lieutenant," Kelly said, almost gleefully as she entered the car.

The Lieutenant smiled in Attorney General Kelly's direction and then his face hardened as he returned his gaze to Mars, "I understand," he said politely pointing to the cameras in the ceiling, "but if you don't leave now, I will have you forcibly removed."

As if on cue, the two guards stepped back and charged their weapons. The harsh metallic sound of the bolts chambering rounds caused Mars to jump. Without a further word she pivoted on her heels and marched toward the elevator. It seemed like an eternity as she waited for the elevator to answer her call. Mars gazed back at the entrance to the hall.

The young officer had returned to the ward. The two security guards were once again standing in front of each door as if nothing had happened.

The chime rang and the doors opened. Mars stormed into the car, spun on her heels and smashed the button.

"Have a nice day," the nurse said cheerfully, as the two doors closed in front of Mars' face.

Jax lay on his back staring at the blank ceiling. It had taken the team eight days to return to District One from the mission. Six of the days were spent hiding in the basement of a bakery while CSF troops swarmed the city like a hive of angry bees. Informants had told them that road blocks were everywhere, searching every vehicle that passed through. No one got through without a thorough check of their PD's. Since the three of them were traveling without devices they figured they would probably have been shot on site.

They did have access to the Netnews broadcast and had watched the reruns of President Ziven and Attorney General Kelly's address to the crowds at the university. They were not surprised when nothing was mentioned about the sniper attack on Commander Adelric.

It was also interesting to note that several of the small netcams were running stories on the

Lottes', especially Dena's life story. According to the reports, the Lottes' were still officially missing and therefore unavailable for comment. This fueled the controversy surrounding the circumstances of their disappearance. Of special note was the fact that the main netcam stations controlled by Sapphire were running other news stories. If one were to watch only these stations, they would have no knowledge of who Dena Lotte was, let alone the circumstances surrounding her death.

Jax heard Rebecca enter his room. She walked very softly but he could still hear her movement. He didn't take his eyes off the ceiling. "Hey, Rebecca, what's up?"

When she didn't answer he glanced in her direction. Immediately he knew something was wrong. The silhouette of the woman standing in the dark was not Rebecca's. He tensed ready to defend himself as he assessed the stranger. Rebecca's body was sleeker, he thought, rock hard from her constant physical training. This person, while still showing athletic features, was more curvaceous. Her long legs, he noticed, were iron-muscled but erotic.

"Hello, Jax," she said softly. "Miss me?"

"Emily?" he said, after a moment's hesitation.

The figure slowly reached over to the small lamp on the table. With a muffled click, the lamp partially illuminated the room with an uneven pastel glow. McKee was dressed in a one-piece non-military black jumpsuit; the zipper running down the middle of the garment was pulled all the way up to her collar. Jax noticed that the jumpsuit did nothing to hide the sensuous curves of her breasts and hips.

"Why…why are you here?" he stammered, trying to regain his composure.

The cobalt color within her eyes seemed to glow iridescently at the question. She took one step forward, her hand reaching up grasping the zipper. Slowly she pulled downward. The two halves of the jumpsuit parted easily as the zipper glided downward. "I was hoping you were going to ask that," she answered with malicious delight.

Jax eyes were frozen on her. The zipper stopped at the end of its track just below her waist. With one smooth motion, the two halves dropped away from her shoulders exposing her bare breasts. A slight shift of her weight from one side to the other caused the jumpsuit to fall to the floor.

Jax's eyes took in the small pair of black panties, the waistband resting precariously on her hips. "I don't think those are regulation," he said, the excitement obvious in his voice.

She gazed at him candidly, "There are some things I refuse to go military on." She leaned back to the light and turned it off. He watched her silhouette, outlined by the light entering through the window, as she removed her panties.

In a single motion Emily stepped up to the bed, pulled the covers up and slid in next to Jax. The scent of her skin, coupled with the warmth of her body, sent previously suppressed urges racing through his body. "I don't think this is a good idea," he whispered.

Emily's body pressed against his, her hand followed the lines of his abdomen down to his crotch. A moan escaped his lips as she took a firm hold of him. "I think parts of you agree with me," she almost breathed into his mouth.

His lips met hers, a molten fire ignited when they touched. The kiss was long and lustful. He pulled her closer. "You have a demon inside you woman," he whispered.

She gently kissed the lower lobe of his ear. "If not now," she said softly, I will have shortly."

Jax woke with a start. He reached over searching for Emily. The movement of the sheet stirred the air, wafting traces of her scent. The bed was empty. He scanned the room for her presence but all evidence of her was gone. He got up and stumbled into the bathroom and within seconds was standing under the warm spray of the shower. Minutes later he was making his way toward the kitchen stove. Passing the kitchen table he scooped up a mug deciding that coffee, not tea was needed.

He plodded down the stairs toward his desk, his head still filled with the memory of he and Emily's evening together.

"Good morning, Jax," Emily said, greeting him from behind his own desk.

She had changed clothes and was now dressed in the camouflage shirt and pants of the Special Forces troops. He imagined the black panties or something similarly provocative under her cotton utilities. He took a deep pull on his coffee trying to drown out the thought.

"Have a seat, Captain," she said.

Reality settled in. Any remaining erotic thoughts were pushed to a far corner of his brain. "Morning," he said, as he took a seat, wondering if his mission was coming to an end. After all, McKee's presence certainly represented the start of phase three. "I guess I'm relieved," he said stating the inevitable.

"At least twice," she beamed fondly, "the way I remember it anyhow."

Jax felt the heat spread across his face. "That's not what I meant," he said, "and you know it."

Her head titled slightly to one side. "Why would I relieve one of my best field officers?" she asked.

He shrugged his shoulders, "I figured my work was done," he offered. "Aren't you here to start the next phase of the operation?"

"If I am; does that mean your job is finished?"

"Well," he responded, "I stirred the pot up for you like you asked. I understand that the Government and Core Council's approval ratings are at a record low."

McKee leaned forward on her elbows. "I didn't say I wanted the pot to boil," she reminded him. "I said I wanted it to boil over; blow its lid."

Jax nodded his head in understanding, "OK, we'll continue to stir things up until you get what you asked for," he answered. "By the way, when did you get here?"

"Four days ago," she offered.

Jax's ego was slightly bruised when he discovered that he wasn't the first stop after she arrived.

"That tip you gave us on the missile silos was correct. We've located two of the Trust silos outside the perimeter fence. It was just a matter of repelling down through the debris and getting the inner silos doors open to gain access to the complex. Now our troops are able to enter in larger numbers."

"How did you know they weren't the real thing?" he asked. "You could have opened one of those things and had a live missile staring you in the face."

Her eyebrow went up, "The nuclear missile silos were decommissioned in the late 1990's and early 2000's" she reminded him, "The missiles were removed and dismantled. The sites were imploded. Therefore any remaining sites had a good chance of being part of the Trust's secret launch system," she stated. "Didn't you cover that in your history classes?"

"Can't say that I remember going over that material in my *Political Science* history classes, but I could have skipped that lecture," he offered.

"One funny story," she continued. "We did come across one of the original silos that had been converted into a private home."

"Really," he laughed, "what happened."

She shrugged her shoulders, "Nobody home," she smiled.

"Tell me about Commander Adelric," she asked, becoming serious again. "You had to have titanium balls to make that head shot."

Jax wasn't sure if that was a compliment or a reprimand. "I was told to scare the shit out of the man," he said, "I thought the shot I took was up to me."

McKee studied his face for several seconds. "If that had been me; I would have gone for a shoulder shot."

A reprimand? he asked himself. Jax shook his head, "A shot to the shoulder could have killed him. That type of shock to the body could have caused more damage than anticipated. I could have caused serious damage to any number of internal organs. He could have bled out before they got him to a hospital."

McKee nodded her head as she thought through his answer. "I bullet to an arm would have sufficed. Your choice could have blown his head clear off his shoulders," she offered.

"If I could hit him in the arm; I could have grazed his helmet," he replied. "Besides, in their mind there is no doubt that someone was trying to kill him, not just wound him. Isn't that what you were after?"

McKee nodded her affirmation, "Like I said, titanium balls, Jax. Good job!"

Phil knocked on the wall adjacent to the staircase. "May I come in Colonel?"

McKee looked over Jax's head, "Hey Phil, come on down, glad you stopped in. You saved me the troubles of having someone find you."

Phil walked in and patted Jax on the shoulder as he sat down. "Thanks, Colonel," he said, "Rebecca told me you where here so I thought I'd report in."

"Excellent," she beamed, "I was just about finished lavishing Jax here with compliments so I should just continue with you. Your work with the multimedia presentation of the Guardians is outstanding!"

"Well," he said blushing, "it was Jax's idea. I just followed through."

Jax nudged him with his elbow, "Take your compliments where you can get them," he offered.

McKee grinned, "Jax is right. Never give up a compliment when you've earned it. You and your group have spliced together a technological masterpiece. I want to hear about the hospital. Damn, an interactive holo with the man?"

Phil beamed, "We had help from some of our people in the hospital," he began. "We rigged some of our equipment into the medical scanners that were placed in his room. Then in a different area of the hospital we were able to monitor his condition. From the same room we were able to dress Donna up as the Guardian leader, project her image through the equipment and have a two way conversation with the Commander. The Raven was a 3D photo character super imposed onto the Guardian image. "

"Crap!" she laughed, "do you think he caught on?"

Phil shook his head, "The man was so doped up he didn't know which end was up. One of the nurses working the floor told us that he never mentioned it to anyone, not even his private doctor. But the next morning he gave orders to his troops that no one was allowed into see him."

"Excellent," she beamed. "You guys have done well."

Jax looked over at Phil, "The boss wants us to turn up the heat."

"Really?" Phil asked, looking at McKee.

"Yep," she answered, "I want the shit to really hit the fan. You're to push it to the brink."

"What about Ziven and his merry band of misfits?" Jax asked.

McKee gave the two of them a stern look. "He is no longer your concern," she answered flatly. "Don't go out of your way to involve them, but don't cut them any slack either."

"I'm glad you said that," Jax answered. "The Council and the Government are still tied at the hip as far as the people are concerned."

"They'll be at each other's throats soon enough," McKee stated.

"Do you think the Council is part of the Trust?" Phil asked.

Jax noticed that McKee stiffened at the mention of the Trust. She seemed to be lost in thought for several seconds.

"You don't have to answer," Phil said, worried that she may chew him a new ass for asking about the Trust.

"No, it's alright," she stated, "I was trying to go through it in my own mind for the thousandth time. "It's a complex answer," she started. "Our guys in the think tank back home have run dozens of scenarios and it boils down to a few educated guesses. From what Jax and Rebecca have told us about their meeting with Ziven; it is uncharacteristic of this Trust to openly take such a position of obvious power. It seems that in the past they have been happy to manipulate things from behind the scene and that might be exactly what they're doing now."

"That would be bad for us," Jax offered. "We would have no idea who these people were."

"Correct," she answered. "If that's the case, we're taking shots at the puppet and not the puppeteer."

"It would be like pulling up a weed, but not killing the root," Phil offered. "They could just sprout up again at another time."

"Exactly," she said, "but they had twenty years to reformulate their game plan while in those bunkers. Maybe, with their ability to limit the outside influences and therefore, a majority of the variables, they felt comfortable with stepping into the driver's seat."

"Then," Jax said, "I think we better discover how deep the roots are before we pinch off their head."

"And that," she said smiling mischievously, "is what the next part of your operation is."

Jax frowned at the comment. "I thought we were to continue turning up the heat?"

"Absolutely," she agreed, "but what I'm hoping is that when you're doing, that the Trust will tip their hand. We have to destroy their hold on the country or all of this is for nothing."

Mars stepped off the elevator onto the 21st floor. A savvy looking Major was waiting for her.

"Good morning, Ms. Tansy," he stated, "Commander Adelric is sorry that he couldn't meet you personally, but he has sent me in his stead; I hope you don't mind."

"Not at all," she smiled thinly, "how is the Commander doing?"

"It's his first day back in the office so we in his senior staff are making sure he's taking it easy."

"Totally understandable," she said, stepping in line with the Major, "I won't take up much of his time," she said graciously.

"Thank you for the consideration."

Mars followed the man through the usual maze of corridors until they came to an unmarked door.

"He's waiting inside," the Major said, opening the door for her.

If it wasn't the same room they had met in the last time, it was one very similar. She observed that once again, there were two large leather chairs with a small table between them. Mars noticed that there were two items on the table. One was a single glass of ice water and the other an CSF combat helmet.

"Come in Ms. Tansy," Adelric said in a very friendly tone. "Please excuse me for not standing, you understand."

"Of course I do," she said, taking the chair opposite him. "How are you feeling?"

Adelric still wore a lighter version of the neck brace he had been given in the hospital. Mars noticed that the bruising was fading but was still quite large.

"I feel like an old man," he smiled "but the doctors say I'm healing nicely."

"Good, good," she said pointing to his eye. "That's still a hell of a black eye though."

"I know," he grinned, "thankfully it looks a hell of a lot worse then it feels."

"Martin," she said compassionately, "I tried to visit you in the hospital."

"I know Marci, thank you, but please understand the circumstances at the time. Until my staff felt that I was out of danger, they wouldn't let anyone in."

"And, Kelly?" she asked, not even trying to hide her feelings for the woman.

"I heard she had come to see me," he laughed, "but I was so out of it they tell me I didn't recognize her."

"How did she get past those two bruisers you had stationed at the door?"

"I'm told she bullied her way past them," he answered. "When Major Thoren saw her enter the room he stepped out into the hallway and chewed the young lieutenant's ass within an inch of his life."

Mars nodded her understanding, "So, I walk in the door after Kelly stirred up the hornet's nest and I'm the one that gets stung," she laughed.

"Sorry about that," Adelric apologized.

"No problem," she said, pointing to the helmet on the table, "are they making you wear that thing?

Adelric grinned as he slowly picked up the combat helmet. He turned it 180 degrees so that she could see the left side. There was a four inch gash sliced into the side of the armor plating. "I was lucky that I didn't have my chinstrap fastened," he said letting her take the helmet from him. "It could have torn my head off when it went flying."

Mars studied the narrow gash for several seconds before placing it back on the table. "Any leads to who the perpetrators were?"

"Not really," he sighed, "what was recovered of the round indicates it was probably from one of our own sniper rifles; almost certainly stolen from the armory."

Mars nodded her understanding. "Martin, we have to get our hands around this situation." The numbers are starting to show that the President is gaining in popularity. He made another public appearance this morning."

"Another campus speech?" Adelric asked.

"I wish," she sighed. "He was seen in Old Town today, walking down the street shaking hands with everyone. You would think he was back on the campaign trail running for office."

"Maybe he is," Adelric said thoughtfully. "He may be drumming up support among the people to distance himself from the Council."

"Why would he do that?"

"Someone is going to take the hit for everything that's happening," he said, as he worked through the issues. "This isn't going to stop until the Raven and or the Guardians are gone." He raised his finger into the air, "and this Dena Lotte thing isn't over. The President has promised to get to the bottom of the incident."

"What if he doesn't?" Mars asked.

"What?"

"What if *we* get to the bottom of the incident? What if *we* are the ones to discover what truly happened that night?"

Adelric's lip curled upward, "Marci, we ordered that raid, don't you remember."

"I know who ordered it," she hissed, "but what if your man admits he went against orders?"

"You want me to string up one of my own men?" he asked incredulously. "And if I were to do that, which I won't, we still raided the wrong house."

"The raid part won't be as big of a problem as you think," she said. "We'll offer the Lottes' credit compensation. The amount will be large enough to please the crowds, I'm sure. Besides, they would have to reappear to claim it."

"There's still the issue of my man."

"I have a way to handle that also," she smiled wickedly.

Ziven sat with his top aides after spending the morning on a Flash Netcast. He had generously given his time to the small time reporter once again avoiding the censorship Sapphire had imposed on government broadcasts. The reporter wasn't as prepared as Ziven would have liked but he did manage to hit all of the bullet points he and Lars had identified as top priority. They were watching it for the third time, dissecting the interview for areas of weakness and discussing how to make future broadcasts more effective.

"I wonder how much longer Sapphire is going to allow us to get away with this?" he asked the group.

"I'm sure they're losing sleep over the issue," Lars said, "we're just going to have to make the best of it until they figure out a way to keep the Flash reporters off the net."

"I'm monitoring that very scenario," Kelly stated. "We're ready to file injunctions to block the Council when they try."

Ryan entered the office at a fast clip. "You guys are going to want to watch this," he said, activating the main net viewer.

The screen quickly flickered to life showing a close up of Tansy. She was flanked by a group of staffers on either side. She smiled to the audience. "I have several pieces of information to share with you today," she said. "The first involves the Council's decision to step forward and help our community in a time of need. We have unanimously agreed that compensation in the amount of One Million credits be remunerated to the Lotte family for the pain they sustained when the rebel group known as the Raven, tricked our forces into mistakenly entering the wrong home in pursuit of them." Mars held up her hands, "I know this can never make up for the loss of their lovely daughter, but we felt it was something we can do and should do."

The camera angle switched to show Tansy from a different direction. "Also in honor of Dean Lotte, the Council has authorized the creation of the Dena Lotte Scholarship Fund not just for Core Central University, but in all Universities across all districts. This scholarship will be used to help young freshman students defray some of their first year costs, helping them achieve a goal that young Dena was tragically kept from accomplishing.

"Son of a Bitch," Lars said, throwing a handful of papers down on the desk.

"Quiet," Ziven ordered not taking his eyes off the view screen, "the other shoe is about to drop."

Mars' expression became solemn as if she had heard Ziven's comment. "In a matter connected to this travesty, Commander Adelric and our legal group have been involved in thorough investigation of the terrible mishap that caused Dena's death." The view changed again. "After the initial portion of our investigation, one of the CSF troopers was called in for questioning. His name is Trooper John Manning. It was believed that Trooper Manning was the solider that, without orders, fired the shots that killed Dena. When the trooper failed to show up at CSF headquarters for the questioning; an officer was dispatched to his home."

Mars paused for several seconds as if pained to go on.

"Here it comes," Ziven commented.

"Sadly, upon arriving at the trooper's home it was discovered that the man had taken his own life." Tansy held up a memory wheel. "He left this recording behind." Again she paused, "I have been authorized to show you a small portion of the file." Mars nodded to someone off screen. Her image faded and was replaced with the video.

A young man dressed in a mussed CSF uniform entered the picture and sat on a chair facing the camera. It was obvious that he hadn't slept in several days and from the plastic bottle of liquor in his hand, he had been drinking heavily. "I would just like to say," he started staring towards the camera, "that I am so sorry for what happened to that young girl, Dena. I've gone over it in my head for days now and can honestly say that I was…scared and wasn't thinking. When the young woman ran down the stairs toward me I…I just…panicked. I don't remember pulling the trigger. I don't remember why… I did that. Like I said, I was just scared. The rebels had been killing troopers, some of them were my friends and… I just didn't want to die." He placed the liquor bottle down on the floor out of camera range. When his hand came back into view he was holding a pistol. "I am so sorry, "he said, as he put the gun to the side of his head.

The video went blank and the screen stayed

blank for several seconds. When it came back on it caught Ms. Tansy in a very vulnerable moment. She was wiping hers eyes on a tissue. "It's OK, it's OK," she sniffled not knowing the camera was on again, "I have to go back on."

Mars straightened her jacket and stood erect. She handed the tissue to an aid. "OK," she almost whispered, "put me back on."

"You are on," said the voice of the cameraman.

"I'm sorry," she started slowly, "to have to show that to you, but I believed you all deserved the truth." She smiled weakly. "Now is a time of healing for us all," she said gaining strength as she spoke. "Now is a time for us to stand united against these rebels and send them back to the hell they came from. I ask you to stand with your Core Council and regain our freedom, as it was before they came here and killed our troops, bombed our citizens and…killed a wonderful young woman." Tears ran down her check, "Thank you for allowing me into your homes." The staff behind her broke into applause and cheers. The screen faded.

Kelly jumped up and started out the door. "Where are you going?" Ziven shouted after her.

Kelly made a beeline for the outer door. "I'm going over there and kill that Bitch myself!" she yelled.

Ziven quickly picked up the phone and punched a speed number. "Yes," he said into the phone, "Please do not let Mrs. Kelly leave the building." There was a short pause, "No," he said, "She is not to be harmed in any way. Let me know when you have her." There was another pause, "Thank you."

Jax, Rebecca and McKee watched in silence as Ms. Tansy faded from the view screen. Jax pushed the off control and the screen went blank.

"That's not going to help us turn up the heat, "Rebecca said, as she stood and stretched.

"That wasn't Trooper Manning either," McKee said.

"How do you know?" Jax asked, trying to figure out how she knew that.

McKee followed Rebecca's lead and stood to stretch. Jax noticed that her utility shirt move upward exposing her belly. *Christ*, he though feeling the urge tingling in his crotch area, *not now, please.*

McKee retook her seat placing her face into her hands and rubbing, "That wasn't Trooper Manning because it was actually Sergeant Mike Fadin, second platoon, 87th Raider Group." She looked over at Jax.

"He was sent on a reconnaissance mission three weeks ago. He never returned to his unit. We've been carrying him as missing in action for a week now."

"What was he doing dressed up in a CSF uniform?" Rebecca asked.

"My guess," McKee said, "is that he was drugged and forced to act out that little charade we just watched."

"He did look very drunk," Jax admitted.

"Didn't drink," McKee said.

"What?"

"He didn't drink," McKee repeated. "No drinking or drugs. He was as straight as they come."

Rebecca took her seat. "They drugged him and made him say all that stuff?"

McKee nodded, "We don't know what type of physiological drugs they may have," she offered. "Hell, for all we know, the poor man believed he was Trooper Manning and that he actually killed the Lotte girl. No one can say."

"Hit the replay," Rebecca told Jax.

The video came to life. The three sat in silence as they watched the entire broad cast a second time.

It was more painful, Jax thought, *knowing it was one of their men.*

"Jax, restart the video from the beginning of Fadin's confession, "McKee asked.

Jax repositioned the video back to the section McKee had asked for. Again, they watched in silence.

"Slow it down," she commanded. Jax fumbled with the controller for a second before he managed to push the right button.

"There," she said pointing to the screen, "see how he pauses looking off screen for a split second."

"Yes," they answered in unison.

"It's like he's taking his cue off a teleprompter. Can you enlarge the picture?"

Jax pushed the button once and the image zoomed in one level. He pushed it a second time and the man's' face filled the screen.

"Look at his eyes," McKee prompted. "Look at the size of his pupils, see how they're dilated?"

Jax looked closely at the image on the screen. "So they shot him up with something and convinced him he was someone else?"

McKee stood and began walking around the

room. "I don't know. Like I said, there are drugs out there that under the right conditions could make Fadin do what we saw."

"We didn't actually see him pull the trigger," Rebecca offered. "Maybe he's still alive."

"Doubtful." McKee sighed, "he was no longer any good to them the minute they finished that recording."

Jax replayed the recording in his head, "I can't believe they have drugs that could do that."

"Believe it." McKee stated, "Remember the PD you sent back for analysis? "

"Sure."

"Our medical personnel confirmed that there was a chemical encapsulated within the device that could be released through the porous protective case around the PD. Once activated the chemical would be picked up by the owner's hands. It was only a matter of time before the chemical would cause sterilization in the man or woman holding the case."

"Wouldn't the owner notice this goo leaking out of their PD?" Rebecca asked.

"Doubtful, the pores are microscopic. The carrier wouldn't even be aware."

Jax stood and approached McKee, "That would be a type of selective genocide! Which couples can have children is none of their concern!" He unconsciously locked eyes with Emily as thoughts of having a child with her filled his head.

The momentary glance from him did not go unnoticed. The rims of Emily's eyes moistened as she acknowledged his thoughts with a demure smile. "Yes," she said clearing her throat, "but remember, in their minds they are doing it for self-preservation, culling out the weakest. "

"Bastards!" Rebecca almost cried.

Jax turned his attention toward her. Several tears had carved their way down her cheeks. "*This can't be allowed,* he thought, *women just like Rebecca and Emily will never know what was stolen from them.* "Won't people begin to figure this out?"

"They'll just blame it on the virus. It's an old excuse, but still a good one." McKee stated.

Jax headed for the staircase. "Excuse me, but I've got some work to do."

"What one, Jax." McKee ordered as she turned to Rebecca. "Rebecca please find Phil and Chris. Tell them I would like to see them as soon as possible." She turned to Jax. "I need a few more minutes of your time," she stated flatly.

Jax and McKee watched as Rebecca headed up

the stairs. McKee waited until she was gone before turning to Jax. "I will be leaving in a few days," she informed him. "I will be out in the field for quite some time," she said, as she moved closer to him. "So, I would like to spend as much…personal time with you as I can." Her voice softened, "if that's alright with you."

Jax smiled innocently, "You didn't ask last night," he said placing the palm of his hand gently on her check.

She leaned into his touch, her eyes becoming radiant blue pools of affection. "Last night was last night," she whispered moving closer. "Now, I would like to explore deeper possibilities…together."

Jax touched her lips lightly with his. "Together sounds very nice," he whispered into her mouth as he gave her a second, more passionate kiss.

Jax lay on his back, his hands locked behind his head. He had been staring at the blank ceiling for some time. Peter, Phil, Rebecca and he had worked out some interesting possibilities for blowing the lid off. None of the plans were foolproof and the danger with all of them was much higher than he liked.

Emily stirred next to him. She inched closer,

resting her head on his shoulder. "Didn't I wear you out?" she whispered softly.

He lowered his arm around her. She moved even closer placing her hand across his chest. He stroked the side of her breasts gently. "Yes," he answered, "but I still can't sleep," he admitted. "Too much on my mind I guess."

She reached up and tenderly kissed his cheek knowing what was bothering him. "You have a great team," she told him. "They'll pull everything together."

"Thank you for that, by the way."

"For what?"

"For assigning such great people to my team."

She squeezed him lightly around the chest, "Well," she yawned, "for someone who doesn't play well with others, you've certainly earned their respect."

Jax looked down at her, "How do you know that?" he asked. "Have they told you that?"

Emily rocked her head back and forth on his chest, "Nope, they didn't have to. I can tell by the way you guys interact. You have a solid team."

Jax looked back up at the ceiling. "I never gave it much thought," he admitted. "Emily?"

"Yes."

"Have you ever thought what will happen if we should win?" he asked.

"Not really," she said, "I've spent most of my energy just trying to end this civil war, not worrying about how the wounds will be healed…figured that would be someone else's job."

"Civil war? Is that how you see it?"

She lightly ran her fingers through the hair on his chest, "You're the Political Scientist. What would you call the fighting between factions of a single nation divided by differences in ideology?"

Jax was silent for several minutes as he pondered Emily's question.

"You fall asleep?" she whispered.

"No," he answered, "I can't believe that possibility went right over my head. I grew up in Middle-earth thinking that it was my home, my country. I didn't see the bigger picture of our living in a region of the same country."

"Interesting," she yawned, "why do you think they call us rebels?"

"That's just it," he said, "we didn't rebel, we were forced out."

"Because we rebelled against their rules," she

reminded him. "Jax, sweetheart."

"Yes?"

"Please shut up and go to sleep."

CHAPTER 25

TIGHTENING THE NOOSE

The molecular model of the synthetic compound discovered hidden within the PD's was slowly rotating an inch above the Guardian's hand. To the untrained eye the multicolored spheres could be considered beautiful or even artistic, but to someone understanding the chemistry, it was deadly.

"Your Core Council," the Guardian said, "several years ago concluded that the decision to bare children should no longer be left up to you, the parents. They decided that this was just one more freedom that you didn't need" she continued, holding out the model. "So, they unilaterally took it away from you by giving you the new PDs laced with this substance. They didn't bother telling you this because they consider you infants; too child-like to make up your own minds."

Sixty-seven Flash reporters had received the video recording that was now being simultaneously played across the country. Every non-Sapphire controlled method of broadcasting the video was being used. Jax and his small group had spent the last few weeks meeting individually with the reporters and allowing them to view the video. Many of the reporters, not taking Jax and the others at their word, began researching the story on their own. A number of the new PD's had been pried open revealing the encapsulated chemical. The word began to spread through a weakly constructed underground network set up by the Flash reporters; a network that included a large number of young people willing to be tested for sterility.

Of the young people tested, all were currently attempting to become pregnant and had so far been unsuccessful. Of those tested, eighty six percent of them had been among the first groups to receive the new PD's almost a year ago. It was discovered that in every case where a new PD had been issued, either the male or female's capsules located inside the personal devices had been ruptured and were now empty. It was also discovered that all of the members of this group had experienced problems with their new PD's and had been issued replacements; replacements that had inoculated each of the owners with a second dose of the agent. In a smaller number of participants, the couples were now on their third new device.

The molecular model faded from the palm of the Guardian. She opened her arms to the audience. "When we discovered this terrible news we began sharing it with others. They in turn, did their own research which confirmed our conclusions. The Core Council through Dr. Ned Grady, Director of Core Systems Medical Network and Ms. Marci Tansy, Director of Sapphire Systems, has co-conspired to inflict this genocide upon you, their own citizens."

"The same Core Council," she continued, "that recently tried to buy your loyalty with the credit programs they offered to purchase their way out of what they did to Dena Lotte. The Angelic face of the Guardian twisted in pain. "One can only wonder" she said, her voice raising an octave, "if sterility was in Dena's future if they hadn't murdered her."

Adelric sat back in his chair. The signs of fatigue were evident on his face. "Sapphire," he commanded, "replay the security camera video from the Lakeside incident."

The room darkened as the video was started. It was obviously close to sunset when the video was taken. The sky was filled with a purple and amber glow of the early evening. There was still enough light to watch the young woman rapping on the glass of the store. The Council watched as the center manager came to the door and spoke with her.

"On the separate internal store surveillance we were able to pick up parts of their conversation. This young lady was pleading with the manager to let her in to replace her broken PD. The store had just closed." Adelric pointed to the screen, "As you can see, the manger allowed her to enter the shop and issued her the new PD. Sapphire, advance video to the point where the young lady comes out."

Without giving a verbal response, Sapphire advanced the footage to a point where the woman was exiting the building. It could also be noted that the store manager was locking the door behind her.

"Pause video," Adelric commanded. "Split screen, show scenes of the woman entering and exiting the store. Again, Sapphire complied without a verbal response. "Pause second video," he commanded. "Notice anything different?" he asked the other members of the Council.

"She has the box with the new PD under her arm," Kinsley noted.

"Her backpack," Pyrs said pointing to the screen, "she has it going into the store, but it's missing as she leaves."

"Single screen," he ordered. "Start with woman leaving the store; begin play."

The Council watched as the woman once again leaves the store and walks away. Seconds after she is no longer in the scene, the front of the building erupted in a ball of fire temporarily causing the security cameras to shut down in order to protect their delicate light sensors. For several seconds the screen remained blank until the sensors reset and show the wreckage of the store.

"That is the seventh PD store to be either blown up or set on fire in the last several days. Several of the stores have been center points for demonstrations and riots. Over one hundred and eighty people have been arrested," he sighed. "Sapphire, report on the status of civil unrest since the last Guardian broadcast."

"There have been one hundred and sixty-six acts of civil violence since the broadcast. Twenty seven are currently in progress throughout the nine districts."

"How many personal PDs have been destroyed?" he asked.

"To date, 47,476 PD's have been destroyed. That number is of course, being constantly adjusted. 2,296 were destroyed in a single incident involving a riot where the perpetrators started a bonfire. The devices were then ceremoniously thrown into the fire. It may be noted that all of the devices destroyed were not just the new issue units. There is an increase in the number of later models also being destroyed."

Adelric looked toward Mars. "Marci, do you have anything to add?"

Mars' nostrils flared at the thought of Adelric speaking to her as an equal on the Council. *I'll address that with the Executive Council,* she thought, *as soon as this meeting is closed.* "As you already know," she started, "we have shut down every one of the Flash reporters that broadcast the Guardian message."

"Seventeen," Adelric said interrupting her, "have been arrested and are currently being questioned. The others have gone into hiding."

"Correct," she said, "Attorney General Kelly has issued five different restraining orders against the council in reference to our action. She has, as of today, filed two separate lawsuits in the Core Judicial Courts against our actions."

"Isn't there a couple of 'cease-and-desist' orders?" Pyrs asked.

"Yes, but they were turned into the lawsuits when we ignored them," she reminded him.

"Commander," Pyrs asked, "what is happening out in the districts?"

"Civil unrest is growing," he answered. "Every day there are more attacks on the CSF's station out there. I have given my men orders to shoot if they believe their lives are in danger."

"Commander," Mars challenged, "shouldn't you have asked for Councils permission to give that order?"

Adelric smiled curtly, "May I remind the Chair that the CSF does not answer to this council and that the position I hold here is that of an Associate member. I still report to the Attorney General's Office."

"This council," Mars said bluntly, "is the source of all your power!"

"This council," Adelric fired back, "is the source of all my headaches. If you would like me to resign my position on the council," he stated smugly, "I'm sure I could find accommodations for myself and my men in Government Plaza."

"Settle down," Kinsley interjected, "we're all under a lot of stress. It will do us no good to start quarreling among ourselves."

Mars bit her tongue, *another time*, she conceded to herself.

"Commander Adelric has brought up a very good point," Kinsley said after order had been reestablished. "I believe we should consider making his position into a full Directorship."

"No!' Mars shouted out. "That is impossible!"

"I believe that it is quite possible," Kinsley stated. "We should vote on it. I motion that we vote on raising the position of Commander of the Core Security to a full Directorship."

"I would like to table the motion," Mars interceded, before the motion could be seconded, "until such time as Dr. Grady is present to vote." She figured it was the only thing she could do to slow down this madness. Given more time she could persuade the other members to vote against such a motion.

"Where is Dr. Grady?" Pyrs asked.

"He's been detained," Mars lied. In fact, she didn't know why the man was late. "Does someone wish to second my motion to table?" she asked, looking toward Pyrs.

Pyrs moved forward in his chair, "I will second the motion to vote on the Directorship for the Commander of CSF."

"We can't vote until Dr. Grady arrives," Mars stated, trying to stall the vote.

"We don't need Dr. Grady here to vote," Kinsley responded.

"The charter clearly states that all members must be present for such a vote." Mars said, "or, in the case of a member's absence, a second must be appointed by that person in their stead. Again, I make a motion to table this vote."

"I think you're mistaken, Marci," Kinsley said. "This is a vote for the Executive Council to make and we are all present."

Mars felt betrayed as the reality set in. *I've been set up*, she cursed to herself, *obviously Kinsley, Pyrs and Adelric have already discussed this matter without me. They all knew going into this meeting that they were going to press this matter to a vote.*

"A second has been made," Kinsley stated for the record. "Sapphire, a vote will now be recorded."

"Yes Councilman Kinsley. On the matter of promoting the Commander of the Core Security Forces to a full Directorship, how do you vote?

Mrs. Iris Kinsley?"

"I vote, yes," she stated clearly.

"Mr. Stephen Pyrs?"

"I vote, yes."

"Ms. Marci Tansy?"

"I abstain," she answered bitterly.

"Ms. Tansy," Sapphire said, "per Council protocol it is my duty to inform you as Chairperson, that a vote to promote the position of Commander of the Core Security Forces to a full directorship has been taken. The final vote of the Executive Council is two in favor of the motion and one abstention."

Mars knew that it was now her duty as Chairperson to confirm the vote and announce that the position was elevated to a full Directorship. Mars rose from her chair and looked around the room. "This meeting is adjourned," she said and walked out of the conference room.

Dr. Ned Grady tapped his driver on the shoulder. "Can't you get around this mess?" he asked.

Protesters had moved in around the vehicles as they marched toward the Central Exchange building. Vehicle traffic had come to a standstill as the crowd continued to march down the street.

"Sorry, Sir," his driver stated, "they've got traffic stopped in all directions, but from the looks of things we will be able to start moving in a few minutes."

Grady had tried to call in to the meeting to tell them he would be late, but the meeting had already started. He knew that it would take a Class Four emergency call to get anyone in the conference room to answer once the meeting started. Using a

Class Four emergency to tell them that he was going to be delayed didn't sit well with him. *They'll figure it out that I'm late when I don't show up,* he mused.

The car slowly started to move as the crowd began to thin out toward the rear of the marchers. Following behind the large group would take forever.

"Steve," he called to his driver, "take a left at the corner."

"Sir that will take us to the north side of the building. We'll have to circle the block to get to the south gate entrance to the underground parking. I just heard that another large group of protesters is approaching from the west. I don't think that will help."

Grady nodded his understanding, "That's OK," he said, "you can let me out at the corner and I can go through the front entrance. It'll be much quicker. If we hurry we'll get there before this damn crowd reaches the steps."

The driver nodded his understanding, turned left and sped down the avenue. Minutes later he quickly pulled to the curb.

"Don't get out," Grady said as the man started to unfasten his seat-belt, "I'll jump out here. You circle around to the parking garage."

The door lock popped to the open position and

Grady slid across the back seat toward the curb. He squeezed out of the back seat and onto the sidewalk. As he headed up the front steps he noticed that a small group of protesters had already arrived. The crowd was holding a multitude of different size signs, mostly hand painted protesting the actions of the council. The crowd seemed disorganized as several different chants were being shouted simultaneously.

Grady started up the long sets of steps leading to the front entrance. At the midway point he was able to look over some of the protesters heads and could look down the central avenue. The large group that he was behind earlier was still about eighty yards down the street. He smiled to himself knowing he would be up the steps and through the security barriers long before the protesters would merge with the group already there.

He pushed his way through the crowd politely and most people begrudgingly moved out of his way. He was twenty yards from the barricades and the crowd began to thin out. The protesters were keeping their distance from the CSF barriers and the red line painted five yards in front of it. Official signs stating that any person caught crossing the red line were subject to immediate imprisonment. None of the protesters seemed to want to test the rule.

Grady dug out his identification card and

looped the lanyard over his head as he approached. He was almost to the red line when a woman behind him called out his name. Grady turned around smiling. The young women smiled back as she approached. When she was less than ten feet from the man she removed an automatic pistol from her bag and began firing toward him. Grady had no chance to react to the woman's attack. The women fired seven shot into his chest before the small pistol suddenly stopped when the seventh shell casing wedging itself in the ejection port. She tried once more to pull the trigger but when that failed, she threw the weapon at Grady's body. She stood there for a second. "That's for the baby I'll never have you Bastard!" she cursed. She turned around and melted back into the crowd.

Rebecca led her small band of organizers down a side alley of a strip mall located in the District 8's city of Thurman. Thurman was the governor's seat for the district and she had been assigned to organize the protest there. As they had discussed with Jax, each of the small groups would enter a predetermined area, usually a neighborhood and begin their door to door rallies. They would invite neighbors and friends to join them as they gathered in the street to voice their opinions. Other members of the team were spread out over several blocks with the two-fold purpose of warning the group of the approach of the CSF and to impede the response time of these troops.

The strategy to slow the troops down usually involved blocking roads with shopping carts, trash bins or any other item big enough to slow their progress. In some instances people who had left their vehicles unlocked found their cars pushed out into the middle of the street. When the responding troops were close enough, smoke grenades were ignited in the area. The security force vehicles were required to slow to a crawl in order to weave their way through the mess. When the CSF started using heavier ramming style units, disabling mines were used. As the name implied, the mines could quickly disable the larger vehicles and also cause minor physical damage or psychological damage to the personnel inside. After several weeks of having their heads rattled, the troops abandoned this tactic especially after they started finding nearby signs stating '*If this had been a real mine, you would be dead!*'

The troopers had also learned not to abandon their vehicles and pursue on foot. Upon returning to the vehicles they would find the vehicles covered in stickers or the signature blue-gray paint of the guardians. Also, more often than not, the vehicles could not be restarted. A tow vehicle would have to be called. When they decided to start leaving a guard behind to watch the vehicles the protest teams had expert snipers assigned to them. These snipers would fire a tranquilizer dart into the unsuspecting guard. Again when the CSF team returned they would not only find their vehicles vandalized but the drugged guard naked and painted Guardian blue.

Rebecca's team scattered amongst the homes knocking on several doors at once. In the last few days the response from the home owners had been very good. Jax had been right when he said most people would feel more comfortable staying in their own neighborhoods to protest the Core Council's actions of late. This type of mini-protest was designed to keep the CSF available troops spread out over a large area. At any given time, there could be six or seven mini-protests occurring at the same time. The groups had counted on some neighbors remaining loyal to the council and fully expected them to alert the CFS. The emergency calls made through these Loyalists PD's would cause the troops to respond. By the time the troops had gotten through the delayers, the block protesters would have disbanded. The soldiers would usually find one or two people posing as Loyalists helping the troops by pointing them in the wrong direction. When it was safe, the group would reassemble and move to a different area and start over.

Rebecca yelled through the bullhorn as more and more people gathered on the street. Two of her people were busy handing out flyers and stickers to anyone who would take them. Still others were busy posting the flyers anywhere they would stick.

"Troops arriving," her headset buzzed, "from the west side of 147th street."

"West side of 147th," she confirmed looking over the crowd. She held up a portable air horn and released three rapid blasts. It was the prearranged signal that the groups needed to start wrapping up their activities. She stuffed the larger bullhorn into her back pack. Three minutes later she once again triggered two blasts from the air horn. She watched as her team began to scatter. When she was satisfied that everyone was moving she chose her own avenue of escape. She ran between two houses and over the four foot fence in the rear of the yard. Clearing the fence she was now standing in the service alley used by the utility vehicles to service the homes. She trotted down the alley and at the junction, turned away from 147th street. It was there that she ran into the armed CSF foot patrol.

"Move and we'll fire!" yelled one of the troopers.

"Hands in the air!" commanded the second.

Rebecca looked around her for an avenue of escape. Her hopes sank as she determined that there was no place to run.

"Go ahead," one of the soldiers stated as if guessing her intentions, "let's see if you can outrun a bullet."

Rebecca kept her hands over her head but somewhat relaxed her stance. She knew that in their heightened state of alertness either or both of them would open fire instantly. It was better to surrender now and hope to escape later.

"Smart move, asshole," one of them shouted, noticing her decision not to run. "Now on the ground, face down."

Rebecca slowly lowered herself to the ground.

"Cross your feet at your ankles" they ordered, "hands in the small of your back."

Again, she had no choice but to acquiesce. One trooper circled around to her side while the other kept his weapon trained on her head. She could feel the restraining strap being placed over her hands. Suddenly she cried out in pain as the man over tightened the restraint. A second set of thick plastic leg cuffs where placed on her ankles. They were manufactured in such a manner as to allow the captive to waddle forward, but not run. Again, he tightened them without mercy.

"Perfect fit," he said smugly as he jabbed her in the ribs. "Get up!" he commanded, roughly pulling her to her feet.

"Team one, one, eight to central," the other soldier said into his headset.

"Central, go ahead one, one, eight." Rebecca

heard as a response.

"One in the bag," he sneered looking at her.

"Affirmative, one, one, eight," was the scratchy response. "Return for processing."

Ziven sat at his desk, the bottom drawer pulled out far enough to allow him to rest his foot on its rim.

"How are things going?" he asked Lars sitting on the opposite side of the desk.

Lars was slouched down in the chair, his feet out in front of him, crossed at the ankles. As usual, his tie had been loosened and was slightly pulled to one side. "Good," he offered as a short answer, and then continued with a longer report. "Kelly is piling up the injunctions against the Core Council as well as individual injunctions against each of the members. Between the court orders and her public appearances, she is effectively burying them up to their necks in paperwork."

Ziven looked up from is work, "Is it doing any good?"

Lars nodded, "I think so. Psychologically, she is keeping the pressure on them. Ryan's men have been successful at infiltrating the protest gatherings. If they feel the protests are too peaceful, they stir things up at bit."

"What about the rebels?"

Lars laughed out loud at the question, "I have to give it to them; they're keeping the CSF jumping. The CSF no sooner puts out one fire when the rebels start two more."

Ziven locked eyes with Lars, "I hope we're learning from this experience," he said, "I don't want this type of thing to happen again." He dropped his eyes back to his work. "What about the armed groups?"

"As arranged, they are making a mess out of the outer CSF infrastructure. They continued to raid CSF outposts, destroy bridges and tube stations. PD's stores have become a favorite target for the rebels as well as a number of disgruntled parents. A single irate woman took out the Lakeside PD shop with a homemade satchel charge planted in her knap sack. Killed two employees and wounded two others."

"Did they catch her?" Ziven asked not looking up.

"Nope," Lars answered, "but they are hauling people off to their interrogation centers as fast as they can."

The phone buzzed at the edge of Ziven's desk. "I'll get it," stated Lars.

He leaned forward and picked up the receiver, "Presidents Ziven's office Bob Lars speaking." Lars listened for a second, "Hi Mike, what can I do for you?" Again there was silence as the other man spoke. "Has it been confirmed? I see...I see. Alright then, keep us posted."

Lars replaced the receiver in its holder. He returned to his previous relaxed position. "That was Mike Russel down in Information. He just got word that Dr. Grady was shot while he was walking up the front steps of the Tower Exchange building."

Ziven sat up in his chair, "Now that's poetic justice; dead I hope."

"Seven times dead," Lars chuckled. "The woman who did it shot him seven times in the chest. The witnesses said she fired her weapon until it jammed then as the coup de grâce, threw the weapon at his head. He was DOA at Core Hospital."

"And the woman?"

"She disappeared back into the crowd as if nothing happened," Lars replied.

"I bet that shook them up on the 22nd floor," Ziven said, as he stood and walked toward his private washroom. "Just remember what I said, Bob.

There's a lesson in everything that's happening."

CHAPTER 26

NEVER LEFT BEHIND

The CSF vehicle rumbled down the road, behind it the larger and heavily armed troop transport stayed within three feet of its bumper. The turret gunner of the transport continually rotated the twin 50 caliber machine guns scanning the surrounding landscape. Both units showed the scars of recent encounters with rebel forces. The once putty white paint was blackened in several areas of each vehicle. The lead unit had bullet holes in the rear door and fender. The troop transport wore a single line of holes received from automatic fire.

It was almost dusk and as they crested the hill and turned into the forest, the lights on both vehicles came on automatically. They twisted and turned on the single lane dirt road until they approached the sentry post. Both vehicles slowed in unison maintaining their three foot distance. The sentry approached the first vehicle on the passenger's side. His counterpart stayed behind the barricade pointing his MR 50 in the general direction of the car.

"Good evening Captain," the guard said, as the officer inside the vehicle lowered the window. He took notice of the condition of the man's general appearance. His face looked as if it had been wiped with a greasy rag. His hair resembled a rat's nest that had been long abandoned. Somewhere under the dirt and grease was two day's growth of beard. His uniform also showed the recent signs of combat. "Your PD Sir," the guard commanded.

The Officer held his PD out to the guard. "Are we too late for chow? My men and I haven't eaten since this morning." The guard lightly tapped his PD against the officer's and then read his screen. "Food service will end in about forty-five minutes," he answered looking at the young officer. "What can I do for you...Captain Dunson?"

"We have seven prisoners in the rear," he answered, jerking his thumb toward the armored transport. "Once we sign them over to you we'll get something to eat and get back into the fight."

The guard stepped back from the door. "Captain, I need to look in the rear of the vehicle."

"As long as you don't use up the next forty-five minutes," he said, stepping out of the car.

Together they walked toward the rear of the second vehicle. The turret gunner looked down at them as they passed. "Captain, they got any food?" the gunner asked.

"Yep," Captain Dunson answered, "as long as we get there in the next forty-two minutes." As they reached the rear hatch, Captain Dunson looked back at the gunner. "Release the lock on the hatch Jimmy," he ordered.

With a hiss the rear hatch cracked open. As he opened the door they were met by the rifle barrels of two CSF soldiers' weapons. As soon as the two men recognized the Captain they lowered their weapons.

"Chow in forty minutes," Captain Dunson said anticipating their question.

The guard looked past the two men seated at the door. On both sides of the van were a total of seven, hooded and shackled men and women.

"That's a lot of crap you got there," the guard laughed.

"Well I'm going to dump them and get the hell out of here," he answered, "after we eat."

The two men returned to the first vehicle.

Captain Dunson climbed in the front seat while the guard waved his hand at the man behind the MR 50. The barrier guard lowered his weapon and activated the barrier, the center portion dropping into the ground.

The guard pointed past the barrier. "Straight ahead about six hundred yards you'll come to the main compound," he instructed, "they'll have you back up to the processing door and take your prisoners." He looked at his PD. "Would you like me to call ahead and make sure they keep the chow line open?"

"I'll put you in my will if you'd do that," Captain Dunson grinned.

The two vehicles entered the main compound and, as promised, the transport vehicle was instructed to back up to the double doors. The vehicle came to an abrupt stop several feet from the building. The two security personnel supervising the area opened the back hatch.

As the door opened, two muffled pops came from inside the transport and both of the guards went down. Nine members of the rescue team exited the back of the vehicle. The two that had been dressed in the CSF uniforms had stripped off their jackets. Each member of the rescue team wore gray shirts impregnated with small white specs. Jax came around the back of the truck similarly dressed.

"Steve and Reese" he ordered, "around the side. Find the power coupling to the building and wait for my orders to kill the power."

He moved back to the front of the armored transport. "Serra," he said speaking to the driver, "Pull your vehicle over there." He looked up at the man in the turret. "You're going to have to cover the building and the road."

"Good to go, Jax," the gunner assured him.

As the vehicle pulled away from the doors Jax and the other began checking their weapons and gear. Each was now wearing a night vision helmet.

Once the two men had control of the power coupling Jax gave the order to kill the lights. The entire compound went dark all at once. Each soldier switched on their helmets and stood alongside the double door waiting for Jax's orders. Jax made a quick sweep of the compound. The small white specs on his team member's shirts glowed bright greenish yellow in the visors. There would be no mistaking his men from those of the CSF. The thin targeting beams of their weapons also glowed under the aid of the visors. Jax remembered the first time he had used the gear back in training. Like everyone else, he thought it was stupid to give away your position with the targeting beams. Under the effects of the visors, they seemed like long thin beacons directing the enemy straight to their position. It wasn't until you turned off your visor that you understood that without the help of the night vision gear and the proper frequency, everything was again in total darkness.

Jax gave the team the hand motion to move out. Quietly they entered the building through the receiving doors. When a CSF soldier was encountered he or she was dropped with a quick burst of fire. The weapons silencers made it almost impossible to hear the weapons from very far away. The larger team split into several small units each continuing with the methodical task of securing the building. Several times short bursts of gun fire could be heard within the complex. It didn't last long.

After six minutes, the building was cleared. Jax gave the order for the power to be restored. The two men at the power station were to remain outside and back up the transport vehicle in securing the perimeter. A neatly dressed officer was presented to Jax.

"Is this your facility?" he asked the man.

The man did not answer. Jax quickly pulled out his side arm, chambered a round and held it to the Officers head. "I'm on the clock here so one last time," he hissed, "is this your facility?"

"Yes," he finally answered.

"Where are the prisoners kept?" Jax asked, still

holding the gun to the man's head.

The Officer slowly raised his hand pointing. "Down there, through that door."

"Lead the way," Jax commanded.

The man led the six of them down the hall and held his PD up to the lock. The door opened with a loud metallic click. Jax pushed him to the rear and pushed the door open with the barrel of his gun. The man behind the console was just turning to see who had entered the room. Jax caught him across the side of his head with the butt of his gun. He fell to the floor. Two team members stepped forward and began securing the man.

The room was long and narrow. Ten cell doors lined each side of the corridor. At the far end was another door.

Jax turned to the facility commander, "How do I open all of the cells at one time?"

The man pointed to the key pad on the console, "Press one, zero, one, zero than enter.

Jax stuck his gun in the man's crotch. "If the alarm goes off, so do your balls," Jax said with conviction.

"One, zero, one, zero then enter," the Officer repeated.

After entering the code Jax pushed the enter key. Instantly the doors began to unlock with almost the same metallic click that the entrance door had made when they arrived. The cell doors slid to one side. The team waited for people to start exiting the cells. After what seemed an eternity no one had walked out of the doors. Jax looked over his shoulder. "Chris, go check, but be careful."

Chris ran to the first set of cell doors and stopped just short of the openings. With a quick motion he peered in the cells his rifle at the ready. He repeated the procedure ten times then trotted back up to the control center.

"Empty?" Jax asked incredulously.

"No," Chris said catching his breath, but they're all going to need help to the transport. They look pretty bad, Jax."

"Rebecca?"

"Not in a cell, but a few of them are empty," Chris answered.

Jax shoved his gun back into the crotch of the Officer. "A young woman," he said shoving the gun harder into his crotch. The man doubled over letting out a moan. "She was brought in here three days ago; auburn hair, probably has told you to go fuck yourself repeatedly."

The man nodded his head quickly pointing to

the door at the far end of the hall. "Through there."

Jax turned to Chris. "Chris, get some of our guys to help you with the people in the cells. Don't forget to video everything you see."

"No problem," Chris said as he turned to go. Jax grabbed him by the shoulder. "Send Mat in here to find me."

Chris' eyes widened at the command. He nodded weakly then left.

Jax turned back to the Officer, "OK, let's go see what's behind the door."

They pushed the door open with the same caution they had used before. As the door opened the smell assaulted Jax senses. It stank of human sweat and body odor. There was also the strong smell of urine. The room was devoid of any soldiers but there were three people in the room. Two were shackled to the wall. Both seemed unconscious or maybe dead. The third was loosely stretched over a large upright metal frame. Her hands were fastened to the two upper corners by leather straps. Her feet were similarly secured at the bottom. She was totally naked, drenched in her own sweat. Her head sagged forward; her auburn hair was knotted and filthy. Electrodes were fastened to several parts of her body. Jax felt as if a cold hand had just crushed his heart. "Get her down from there he ordered, his voice quivering. "Don't let Mat see her that way."

Two of his team unfastened her from the device. She crumpled into their arms and hung limp in their grasp. They lowered her gently to the ground. Cindy, a member of the team and a good friend to Rebecca's felt the side of her neck for a pulse. She turned and sobbing lifted her thumb upwards to Jax. She then removed her own jacket and pants and began placing them on Rebecca's frail naked body.

Jax looked at the now half naked woman kneeling next to Rebecca. He turned to the Officer. "The lady needs your pants and jacket." He said, his lips curled in disgust. "Now!"

By the time Mat had entered the room, they had moved Rebecca to a stretcher. Somewhere Cindy had found a towel and wetting it, cleaned Rebecca's face as best she could under the circumstances.

Mat looked around the room in horror. He wept openly when he knelt down beside Rebecca and touched her face. Eyes blazing murderously, he leapt toward the Officer, his dagger in hand. It took both Jax and Chris to restrain him from killing the man. "I'll cut your cold heart out before I leave," Mat promised as they restrained him.

"Easy, Mat," Jax whispered in his ear, "let me handle this."

Jax felt Mat go limp in his arms. "Cindy," he said looking down at the woman by Rebecca side, "take Rebecca out of here and get her in the back of the transport. There's a med kit there."

"Yes, sir," she answered, placing her hands on the rear handles of the stretcher. Another member took the front and they lifted together. Mat gently touched her as they walked by.

Jax turned his attention back to the officer. "I'm going to have this gentleman escort you to your office," Jax said pointing to Chris. "I want you to open your security locker and give the contents to him."

The Officer's eyes hardened as he shook his head from side to side. Jax leaned against the console that controlled the electrical current that they had been feeding through Rebecca's body. "You know," Jax started, "I don't know anything about torture other than what I've read in a few books." He looked at the officer with distain, "nasty business."

Jax walked over to the metal frame on which they had found Rebecca. He ran his hand along the cold metal. "I understand though, that forcing others to watch a person being tortured can be quite valuable. Once they've been required to watch the agony of several other people being tortured; it's said that it softens them up. Often, the poor person that has been forced to watch spills their guts in order to avoid the same fate." Jax walked up behind the Officer. "I'll bet you watched countless people scream uncontrollably in agony on this thing," he said, pointing to the device. "I also understand that attaching one of the electrodes to the person's genitals really makes them dance when the switch is turned on."

Huge beads of sweat covered the man's face until they were too large to defy gravity any longer. They then came crashing down like rain; the collar of his shirt soon became soaked. "Now you have a simple choice to make," Jax whispered into his ear. "Open the security locker and give my man the contents or, I let Mat strap your naked ass to that frame."

Again he shot Jax a defiant look and shook his head negatively. "Chris, Mat," he ordered, strip him down!"

Mat grabbed the man's shirt and ripped it open sending the buttons flying across the room. Chris had his boxer shorts down to his knees when he shouted, "No! Wait!"

Jax leaned toward him as if it were difficult to understand what he had just said, "Excuse me," Jax teased, "have you changed your mind?"

The man breathed heavily, "Alright," he agreed, "Alright!"

Jax motioned for Chris to take him to his office. "Mat," he commanded, "you stay with me."

It was several minutes before Chris returned

with the man in tow. The Officer's face was bruised and puffy in several places. A thin line of blood trickled down from his left eyebrow. Jax made an inquisitive gesture toward Chris.

"He tripped…several times," Chris offered as an answer.

"The contents of the locker?" Jax asked.

"On its way to the car," Chris assured him.

"Excellent," Jax beamed pointing toward the metal frame. "Gentleman," he prompted.

Instantly, Chris and Mat began to strip the clothing off the man. "Wait," he protested, "You said you wouldn't."

Jax watched as they fastened the man's arms and legs to the straps on the frame. Chris threw a bucket of dirty water toward the man. The stream of filthy water hit him mid-chest and splashed up into his face.

"Please," he sputtered, please!"

"While you were gone, Mat here was studying up on the control panel," Jax said without emotion. He turned to Mat. "Chris and I will be waiting in the car. Don't be late."

Mat gave them a wicked smile, "There's an automatic feature on this thing," he said, pointing to the controls. "You can set the intensity and time duration right here," Mat informed them.

"You said you wouldn't!" the officer screamed. "We had a deal!"

"This one," Mat said, ignoring the man's pleas, "controls the time intervals between each shock treatment."

"You promised!" he screamed again, his eyes wide with terror.

Jax walked up to the man. "Alright," he said calmly, "here's what I'll do. You tell me how many times you've strapped people into this device and the number of times that you've acquiesced to their pleas for mercy. If it equals at least once; I'll have you released.

The man began to cry openly. "You don't understand," he sobbed, "I was ordered to do it."

Jax motioned for Chris to follow him out the room. "Mat, don't be long."

Jax and Chris exited the building together. Jax quickly checked with all of the teams and had them prepare to move out. He checked on the prisoners that had been carried to the transport. The words caught in his throat as he watched Cindy attending to Rebecca. "How's she doing?" he asked weakly.

Cindy offered him a reassuring smile, "Much

better I think," she answered, "but it wouldn't hurt to have one of the Doctors look at her."

"That's first on the list when we get out of here," he promised. His thoughts turned to Emily and what she might be doing. A lump tightened in his throat as he thought of the possibility that Emily could be injured or killed.

Mat ran out of the building a few seconds later. He stopped in front of Jax and Chris. "Do you mind if I ride in the back of the transport with Rebecca?" he asked. "Not at all," Jax answered, pushing his thoughts of Emily into a deeper place. "I had them save you a seat."

Chris touched Mat's shoulder, "did you kill him?"

Mat shook his head from side to side, "No," he admitted. Jax talked me out of it while you were in the man's office. I put the machine on the lowest power setting. Set the interval for once every ten minutes."

"And the duration?" Jax asked.

"I thought eight hours was a nice round number," Mat smiled.

Jax returned his smile, "Get in the back of the truck, we're leaving."

The small convoy once again rolled up to the

check point. The barrier was automatically lowered before they reached it. *Obviously,* Jax thought, *it's easier to get out of here than in.* Jax motioned for Chris to slow down as they reached the two guards.

"Did you guys get you fill?" the guard asked.

"We got more than we were hoping for," Jax smiled. "How much longer do you two have to stand out here?"

The guard looked at his PD for the time. "Another three hours then we're off," the guard answered.

"That's not too bad," Jax said as he nudged Chris to get moving. "We left something with your Commander for you when you go back inside. You guys have a good night and thanks again," he said as they drove away.

Jax sat lightly on the edge of the bed. He studied Rebecca's face. Except for a few minor abrasions and cuts, she looked almost normal again. The Doctor had cautioned him that she would still have to be checked out by the physicians and psychiatrist back home. *Lingering psychological issues,* he remembered the Doctor saying, *may appear later.* She was scheduled to be shipped out in a few days.

"Jax?" she whispered hoarsely.

At the sound of her voice he remembered something else the Doctor had said. *Her vocal cords may have been injured or at least strained,* he had said. *The intense uncontrollable screaming caused by the electrical shock…*

"Hey," Jax smiled, "you look a lot better than the last time I saw you."

Tears formed around her eye lids, "If you're trying to cheer me up."

"Well, it's the morale portion of my job," he said, "you know, keep their spirits up."

She managed one of her beautiful smiles that he had become so accustomed to. "You came for me," she said, almost weeping.

"Well," he said looking toward the ceiling trying to maintain his composure, "I couldn't stomach the thought of breaking in another second in command."

"You lying sack of dun," she said through watery eyes. "Just admit it, you came for me."

"Alright," he said giving in, "since there's no witness here I can admit it. I did come to get you out."

She removed her hand from under the sheet and placed it on top of his. "Why?"

"Why?" he asked for the first time, actually

trying to work out what he had done, "I guess there are a couple of reasons," he thought out loud. "The first is…" Jax looked at Rebecca affectionately, "you're the first friend I've ever had, Rebecca. Colonel McKee has told me on several occasions that I don't play well with others."

"That's not true," she rasped, "everyone on your team respects and loves you." She squeezed his hand, "Emily loves you."

Jax's left eyebrow rose in a questioning slant, "She tell you that?"

Rebecca shook her head slightly, "She doesn't have to, Jax. I can see it."

Jax quickly nodded his head, "Oh, it's that woman thing, right"

"Yes, that woman thing is never wrong." She squeezed his hand lightly, "What's the other reason?"

Jax took a deep breath and let it out slowly. "I've spent a lot of time studying the pre-apocalypse United States. I always studied the craziness and stupidity that was happening. I searched for the reasons why a country and the world would go so far as to destroy everything." He squeezed her hand, "I discovered that when you stand so close to the edge there's a tremendous possibility of going over by accident." He smiled at her and continued, "But in the middle of all the horrible things that were going on, I found out that there were so many people still trying to do good. One thing in particular I found that caught my attention was in, of all places, their military."

"The military?" she asked.

"Yes," he nodded, "they had a creed back then, "it was simple, but powerful."

"What was it Jax?"

His face brightened, "Leave no man behind," he said, regarding her with open fondness. "Rebecca, you are my best friend and a great soldier, there was no way I was going to leave you behind."

Tears ran freely down her cheeks, "Damn it, Jax," she sniffled, her voice almost gone.

"What? What did I do?" he asked bewildered.

She smiled affectionately, "You just made your best friend cry."

Director Iris Kinsley rode in the rear seat of her chauffeur driven car. In the front seat next to the driver was her newly assigned bodyguard. There was no traffic on the road since it was several hours after the mandatory curfew. It had been imposed by the CSF several days ago after the peaceful protest in front of the Tower Exchange building had turned ugly. They had assured the country that the clampdown would be lifted as quickly as possible.

Kinsley was quite pleased with the way things had progressed through the week. Commander Adelric had been elevated to a full Director and Mars had been knocked down a few pegs. *The look on Mar's face,* she smirked to herself, *was priceless. The next part of the plan,* she thought becoming serious, *was going to be a lot more difficult.*

Kinsley caught a flash of light reflecting off the window frame of her door. "Is there someone behind us?" she asked the two men in the front seat.

The driver's eyes shifted to the rear view mirror for several seconds, "Yes, Director," he said, while keeping his eyes on the road. "It's one of the council's fleet vehicles," he said.

"Probably Pyrs," she said in the direction of the front seat, "he doesn't live too far for me you know."

"Yes, Director," the driver answered, checking the rear view mirror once again, "I've taken him home on several occasions."

She turned her attention back to the problem at hand. The charter required that the executive council be made up of at least three members but it didn't stipulate which three council members it had to be. *Dr. Grady had been too soft*, she thought, *he had a difficult time standing up to any of the others; especially Mars. Grady was not what they needed on the Executive Council. Of course, his murder took care of any consideration he may have received. But,* she recalled Pyrs saying, *it could be problematic if they were to promote Adelric to the Executive Council so soon after he had become a full Director.* Pyrs was in favor of waiting a few months before bringing it up for a vote. *Mars will have us into a full blown civil war before then*, she thought. *And then*, she reflected, *there had been the message from Government Plaza.* She had committed the exact words to memory: *The government would become more agreeable and would possibly work closer with the council if a wild card, such as Tansy, was removed from the equation.* She and Pyrs had decided that the note did not mean that they wanted Mars to be killed, but simply distanced from the upper echelon of the council.

Pyrs' car picked up speed and would soon pass. She looked out the window hoping to catch a glimpse of the man. *A conspiratorial wave*, she thought, *would be in good taste.* She waited until the car was directly across from hers. She noticed that Pyrs rear window was being lowered. *Great minds think alike*, she smiled to herself. She pushed the button to lower her own window. When it didn't respond she looked toward her driver.

"Driver, my window won't go down," she complained.

"No, Director," he said, watching the car pull next to them, "the button is locked."

"Well," she huffed, "release it."

"Get on the floor," he responded.

"What, are you crazy?

"On the floor," he hollered.

Kinsley looked out the window at Pyrs car. The rear window was completely down and almost even with hers. That is when she first noticed the barrel of the machine gun resting on the window ledge.

The MR 50 belched out its rounds with a brilliant flash of light quickly followed by the deafening roar of the explosions. The windows were the first things to confirm that an attack was in progress. Even though the windows were bulletproof, the close range and repeated firing caused the glass to explode into a shower of sparkling fragments spraying the inside of the vehicle with tiny particles. Kinsley heard the horrifying sound of metal slamming against metal as the projectiles punched holes into the light armor of the door frames. She was tossed from side to side as her driver attempted to get away from the attack. The noise seemed to be moving toward the front of the vehicle when, without warning, the car suddenly tilted to the left, crashed through the safety rail and rolled down the embankment. When it finally came to rest at the bottom of the stone gulley there was only silence.

✱   ✱   ✱   ✱

Mars sat at her desk rubbing her temples in a futile attempt to ease the throbbing. She opened the top desk drawer and removed the bottle of pain relievers. She quickly removed the cap and shook three of the tiny pills into the palm of her hand.

"Commander Adelric," Sapphire reported, "is here to see you."

"Let him in," she said, popping the pills into her mouth.

Adelric strutted into her office bearing a victorious grin across his face. "Working late I see," he said. "Everyone else has gone home." He didn't wait for permission to sit but took a seat directly in front of her desk.

"I was just getting ready to leave," she lied. "I could say the same about you. Why are you still here?"

"The rebels have been busy tonight," he said, reaching over her desk and picking up the bottle of pain killers. He looked at the label suspiciously. "Too many of these," he said, holding the bottle out toward her, "can cause an overdose."

In a single fluid motion, she snatched the bottle from his hand and tosses it into the desk drawer. "Is there something you want?" she asked, closing the drawer.

He shook his head from side to side, "Just thought you would want to know," he said studying her eyes, "Iris Kinsley's car was ambushed on the throughway an hour ago; machine gun fire from one of our own fleet vehicles."

Mars' face remained cold and stony, the news having no affect on her, "There had to be a survivor for you to know that. Did they identify anyone in the other vehicle?"

Adelric shook his head slowly, "No," he said, "I don't think it was possible to look around the inside of the other vehicle when someone is trying to kill you with a machine gun."

"Did she survive the attack?"

Adelric continued to study her face, "Yes, she was lucky enough to drop to the floor. The lowered portion of the vehicle has better armor protection," he answered. "She's in guarded condition at Core Hospital."

"Well that's a relief," she said, "losing two Directors in the same week would look terrible for the CSF, not to mention you personally."

Adelric ground out the words from behind

clenched teeth, "We can handle it," he responded.

"I'm beginning to doubt that, Commander," she said with contempt. "You, yourself was shot, almost killed. Dr. Grady was murdered on the front steps of this very building and now you're sitting here telling me that Iris just barely escaped with her life. I would hate to see what it looked like if you couldn't handle it."

"Careful, Mars," he warned.

"Don't threaten me," she shot back, her eyes smoldering, "you're in charge of security and it's been inadequate at best. Maybe we should ask President Ziven to allow his Secret Service to take over the responsibility of protecting the Council!"

Adelric shook his head grinning, "Is all this anger coming from the fact that I was promoted to a Director today?"

"The anger," she answered bitterly, "is because there are only two of us left on the Council that haven't been killed or shot at." She pointed her finger toward him, "And just for clarification, the position of the Commander of the CSF was promoted to a full Directorship; not you personally. *You*, can be replaced."

"That would take a majority vote of the Executive Council," he reminded her.

Mar's punched several keys on her console. The

holographic image of Pyrs' face filled the area, "What do you think, Steven?" she asked.

It became obvious that Pyrs had been listening to the entire conversation. His face was grim, almost ghostly. "Commander, I have to agree with Marci on this issue. If you can't guarantee our protection, I'm afraid we will have to find someone who can." His image turned to face Mars, "I'll see you in the morning, maybe we can ride over together to visit Iris."

"That sounds good, Stephen," she smiled graciously, "see you then."

Pyrs' image faded. Mars turned her attention back to Adelric. "Is there anything else you would like to gloat about, Martin?"

Adelric stood and walked to the door. "I should have guessed the three of you would be watching each other's backs." He smiled coldly, "I'll repeat myself, Marci. Be careful."

"Sapphire, did you document the Commanders threat?" Mars asked flatly.

"Yes, Ms. Tansy. Recorded and filed."

Mars regarded Adelric with disgust. "Maybe you should take a walk around the outside of the building to cool off," she offered. "Who knows, maybe we'll get lucky and they won't miss this time."

Adelric stormed out of the room without speaking further.

Mars eyes sparkled with pleasure as Adelric disappeared from site. *He's such a child when it comes to politics,* she thought.

There was a sudden thud at the large window behind her head, the pane rattled violently as it splintered into a spider's web. Mars threw herself to the ground, her face pushed firmly against the carpet. After a moment of silence, she turned over to examine the window. The armor coating had done its job. She mentally assessed where the center of the spider's web was in relation to where her head had been. If not for the protective glass, she realized, the bullet would have passed through the base of her skull.

CHAPTER 27

HEART OF THE DRAGON

Jax had spent most of the morning with Rebecca. He had mostly stood around watching Cindy help pack her last minute things for the trip. He had discovered that trying to stay out of the way was a full time job. Their good-bye was as tearful as he had expected, but he would not have missed the chance see her one more time. The previous day he had gotten an earful from her when he informed her that Mat was going to be assigned to the team escorting her all the way home. When Mat joined them he received the joint assault from the two of them. While they both appreciated what he was trying to do for them, they had convinced him that Mat's place was with his unit. Jax begrudgingly gave in. Mat was one of their best men and Jax knew he needed him. As a compromise, Mat would be part of the escort taking her to the complex that lead under the barrier.

Now he was once again huddled with his unit commanders. They were all standing around his desk. It had been cleared of everything that was not pertinent to their upcoming campaign.

"Jax," Peter asked, "have you been in contact with Jay's people"

Jax rubbed the tiny beard that had started growing on his chin. "Yes, we've advised his people of our plan to release the latest video. Everything is dependent on their co-operation on this one. If they don't step forward, we'll be dead in the water."

"Do we have a backup plan?"

Jax shook his head. "Sapphire has got all the media locked down," he offered. "The Flash reporters that have not been put in prison are in hiding. All of their equipment has been destroyed or confiscated."

"No chance of getting access codes to the Sapphire network?" Chris asked hopefully.

"We've tried," Jax answered. "Do you know that no one has the slightest idea where their programmers are? Supposedly the President himself doesn't have access to that information."

"What good are the programmers," someone asked.

"We were hoping to get our hands on one or two of them and sweat the access code out of them," Jax answered, "but we haven't been able to get a lead on anyone with a high enough clearance to even access the programming."

"What about grabbing one of the council members?" Peter asked.

Again Jax shook his head, "After the last attempt on Mrs. Kinsley's life they've been too heavily guarded." He sighed, "Besides, we don't think any of them would have full access to the program."

"Even that Tansy bitch?" Chris asked.

"Possible," Jax admitted, "but again, they're all under extremely heavy guard."

"By the way," Peter interjected, "I was going to wait until after the meeting to bring this up, but I heard back from all of our field people and most of McKee's units. No one in our groups were involved in the attempt to assassinate Kinsley."

"I don't know if that's good or bad." Jax frowned, "It could mean that there is an internal riff happening. Infighting amongst the council members could be helpful." Jax blinked several times. "Let's not worry about that right now," he said continuing, "We haven't sent Jay's people the information yet. I figured we didn't need to supply them with anything if they can't help."

"I think it's some of Phil's group's best work so far," Peter said, "It'd be a shame if we didn't get to use it."

"I'll second that," Phil added, "it was very tough going on my guys to put it all together."

Jax spent the time to look at each of his team leaders. How can you loose with a group like this, he wondered. "Ladies and Gentlemen this will be a strike right at the heart of this dragon. It has way too many heads to try and decapitate it. Any questions?"

Jax waited several seconds for any response. When there was none he continued, "Alright," he said clapping his hands together," if there's nothing else, I want all team leaders heading back into the field by ten tomorrow."

The group began breaking up. Some stood in small clusters, talking, while others made their way up the stairs. Peter moved over to where Jax was.

"Hey, boss," he asked, "how'd it go with Rebecca this morning?"

"I think she's going to be OK," he said, eyes saddening. "I'll miss her as my second."

"She was a tough nut," Peter agreed. "I don't envy you the job of replacing her."

"No envy required," Jax smiled, "*You're* it."

"What?"

"You're now second in command," Jax said, putting out his hand. "You've earned it."

"Wow," Peter said taking Jax's hand, "I was too buried up to my ass with issues to even see that coming." Peter dug into his shirt pocket. "Oh," he said offering a sealed envelope to Jax, "communiqué from the field."

Jax took the envelope and studied the handwriting on the front. "From the Colonel," he said, turning it to the other side. "I'll save it for when I already have indigestion."

Peter pointed to the envelope, "At least it's not big enough for her to put her boot in," he laughed. Peter slapped him on the back and headed toward the stairs. "You going to get something to eat?"

"Sure," Jax said, holding up the letter, "let me read this and I'll join you shortly."

When the room had cleared out Jax sat on the corner of his desk and opened the envelope with his dagger. He pulled the page out and laid the envelope on the desk. It only took him a second to open the single page.

Hello my love, he read, *I hope you had the good sense to open this letter in private. If not, you'll have to assume all of the embarrassment for the both of us. Telling you that I miss you desperately could be the biggest understatement of this war. Jax, you have filled a void in me that I never knew existed. (no pun intended!). It wasn't until I met you that I ever dreamed of having a life outside a camouflage colored uniform. I know, not very sexy, but I know you understand what I mean. I now live for the day when you and I can share something neither of us has ever had in our lives.*

I'm limiting this letter to one page so let me address one more thing. I have received a complete report on your raid to rescue Rebecca and the others. I am so proud of you for what you and your team accomplished. I'm proud of myself for seeing such a strong character inside you at our first meeting. Remember that my love is always with you.

Emily,

ps. I was going to enclose a pair of my underwear, but decided you would rather wait and take them off yourself. And yes, the pair I have on right now would fit inside this tiny envelope. Think about that! All my love...

Ziven sat at the small conference table with his closest advisors. The hour was late and he wore a pair of slacks and a dark blue them by Jax. pullover shirt. The other men were similarly dressed. Kelly was still in a three piece suit, but she had removed her jacket. They had just finished watching, for the third time, the video sent to

"Well, Lars said, getting the ball rolling, "they really put us in a corner on this one."

Ziven looked down at his fingernails, "Ryan?" he prompted without looking up.

Ryan removed his glasses and began cleaning them with a soft cloth. "Lars is right, this will upset the apple cart."

"An apple cart that already has a broken wheel or two," Ziven replied. "Kelly, what do you think?"

"It's what we've been pushing for all along," she answered. "It's what you promised them months ago at your meeting. The real question is, are we ready for this?"

Ziven leaned back in his chair, "Kelly's right," he stated, "this is exactly where we projected we would be at this time in this particular scenario. You all remember our discussing the possible avenues at this juncture. The only difference between back then and now is that two years ago, it was just an exercise on a computer screen. Two possible hypotheses with two entirely different end games. Now it's reality."

"There is one big difference now," Ryan interjected as he held his glasses up to the light. "We did not run the games with the possibility of armed rebels within our borders." He gently placed the glasses back on his nose, "What the rebels are asking you to do could change the entire outcome."

"We've made allowances, for this new variable," Lars offered.

Ryan looked in Lars' direction. "I can't remember… did those allowances include the popularity numbers the rebels are currently enjoying?"

"They most certainly did not," Kelley interjected before Lars had a chance to counter. "They have liberated two of the CSF interrogation camps in the past few weeks. The second camp contained the sixteen Flash journalists that were arrested for their part in the broadcast from the steps of the Administration building. We're catching some crap on that," she continued. "Some of them are saying we should have stepped in on their behalf not the rebels."

"We did," Ryan said smiling, "we sent in a group of covert operatives disguised as rebels to free them."

"I like that," Ziven said pointing to Ryan. "Can we sell it?"

"I don't see why not," Lars said, "after all, the rebels aren't carrying around ID devices stating they're rebels. We have good relations with six or seven of the journalists. We could always let it leak that we had to use the rebel cover to maintain a position of deniability to the Council."

"Any thoughts on that?" Ziven asked.

"We could sweeten the pot by giving those six an exclusive interview with the Lottes'," Kelly offered.

"Where are the Lottes' anyway?" Ryan said with a grin.

"I have no idea," Kelly shot back returning the grin, "vanished, but I'm sure they could be found in time for an interview."

Ziven leaned forward resting his elbow on the table. "This could play very well for us if it's handled correctly." He pointed to Lars, "Get a group of our most trusted PR people together. They're going to be sent to a secure area to work on this so make sure they understand they may be gone for a week or so. There will be no leaks before we set this in motion. Lars, you and I can go over a possible script after this meeting."

"What about the rebel's video and their request to air it?" Ryan asked.

"Tell them we agree to their plan, but not the timing. Tell them we'll need some time to get everything on our side in order," Ziven said, quite pleased with the outcome of the meeting. "We're going to drive a stake in this demon's heart before this is over. Now, if there's nothing else, I would like to spend the rest of the evening with my lovely and of late, lonely wife."

They all shook their heads. "Oh," Lars said as he stood, "there is one more thing Mr. President."

"What's that."

"You sent a very large bouquet of fresh flowers to Director Kinsley's hospital room today. I do believe they were her favorites," Lars smiled.

CHAPTER 28

NEW REVELATIONS

The compound was 100 yards directly in front of Jax's position. He and Peter both had been watching the troop movements through their night vision equipment for over an hour now. It seemed that no sooner had one group entered the area than another began to move in. Jax had counted over 100 heavily armored personnel carriers in just the last forty minutes.

There was also something new added to the standard Table of Organization and Equipment for a CSF company. They had seen the first of these new attack vehicles in the last fifteen minutes. They were somewhat larger than the usual armored transport that they had become accustomed to. These vehicles were also equipped with much heavier armament than the standard troop carriers. The troop carriers were armed with either the standard MR-50 or, in some cases, what was known as a twin MR-50. These new vehicles had a primary weapon that was a single barreled cannon. Peter and Jax agreed that it was most likely a 25 to 30 mm rapid fire cannon. The vehicle's armament didn't stop there. To the right of the cannon was the familiar MR-50 machine gun. Several of the ones they had seen were also equipped with rocket launchers. There was no doubt in their minds that these new vehicles were not designed to transport troops. These vehicles had a crew of three with space for a full combat load of ammunition.

Jax heard the steady click, click, click as Peter continued to take photographs of the units as they rolled in.

"Have you seen enough?" Jax asked.

"More than I cared to," Peter said, lowering his camera. "Where did they get these things?"

Jax shook his head, "I'm not sure but I would guess they've been sitting in some storage bunker. They didn't need to pull them out until now."

"Makes you wonder what else they have hidden away."

Jax's throat tightened at the thought. "Let's get out of here; we have to get these photographs to

McKee ASAP."

Together they made their way through the wooded countryside, neither speaking. They came to a small dirt road after about five miles. Jax looked at his watch. "We're a little early," he said, pointing to an area that would offer them some cover, "Might as well have a seat over there and wait for our ride."

Jax thought about what they had just witnessed. He jumped when Peter spoke, "Why now?" Peter asked. "Why not bring those things out a month ago?"

"I was just wondering about that myself," Jax said, "and the other question is, how many? I'm sure this is not the only area they are gathering in. I'm willing to bet that they have groups like this one spread out over the entire countryside."

"Should we tell, Jay?" Peter asked.

Jax thought about the question for several seconds. "Probably not," he said slowly. "If he doesn't know about them there's nothing we can do about it now. We can't have him getting cold feet because a new attack vehicle rolls onto the scene."

"New, with heavy weaponry that could kick their ass and ours."

"The bulk of the fighting is going to be in Core City," he said. "If McKee's troops can keep these guys out here in the countryside, the whole thing could be over before they had time to reorganize and head into the city."

"How do you expect them to do that?"

"Simultaneous assaults on several of the solar collector stations could do that," Jax said. "They'll commit these troops there first. They can't afford to lose any of those stations. Josh told me that they didn't have any replacements."

A single vehicle came down the road and stopped at the designated pick up point. Jax and Peter remained hidden until they could be sure that everything was as planned. The car door opened and Chris stood by the driver's side. "Someone call for a taxi?" he asked into the dark.

Jax and Peter left their hiding place and headed to the car.

"This is out of my zone," Chris said as they approached, "so the fare will be triple."

When he got no response out of either of the two men he climbed back in behind the wheel, "What's up?"

Peter pushed a button on the camera and handed it to Chris, "This is what's up," he said flatly.

Chris began flipping through the photos,

"Damn," he said, continuing to scan the photographs. "What the hell is this?" he asked holding up a picture of the new attack vehicle.

"It's a whole lot of trouble," Jax stated. "Let's get moving, sitting out here in the night air is bad for our health."

Colonel McKee looked over the shoulder of one of her Platoon Captains as he flipped through the photographs. When he had finished for the second time he laid the data pad on the small field table.

"What do you think, Jeff?" she asked after a few seconds.

The man pointed to the photograph still displayed on the data pad. "I agree with Jax's assessment of the vehicle. It's an attack vehicle that we haven't seen before. That cannon, from the looks of it, is just as they said, 25mm rapid fire assault weapon. Along with the rockets these things can do a lot of damage to ground troops."

"Hmmm," McKee said as she reviewed the pictures again. "Armor looks to be of a medium class. Our shoulder fired rockets would most likely penetrate it."

"If you got close enough," he said. "These things are made for quick surgical strikes. That cannon can out-distance anything we have. Depending on how they deploy their ground troops and how we set up our defensive perimeter we could give them a hell of a fight. How many did Jax say he saw?"

"Roughly 125 armored troop transports and 40 of the new attack vehicles. Of course he believes there are additional units being staged elsewhere."

"Have any of our scouts reported seeing these things?"

"Not yet," McKee answered, "based on the location of this staging area I have had them redeployed," she said pointing to the map, "along this line. We should have something back soon enough."

"How did Jax and Peter find them in the first place?"

"By pure luck," she laughed, "Peter was heading back to his area of operation and decided to stick to the back roads to avoid detection. He heard them long before he saw them. He turned around and went back to get Jax as soon as he figured out what he had stepped into."

The Captain scratched up under his cap, "So what are you thinking, Colonel?"

"They're too far from the major cities to lend them any support and again they are almost as far from the nearest solar collection station. Right now I think they're gathering for some type of redeployment; but to where is anybody's guess." McKee picked up the data pad and flipped through several photos, "We'll keep a tight watch on them and see what happens." She pointed to the map next to the pad. "I agree with Jax," she began. "If they are going to move out we have to make sure it's in the direction of the solar collectors and not our main area of attack. We have to keep them as far from Core City as possible."

"Did Jax have any info on Jay's next move?" he asked.

"Jay's agreed to the plan in principal," she answered nodding her head, "but not the timing. He wants another ten days."

"Well," he sighed pointing to the pad, "we should have a better handle on these guys before then. Colonel, are you planning to inform Jay?"

"Jax suggested that we hold off on bringing them in on this too soon and I agree," she answered. "Let's get some more Intel before we spill the beans."

"Sounds good to me, Colonel," he replied. "If you don't need me any more I'll head back to my outfit."

"That's fine, Jeff" she answered, "but keep this

to yourself for now. I'll call a meeting of all the unit commanders once we have some more information."

"I understand, Colonel," he said coming to attention, "by your leave."

"Thank you, Jeff," she said, dismissing him.

After he had left her tent she eased herself down into the folding chair next to the table. She picked up the pad one more time and flipped through a dozen or so pictures. She turned the unit off and placed it back on the table. She sat there for several minutes going over her plans for the morning. When she was satisfied that there was nothing left to do until daybreak, she pulled the envelope out of her jacket pocket. She lightly ran her fingers over the letters spelling out her name on the front. Carefully she opened the flap and removed the letter inside.

Hello, sweetheart, Jax had started the letter. *I'm sorry that this letter couldn't have accompanied something better than the pictures I sent, but times being what they are I wanted to take the opportunity to thank you for your note. I can't tell how much it meant to me to hear from you. Knowing that you love me and want us to share our future together only makes being apart from you all the more difficult. Please take care of yourself and I'll promise to do the same. Emily, you are in my thoughts constantly and never out of my heart.*

All my love…Jax.

She held back her tears as she kissed the letter and returned it to the envelope.

CHAPTER 29

THE BROADCAST

Jax found himself once again in the basement of the Core City bakery where he and the others had taken refuge after the sniper attack on Commander Adelric. Being in the room again rekindled thoughts of Rebecca. He had received word that she had made it back safely and was undergoing treatment for the trauma of her captivity. Early reports from her doctors were very encouraging. He turned his attention back to one of the multiple screens mounted around the large room. Each screen showed a different channel but, the one he was watching was the only available channel that seemed to spew out the least amount of propaganda about the Government and the Core Council.

The show they were watching was titled 'Family Fun'. Its sole purpose was to promote strong family values within the community. On the whole, Jax saw nothing wrong with the broadcast. The show reinforced the importance of families interacting as a unit to conquer whatever problem the producers had scheduled for the episode. It was the underlying messages he had issues with. The episodes never missed an opportunity to show one family member or another posting their weekly message on Sapphire. The producers were even clever enough to center a few episodes on the events of an individual's postings. The show would begin with someone entering their posting for the week. Everything would then be from their point of view. The episode would then become a flashback to the beginning of whatever event the poster was writing about. The character would supply the voice-over where appropriate. No episode failed to interweave the importance of spilling your guts to Sapphire each week and they never missed an opportunity to promote united family support for the Core Council.

They were always able to remind the viewers that it was the Core Council that supplied all of the clean energy they used at a nominal free, that is, as long as you didn't lose your discount by failing to post. They reminded the viewers of the wonderful medical care supplied by their Core medical system. *I wonder what they get charged for the sterilization program*, Jax thought. He broke away from the program and looked around the room.

His team of protest navigators were scattered

around the room. Some, like him, had been watching the program. Others were either involved in private conversations or by some other means, biding their time until given the order to move out. Once engaged with the protesters his navigators would orchestrate the crowd in a way to meet their overall goal. There were fifty-two other teams scattered strategically throughout the city. The main purpose of each team was to get their group of protesters to the central rallying point with the minimum amount of damage caused along the way. Today it would not do them any good to be broken up into segregated disputes with the CSF. It was critical to deliver all of the groups to the rally point intact.

From each of the screens around the room came the same long piercing tone as the programming faded. The screens were now projecting a flat gray background. The obnoxious tone began to pulse. *That's worse than the long solid tone*, Jax thought.

Suddenly, in the center of all of the screens the Presidential Seal did a fade in.

"Ladies and Gentlemen, this is your emergency broadcasting network." A very pleasant, but stern voice began, "A message from the President of New America."

Marci raced down the hallway and

almost skidded by the door to Kinsley's office. She was able to correct her course with only a minor bump against the door frame. Inside the office Pyrs and Kinsley were waiting.

"Is Sapphire going to shut this down?" Pyrs asked, his eyes glued to the screen.

"No," Mars answered, slightly out of breath.

"What?" Pyrs asked indignantly.

"Why not?" Kinsley asked right on the heels of Pyrs question.

Mars had her right hand inside her coat jacket rubbing the pain in her stomach. "He's using the National Emergency Broadcasting System," she explained. "The Emergency Broadcast Act prohibits any outside interference."

"Shut it down anyway," Pyrs demanded.

"You can't," Mars insisted. "It was programmed into the Sapphire System thirty years ago. We would have to rewrite code to do that."

"Did you ask Sapphire to shut it down?" Kinsley asked.

"No, Iris," Mars shot back, "I only asked in a dozen different ways. The answer is always the same; it's prohibited by the Emergency Broadcast

Act.

"Quiet," Pyrs shouted, "he's coming on."

The camera showed a full body view of the President standing behind the podium located in the White House news room. Standing behind the President was his usual band of supporters.

"Good morning," President Ziven started, "I am standing here before you today to share what will be disturbing news to everyone in New America. First of all I must tell you that the information I am about to release has been investigated by Attorney General Kelly and Secretary of Intelligence Ryan. Their joint investigation of this information has been found to be true without a shadow of a doubt. Secondly, after disseminating this information to you, I will share with all of you what steps are being taken to correct it."

"Augh crap!" Mars said.

"Quiet!"

Ziven shifted his position slightly behind the podium. "Here is the recent communication I recently received from The Guardian."

Instantly a full body view of the lead Guardian was standing next to Ziven.

"Mr. President," she said bowing slightly, "I come before you today with another horrible atrocity that is being inflicted on the citizens of New America. My fellow Guardians and I have uncovered proof that the Core Council, through the Core Security Forces have been abducting New American citizens without due process and imprisoning them in secret internment facilities."

On cue, the video showing several of the camps began to play behind her. "Once in these facilities, your citizens are subjected to physical torture and abuse." Again, the video switched to scenes of overcrowded prison cells and what clearly appeared to be battered and tortured prisoners. Different torture devices were shown.

"In many cases," The Guardian continued, "your citizens are murdered, never to return to their loved ones. We know of no case where anyone has been released from one of these facilities." She stretched out her arms toward the President. "Sir, I implore you to reach out to your citizens and rescue them from this situation." She turned toward the audience, "Citizens of New America, you must stand up to these injustices of sterilization and torture of your fellow friends and loved ones." She pointed toward the audience, "It is up to you to end these blatant misuses of power by the Core Council!"

The images faded leaving the President standing alone. "My friends and fellow citizens" he started solely, "as I informed you at the beginning of this broadcast, we have looked into these allegations in depth and have found them all to be true." He pointed to the seat reserved for the press in the room. The cameras followed his gesture. There in sixteen of the seats sat the Flash journalists who had been imprisoned. "Here in this room tonight," Ziven continued, "are sixteen men and woman of the press who have experienced the terrible things that were going on in those facilities. You may remember that these are some of the same reporters that covered my speech at Core Central a few weeks back. For that, they were rounded up like criminals and taken to the interrogation camps and subjected to criminal methods of torture. As you also heard before, they were taken against their will and without the due process of law."

Ziven looked down at the podium for several seconds. "If you remember back at that rally I promised you that we would look into the allegations of mass sterilization being performed on members of our society. We have completed our investigations of both the allegation of sterilization and of unlawful detainment and torture committed by members of the Core Council. I will now read to you our findings." He continued as he picked up a data pad. "On the issue of mass sterilization, we have found that the Core Council in its entirety has violated numerous laws with regard to their program of human genocide," he looked up toward the audience for a moment then looked back to the data pad. "On the charges of unlawful detainment and torture we have found that the entire Council has again violated our most basic and sacred rights."

"Where's Commander Adelric?" Mars asked the others in the room.

"Probably running for the hills by now," Kinsley stated caustically. They turned their attention back to Ziven.

"Now for our plan of action," Ziven stated. "First, Commander Adelric has been formally relieved of his position as Commander of the CSF and a warrant for his arrest has been issued." Ziven gestured to a senior member of the CSF standing next to Attorney General Kelly. The man took several steps forward. "Effective immediately, Colonel Francis Langston, has been promoted to the rank of Commander of the Core Security Forces. He will be replacing Martin Adelric." Ziven nodded toward the new Commander and the man stepped back into line with the others. "Secondly, I have put forth a resolution to our Board of Governors to temporarily disband the Core Council. In a closed session they unanimously voted in favor of this measure. Therefore, effective immediately, an order has been sent to the Core Council informing them of this decision."

"They can't do that!" Mars shouted. Before any of the other members had the chance to voice their opinions each of their PD's chimed simultaneously.

Mars looked down at her screen. There was one new message from the President of New America. It was marked *Urgent*! "Sapphire," Mars commanded, cut off all communication to and from Government Plaza."

"I'm sorry, Ms. Tansy, but an executive override has been legally entered into the system. I cannot comply with your request.

"Well," Pyrs stated calmly, "I guess he can." Pyrs stood and started out the door.

"Where are you going?" Mars asked.

Pyrs turned as he reached the door, "There are a few personal items in my office that I would like to remove," he smiled.

Mars turned back to the screen.

"Also" Ziven stated. "Warrants for the arrest of the following people have been issued. Iris Kinsley, Stephen Pyrs, and Marci Tansy."

Adelric walked into the room. Pyrs returned right behind him. It was the first time Mars had ever seen him wearing combat armor. "The building is in lockdown," he stated. "My men will keep anyone out until we can bring in more troops from the field."

"But, Martin," Kinsley said, "the President just announced that you were no longer in charge of the

CSF."

"Iris," he smiled, "I have enough troops loyal to me and this council to put an end to this uprising. As we speak, my men are mobilizing."

"Iris," Mars said, giving her a sinful look, "Can you cut power to Government Plaza?"

"Yes, I think so," she answered giving it more thought. "That complex is on its own power grid."

"Then get on the line and get it done," Mars said impatiently, as she turned to Pyrs. "Stephen, cut off all funding to the government, I don't want them to have a single credit to spend." She turned back to Kinsley, "Also, put your facilities on full alert. No one is allowed to get within six hundred yards of any facility without your express permission. Tell them that we are in a national emergency and give them orders to shoot to kill."

"And what are you planning to do while all this is going on?" Adelric asked.

"We have Sapphire," she answered smugly. I have a protocol especially written for just such an occasion as this."

Jax and the others sat in complete silence as President Ziven began to wrap up his speech.

"People of New America," he said, "we will get through this dark blemish on our history and you can rest assured…"

The room in which the President and the others were standing suddenly went completely dark.

"What happened to the lights?" someone asked from the darkened room.

"Get the emergency light up," Jax heard Ziven command. Jax stood and walked over to the screen. He turned it off motioning for others to do the same on the other receivers. When the screens were all powered down Jax studied the faces of his protest navigators. Suddenly a large grin covered his face. "Alright people," he said, "you all know what needs to be done so it's time to go to work."

They began to head up the stairs and out of the building. Jax saw Chris waiting for him at the top of the stairs.

"You in contact with the other groups?" Jax asked.

"Most of them," Chris confirmed, "I might have to relay the commands to those on the other side of the city. We hadn't counted on so much interference from the buildings. It's playing hell with our portable communicators, but we'll manage."

"Excellent," Jax said moving toward the door, "anything from Peter?"

"Yes, he says that Colonel McKee has deployed their forces as best she can, but wanted to remind you that theirs is only a delaying action. They can't keep those troops from eventually reaching the city."

"Well then," Jax said, checking his pistol before placing it into the shoulder holster under his jacket, "we better get marching!"

Like precision clockwork, the four huge groups of protesters marched toward the Executive Towers building from the four points on the compass. Skirmishes had broken out against CSF troops loyal to the council, but did little to delay the massive bodies moving ever closer. Luck had been on their side when it came to the local CSF troops that were there in the city. Most of them were not combat soldiers, but municipal employees performing police functions. They did not possess the heavier weapons that Jax and the others had seen out in the countryside. Jax's own troops possessed the firepower to handle the threats so far. He knew it would be a different story once they reached the tower building.

He was surprised when they reached the building and found no one manning the police barriers. He had fully expected to be facing a strong resistance force behind the barriers. What he found instead was a building that was locked down tighter than a drum. Large interlocking metal plates had come up out of the ground directly in front of the windows and entrances sealing off the entire front and sides of the building.

Several protesters had been gunned down when they had first approached the armored walls. Portals spaced along the entire perimeter allowed the CSF soldiers inside to fire on anyone coming within range of their guns. Shoulder fired rockets had no effect on the armor plating and it would be days before he could receive any heavier ordinance from McKee. Jax had ordered his sharpshooters to shoot out all external surveillance cameras that they found. He was positive that they had not destroyed all of them, but he was sure that poking out some of their electronic eyes had to have some psychological affect on the forces inside.

At the end of day two, Jax staged his operations base in a building directly across from the tower. On a minute to minute basis runners would enter the headquarters and pass on the latest intelligence.

Chris found Jax sitting in a small secretary style chair at the corner of a large conference table. Maps and recent photographs were scattered across its surface.

"You couldn't find a better chair than that?" he asked, entering the room.

"It works just fine," Jax answered. "What do

you hear from the battle outside the city?"

"As we suspected," Chris frowned, "Peter and McKee are blowing up roads and bridges while some of the platoons are fighting a delaying action. They have brought them to a crawl but they'll be here in a couple of days. What's happening here?"

Jax shook his head, "I wish I had paid more attention to the 'Storming the Medieval Castle' class back in school. We're getting nowhere. That armor is too thick for anything we can throw at it."

"Didn't you request some heavier explosives from McKee?"

"Yes, but she either hasn't sent them or they haven't reached us. Either way we can't penetrate their perimeter."

"What do you hear from Ziven?" Chris asked.

"Not much," Jax frowned, "his Secret Service doesn't have anything heavy enough to break through either. His new CSF commander is trying to get the forces loyal to the council to break ranks but there hasn't been any movement there. He believes that most of them are playing their cards close to their vest, waiting to see who's going to win this thing?"

"Does the new commander have enough troops to support McKee?"

"No go." Jax answered, "their primary duty right now is protecting the residents of Government Plaza."

Chris studied Jax's face for several seconds, "When was the last time you ate?" he asked.

Jax shrugged his shoulders, "I don't know, what day is it?"

Chris motioned with his hand, "Come on, there's a chow line set up around the corner. I'll buy if you're too cheap to."

Jax pushed himself up and out of the chair with a heavy grunt. "Damn," he said shaking his legs, "I've been in that chair so long my legs have fallen asleep."

"Chris shot him an inquisitive look, "When was the last time you slept?"

Jax stretched, "I don't know, what…"

"day is it?" Chris finished for him, "let's go boss. First some food and then I know where there is a nice soft bed with your name on it."

Jax and Chris walked down the street toward the chow line. Chris didn't speak much knowing that Jax was not mentally awake. He was more concerned with getting him to eat and then, get some shuteye.

"Hi Jax," the person standing in front of them said with a smile. He wore an old pair of blue jeans and a faded pullover sweatshirt with a hood. The hood was loosely pulled up over his head.

Jax and Chris both looked at the man as they moved to step around him. The only difference was that Chris had his fingers around the butt of the gun in his pocket.

"Hi," Jax answered, not bothering to slow down. Ever since Chris had mentioned food, he had a hollow feeling in the pit of his stomach. The quicker he got to eat the better he would like it.

The man reached out and placed his hand on Jax's shoulder. The stranger immediately noticed the gun Chris had pulled from his pocket. "You don't recognize me do you?" he said to Jax.

Jax took a closer looked at the man. "Ryan?" Jax asked astounded at how much different the man in front of him looked from the day he took Rebecca and he on the tour of the missile silo.

"Yes, it's me," he confirmed looking toward Chris, "that gun won't be necessary Chris."

"How do you know my name?" Chris asked, his gun still trained on the man's chest.

Jax put out his hand toward Ryan, "This guy knows everyone," Jax said shaking Ryan's hand. He turned to Chris. "It's OK," he assured him, "put your gun away." Chris complied, but didn't remove his hand from his pocket.

"What are you doing down here?" Jax asked.

"Looking for you actually," Ryan said, motioning his head toward a parked car. "Got time for a ride across town?"

"Jax looked at the vehicle and then back to Ryan, "We're headed to get something to eat. Want to join us?"

Ryan laughed, his glasses riding up on his nose. "You guys come with me," he offered, "I saw what they're serving around the corner; I'm positive I can offer you better."

"Are we going to be gone long?" Jax asked jerking his thumb over his shoulder. "We're busy storming the castle you know."

"Yes," Ryan said, looking past the two of them at the tower building, "how's that going?"

"It's a big castle," Jax offered.

"Alright," Ryan said, "we'll take a ride, have some lunch and I'll have you back here in time for the pouring of the boiling oil."

Jax gestured toward the car. "After you, Sir Knight," he smiled.

* * * *

They sat in the private dining room of the President. A simple table had been set with more than enough food for the two hungry men. After they had both helped themselves to seconds, Jax finally laid his fork and knife on the plate.

"I'm not sure how that compared to the chow line," Jax said, "but it was delicious."

Chris nodded while still chewing on a piece of roast chicken. "Much better," he mumbled with a mouthful.

"Would you like some coffee?" Ryan offered.

"I would prefer some hot tea," Jax answered looking towards Chris. "Chris, coffee?"

Chris placed his knife and fork on the plate and sighed, "Coffee would be great."

Ryan nodded to one of the servers who immediately left and returned with both the hot water for Jax's tea as well as a pot of fresh coffee.

"Well, Ryan," Jax smiled innocently, "you've fed the condemned men and I assume you will now inform us of our fate."

Ryan laughed out loud, "You really have a flair for the theatrics, don't you."

Jax laughed politely, "I'll answer that after you've explained why you brought us here?"

"What?" Ryan asked with a look of innocence, "can't a couple of old friends share a bite to eat?"

"I wish I could add you to my list of friends, Ryan," Jax said, continuing in a light tone, "but I think that currently we are just two people thrown together by a common goal."

Ryan's eyes sparkled, "President Ziven told me that I didn't need to ply you with food, he said that it would be best if I just got right to the point."

"Smart man," Jax smiled, "why did you waste the food then?"

"Because, Ryan grinned, "I really did get a good look at what they were serving in that chow line." The three laughed together then Ryan's face became very serious. "We might have a way for you to get into the Tower Exchange building."

Jax motioned with his hands, "Come on, I can hardly wait to hear it."

Ryan pointed to Jax's tea cup, "Finish up and we'll go for a little walk."

Jax took another sip of his tea, "The last little walk you took me on turned out to be a twenty mile hike around an apocalyptic bunker."

Ryan shook his head, "Nothing quite that grand this time, Jax, I promise.

Ryan handed each of them a large flashlight as they headed down the hall. "The main power is still out," Ryan stated. "I guess Iris Kinsley is still pissed at us for issuing an arrest warrant for her."

Jax looked around the hallway at the paintings, "It's amazing how the little things can break up a friendship. By the way, where is the President?"

"Spending the day with his wife," Ryan stated, "it's her birthday."

Crap!, Jax thought, *I don't even know Emily's birthday!* A more foreboding thought came over him; *I bet she knows mine down to the hour and minute, shit!*

"You alright, Jax?" Chris asked, "you look a little pale."

"I'm good," he said. "Where are we headed?"

Ryan turned down a narrow hallway. The farther they got away from the windows, the darker it became. "Just up ahead," he said turning on his flashlight, "then down."

They reached the end of the hall to find themselves facing a single door. He reached into his pocket and removed a small, flat metal tool for Jax to examine. "You ever see one of these?"

Jax studied the tool for a few seconds, "Nope, can't say I have. What is it?"

"It's an antique device for locking and unlocking doors. It's called a key." Ryan smiled, "this may be one of the only key locks left in existence." Ryan ceremoniously inserted the tool into a narrow slot in the door. With a quarter turn Jax heard the metal bolt release the door. Ryan looked over his shoulder back toward Jax and Chris. "This way. Watch your step."

They followed him down three full flights of stairs until they were at last standing on a small platform. Before them was a small vehicle.

Ryan shone his flashlight on the vehicle, "this is a tube transport vehicle," he said then shone his light on the elevator to his right. "The elevator goes from here directly to the President's private office complex." He then pointed his light down the dark tunnel. "This tunnel leads to the Executive Tower building. At the other end is another elevator that goes directly to the 22nd floor. It opens onto the Council's private chambers."

"Sounds interesting," Jax stated, "So you want four of us to ride in this thing and what?"

"There'll be no riding," Ryan said shaking his head, "that would activate the system and probably alert someone at the other end. No, what you need to do is walk the twelve and a half miles through the tunnel to the other side."

"And once there...what?" Chris asked.

"Well, there are two possibilities," Ryan said. "First four or five of you could ride the elevator to the 22nd floor and kill everyone you see."

"Or?" Jax prompted.

Ryan held out the key, "Take this key and twenty or thirty of you walk up the stairs to the first level and retake the ground floor. After you do that you could disengage the armor walls and let the rest of your people into the building."

"Then it becomes a floor by floor fight to the top." Jax said.

"What was your plan once you broke into the plaza before?" Ryan asked.

"Take each floor one at a time," Jax sighed. "Is there no other way?"

"I don't know," Ryan said, "we can provide you with the floor plans, but I think most everyone will be on the top two floors."

"Why top two?" Chris asked.

Ryan rubbed his chin, "Because the 22nd floor is the offices of the Core Council."

"And the other floor?" Jax prompted.

"That's where the CSF troops protecting the council are housed," Ryan said slowly.

Jax's right eyebrow rose in a questioning slant, "How many troops?"

"At max, thirty five," Ryan said.

"Thirty five!" Chris almost shouted, his words echoing down the dark tunnel.

"At max, Chris," Jax said facetiously.

"At max is right," Ryan interjected. "As you know, we made the broadcast on the weekend. We had a purpose in mind."

"So that the staffing on both floors would be at a minimum," Jax commented.

"Correct," Ryan smiled, "and you're forgetting that some of those troops will be on the first floor; reducing the number left on the 21st floor."

"At least it's something to think about," Jax said.

"Or," Ryan said flatly, "we can just wait for the Council's reinforcements to arrive here sometime in the next two or three days."

"Alright," Jax stated, "when would you like this to happen?"

"Sometime before the reinforcements arrive."

Ryan grinned and added, "With a little time to spare."

CHAPTER 30

INTO THE LAIR

Jax had the hyper tube team take a break at about the ten mile marker in the tunnel. It wasn't that their men weren't used to a full pack march, it was the mere fact that they had traveled the ten miles brutally hunched over like a person with a severe spinal defect.

While the team rested, Jax sent two scouts ahead. They had no idea if the CSF had considered the tube as a possible breach point into the building. Ryan had assured him that there were only a half dozen people who even knew about the transport system between the two buildings. That, Jax had concluded, was about six people too many.

A light tone rang in Jax ear, "Go ahead," he whispered into the tiny mike.

"We have reached the platform," the scout on the other end stated.

"Roger, what is your status."

"Platform is identical to the one on the other end. There are no signs of troop activity here."

"Roger," Jax said softly. "Is there a stairway door like on the government end?"

"Affirmative."

"Excellent, secure the platform. We'll be there shortly," Jax ordered.

Jax gave the signal to move out. Thirty-six men and women picked up their gear and, hunched over, began to travel toward the platform.

He stopped the group once he could see the light of the tunnel opening. He motioned for Chris to move forward.

"What's up boss?" Chris asked.

"Get the *Hushers* up front," he commanded. Their plan was to send the eight men with the silencer equipped weapons up the staircase first.

The team moved forward entering the platform area first. Jax quickly followed. He walked over to the door stretching his cramped muscles as far as they would go. He inserted the key into the slot as he had been shown by Ryan. He turned it counter-clockwise hearing the metal clicking sound as the bolt gave way. Two of the Hushers positioned themselves at the right side of the door waiting for Jax to open it. The two men slipped into the stairway as soon as there was enough room to squeeze by.

Jax opened the door to its full extent and the rest of the Husher team moved forward. Jax waited until he figured that the sniper teams were halfway up the stair-case before signaling the men behind him to move into the narrow stairwell. Having the entire strike force crammed into the confined space could lead to a disastrous outcome. They continued up to the 1st floor landing. The Husher teams had already opened the door and moved out onto the main floor of the building. Jax stopped short of the exit and waited.

What seemed an eternity finally ended when he heard the double click in his earpiece. The signal confirmed that the Husher team had reached the tactical position they needed. Jax keyed his microphone three times without speaking. The sound made by opening the channel and closing it again transmitted the three clicks notifying the Hushers that he was cueing the outside team to begin their ruse.

Jax switched to an auxiliary channel and clicked the mike three times again. Within a few minutes the sound of heavy gunfire echoed into the stairwell. Jax turned to the remainder of the troops. "Lock and load," he ordered. The sound of multiple weapons arming filtered up the staircase. Jax found comfort in the fact that the heavy automatic weapons fire coming from the lobby was most likely masking any noise they were making.

Jax left the safety of the stairwell and moved into the open area of the first floor. The remainder of his team followed him out and began dispersing to both sides of him. When in position, he gave them the hand signal to move forward.

The lobby area was littered with dead CSF troops. The two troopers manning the control desk had been shot and removed from behind the control panel. Several of his team moved up the escalators to the mezzanine level of the lobby. Two of the teams had positioned themselves around the four banks of elevators on both the first and mezzanine levels.

"All clear." Came the report from the Husher team leader.

"Roger, secure your positions," Jax ordered. He looked over to Chris, "Where's the maintenance guy?"

Chris walked forward with another man. He

was not dressed in combat gear like the rest of them. Instead, he wore the custodial uniform for the building. He had been supplied with an armored jacket to wear over his uniform. Jax had requested that Ryan find him someone who would be helpful with the operations of the electrical and maintenance functions of the building.

"Do you know how to lower the defensive panels?" he asked the man.

The custodian walked behind the panel and looked over the controls. "It's not here," he said, after checking the controls several times.

"Where is it then?" Chris asked.

"I don't know," he answered flatly, "I never knew we had defensive panels before today."

"OK," Jax said in a calm voice, "where would you put them if they were your panels?"

The man stood in front of the controls for several minutes pondering Jax's question. Then he slowly took off his armored jacket and laid it on the floor in front of the panel. He then slowly lowered himself down onto the jacket and used it to scoot under the panel. After several seconds he shouted to Jax and Chris. "I think I found it. Do you want me to lower them?" he asked.

Jax looked toward Chris and rolled his eyes, "Would you please," he asked in a pleasant voice.

Instantly, they heard the powerful whining of the mechanical motors. Slowly the motors lowered the shield back into the ground. The sunlight poured into the lobby. Outside he could see hundreds of people waiting to enter the building.

He turned to Chris, "Get all of the teams in here. I want thirty people per floor. Stop at the 20th floor. No one above that level."

"I'm on it," Chris answered, as he headed to the front entrance.

Jax made a conservative estimate that there were forty five CSF troops in the building at the time of the shut down. Taking away the ten they had eliminated in the lobby, left the 21st floor with thirty five soldiers remaining. If they had decided to have personnel on every floor that meant that the CSF Commander could only place one man per floor, leaving him with just fifteen men available to guard the top two floors. Jax felt that the man would not thin out his troops like that. So Jax considered that sending thirty people to each floor was of little risk. If there were troops on the floor when the people arrived they were instructed to tell the guards that the lobby had been opened and they walked in unobstructed. If asked why they were up on the floors they could simply tell the one or two guards they were souvenir hunting. Of course the guards would order the people to leave. This would give the hidden operatives within the group a chance to eliminate the guard.

Jax cleared the surface of the 1st floor control desk and rolled out the building blue prints. He motioned for the custodian to join him.

"Is there any way to enter the floors without using the elevators?" he asked the man.

The custodian pointed to the blueprint. "On the North and South side of the building there are fire escapes that lead from the roof all the way down to the first floor."

"Can you get us into the fire escapes?" he asked.

"That would be easy enough," he said looking at the prints, "but the fire doors are one way."

"One way?" Jax asked, "What do you mean, one way?"

"Let's say for example," the man said pointing to the 15th floor, "that you exit here on the fifteenth floor. If you let the door close behind you there is no exit until you get to the first floor or go up to the roof. All other doors only operate from the inside."

"Meaning," Jax said, "that if I wanted to get from the 15th floor to the 14th floor I couldn't go into the fire escape on the 15th floor then re-enter the building on the 14th floor without somebody opening the door for me."

"That's correct," he nodded.

"Then how would the firemen have access to the floors from the fire escape?"

He pointed to the control panel, "They could activate an emergency open of all doors from this panel or several access panels in the stairwells."

"How's it going?" Chris asked, as he walked up.

"Are the teams on their way up to the floors?" Jax asked.

"On their way now," Chris assured him. "Once they are in position we will return the elevators to the first floor and lock them down."

"Excellent," Jax smiled. "We can access the fire exit doors to any floors from here."

"A single door is a very small opening." Chris said, shaking his head. "A few well placed machine guns could keep us out for ever."

"Can you cut the power to a given floor?" Jax asked the custodian.

"Sure, that wouldn't be a problem."

"What about blasting through the floor?" Chris asked.

"That would take a ton of explosives," the

custodian said shaking his head. "And I don't know what would happen to the building's overall integrity."

"What about the building's sprinkler system," Jax asked. "Can you activate the sprinklers on a single floor?"

"Yes, we can do that," he said.

"What about the AC system can you override the thermostats?" Jax asked grinning.

"Sure, but what good would that do you?"

Jax turned to Chris, "Get as much night vision gear as you can," he said. "I have a plan for getting in after dark."

"I can't wait to hear it," Chris said, walking toward the front entrance of the building.

Chris looked down at his mission timer and then over at the building's custodian. "What's the temperature now?" he asked.

The man looked at his gauge, "fifty two degrees," he stated. "I don't know how much lower we can get it without seriously damaging the system."

Chris keyed his radio, "Jax, we're at fifty two

and that's about it."

Jax stood in the south stairwell outside the fire exit on the 22nd floor. His team was standing by for orders. The sprinkler system had been flooding the entire floor for the last twenty-two minutes.

"OK, Chris," Jax said, "you ready on the north side?"

"Awaiting your orders."

"Alright, go!" Jax ordered.

Simultaneously the power was cut to the 22nd floor and the fire door opened. One of Jax's team pulled the door open and two men rushed into the hallway. Jax was right behind them. Within seconds both teams were through the fire doors and heading into the main sections of the floor. Gun fire erupted from the north side of the building within seconds of entering. It stopped after a few seconds.

"Chris, report." Jax commanded.

"Two guards down," he said, "we have one man down."

Before Jax could respond three of his team began firing down the hallway. Weapons fire was returned for several seconds then died out when a flash grenade was tossed by one of his soldiers and exploded thirty yards down the hall. Members of the team split off as doors appeared. If a door was locked, it was blown off its hinges; a flash grenade was tossed into the room to be followed several seconds after the explosion by two team members.

Soon they could see the targeting lasers of the north team. "Chris, what's your sit?"

"We're clear up to the elevator doors."

"Roger, will be there in three minutes," Jax confirmed.

They rounded the last turn to see Chris and one of his team members standing by the elevator. "Everything secure?" Jax asked.

"We're good," Chris answered.

"Alright, kill the cooling and water and get the lights back on," Jax instructed. "What do you have on your side?"

"There were only three CSF soldiers and," Chris said, motioning to a team member, "Mr. Pyrs here."

Pyrs was sopping wet from head to toe and was turning a light shade of blue when he was brought before Jax.

"Where are the others?" Jax asked.

Before Chris could answer, the radio screeched in Jax's ear. "Jax, we got Kinsley," the voice said. "We found her hiding in a closet under a pile of coats."

"Roger," Jax said, "bring her to the elevators." He turned back to Pyrs.

"Where are the others?"

Pyrs, still shaking, tried to answer the question with the most dignity he could muster. "Commander Adelric and Tansy are down on twenty one with the rest of the Commander's troops."

"How many troops?" Jax demanded.

"Eleven, I think," his teeth chattered, "but that floor is a fortress. It won't be as easy getting them as it was with us."

Kinsley was brought around the corner and pushed next to Pyrs. Jax looked at the two standing there wet and shivering. *These were the most powerful people in New America,* he asked himself. "Alright Chris, have some people escort them down to the first floor."

"Right," he said, "what are we going to do about the 21st floor?"

Jax turned to Pyrs, "do you still have your PD?"

"Yes" he said, still visibly shaking. Slowly he placed his hand into his jacket. He then removed it and offered the PD to Jax.

"No," Jax ordered, "you keep it. I want you to

message the Commander and tell him that I'm coming down in the elevator to speak with him. I will be unarmed."

"Jax?" Chris started to protest, but fell silent when Jax waved him off.

"OK," Pyrs said reading his PD, "he'll meet you at the elevator.

"Get everyone downstairs, Chris," he said, as he pushed the elevator button. "I'll be down in about five minutes."

"Be careful," Chris cautioned, as the elevator opened.

Jax handed Chris his weapon and stepped into the car. He offered Chris a faint smile as the door closed.

As promised, Commander Adelric met him as the elevator opened. He, unlike Jax, was armed with an automatic rifle.

"Step out of the car," Adelric ordered.

Jax complied but only stepped as far as the door. He then leaned casually against the door frame blocking the doors from closing. It was then that he first noticed Tansy standing just left of the elevator door.

"I assume that you've come to offer us some

type of terms," Adelric stated in a military manner.

"Something like that," Jax answered. "This won't take long.

"You understand," Adelric grinned, "this floor is impregnable to your attack."

"Probably," Jax affirmed.

"We only have to hold out another sixteen hours before my reinforcements get here."

"I understand," answered Jax, "but you and all your people will be dead by then."

"Why do you say that?" Mars asked.

Jax pointed up to the ceiling above their heads. In several areas the walls were starting to show the signs of water seeping down from the 22nd floor. "Because," Jax said firmly, "in about twenty minutes the sprinkler system will be activated and instead of water coming out of those little nozzles," he said pointing to the ceiling, "a highly flammable liquid will be flushed through the system. Several seconds later it will be ignited. If the fumes don't kill you the flames and explosion certainly will." Jax had no idea if what he had just told them could even be done. He had just thought of it while riding down in the elevator.

"You wouldn't do that," Mars hissed, "that would be cold blooded murder."

Jax eyes hardened, "And what you did to my friends at the internment camps would be considered…what? A mercy killing?" Jax asked, stepping back into the car. "I'll be waiting on the first floor for you and your men. If the elevator doesn't start down in twenty minutes, I'll know your answer." The doors closed.

CHAPTER 31

THE RECKONING

Commander Adelric, Stephen Pyrs, Iris Kinsley, and Marci Tansy sat around the conference table that Jax had used as his temporary office while assaulting the Tower Building. The four had their hands bound before them when they had come out of the elevators in the Tower. It took every man Jax had to keep the angry crowd at a safe distance from the four. Even now angry shouting filtered through the closed windows. None had spoken except to demand to speak directly with the President. Jax had relayed the request through Ryan.

Ryan entered the room accompanied by two Secret Service agents. The men circled the room taking the time to stop by each of the Council members for a quick search. When they were satisfied they nodded their approval to Ryan. Ryan then in turn stepped out into the hallway and signaled the President.

Two additional Secret Service agents preceded President Ziven into the room. The two agents that were bringing up the rear stationed themselves at the door.

The President studied the four. "Stephen, Iris," he said noticing their wet condition, "you two look like hell." He turned to Jax, "Couldn't we supply them with some dry clothes?"

Jax did not move from where he was standing, "The thought never crossed my mind," he stated flatly.

Ziven made an emphatic gesture toward Jax, "Could you have someone find something now?"

Jax motioned to Chris without speaking. Chris nodded his understanding and started out of the room. "I hope whatever I find is gaudy and ill fitting."

Ziven turned his attention back to the four. "Well I guess our first order of business would be to have Martin tell his troops to stand down."

Adelric offered an insolent smirk as an answer.

Ziven walked over to the table and eased his leg up on the surface and sat on the corner. "Martin, if I have to take you to the outskirts of the city and have you publicly executed in full site of your advancing troops," he stated firmly, "I will."

"I believe that a trial is in order before any sentence could be passed," he said with a sneer, "I'm sure the trial would take months."

Ziven turned to Ryan, "Please inform these people how much crap they are in."

Ryan stepped forward. "The Board of Governors has recently convened and voted unanimously to grant the President emergency war time authority to put down your rebellion." Ryan looked at the four waiting for each of them to look at him. "Under the war time act, the President of New America has the power to order summary executions as deemed necessary for the good of the country."

Ziven looked directly at Adelric, "I believe stopping an aggressive attack from a band of rebel soldiers would fall under that act, don't you?" Ziven stood up and then placed his hand on the table and leaned toward Adelric. "Don't push me, Martin. I am in no mood for any of your superior bullshit this morning." He pointed to the outside of the building. "I have a transport waiting for you right now. So what will it be?"

Adelric looked down to the table in front of him as he contemplated Ziven's words. "I would like to be taken to Government Plaza to discuss my terms of surrender," he offered.

"Sorry," Ziven said curtly, "but we're having a small power problem at the Plaza right now. So…"

"I can fix that," Kinsley offered timidly, "I mean I could get the power back on, if you like."

Ziven turned and smiled toward Ryan.

Ryan grinned back, "Would you like her to be taken to the Plaza?"

Ziven stood and pushed his coat behind him so that he could comfortably rest his hands on his hips. "That's a very good idea," Ziven nodded, "why don't you have Iris and Stephen taken there." He looked at the two of them, "have you eaten lately?"

Both shook their heads confirming they had not. "Ryan, escorted them to a car and have them taken to the Plaza. Mrs. Kinsley can contact the power plant from the vehicle on the way over. By the time they get there, I'm sure the chef can have something prepared for them."

"This way," Ryan gestured and the two followed him out of the room.

Ziven turned back to Adelric. "Alright, Martin, you've had enough time to decide. Your terms better be short and sweet. What are you going to do?"

"Amnesty for any wrong doing," he offered.

Ziven thought about the request. "Alright, you'll receive amnesty for the crimes you committed against the people; *after* you have your men lay down their arms."

"Adelric stood up, "Agreed," he said as he walked from behind the table. "Get me to a PD so that I may contact my officers."

Ziven motioned to one of the agents standing in the room. "Take him out of here," he said, his voice dripping with disgust."

Ryan re-entered the room as Adelric reached the door. Ryan ignored the man and continued over to the President. "Power is restored and the two of them are on their way to the Plaza."

Once Adelric had left the room, Ziven turned to Ryan. "If his men lay down their arms and end the fighting, I want you to arrange for Adelric to be taken to the Eastern frontier. Lower the fence and throw his ass out."

"You promised him amnesty," Mars protested.

"And he got it," Ziven spat back now facing her. "And now, what to do with your scheming ass?"

Mars smiled politely, "I'll be much better treated than you've treated the others," she stated.

Ziven's left eyebrow slanted upward slightly,

"And why's that?"

"Because I still control Sapphire," she said flatly.

"Not once I get hold of the programmers," he replied.

"Good luck with that," she huffed, "and besides by the time you find them Sapphire will have shut down every system in this entire country."

"What are you saying?" Ziven asked her suspiciously.

"I have activated a failsafe protocol with Sapphire," she said in a triumphant tone. "If I am not given what I demand, your little country will come crashing down."

Jax moved closer to where Ryan was standing and leaned toward his ear. "What is she saying?"

"The Sapphire programming runs almost everything we have in the country. Power, water," he sighed, "hell even the solid waste management facilities."

"That sounds like it could become very messy," Jax whispered.

"You don't know," answered Ryan.

"Like I said," Ziven continued, "we'll get the programmers and get them to clean up whatever you think you did."

Mars laughed wickedly, "Not a chance," she said, "it would take months, if not years, to dig through the code and find the failsafe. Oh, and by the way, there are several sleeper programs hidden within the code. If they should stumble across one of them it would cause the entire system to be reformatted."

"Reformatted?" Jax whispered to Ryan.

"It would wipe all the programming from the system," Ryan whispered back. If that happened all that would be left is a very big paperweight."

"Crap!"

"Crap is putting it mildly," Ryan assured him.

"So," Ziven said, "let me get this straight, "you're the only one with the access code to get in and abort this failsafe?"

"That's correct," she smiled.

"And you'll give it to us if we cut you a deal?"

"A very good deal," Mars said correcting him.

"And when is this doomsday program of yours going to bring us to our knees?"

"You have about eighty hours left before it activates," she said, "not enough time for you to even find the programmers, let alone, stop it."

Ziven began pacing the room, his hands again on his hips. After a few minutes he turned back to Mars. "I'll tell you what I'm going to do," he said, pointing toward her. "I'm going to make you a bet."

"What's that?" she sneered.

"I'm going to bet you that, you are going to leave this room and be transported to the closest interrogation camp that you and Adelric set up. "There you will be subjected to the same methods of interrogation you have been using on the citizens of this country." He smiled before continuing, "I will order that your interrogation be as slow and painful as they can possibly make it." He leaned down to look her straight in the eyes. "I'm willing to bet that your weak ass body will scream out the code before the end of the first hour."

Her eyes became the size of saucers, "You wouldn't dare!" she threatened.

He leaned closer still. "Not only do I dare, but I want to be there to watch you scream. As a matter of fact," he said his eyes blazing into hers, "for every ten minutes under torture that you don't reveal the code, I'll have that time added on to the end of your session after you finally do tell us."

Mars looked down at the table for several seconds then raised her head to meet Ziven's eyes.

"I'll die first."

Ziven stood and motioned for his agents to take her out, "I was hoping you would say that," he said, following her out the room.

Chris reentered the room carrying a pile of colorful clothing. "What, what did I miss?" he asked as he approached Jax.

"Everything," Jax laughed.

Ryan turned to Jax putting out his hand. "You are a very interesting person, Jax."

Jax reached out his hand and shook Ryan's. "Thank...you," he said feeling the note that was being passed to him.

"I have to go now," Ryan said, pulling his hand back leaving the note in Jax's palm, "I don't think we'll be meeting again."

Ryan turned and walked out of the room without allowing any further conversation.

Jax opened the note and read it.

"What's it say?" Chris asked, dumping the clothing on the conference table.

Jax slipped the note in his jacket and turned toward Chris. His face was covered by a dark shadow of understanding. "We got to go," he said in a tone that was not to be challenged. "Get all of our people out of the city."

"What?" Chris said, frozen in place.

"Ziven is the Raven," Jax said bitterly, "he's going to attack us."

It had been three hard weeks of fighting. Within hours of Adelric's men laying down their weapons, the President ordered the attack on the Outlanders and Jax. Many of the Flash reporters rescued from the interrogation facility were duped into believing that the Outsiders had been at the root of their arrest. Ziven had convinced them that it was his forces posing as rebels that carried out their rescue. Pictures of many of the rebels were broadcast over the networks including images of Jax and Chris. They were wanted for murder, espionage, and conspiracy to aid the Core Council in overthrowing the government. If not to add insult to injury, the Lotte's went on an all district Netcast and swore that for the last several months their disappearance was due to being kidnapped by Jax's rebels. They were only freed after a heroic battle in which the President's own Secret Service had managed to free them.

For the last three weeks the rebels were being forced northward by three pursuing armies. Soon they would be trapped up against the northern corner of District One between the solar fence and the armies of the President.

Jax waited at the edge of the clearing with Emily. They had been hiding there for nearly an hour when finally a single figure broke cover on the opposite side of the small glade and walked toward the middle. The figure looked around for a brief moment then decided to sit on a fallen tree and wait.

"You ready?" Jax whispered to Emily.

"Let's go."

The two rose together and made their way toward the figure. The man stood at their approach.

"Hello Jax," Ryan said.

"Ryan," Jax replied.

Ryan offered his hand to Emily, "And this is?"

"No one you need to know," Jax answered.

"I understand," Ryan said lowering his hand. "Jax, I'm sorry it had to end this way."

"Which way?" Jax asked bluntly. "You're using us to rid yourselves of the Core Council and turn your backs on us."

Ryan raised his hands in an emphatic gesture, "Again, all I can offer you is my personal apology. Ziven is not a man to be messed with."

"So all this time," Jax started, "it was Ziven who was murdering the CSF troops and spray painting the Raven emblem on their vehicles."

"That's correct."

"Why?" Jax asked.

"Because Ziven didn't think you were moving fast enough so he kind of helped you along. He knew that the Raven attacks would bring things to a boil faster and then at a later date, he could dump the whole mess in your lap. He also set up the attack on Kinsley and took the shot at Tansy; all in a pre-planned effort to keep everyone on edge not knowing who to trust."

"I didn't think he was smart enough," Jax sighed.

"That was your biggest mistake," Ryan confirmed. "He didn't lie to you that day in the bunker. The *Trust* as you guys call it, are masters of manipulation. Come on Jax, they manipulated the entire world into Armageddon. Do you really think they would have much trouble with you?"

"They?" McKee said, speaking for the first time.

Ryan nodded, "Ziven was part of the Trust or at least his ancestors were. Let me back up some," he said as he tried to organize events in such a way that Jax and Emily could understand them. "Back in the pre apocalypse days, members of the US

Government were in fact part of the Trust. Their fingers were woven into the House and Senate as well as many of the Lobbyists. Then, sometime during their time underground, a riff developed between several factions of the Trust." He scratched his head. "OK, to try and make it simple, I'm going to use the names of the people you know. Just understand that they represent a faction."

"OK, just continue," Jax said. "This night air is not good for my health."

"The groups Tansy, Pyrs, and Kinsley, came to the conclusion that they would not need the group Ziven, once they repopulated the surface. In a post Apocalypse analysis they discovered, or at least they believed they discovered, that the government had become too unstable for a small group like the Trust to control. Too many power hungry people entered the government to twist it to their advantage. The government grew so large and the factions within the government so fractured they ended up causing more damage than you can possibly imagine. The government became gridlocked. It was the first time in the history of the United States that 95% of the general populace disliked or didn't trust their elected officials." Ryan stopped and checked their faces, "You keeping up?" Ryan asked. "So a mini-civil war took place in the bunkers with the winners being the three aforementioned names. The fourth, the Ziven's, were censured to silence."

"By censured, you mean killed?" McKee asked.

"Some," Ryan agreed, "but not that many. When they came out of the bunkers the new order was established. It was their intent to take a more direct position of control but still maintain the government, in its new form, as the ruling body."

"But it was a façade," Jax offered. "The Government's power was diminished and they weren't allowed to be part of the Trust – Council."

Ryan nodded his head. "It's taken Ziven's people all of this time to retake what they feel was stolen from them. Like I said, very methodical."

So how did we fit in to this mess?" McKee asked.

"Well, actually you didn't. You stumbled into the middle of everything. You were another wild card that they hadn't counted on," "Ryan admitted, "but once you were discovered, Ziven used you to his advantage. Remember our mentioning Tapio's Theory of 21?"

"Yes of course," Jax answered.

"You don't think they just dumped all that work into the trash pile before entering the bunkers, do you? Tapio had a reservation for a VIP suite in the first bunker. He continued his work until his death. By that time he had advanced his theories and left a legacy of brilliant understudies behind.

Very simply put, Ziven just added you into the equations."

"So now it's just Ziven, Ruler Supreme," McKee offered.

"No, not really," Ryan said, "next week Ziven is going to announce the creation of the new position; Secretary of the Treasury. Stephen Pyrs will be its first Secretary."

"You have got to be kidding!" Jax said, a sour look on his face.

"Pyrs was on Ziven's side all along," Ryan confirmed. "In three weeks there will be the announcement of another new position; Secretary of Energy. Want to guess who's going to fill that position?"

"Crap!" Jax shouted, "I'm going to be sick."

"Masters of manipulation." Ryan stated.

"And I guess Tansy will be his Queen?" Jax said caustically.

"Tansy gave up the codes within the first fifteen minutes of her interrogation." Ryan smiled coldly. "Ziven had her tortured for three days until she finally died. He also had her entire family killed."

"Why?" McKee asked.

"Tansy represented the faction that almost

wiped out his family in the bunker," Ryan explained. "It was their idea to rid themselves of the government entanglements of the past and they had enough support to do it."

"So pay back is a bitch after all," Jax said. "Looks like Adelric cut the best deal."

Ryan shook his head, "As promised, he received amnesty and was released into the Eastern frontier. He had taken about six steps past the fence when he was shot in the back of the head." Ryan looked to each of them, "Now do you understand what you're up against?"

"Are you a member of the Trust?" Jax asked.

"No, none of his aides are, but we are loyal to him," Ryan confirmed.

"I don't think you would be considered very loyal if he knew you were talking to us," McKee said.

"He would be even more concerned if he knew I have arranged for your escape," Ryan said.

"Our escape, why?" Jax asked.

"I'm not really sure," he said truthfully, "let's just say I got to know you and against my better judgment like you."

"So what happens next?" Jax asked.

Two nights from now, the power to sections 1-7 and 1-8 will be shut down for routine maintenance. They will only be shut down for forty five minutes, no more."

"So you expect us all to gather at this pre designated spot," Jax said icily, "so you can shoot us all down."

"I could have stayed home in a nice warm house and let you fin for yourselves," Ryan stated. "It's up to you, you can get out or wait for the troops to trap you against the fence and kill you. Ziven has given orders that none of you are to be left alive."

Jax thoughts turned to Emily; he could not let her die like that. "Alright, we'll be there and we'll leave," Jax agreed. "I have one more question since you're so talkative."

"Yes," Ryan prompted.

"None of this solves you little problem of overpopulation or lack of infrastructure to support it. What happens there?"

"I'm afraid," Ryan sighed, "Dr. Grady has already solved that problem. Our latest calculations predict that with the number of people sterilized by Dr. Grady's program, New America will undergo a Zero Population Growth for the next twenty to thirty years. We could even see a slight negative dip in our numbers."

"How nice for you," McKee said caustically. "If we had known that, we would have made sure Dr. Grady and his programs were alive and well today."

Ryan smiled weakly, "It's time for me to go," he said, "I've already said my goodbyes back in Core City so I'll just say good luck."

With that Ryan turned and headed back the way he came.

McKee nudged Jax in the ribs, "Come on," she said with a sense of urgency, "we don't want to be standing in the middle of this field when the music stops."

CHAPTER 32

HOMEWARD

Jax was sitting in the overstuffed chair when Emily came tromping down the stairs. "Jax, honey," she said as she passed him and went to the desk, "you are not taking that chair with you. So get your ass up and finish packing. We're out of here in twenty minutes."

He pulled himself out of the chair, "I'm already packed," he said, "but I'm not going with you."

Emily turned to face him, "What do you mean? Of course you're going, that's an order."

"Emily," he said with an even tone, "I'm staying to finish what I was sent in to do."

She walked over to where he was standing, "Jax, that's not possible," she said, "they will kill you."

"They won't even know I'm still here," he said confidently. "If nothing else, I'll take those bastards down starting with Ziven."

She rested her arm on his shoulder. "That's crazy, baby, you can't hope to get near those people. Your picture is plastered from one end of this country to the other."

"One person can blend into the countryside," he stated. "I can stay hidden till this all blows over. Then, when they least expect it, I'll kill them."

She moved her hand to his face and gently stroked it. "What will that accomplish, Jax," she asked, "they probably have their replacement all lined up. You know the hundred year plan or whatever."

"Many of our people suffered and died here," he said. "I couldn't face their families back home if I didn't do everything I could."

Emily dropped the piece of equipment she held in her one hand and placed her arms around him, "Jax, you've done more for our people than anyone, including me, could have asked. You don't owe us a thing," she stated. "The only thing you owe me is to live a long and happy life."

He gazed into her eyes, "Emily, I love you, but I'm staying. I'll get out later when I'm finished."

"Then I'm staying with you."

Jax shook his head, "not possible."

Emily searched his eyes for any sign that she could change his mind. When she finally convinced herself that it was futile, she hugged him tightly until his body relaxed and melted into hers. "Jax, I once told you that I knew I could never make you do something you didn't want to do," she said pulling back just far enough to look him in the eyes. "I know that's still true today. I love you, baby and I don't want to lose you." She pressed her lips to his, kissing him deeply. He flinched when the needle penetrated his buttock. He pushed her away from him; a look of astonishment across his face.

"What did…" he said, his words failing him.

She held up the syringe. "Sorry, my love," she said, "but on this issue I'm going to be very selfish."

"You bitch," he slurred falling back into the overstuffed chair.

"I love you too," she cooed, checking his eyes then his pulse. She stood erect very pleased with herself. She released a short, but very loud whistle. Within seconds Peter and Chris came down the stairs.

"How long will he be out?" Peter asked.

"Yeah," Chris agreed, "I don't want him waking up when we're dragging his ass to the fence."

"We will be long gone before he comes to," she confirmed. "Let's get him upstairs with all the rest of the baggage," she said, tossing the syringe over her shoulder.

Ziven stood next to Ryan both of them fixed on the images in their night vision binoculars. They watched as hundreds of rebel troops made their way between the hundred yards of fence that had been deactivated. Ziven looked at the time display just at the corner of his vision. "They're all through with eleven minutes to spare."

Ryan grunted his agreement. "Neatly done," he added.

"I'm still not completely convinced it was the right thing to do," Ziven said, still watching the troops move off in the distance.

"It saved the lives of countless numbers of our troops and still accomplished the same end game," Ryan reminded him.

"I disagree," Ziven said, lowering his binoculars to face Ryan. "They could come back, Sir."

"If we had murdered all of them," Ryan said, "others would have defiantly come back to avenge their deaths." Ryan handed his binoculars to Ziven, "Remember, Ziven, you never want to give a rebel a cause to fight for."

"Yes, Sir," Ziven answered. "Sir, do you think they will ever suspect your hand in all of this?"

"If they do," Ryan smiled wickedly, "then I didn't do my job correctly; did I."

EPILOGUE

The fire crackled and popped sending tiny hot embers into the air. From there they were picked up by the air currents and sent spiraling above Jax's head. From where he sat he poked at the center of the logs with a long stick. The fire answered his attack with more crackling and a new wave of flames. He reached over and threw another log into the center. *Sunrise will be soon*, he judged by the tell-tale sign of the razor thin yellow line on the far horizon.

From his vantage point atop the bluff he would soon witness the entire foothills and further out, the flatlands, become flooded with the morning light. He would gaze at the light as it filled every dip and gully; effortlessly climb over and around every bush and tree. *There was always something magical about sunrise*, he mused, it always stirred deep emotions within him.

Soon after returning from New America, he and Emily had resigned their commissions and together, set out to find a new world for themselves. For the last eighteen months they had made their home in the converted Titan missile silo Emily had found on her way to New America. It turned out to be a wonderful place to live. They had planted several gardens and were able to reactivate a nearby deep water well for drinking water and irrigation. Both were adept at hunting and preserving the meat they killed. They had even found several goats and sheep that they put in pens.

Emily walked up and knelt behind Jax. She opened the blanket that covered her and draped it around him. As she closed it across his chest, her bare breasts pressed into his upper back. Jax closed her hands in his as she gently kissed him on the neck.

"It will be sunrise soon," she whispered into his ear.

"Yes," he answered staring off at the horizon. "Come sit with me."

She stood and removed the blanket from around herself and draped it over his shoulders. She stepped in-between Jax and the fire, her naked body silhouetted with an amber glow, her belly just starting to show signs of the baby. Slowly she lowered herself to the blanket on which Jax was sitting on. She snuggled up against his chest as he closed the blanket around them both. As always, she took hold of the front of the blanket keeping it closed about them as Jax wrapped his arms around her, the one hand that usually cupped one of her breasts was now resting gently on her stomach.

"I never grow tired of your touch," she sighed as hot waves swept across her belly.

He gently kissed the nape of her neck in response.

"Soon now," she said softly, noticing the predawn shimmer massing.

Instantly the morning sun pierced the horizon spilling its light across the rim of the earth's sphere. Together they watched in silence as the darkness of the night gave way to the new morning. The light raced across the countryside heading in their direction. Suddenly, without warning, a brilliant glowing fiber pierced the cloud layer above sending a bright stream of light downward. The golden strain continued toward the ground until, hitting the solar collector below, it showered the surrounding area in a dazzling white glow.

"That always amazes me," Emily said softly, not to disturb the special moment.

"I've never seen anything else like it," Jax agreed.

Emily rested her hand over his. "Jax, are you

sure that you don't hold the slightest grudge against me for what I did back there?"

Jax hugged her tenderly, "It was sneaky, I grant you that, but I've never had any feelings for you other than love."

"The way you sit out here on some nights and wait for the sun to come up." she said, "and when the sun hits that solar collector; it makes me wonder."

"Wonder what, baby?" he asked.

"Wonder if I did the right thing by stopping you from staying," she admitted.

He twisted slightly causing Emily to slip off his shoulder and into his arms, "Let me tell you here and now, there is nothing that I want on the other side of that fence. My life is here with you and our baby. Let those idiots have their games of manipulation. We have a freedom that they will never know; a freedom that a thousand Sapphires could never give them."

"Then you really don't want to go back there?" she asked.

"Not there," Jax smiled, "but maybe after the baby's born you and I can take a trip out to the west coast; Catalina Island perhaps."

"Maybe," she agreed. "Jax?"

"Yes."

"The doctor said I could still have sex for a couple of months," she beamed fondly, "that is, if you don't mind bedding a pregnant woman."

Jax eased her down to the blanket beneath them. He leaned over and kissing her gently said, "When have I ever refused you."

Made in the USA
San Bernardino, CA
13 November 2014